A Spell in the Country

A Novel of the Averraine Cycle

Morgan Smith

This book is a work of fiction. Nothing in this is remotely based on actual events nor does it take place in any earthbound locale. None of the characters or situations has even a smidgen of reality about them, nor did I write it to get back at my legion of enemies or my arch-nemesis. If you see yourself in one of the characters, you either need a stiff drink, a change in your medication, or a long, hard look in the mirror.

This book is dedicated to many people, but mostly to Pat, because he believed.

Cover design and artwork by Julie Nichol. Photographer: Rod Heibert. Model: Chaleur Jones. Many thanks to Dark Ages creations for loaning the armour and weapons. If anyone is in Calgary and needs a nice chainmail shirt, those are the people to see!

Table of Contents

Chapter 1   7

Chapter 2   11

Chapter 3   19

Chapter 4   26

Chapter 5   31

Chapter 6   35

Chapter 7   39

Chapter 8   45

Chapter 9   51

Chapter 10   55

Chapter 11   60

Chapter 12   65

Chapter 13   70

Chapter 14   75

Chapter 15   81

Chapter 16   86

Chapter 17   90

Chapter 18   96

Chapter 19   102

Chapter 20   109

Chapter 21   113

Chapter 22   119

Chapter 23   129

Chapter 24   134

Chapter 25	140
Chapter 26	144
Chapter 27	147
Chapter 28	153
Chapter 29	159
Chapter 30	169
Chapter 31	174
Chapter 32	180
Chapter 33	182
Chapter 34	189
Chapter 35	196
Chapter 36	204
Chapter 37	212
Chapter 38	222
Chapter 39	230
Chapter 40	237
Chapter 41	241
Chapter 42	247
Chapter 43	251
Chapter 44	257
Chapter 45	263
Chapter 46	270
Chapter 47	277
Chapter 48	284
Chapter 49	290

Chapter 1

The carrion birds were circling overhead.

The bodies covered the fields, twisted in final agonies, toppled into untidy heaps, or outstretched as if in supplication. In the dying light, the blood lay black and slick on the grass.

Really, we'd been doomed from the start.

Oh, we'd had ground. We'd had numbers.

What we lacked, as soon as battle was joined, was the heart to fight at all. From the moment our opponent showed himself, boiling up out of the defile, with the Prince's own standard flying at the fore, we'd known how completely we'd been had. My own troop had watched in horrified fascination as Alcuin's troop had desperately tried to wheel away, while the hapless units behind recoiled and attempted to run.

Failing this, they'd tried to surrender, but Prince Tirais' troops had been in no mood for that. It had been unmitigated slaughter, from the start.

I, for one, didn't blame them. For what we'd done, death was the only answer. And if I were to die, it seemed at least marginally better to die here, than to swing from the gallows later.

But battles are ugly, and battlegrounds in their aftermath even uglier. Near me lay the severed arm of one of my luckier soldiers, his body only inches away, bleeding quietly into death. A few yards down the hill, I saw Gille's corpse, his throat cut and grinning, a second mouth. Beyond him most of his troop lay dead or dying.

I moved my head to avert the sight; wished I hadn't. Pain lanced through my skull, and now I could feel blood, hot and sticky, trickling down my neck.

I shut my eyes. Opened them.

Nothing much had changed.

I must have passed out. I could remember nothing, but I was lying now on a cold stone floor, in darkness. There were others here too, the sounds of laboured breathing and occasional groans told me that. I reached up carefully and touched the base of my skull: someone had done a cursory job of cleaning and bandaging the wound in my head.

The gallows, then. They were taking some trouble keeping me alive enough to make it that far. I could understand it; I would have wanted some examples made myself.

In the pain and the darkness, I kept thinking that my parents would never forgive me.

In the epic tales that I grew up on in my father's hall, the heroes were always victims of some singular circumstance of birth. They were the fruit of wandering gods, or the heirs of great realms, fostered out in mysterious ways, kept hidden from evil enemies until the time for their great deeds was ripe. I might have known, then, that I was not the stuff that heroes are made of.

My family was a large and happy one. I was the youngest, a last tribute to my parents' long love, and I won't deny that I'd been somewhat indulged. Only somewhat; my father's rigid principles and sense of duty didn't allow him to forget that as a minor lord, he had little to offer me for the future. There were no lands left to make me a living, and little advantage to marrying the daughter of an unimportant man holding not very strategic lands.

Fortunately for all of us, I was fascinated by swords and soldiers, and he had himself been well-trained as a warrior. I got a fairly thorough education and, when autumn storms were late and Istaran raiders harried our fishing villages, some practical experience. It was just an accepted fact for most of my life that I would have to go out and seek service with some other lord, and in the spring of my seventeenth year, my mother dug out my grandmother's old chainmail shirt, my oldest brother conned his rent rolls and came up with the coin for a decent horse, my sisters chipped in with a newmade sword, and my father sat down at his table and wrote a letter of recommendation to a man he'd been a squire with, long, long ago.

If I'd been prettier, or more inclined to my books, there might have been some other option, but by the time I was ten, it was obvious that I had no other future than what strength, a good eye and an unlimited appetite for war stories would bring me. I rode out on a perfectly ordinary spring morning, on a perfectly ordinary task: to search out a perfectly ordinary position as a simple soldier in some as-yet unknown, but surely ordinary lord's troop.

It's funny, really, how perfectly ordinary dreams turn sour.

My eyes grew more used to the darkness, which turned out not to be as total as I'd first thought.

This was not the blessing it sounds.

I began to recognize my fellow-captives, and some of them were not people I especially wanted to spend my last hours with. Notably there was Alcuin, whom I'd loathed for months. I could not, for the life of me, conceive of how he had survived that first brutal clash. Probably, I decided, through some coward's trick; I found comfort in ascribing the worst behavior to him.

I don't think I wronged him; he was hunched into the farthest corner, groaning. It was all you could hear after a while, his incessant mumbling that "He wasn't supposed to be there", over and over. Annoying, and eventually maddening to all of us. Finally Gruffudd, one of my fellow-captains, crawled over and bellowed in his ear for him to shut up.

It worked after a fashion; Alcuin blinked, groaned, and fell to muttering his little incantation in a whisper. I personally would have shut up altogether; Gruffudd was about the size and shape of a small barn, with very little more intelligence. Still, with all the anguished shifting about as wounded limbs began to cramp, and the distant noises of guard changes, Alcuin faded into a minor aggravation.

I didn't see Lord Uln among my companions. I hadn't really expected to. If he lived, his prison was undoubtedly a finer one than this: rank does have its privileges.

It was also possible that the man who'd led us to this end had met with his fate already. If I'd been Prince Tirais, I wouldn't have given him any quarter on the field at all. For my own part, I'd have cheerfully strangled the man myself, if he'd been here.

They came for us eventually. The first warning was the tromping of several pairs of heavy feet, then the wrenching squeal of the cell-door being thrown open and the blinding light of six torches in our eyes. Alcuin was trying to scrabble further into his corner, along with several others; I felt suddenly as if my stomach was attempting to work its way into the floor.

If you are going to die, though, you've got little left to lose but pride. Without quite knowing I was doing it, I faced up to the final realization that I was a corpse already, that my body simply didn't know it yet, and that the only course left was to meet the end with whatever dignity I could.

I found myself, in that sea of crawling, begging men and women, standing on my feet.

It took some time to sort us out, but eventually, hands bound and surrounded by guards, we were marched into the main hall, up stairwells and through corridors, until, confused and exhausted, we came to a long wide hallway. Benches had been placed down one side on which we were told to sit. There were several guards on duty, watching us with contempt and curiosity, and singly, each of us was escorted in through one of the doors, questioned, and taken away.

Alcuin was one of the first to enter, and he went quietly enough, but a surprisingly short time later he was being hustled out, ashen-faced and sporting the beginnings of a nasty bruise on his face. Apparently he had failed to give an adequate reason for taking up arms against the heir to the throne. I made a mental note to duck if I could. My reasons for being here were undoubtedly less logical.

The line moved slowly. It was only captains and commanders here and I used up a full minute wondering where my troop was housed, if any of them had survived. It kept me from speculating on what or who was beyond that door, and what they wanted from us.

We were guilty of treason. I couldn't imagine what else there was to say. Each of my comrades was escorted immediately away from us when they left the room, and all of them looked shocked and terrified by whatever they had gone through inside.

The soldier on duty yanked me up. I moved forward, through the doorway, then stopped in dismay.

Chapter 2

It was a room chosen for its magnificence, as long and formal as a throne room. Halfway down, there was a fireplace with a small fire going in the grate, and beyond that a table with two chairs. My eyes were drawn instantly to the man seated there.

He was, quite simply, the most beautiful man I'd ever seen. He was all those things the bards sing about: golden, young, with broad shoulders and deep blue eyes, the whole poetic rigmarole. My instinct was almost instantly hostile. There was something so calculatedly unfair about his immaculately dressed appearance, in comparison to my own filthy state, that I mentally girded myself against it.

I barely noticed the other man in the room, as he turned from the side table and brought a cup of wine to Prince Tirais. The guard shoved at my back, and I moved slowly, unwillingly, down to face this not-quite-final ordeal.

"Sit down" said the Prince coldly, indicating a low bench just a few feet in front of me.

"Thank you," I said politely. He gave me a slightly exasperated look.

"Name?"

"Keridwen, sir."

"And you've been in Lord Uln's service how long?'

"Four months, almost exactly."

"Rank?"

"Troop captain."

There was a pause, while he looked me over.

"How old are you?' he asked. He sounded careful, wary, as if he expected a lie.

"Eighteen, come the Festival of the Merydd."

The prince's expression was derisory. I knew how it looked. Damned stupid is how it looked. I could have been Bronwyn the Brave herself come back to life, and no sane commander would put me in charge of a troop. Not at seventeen. With four months of command behind me, I wouldn't have put a seventeen year old in sole charge of digging a ditch. I'd learned that much at least.

"Can you tell us why, at so tender an age, without experience or long loyalty, you merited such an - er - honour?" he said finally. He seemed to be struggling with some inner emotion. I suspected amusement.

"Because anyone older would have wondered what the hell was going on a lot sooner than I did…Your Grace."

The honorific, coming out as the afterthought it was, sounded perilously close to an insult. The man beside him tensed.

I said, to fill in the silence, "Actually, I'm not totally inexperienced. Compared to most of them, I'm a veteran. I've had some training, anyway."

"All right," said Tirais. "Let's have it from the beginning. No, no," this to his companion, "I want to know. Maybe she can shed some light on whatever is going on here. Goddess knows she's the first one who isn't groveling on the floor begging for mercy - we may as well find out what we can."

Telling one's life story while waiting to be sent to the gallows is not a course I would recommend to anyone. I would have kept to the recent past, if I could have, but I knew that was hopeless. The moment I mentioned the letter my father had written to Baron Gallerrain, my parentage was out in the open. Not surprisingly, it pleased them not at all. Hanging even minor gentry's daughters is not pleasant, especially when their father's honour is practically a legend. They took the news stoically.

"So you went to Gallerain for a job," said the Prince.

"No, not that. My father's letter was just asking him to recommend me to someone who might have a place for me, either as an armsman, or a guard , or something like that. He vouched for me being well-trained and not - er - unintelligent."

"You read the letter?" The prince sounded indignant.

"He read it to me. To all of us, at dinner, before he sealed it. My brothers found it particularly amusing."

"And you resented it, I'm sure."

"Oh, Goddess no." I grinned suddenly, remembering. "It was nice of him, really. Considering what he'd said about my forgetting to shut the dog-kennels off properly, the week before, it was pretty generous." But this was dangerous ground, these pleasant memories. I concentrated on confession.

"So, you went to Gallerain Castle." His voice was neutral, unemotional.

"Yes."

"And he sent you to Uln?"

"He said Lord Uln had asked him to look out for some good prospects, for new patrols on the roads. Something about more bandit raids this year."

Gallerrain had, in fact, been quite kind to me, in a remote sort of way. I hadn't expected to see him myself - I'd turned the letter over to a guards-captain, hoping that the Baron would be nice enough to send me on with a note to some caravanmaster or town-watch captain, vouching for my identity.

Instead I'd been ushered into a well-appointed room and plied with wine and questions about my family. I hadn't thought that he'd known my father all that well, even as young men together, but the arrogance of youth asserted itself. He was of an age, I'd thought, to be nostalgic about his past. I'd noticed the same tendency in my parents.

"Anyway," I said, clearing my throat, "he'd found a few farmhands who wanted a change, and was sending them on. He thought that if I took charge of them, and got them there, I would look more, well, useful, I guess. He thought maybe a position as a squad leader, or even, if Uln were really shorthanded, a troop second. He said anyone trained by my father would be capable of that no matter how young. He was very nice to me."

In fact he'd dazzled me. Gallerrain Castle was huge and rich, compared to Orliegh. I was invited to stay the night, so as to get a good start on the morrow, and given a place, not at the high table, but far enough up from the salt as to impress my seatmates, and myself. I was treated like an important guest. It was flattering, to say the least.

"And is that what Uln offered you? A troop second?"

"No, sir. He gave me the troop."

The man beside the prince got up with a muttered curse. "Tirais, what is this idiocy? What would it matter if he made her his commander in the field? it changes nothing."

"But I'm entranced, Gervase. A warrior out of nowhere, whose talents reveal themselves to all who behold her. It's like some bard's tale!"

I squirmed. This was too near my childhood dreams.

The prince noticed my discomfort, and smiled, not very nicely. Gervase sat again, with an expression of extreme distaste. He was older than the His Highness, a huge bear of a man, with rusty-coloured hair, and the look of a seasoned veteran.

"Well, go on," said Tirais. "You walk in, with a halfdozen farmhands in tow, and Lord Uln hands over fifty souls into your charge, just like that."

"Yes." I sighed. "Pretty much."

Uln had asked me some questions, about training and experience, but I'd had the distinct impression that I could have made any answers at all, he wasn't actually listening. After twenty minutes, he'd announced that he was forming a troop exclusively for patrolling the main roads, and did I think I could train them up for that sort of work?

I'd said yes without thinking, he'd said 'Wonderful', and called in Alcuin and Ralf, his commanders, introduced me as his new troop captain, and two days later I'd been in a fort on the westernmost edge of his lands, trying to teach some completely unskilled young men and women how to use a sword without killing themselves.

"The other captains didn't resent you? They didn't wonder how a seventeen year old from the back end of the country got such a plum job for nothing?'

"That was the thing I couldn't understand," I said. "The other captains. They weren't all as young, but I had more experience than they did. Even Alcuin and Ralf. They'd done a lot of guardwork and patrol, but they'd no real battle experience. And outside of the household guards, no-one had been there for more than a year."

"But you didn't question it?'

I stared at my feet. What would any young soldier say when handed a command so easily? I had questioned it. Added together, the eight captains wouldn't have amounted to anything like a single decent commander, quite the reverse, and to someone raised by Gareth ap Guerin, it had seemed idiotic; on the other hand, it was a job.

"I did wonder, Your Grace. I talked to some of the other captains. We all thought it was odd, but, well, you know, we couldn't really see…Gilles, one of the others, that is, thought maybe Uln was trying to cut an important figure, at court, you know, or something…"

I listened to my voice trail off, embarrassed. Far from explaining anything, I sounded like a fool.

"All right," said Tirais. "You wondered. Maybe. What then?'

"Well, we spent the summer chasing bandits. Nothing exciting. There were some raids, we'd go check them out, follow the trails, the usual drill. Other than that we never caught any, hardly. And there weren't that many raids even. I figured Uln would probably discharge most of us after our year was up."

I stopped; swallowed hard. We were getting to the hard part now, the things I didn't want to think about. The things I would have given anything in the world not to have been part of.

"It's just the last seven-day, Your Grace. Or ten days, I guess. That it changed, really. And I'm guilty, and my life's forfeit, I understand that. But we, none of us had been there long enough. If we'd known what kind of man he was, at the start, but then - we didn't know what he meant to do, it was just a job, really…"

I closed my eyes and reminded myself that I was already dead, and that none of this mattered. I drew a breath and said

"About ten days ago, Uln got us all back into the keep. I thought it was stupid, this close to harvest. I mean, if I were a bandit, I'd be pretty busy about then. But those were the orders.

"And then five, no, six days ago now, Uln called us all into the courtyard and said that he'd just gotten word that the Lord Steward of Fairbridge had turned against the queen, that when the local people heard of this perfidy, they'd risen up against their lord, and that he'd slaughtered a whole village, just to frighten them. And that we were going to march on Fairbridge, and punish him. He got everyone all fired up.

"And I knew there was something wrong, and I did nothing. I'm sorry."

"Yes, I'm sure you are," said Tirais, coldly.

"How did you know something was wrong?' asked Gervase, at the same moment. I looked at him. It was the first time he had said anything to me, and his tone was neutral, as if he were merely curious.

"I was duty-officer, all week. If Uln had had a message, I would have known. No-one came through those gates for four days. And if no-one brought him the news, how did he know it?"

"But you marched out anyway?' Tirais' voice was still cold.

"I hardly had time to think. I didn't really think about it till we were on the road, and then I thought maybe he'd some secret way in, for special, urgent things. Oh, I know" I caught the Prince's look of contempt, "Not very plausible, I agree. But you know how it is, on the march. You haven't got time to think about anything except keeping your troop together, in decent order, and who's going to dig latrines, and settling disputes over watch-shifts. And with my lot, it was worse. They weren't used to sleeping rough, or long marching, or anything. I found every reason I could to put it out of my mind."

"So then you came to Fairbridge." His voice was almost a whisper, he seemed as reluctant as I to come to grips with this part. Small wonder.

"Ye-es. We camped about three miles out. The idea was to take them by surprise, I guess."

"And then," his voice was still strained and low. "Go on, tell me."

"The night we camped, Alcuin took out some of the household guards. The ones who'd been in Uln's service a long time, his own troop, originally, I think. They said scouting. They came back, a couple of hours before dawn. I'd just gotten up, I saw them ride in. I thought they must have happened on some patrol or something. They were like that, strung up, and overconfident, the way you are when you've had an easy win.

"We got on the march. And just after dawn, we came to the village."

It had been the most horrible moment of my life. That there was more horror to come, I didn't know, and couldn't have imagined. In the face of that senseless brutality, it seemed nothing could be right and whole again in my life. Even now, I could not fathom how anyone could commit such atrocity. The dead had been everywhere, in a welter of blood and stench that lingered in my soul. I could not bear it, I could not bear myself, for having been in such a tiny way, part of that evil.

"And you just continued on to Fairbridge, after that?"

I could learn to hate that voice, I decided. It was too much like my own conscience.

"I didn't want to. Alcuin and the others were saying it was what Fairbridge had done. And the troops believed it. They were really hot for a fight, you see. All those women and children. And they were all just farmhands and all, anyway, they didn't know that bodies dead for four days don't look like that, all nice and fresh. Or if they did know, they weren't thinking, just being angry and rushing around."

I'd known though. And I'd taken all my courage and gone to Lord Uln and taxed him with it. I was not proud of myself. I had couched my suspicions and my objections so carefully and so courteously that it was likely that only his own knowledge allowed him to understand what I was accusing his commander of. I had not noticed his amusement at my hedged comments until much later.

"I asked Lord Uln, I mean I said that I had my doubts, about what had happened, I mean. And he admitted it, my lord. He said that he knew the troops weren't really ready for battle, that he'd needed something to spur them on, and give them courage. It wasn't entirely a stupid answer, either. I'd been worried about keeping them on the field once we joined battle, myself, and I guess I let myself be, well, persuaded. That's all really. We marched up into the hills, and, well, you know the rest."

"Do I?' his tone hardened. "Do I, really? I think I have several unanswered questions about that battle. For a start, I'd like to know where Uln is. And when did he contrive to leave? And I'd like to hear you tell me the answers, if you please."

But now I was on my feet and shouting.

"Uln's gone? Do you mean to tell me that the bastard got us here and left us to face the music? And you let him? Oh, Goddess' tits, do you think you can hang us and let him run off free and clear?"

I was lucky, I suppose, that Gervase was there. He caught at the prince's arm as he rose, and Tirais did not shake him off, but stood glaring at me.

"You'll address His Grace with respect, in future," said Gervase.

"I haven't got a future," I said nastily. "If he hasn't got the jam to take Lord Uln, he's no business judging us. What good is it to hang the hens for not noticing the fox?"

"I suppose you think you'd have done better? Seeing as how you sleepwalked through Uln's treason, you feel you're an authority on this?" Tirais was breathing hard, probably with the effort of not throttling me here and now.

I sagged a little. He was only too right. I was no judge of his.

"I'm sorry, Your Grace. But all the same - "

"All the same, you'll hang, in a matter of hours. Enjoy your last minutes, Keridwen."

But instead of calling the guard, he nodded to Gervase, who rose and started to the door.

"One last thing, Keridwen of Orliegh."

Gervase stopped, his hand on the doorknob, and both of us looked back to Tirais.

"All those times, that you suspected things were wrong at Uln, why didn't you leave? Find a new job, with less questions to it?"

I looked at Gervase, at the floor, at the tapestry on the wall behind the table, anywhere but at Tirais, Prince of Keraine. How was I supposed to explain to a prince that a seventeen year old fighter, showing up at any lord's household, having quit midseason from another place for no adequately explainable reason was about as likely to find a job as I was to live till sunset tomorrow? How could I explain that in my world, if you walked away from employment because your employer was not as honourable as the kings of heroic tales, you didn't work for anyone?

One of the logs in the fireplace crackled, giving off a shower of sparks.

"Practically the last thing my father told me," I said finally, "was not to assume that Orliegh was the whole world. That just because we did things one way, didn't mean there weren't other ways of going on. He said to listen and to learn, and to obey my sworn lord. I guess he didn't mean that exactly as I took it, but in the end, it was all I knew."

Gervase opened the door. As I passed out to the waiting guards, I looked back at the prince. Stupidly enough, he looked as if he understood.

Chapter 3

On our way back to the cells, we crossed the main hall again. The doors had been flung wide to let in the fine, late summer breeze, and I could see morning sunlight and a scrap of deliriously blue sky. I could also see the work party, assembling a scaffold. The sound of hammers kept knocking at my heart, long after we'd descended down to the lower levels and the cell door rang shut behind me.

Tirais underestimated my time. The scaffold-builders were slow and my conscience and I had to get through that long, last, interminable, dimly lit day, and then through a yet more miserable night.

In hindsight, he'd had some things right. The intelligent move would have been to quit Uln's service long before it had come to this, and taken my chances on landing a soldiering job out on the Camrhys border. I'd had more reasons than those I'd given the prince for thinking that Uln was a damn lousy man to work for.

The most obnoxious of those reasons lay a few feet from me, still muttering to himself and moaning about the unfairness of it all. Knowing that Uln had left his favoured commander in the same soup as the rest of us was little comfort. In a few hours Alcuin would get the same death I would, and if he was more directly guilty than I was, he would not be more dead. Possibly less mourned, but not more dead.

I don't know if you can understand what it had been like to serve under a commander like Alcuin. All forces have an Alcuin or two, but they seldom rise so high. I've since known commanders who were ruthless, and I've known a few that were corrupt, but Alcuin could only have wound up where he did because Uln had wanted it that way. Which said a lot about Uln, if I'd taken the trouble to think it all through.

Alcuin was simply a bully put in charge of a pack of unsuspecting children. He was cruel, devious, a liar, a boaster, a rapist and a thief.

I'd watched him brutalize a young recruit publicly. I'd seen him pick through a travelling tinker's belongings, openly taking what little of value there was, and laughing when the poor man had protested. He'd bragged about forcing a village girl into his bed, after beating up her brother in the local tavern. He had been the subject of two separate conversations with Lord Uln, during which I tried to convince Uln that morale was suffering from Alcuin's inability to satisfy anything but his own appetites.

I got platitudes and a veiled warning to back off, and the distinct impression that every word had later been repeated to Alcuin himself. After that, I'd concentrated on keeping my own troops away from him, but it became increasingly clear to me that at least some of the "bandit" raids we were chasing after were the work of Alcuin and a few chosen members of the household troops.

Tirais was right. I should have walked away. I knew it, even then. But there was my pride involved: what would my father say if I gave up on my first job after two months? And then there were "my" soldiers, such as they were. I was realistic enough to know that my leaving would change little for them. It might make it worse. The next captain might not take care that none of his troops was ever in sole contact with Alcuin, and Alcuin, after watching me change the mind of a young recruit who disputed my right to give him orders (it's necessary, my father said, to do this sometimes, and had made damn sure I could come out the winner) Alcuin had been at least wary of challenging me directly.

Morning came at last. I knew they couldn't delay much longer. The enjoyable torture of making us wait had to be balanced against the victors' need to see justice done speedily.

The guards came again, this time more of them, and we were herded unceremoniously out into the courtyard. The prince's troops stood in neat, careful ranks, all around us. In the centre were our lot, frightened, lost little recruits who'd gone looking for something a little more entertaining than watching the wheat grow. They'd found it, I thought savagely. Why the hell couldn't he have cut their poor throats on the battlefield instead of putting them through this nonsense?

Someone was bellowing that we were to form up in our units, captains at the fore. There were pitifully few of mine left, maybe half or even less. I was past counting noses. I saw Gilles' troop second, tough little Maeve, and ordered mine over a step to make room for the six shivering souls she was gamely pushing into a line.

"Steady on," I said. "Not long now."

She looked grateful. I felt awful. This was worse than anything I could have dreamed of, to stand with these men and women, most my own age or younger, having brought them to this idiotic pass, because I'd lacked the brains and the courage to -

But at this point my conscience failed me. Nothing could change what was. Most of them would have been here, with or without me.

The prince mounted the scaffold, which lay short steps ahead of us. There were four others with him. I focused up, away from the hangman's ropes, and tried not to think, to hear anything at all.

"You have come here as traitors to your rightful Queen, " he said. He had the knack of command. It didn't seem as if he was even raising his voice, yet it carried clearly through the courtyard. "You've been judged. I can think of no reason to delay."

Good, I thought. Make it snappy. I haven't got all day. Well, all right, I have, but still…

He was going on. About our guilt. I was getting angry. It was his right and his damned duty to kill us, but was it necessary to make us listen to our shame all over again, as if we all hadn't been regretting this for two days?

Finally the voice ceased. I was aware that really he'd only said a few sentences, probably for the benefit of his own troops. There was no reason for him to care about our sensibilities, anyway. I tried to find a calm quiet place inside of me. It might be a while before my turn came.

They ordered up the first units, which happened to be Ralf and Alcuin and the remainder of Uln's erstwhile household guards. I was not much elated. I didn't want to watch anyone's death here, I just wanted to get my own done with and that eternal voice in my head shut up once and for all.

I'd seen hangings before. I know in some places they are considered a high treat, worthy of an impromptu market and much heavy drinking, but those are not places I would personally want to live. I had been raised to believe that punishment ought to be a sober affair, so that the maximum deterrent benefit could be derived. It seemed that Tirais' shared this belief, his troops stood motionless and silent as they dropped my fellows neatly from the scaffold. No-one cheered, no-one even seemed to breathe. It was still an ugly, harrowing sight, and it seemed to take forever. Especially for those of us whose turn was coming.

Tirais stayed on the scaffold through it all. I had to hand it to him, he knew what was required of a good commander, and he wasn't letting himself out of the lousy bits.

The bodies were being taken away. I tensed, waiting for the next signal. It would be me and mine soon enough.

"I want you to think long and hard on this," said Tirais. "I want you all to burn this memory into your skulls forever. I know that most of you followed where others led. If there are those among you who, in fact, understood more clearly where this was leading, I don't wish to know it. I want you to learn the lesson here and go forward. I pardon all of you, and tell you to remember that I, and my mother, your rightful Queen, will never forgive this again."

There was a stunned and complete silence. He was walking to the steps now, coming down, walking away. We, all of us, were merely staring in disbelief. Where was the trick? I thought. No, no, Your Grace, this is too much. You can't do this. There are rules, dammit.

But all around me, people were crying out, in sudden joy and relief. Little Maeve was hanging on my arm, weeping, while I stood, frozen in my fury, waiting for the punchline to this not very funny joke.

Gradually, it dawned on me that it was true. I was not going to die, at least not today. I hugged Maeve. I chatted nicely to the various farmhands-turned-soldiers who assured me of their sudden love of the pastoral life. I accepted the bread and cheese shoved into my hands by a perfectly amiable guard who'd been detailed to see that we were fed.

People milled around, not quite sure what they were supposed to do next, but quite willing to be told. After a time it became apparent, to me, at least, that they would be asked to do various menial tasks the Prince's army needed or wanted doing, and that one of those tasks would likely be burying the residents of the village Alcuin had massacred. I wondered if any of them had figured out that part. I decided it wasn't my problem, or perhaps I just hoped it was not.

I was just working my way to the edge of the crowd when a guard pushed into the knot of rejoicing ex-traitors I'd been detaching myself from and asked if I was Keridwen of Orliegh.

I admitted I was. In my current euphoric state, I might have admitted to anything.

"Well, then, you're to come with me. His nibs wants to see you."

The guard gave nothing away, but the familiarity reassured me. Soldiers on serious business do not use those cute little terms for their commanders. He led me back up through some familiar bits of Fairbridge Keep to the corridor I had spent some rotten time in and told me to sit down on the bench again.

I was still in that pleasant state of wonder. The world seemed a lovely place, I could not fathom why I had been so eager to leave it. The very stone of the walls was beautiful, the hard wood of my bench was dear and familiar. People came and went in an amusing fashion. I relaxed contentedly against the wall and watched happily. I probably looked like the village idiot. I couldn't have cared less.

After some time, Gervase came out of the room at the end of the corridor. He stopped, wrinkled his forehead in an interesting way when he saw me, and motioned to one of the soldiers passing through.

"Take her down to the healers and get her looked after. And feed her. I'll be a couple of hours yet, there's a lot to do."

"I've eaten," I said cheerfully. "And I feel fine."

He looked at me as if I were a defective child and said, "Er, yes. Do it, Bors."

Bors looked as if he would have sooner cleaned the latrines, but he hauled me up and turned me gently in the direction of the stairs. I followed him happily down through a rabbit-warren of rooms and hallways to a brightly lit place full of wounded men and women.

"Lisset," said Bors to one of the greyrobed healers. "Lord Gervase says you're to see to this one."

Lisset looked at the rope-marks at my wrists, and sighed in a longsuffering way.

"One of Uln's, is she? She looks well enough."

"I am," I agreed. "I'm fine."

But Lisset wasn't taking the traitor's word for anything. She sat me on a bench, unwrapped my wound, made remarks about incompetent helpers, and about how many really serious cases she had going, all the while yelling for various items, cleaning, in no very gentle way, the dried blood and dirt encrusted on my scalp, and generally sounding like my mother. When a particularly vigorous swab at my wound elicited a groan, I half expected her to tell me not to be such a baby.

In due course, she rebandaged my head, told me I'd better keep it on for another day or two, and said I'd live.

"I know," I said happily.

Bors levered himself off his bench, and led me to the kitchens, where I ate a small bowl of soup and some more bread. Then we wandered about till I found myself back at the same corridor, and I settled in to more waiting.

I'd known, at the back of my mind that this delightful state of joy could not last. When the crash came, it was more brutal, perhaps, than I'd expected. I became suddenly aware of a hundred things I did not want to face.

Such as how to go home and tell my family what I'd become. Such as what on earth I was going to do with the rest of my massively screwed up existence. There were other things, probably worse ones, if I'd given them house room, but I concentrated on those. They were at least concrete, if insurmountable, problems; the more philosophical ones waiting in the dimmer, dirtier recesses of my mind could wait.

I had just worked my way around my most pressing questions for the third or fourth time, with no appreciable improvement, when someone tapped me on my shoulder and said Lord Gervase would see me now.

The short strip of hallway that separated me from the door seemed awfully long, suddenly. I could feel myself trembling, tried to get a grip on my fears and fantasies, and pushed open the heavy wooden door.

Gervase, Lord Steward of Fairbridge, was seated at a table piled with parchments, tapping his pen impatiently when I came in. His countenance was unhelpful, he studied me with the regard one usually accords to weevilly grain. I waited, wondering what he could possibly have to say to me.

"The Prince," he said finally, "seems to feel that the House of Machyll owes Orliegh something, Goddess knows why. He's instructed me to offer you a place on the border, at a fort called Penvarron."

My heart, in that one sentence, took a leap, and then a colossal dive. Penvarron. The well known dumping ground for useless commanders, incompetent quartermasters, and soldiers on their last ignoble steps to nowhere.

"I see you've heard of it. Well, girl, it isn't an order. You're free to choose it or go your own road. You're not likely to find a better offer, though."

He set a small copper disc, stamped with the Prince's seal, on the table.

I stared blindly at the design. I could get no lower in life, I thought, than Penvarron.

"Go on, take it. You should know," he added, "That we expect the Queen, and Baron Gallerrain here, sometime tomorrow. You might prefer to be on your way by then."

He knew how to apply the spurs. I picked up the token.

"Fine. Try keeping out of trouble for a year or two. You never know, you might make a soldier after all."

Five minutes later, I was back out in the corridor, holding a leather-wrapped packet stamped with the royal arms of Keraine. Another soldier, not Bors this time, was handing me my mail shirt, my sword and belt, and my daggers, and leading me off back to the courtyard. There was a horse saddled and waiting, and he urged me onto it with almost indecent haste. All of Fairbridge, it seemed, was eager to see the last of me.

Chapter 4

I was less than a day's hard ride out of Fairbridge when the storm clouds that had been gathering overhead finally let loose. What began as a determined little drizzle hardened into a steady rain and then progressed into a downpour, and by the time I found limited shelter between a rocky outcrop and some thick brush, it was bucketing down in torrents.

I led my horse up from the soggy, slippery roadbank and unsaddled her, and then half-slid and half-crawled as far back into my damp refuge as I could, by which point I was muddy to my knees and soaked to the skin. My bedroll, when I unrolled it was as wet as I was, and the last of my bread had turned to a sodden inedible mess.

The mare glared at me with malevolence. She was a tough little brute, built for endurance, with an evil and malicious disposition.

"You can't blame the rain on me," I said. "I'll admit to the rest of it, but I'm no happier about this than you are."

When I'd made camp the night before, I'd hoped for a respite from my unhappiness through sleep; I had not gotten it. Though the weather had been more co-operative, my dreams had not been. I'd been wakened constantly by nightmares of the lowest kind: the dead had followed me through the darkness, asking various unanswerable questions, and several of the people I cared most about in the world of the living had shown up to add their own opinions. I had gotten up less rested than I'd been when I'd lain down, and in a thoroughly depressed frame of mind.

I had come to the conclusion that life could not possibly be more hopeless.

Staring out at the rain and the black unhelpful sky, I considered my present condition. I was shivering with cold, I was filthy, wet, hungry, exhausted and miserable, a pardoned criminal facing a future with a garrison that was noted only for its disreputable character and utter lack of usefulness. There was nothing for leagues around it that Kerraine needed to defend, nor anything much to defend against, and my chances at rehabilitating myself, or even earning a transfer to a less unappetizing locale were less than nothing.

Short of the hanging I had expected, I could not be closer to dead.

The weather, as if to mock my mood, turned fine and warm, one of those last, unexpectedly sweet days of summer filled with sunshine and soft breeze. I crossed the River Varre and turned to follow it eastwards, and, looking out over the bare and unlovely hills, I saw in the distance the ancient fortress of Penvarron.

It was less than inspiring, though in other times I might not have thought so. There was no other habitation for miles around, and Penvarron, built out of the gray local stone, rose up like a mountain, dwarfing the already stunted trees. I shivered, despite the day's warmth.

I could, I thought, turn away. I had a horse, a sword. If I rode back north and hired on to some merchant-train headed to Fendrais, I could lose myself in distant lands, and forget myself, my past. The garrison wasn't expecting me.

The thought was attractive, if only for a moment or two. Then I considered my parents, considered the fact that I was alive and hadn't expected to be, considered that His Royal Highness, Prince Tirais, had chosen this for me, and realised that it simply wasn't in me to run.

So I reined in at the river's edge instead, and set about making myself, if not precisely presentable, at least less like a piece of refuse thrown up by an angry tide.

I stripped off my arming tunic and trews and knelt in the shallows and scrubbed at ten days' mud and sweat and blood till they were as clean as they were likely to get, and spread them out in the hot sun to dry. I unwound and discarded my bandaging, and stood waist deep in the Varre and washed every part of me three times over - my body appeared to disbelieve in its clean state and wanted convincing. I used first my fingers, then a twig, to disentangle the knots in my hair. I went over Banshee with the same thoroughness, avoiding her snapping and small outward kicks, so that she, too, was in as good shape as she could be.

Penvarron did not improve on closer examination. A small village had grown up around the walls, to serve the soldiers' off-duty needs; it was tiny, tawdry, and mean-looking, even by my limited experience.

I had dreaded going to Penvarron not least because, in the normal course of events, I thought that I would have to explain myself to my commanders. It would be without excuses, because they wouldn't be interested in anything but the bare facts of my treason. Even in Penvarron, the lowest of the low would look on me with contempt.

Or so I thought.

The main gates stood wide open, and there was no actual guard within sight as I rode up.

No-one was inclined to pay me any attention at all, and when I finally did explain my presence to an apparently off-duty guards-captain, he seemed unable to think what he should do about it.

Penvarron was in an uproar. A patrol captain had been found lying dead at the foot of a set of rickety stairs, in a confused tale involving a famous curse, internal wrangles, and homemade hooch, not necessarily in that order. I heard three separate versions in first hour I was there, as I passed from one group of indecisive and uninterested officers to another. It was with a certain amount of shock that I discovered, in the second hour of ineffective and tedious waiting, that this tragedy was not a fresh one. The man had died ten days before. The garrison, having drunk and diced the month's wages away, had seized on the story and given it a life of its own. Many of my informants could not, at this point, remember the man's name.

It took three full glasses, all told, for someone to realise my presence meant something, however trivial, and that there was someone who might reasonably wish to know of it. Not, as I would have assumed, in my innocence, the garrison commander, Sir Aidan, but his second-in-command, a woman named Sorcha, who unbent so far as to come out of the main barracks and bellow across the courtyard for me to come on in.

Sorcha was the most extraordinary woman I had ever seen. She was, first of all, enormous: well over six feet tall, and hugely, happily fat, and she exuded a terrifying good humor, the kind that ogres in fairy tales are reputed to have. She took the packet of papers that Lord Gervase had handed to me, along with my token, tossed them carelessly onto an already overloaded table, and remarked that Penvarron was no doubt different than what I was used to.

I said that I wasn't really used to anything in particular.

"You'll be all right here, then." She gave me a surprisingly sweet smile, despite a couple of missing teeth. "Just bear in mind that Sir Aidan's, well, a bit under the weather, just now."

"I see," I said. I didn't, really, but who cared?

"Right, then. Well, no time like the present."

The room that Sir Aidan was in was dark and shuttered. He was sitting more or less upright, and the smell, stale and rank, told me immediately what ailed him. He was drunk. Not stinking, on-a-temporary-bender-drunk. Just unpleasantly and habitually drunk. He blinked, attempted to focus and then lapsed into a huddle in his chair, while Sorcha explained carefully that I was just arrived from the Prince, and that it was timely, wasn't it? Seeing as how they were a little shorthanded, just now.

"Shorthanded? shorthanded for what?" said Aidan. "Not like we do anythin-"

But he broke off as Sorcha bent down and began whispering in his ear. Then he made a serious attempt at sitting up.

"Got any command experience?'

"Yes," I began, "But I'm not actually-"

"Perfect. I'll give you a patrol. Just a small unit, not what you're used to I'm sure." He shot me an evil grin.

My heart, not buoyant anyway, sank further. I wondered how many times in my life people would hand me command on the barest of pretexts.

At least this time I knew I was being set up: I had gathered, amid the speculation on the cause of young Diarmuid's untimely demise, that his death posed a certain problem for Sir Aidan.

The patrol's second could not be promoted, for reasons that were unclear to me but apparently were ironclad certainties to the soldiers I'd talked to. No other resident of Penvarron was willing to take on the duties of commanding a patrol unit which had lost its captain in such unsavory circumstances, especially since most of the theories concerning his death seemed to be turning on the idea that his arrival at the bottom of the stairs with a broken neck had not been voluntary.

I said, as calmly as I could, "Thank you sir. I'll do my best."

We went out, after Aidan and I exchanged a couple more idiotically trite and conventional phrases.

Sorcha seemed very pleased. She began giving me a tour of Penvarron, mainly from the windows on the second level, pointing out the practice-ground, the stables and the barracks that housed my troop. I got up my courage and asked about duties.

"Ah, well, you'll be taking them out on patrols, dearie. I post the roster every seven-day. And there's the extra watches, when the supply wagons come in, we all do a little bit of that."

Then, as she began leading me down the stairs to pick up my things, I was struck by an errant thought.

"Sorcha, he didn't take my oath. Oughtn't we, I mean, well, go back and, well…you know…"

"People come and go so much here, dear," she said vaguely. It was news to me.

"But how will I get paid?"

"Oh, don't worry. I'll just put your name over top of Diarmuid's on the roster. No-one cares who you are, dear, just so long as you're here. You just do your work, keep your head down and hope for the best."

"Hope for the best?' I could hear the disbelief in my own voice. She stopped and looked at me, with a kind of rough sympathy in her eyes.

"Look, here. You think this is the end of everything, don't you? Well, it could be. But for some of us, it's the best we can do. Look at me. I never would have got so far, if not for Penvarron. I wouldn't be second latrine digger, any other place. Best thing that ever happened to me, getting sent down here."

"How did it happen?' The words were out before I could stop them.

"Whoring, darlin'. They warned me, but I didn't listen. Short of dumping me out entirely, this was it. And look how well I've done."

Whoring. I stared at her enormous body.

"Who paid whom?"' My accursed tongue, I thought, but to my eternal astonishment she gave a roar of laughter.

"Who paid Who!" she chortled. She dealt me a clap on the shoulder that staggered me forward a pace. "Who paid Who! Oh that's good, dearie. Oh you'll do, all right. You'll do. But you don't want to go askin' those questions too often, now do you? Bad manners, in Penvarron."

Chapter 5

No-one had bothered to turn out the dead man's quarters. It had the musty smell of unwashed blankets and ancient sweat. A jumble of ragged clothes lay strewn on the floor, along with the other bits and pieces of Diarmuid's brief life. I could see that someone, or perhaps several someones, had already gone through and removed everything of value.

There was a second door, one that led to my patrol's barrack-room. I could hear nothing from the other side, but I knew they were there, speculating on my character, and assuming the worst. I had been in Penvarron for several hours now, long enough for the rumor mill to have gotten cranked up and rolling. It took quite a few grains of the glass for my stalwart conscience to convince me that the sooner I got this bit over with, the better.

I opened the door. My suspicions were justified; the entire patrol, twenty strong, were there, carefully posed to look as elaborately indifferent to my arrival as possible, and watching me as narrowly and closely as cats on the prowl. About halfway down the row of cots, one man had decided to pretend to sleep.

Unlucky choice, I thought, as I walked down through that hostile silence, leaned over his head and bellowed in his ear:

"On your feet!"

I could feel them stiffen in shock, but I didn't dare turn round to look. They had actually been startled, which was a point for me, and I couldn't spoil the effect.

"All of you," I called out as I straightened up. "Stand to."

"What the fuck for?" said the man on the bed.

I reached out, grabbed his hair, and jerked him out on to the floor.

"Because I said so."

He got up. I could hear the others shifting around me, tense, expectant. He had the look of the squad strongman, which was lucky, because I didn't want to waste the next week fighting each of them in turn. I gave him just enough time to strike an attitude of insolent nonchalance.

Then I broke his nose.

It was easy. I was taller than he was, and in far better condition than he was, as well as being in a thoroughly foul mood. I looked up and down the barracks.

31

"Anyone else want to discuss who's in charge? No? Fine. You don't want me here. Guess what? I don't want to be here, either. That's life. Full of nasty surprises. I want someone to take this man down to the healer and get him looked after. I'll meet with whichever of you is the patrol second in one half-glass. The rest of you had best look to your kit. I'll see all of you on the practice-ground at dawn tomorrow. That's all."

I shut the door to my quarters with a minimum of force, leaned against the frail wood, shut my eyes and breathed slowly and carefully until I thought I probably wouldn't throw up.

It took the best part of the half-glass I had given myself to open the windows and doors and dump the filthier and more useless of Diarmuid's belongings out into the small courtyard outside our barracks. I kept the straw-filled pallet on the bed; it seemed no dirtier than the floor, after all, and was miraculously free of vermin. For the rest, the only things of value appeared to be a map of the general area, a roughly turned wooden goblet, and a rather prettily carved comb, which I'd found wedged between the wall and the bunk.

A tentative scratch at the door made me look up from my contemplation of the map.

"Come in," I said.

He was a solid looking man, about twenty-five, with the kind of build that turns early to fat, tow-headed, and pale blue eyes that were carefully free of any expression at all.

"Captain?"

"You'll be the patrol second, I take it." He didn't look overtly hostile. He looked nervous, which considering my little performance wasn't unnatural.

"Yes, sir. Tighe, sir."

"Yes. Well. That man, he's all right, is he?"

"Ari? Yes, sir. Healer says he'll manage."

"Well, then. The patrol looks a bit unfit. You and I will have to get them into shape, won't we? But that's for another day. If you could rustle me up something to eat, I'd be grateful. It was a long ride; I'll be getting an early night."

"Yes, of course."

"And, Tighe," I said as he turned to go, "Get someone to shift that crap out there."

He nodded. "I'll see to it."

Someone brought me bread and a piece of hard, sharp cheese, and a bowl of watery porridge. I could hear good-natured complaints outside my door, as a couple of men dragged away the pile of refuse I'd created.

On the other side of the wall, I could hear the muffled sounds of soldiers doing the things that soldiers do when hanging around in barracks. The sound of blades being sharpened, of gear being emptied out onto the floor, the occasional curse or laugh. It was the most familiar and comfortable background I could imagine. I fell easily and deeply into sleep.

They were all on the practice ground on time, even Ari, despite the unwieldy splinting and bandaging the garrison healer had devised. They looked hungover and resentful, but their complaining wasn't beyond the normal limits of any other group of soldiers rousted out for dawn practice. On the other hand, they were unbelievably out of condition, and I had to keep them to basic drills; even so, within an unusually short time, they were huffing and puffing like cattle in labour.

There were two other units sharing the grounds with us, who gazed on my lot with undisguised contempt, which cheered me up. It meant that Penvarron wasn't completely devoid of real soldiers.

It wasn't even a half-glass before Third East Patrol was visibly flagging. I gave them a few more grains, which was only slightly less than they could take, so that they could retain some shreds of self-respect, then dismissed them with orders to be on duty directly at noon. The roster claimed that we were to do a routine swing out over the south trail, whatever that was. I hoped Tighe knew. The map that I had was woefully inadequate.

They were a little late lining up for our patrol, but I couldn't fault them for it; the noonday rations had been delayed by a fight that had broken out in the lineup. Beyond saying to Tighe that he might, in future, get them out of barracks a little earlier, I let it alone. My advice had been more in the nature of letting them know I had noticed their lateness than any real criticism and they knew it. Tighe just grinned and said if I knew any way to shift their lazy butts quicker, he'd be glad to know it.

After the morning drill, the two of us had sat in the sun and discussed, in a guarded, careful way, the status of Third East. It appeared that Diarmuid had been a weak and ineffective captain, and that he had lost control of the unit in an astonishingly short time.

33

Morning practice wasn't the least of it. Squabbles had gone unchecked, theft had been rampant, and since they had missed several patrol missions, Sorcha had docked their pay. They were thoroughly demoralized, undisciplined, and rudderless. Diarmuid had left this vale of tears none too soon, I thought. Two more months and they'd have been unredeemable.

Looking at them now, I wasn't sure it wasn't already too late. We'd started out the still unmanned gates in fairly good order, and marched down the rough track leading south, still maintaining two files, but within minutes, they'd begun to drift and shift around, looking at each other and discussing the local whores, instead of watching the terrain. Despite a complete lack of cover, they would have been slaughtered by an approaching enemy before they'd have noticed anything was amiss.

I stopped them. Pointed out the problem. They listened in sullen silence. We started up again. There was no improvement in the lines.

"Keep to your places," I said again.

"What the hell for?" muttered someone at the back. "We're the bloody walking dead anyway."

"Yes, well, try being a walking dead soldier, instead of a walking dead yobbo at a country fair," I recommended.

This drew a laugh, as I'd hoped. To humor me, they sorted themselves back into two lines, and managed, more or less, to keep to them. They were still uneven, out of step, and there was too much chatter, but at least, I thought gloomily, if we were attacked, they wouldn't kill each other just getting their weapons out.

Chapter 6

It was amazing how quickly time passed at Penvarron. After a few days of drills, my patrol no longer sounded as if they were all about to expire en masse, and they could keep to a line fairly well. They would have gotten no commendations for style, and they still had a tendency to discuss trivialities as they marched, but we no longer ran the risk of being set upon and slaughtered by any passing trader with a murderous impulse.

Our lives had settled quickly into a familiar, if tedious, round of drills, patrolling, and kit inspections, and the number of pointless quarrels had dropped down to something more of an annoyance than a constant menace.

After the first week, I managed to cajole Sorcha into advancing me some of my future wages, partly by agreeing to help her write the quarter's report for the main garrison at Glaice.

"Not that it matters," she said. "They never read them. Still, it's our duty to write them. So I do, dearie, and if you could help out with the spelling and such, I'd be glad."

Sorcha had decided, since I had afforded her some amusement with my arrival, that she liked me. She invited me occasionally for a drink in her quarters, where she regaled me with tales of the garrison's stranger moments. It was fun, although I kept wishing she wouldn't punch me in the arm when she made a point. It hurt like hell; she was incredibly strong.

If anything had saved Penvarron from complete collapse, it was Sorcha. She kept the entire place going.

Considering the nature of the task, she was possibly the most brilliant administrator the Kingdom had. Food got prepared, latrines got cleaned, watches got kept (more or less), units got paid. She wrote, in addition to the reports, endless politely-worded letters requesting money and materials to make much-needed repairs. If the assistance was not forthcoming, it was not due to lack of effort on Sorcha's part.

She understood what her job was and she did it, faithfully and conscientiously. She didn't understand why Penvarron's garrison should patrol the vast expanse of bleak and uninhabited terrain that lay to the east, but since the rules said we should patrol, we patrolled.

Our patrol designations were pure whimsy, though. Sorcha might not be clear on tactics, but she did understand human nature, and the need to alleviate boredom. Third East patrolled whatever direction Sorcha saw fit to send us.

Of Sir Aidan, I saw very little. He emerged at the end of my second seven-day, apparently sober, to issue a stream of slightly hysterical orders, and two draconian punishments, then retreated back to his quarters. The punishments were not carried out, and the new orders were ignored. Sorcha merely noted them, in a tongue-in-cheek way, to the captains, with a direction to check with her if we found they interfered with our normal duties, and we forgot them.

My natural comrades, the other patrol and watch captains, ignored me at first. I was an enigma in Penvarron, appearing suddenly and alone, without warning as I had. They were polite enough, but distant, partly, I guessed, because the entire garrison was waiting to see what fresh disaster would befall Third East.

When the patrol no longer seemed in danger of deserting suddenly as a group, and it looked as if I was remaining reasonably healthy, some of them unbent so far as to offer advice about the two taverns in Penvarron's pitiful excuse of a village, and to invite me to share jugs of ale, provided, of course, I bought them myself.

These evenings were among the least interesting I have ever spent. My fellow-captains' main interests were making wagers they couldn't afford to lose, comparing the relative merits of garrisons none of us were ever likely to be posted to, and complaining about Sorcha.

In fact, the captains' attitude towards Sorcha puzzled me. They were plainly terrified of her; her rages were rumored to be lethal, and they obeyed her orders without question, but they treated her with barely concealed contempt. They were better born, of course, but Sorcha was no fool; she knew when she was being patronized.

People did, I discovered, get transferred out of Penvarron. Orders occasionally came down for a unit to be sent elsewhere. Which unit was entirely up to Sir Aidan, which meant that Sorcha told him who to send. It seemed a little stupid to alienate the one person who could decide your future, when a little ordinary courtesy would have cost you nothing.

People also deserted, I heard, which explained Sorcha's elliptic comment on comings and goings. She gave them two weeks; if they didn't turn up, she listed them as 'discharged due to malingering', which did lend credence to the garrison's firm belief that no-one ever read Sorcha's quarterly reports. Only the dead or the absent could be said to be malingering by Penvarron's standards.

By the middle of my second week, Third East had recovered itself so far as to make disparaging remarks about Second North Patrol. North Two was notorious for marching out to a point just out of sight of the gates, and steadfastly loafing about until they thought they could get away with coming back.

In winter, this would be cutting off your nose to spite your face: the only way to keep warm, I judged, would be to keep moving as fast as you could. In any case, they fooled no-one, least of all Sorcha, who retaliated by putting them on to the worst of garrison maintenance jobs as often as she could without being obvious.

The patrol and I had come to a basic understanding, helped by my spending part of my advance on a hideously overpriced keg of ale, rolling it into the barracks, and setting down to drink it dry with them. Tongues loosened by free booze, they fell to reminiscence, and I learned a lot about them, and Penvarron, in the process.

Third East had been a perfectly ordinary unit, up on the main frontier, until suddenly they had been transferred to Penvarron without reason. They'd had a good captain when they arrived, perhaps too good, according to Tighe, who thought that another commander had seen Fean as a threat and used a quick transfer to Penvarron as a handy way to rid himself of the risk of being outshone.

Both the reputation and the reality of Penvarron had done Fean in. He had hung himself at the end of the first month.

Aidan had then promoted Diarmuid, who'd been a second with Third South Patrol, and the downhill slide, natural enough when a captain chooses a coward's way out, began in earnest. Diarmuid had been at least four years older than I, but he was not what good commanders are made of.

Good commanders win no popularity contests. You do the job. If your unit hates you, it doesn't matter, as long as they'll follow orders. Consistency is the key: no matter how incomprehensible your orders, they should at least know what to expect, but Diarmuid had alternated between officiousness and spineless sucking up. In an attempt to have both affection and order, he had wound up with neither.

Surprisingly, Third East did not subscribe to any of the lurid theories surrounding his death.

Most of them admitted that they had witnessed it, pointing out that lots of people from other units had been there as well, when Diarmuid, drunk to the gills, had climbed the makeshift wooden steps to Guard-tower Three. He had been engaged in cursing the gods, individually and by name, when he had lost his balance, and pitched headlong down the stairs. It was probably that last piece of indiscretion which had given rise to the idea that there was a curse on

37

the unit. Soldiers are almost fanatically superstitious; no-one would touch Third East.

My arrival had saved Aidan from having to commit the social solecism of elevating the peasant-born Tighe to captain's rank, which apparently the other captains had viewed as impossible. Tighe, in fact, agreed with them. He didn't know of anyone without some pretensions to gentility who was in command, except, of course, Sorcha, who would have been an anomaly even outside Penvarron. On the whole, Third East's opinion was that as I didn't seem either suicidal or given to drink, they could bear with my obsession with drills and marching, especially if I was going to stand them a keg every so often.

The rhythm of our days was well on the way to be a traditional, established habit, when the first of the winter supply trains rolled over the horizon, bearing bags of flour, salted meat, and a wealth of disquieting news.

Chapter 7

Penvarron's peculiar culture had prevented anyone from asking me what had been going on in the rest of Keraine, in case the question touched on the reasons for my sudden appearance, and since it did, I naturally had been reluctant to volunteer my own story. The supply train guards, however, were full of Uln's treachery, and other, more frightening information.

At the same time as my doomed farmhands had been marching to treason, two other local landholders had attempted to overrun a couple of the Queen's posting forts along the West Road.

Then two days after Fairbridge, as soon as Tirais had pulled a good number of the border garrisons in to deal with what appeared to be a local insurrection, the Camrhyssi had poured over the border like a plague. The stories were confused and garbled, but it seemed that they had come in real force this time, and apparently taken at least two small border forts by the time the supply train left, reluctantly, for the south.

Speculation ran rampant, among the supply train guards and the garrison. For two whole days, the watches actually patrolled the east walls, instead of camping themselves over the west gate to watch the drunken revelry in the village below, as was their usual habit. Every unit began betting on the chances, if our losses were severe enough, of whether they would be called up to march north in support of the Queen. Penvarron's hapless and ill-trained troops walked with a snap, the gates got manned (although not, in fact, closed, even at night) and the air fairly crackled with hope.

On the third day, the carter who brought supplies for Penvarron's mean little tavern arrived with the depressing news that the Queen's forces had pushed the Camrhyssi back over the border and retaken the two forts, with bad losses on both sides. It seemed unlikely that there would be transfers. With time on her side now, Queen Elowyn could afford to call up the lords' manor-fees, in the form of well-trained household units out of the west ridings. Penvarron sank back into lethargy and routine.

I kept my own counsel. Barring a few sideways looks from some of my fellow-captains, who grasped the relevance of just when I had arrived to the recent news, there was little to tie me, in anyone's mind, to these disasters. I understood now that Fairbridge had been in the nature of a feint, that Uln was more than a simple, garden variety traitor, and that silence, in the face of this larger turmoil, was my only option. I took Sorcha's advice, kept my mind on my work, and hoped, not for glory, but for a respectable oblivion.

After only a few weeks of patrolling, I could understand Penvarron's general air of hopelessness even more.

As a strategic locale, it was pointless: it was, as near as I could figure, at least a two-week march for any sizable force from the nearest stronghold in Camrhys, over some of the most miserable and bleak terrain ever devised. A thin and infertile soil covered the hard gray rock, supporting tough and malignant grasslands, relieved only by some marshy stretches of bog.

The bare hills reached out for miles, dotted with occasional stands of thin and wind-twisted, stunted trees. There were no farms or villages to support an incoming force, so that an army would have to bring everything it could possibly want with it; although there was some game, it tended to the small and scarce. An approaching force would be noticed two days before it got to the fortress, even with the watch's tendency to ignore its duties.

Once at Penvarron, an army had two choices: it could ignore us and march by, leaving us free to harry its baggage train at will, and considering our general attitude towards each others' belongings, it seemed unlikely that we could resist the temptation.

Or they could try taking the fort. This seemed even less likely than the first choice; regardless of Penvarron's troops' ability, the stronghold was, in fact, just that. Assuming that we lacked the wit to send a message to the Queen, we could still shut our gates and expect to hold out for at least a month. If we did send a message, we were only a few hours' ride from the first tiny stirrings of civilization.

For a single rider or a cavalry troop, that was nothing. For an army on the march, it was disaster. And a siege, under those conditions, was worse; Penvarron's walls were incredibly stout and rose from a promontory of rocky soil that overlooked the River Varre. A besieging army would have to sit at the foot of that rise and wait it out. Assaults of the more conventional sort would be suicidal, or pointless. The possibility of breaching those walls was at best slim, if not impossible. There was no easy ground to tunnel under, and any attack on the gates left the attackers pitifully exposed. Fifty well-trained soldiers could expect to hold Penvarron, and we were, if not well-trained, at least numerous.

It all begged the question of why, in this useless and unlikely situation, anyone had built a stronghold here at all.

Penvarron itself was odd, anyway. Despite the high thick walls, it did not conform to any standards of a fortress that I knew.

There were, for a start, two sets of gates, one facing back to the west, and to Keraine proper (you couldn't, over time, think of Penvarron as part of anything, least of all Keraine), and one set facing east, where out somewhere past the mist and the hills, lay Camrhys. Just inside the west gate, a collection of larger buildings had been erected to form a courtyard, and in the upper bailey beyond, time and long occupation had produced a haphazard and muddled collection of one- and two-story barracks, cooksheds, latrines and cisterns.

All of these looked at first glance, to be centred around a huge stone tower that rose high above it all, far higher than the massive walls, but in fact, they were clustered away from the tower, huddling towards the sullen rocks to leave as much space as possible between the living quarters and this huge hovering stone presence.

Additionally, the guard towers themselves were mostly afterthoughts to the general scheme of things. They were of wood, primarily, and had been added at random intervals along the old walls, at wholly illogical points. They did command a good view of the surrounding terrain, but they seemed to have been placed in response to several individual concerns, not with an eye to any general plan involving efficiency or military tactics. Only those over the gates were of stone, and that was of a definitely inferior and later quality than that of the walls themselves.

Although the tower was central in a physical way, the troops at Penvarron never crossed directly to anywhere in the yard. Complex and time consuming routes had been established to get you to your destination while keeping you as far as possible from the tower.

I thought this silly, but camp traditions are always hard to fight, and this was no exception. I could not make my patrol march directly across the yard, and I knew better than to try. Inside of a month, I had gotten used to walking all the way around the alley behind First East's barracks, across the bottom of the yard, and back up another twisting maze to our mess, so much so that it stopped even registering on me that I could save a quarter-glass by walking straight across the centre of Penvarron and hanging a quick left.

In the beginning though, the tower intrigued me. It was the only other building that was of an age with the walls, it looked stout and well-built, and indefinably aristocratic, the perfect place for a commander's quarters. According to Sorcha, during another of our evenings of cheap wine and garrison gossip, most of them had tried to live there, even Sir Aidan. He had lasted three weeks, when suddenly, without warning, he had ordered his belongings moved to the main barracks, transferred Sorcha down to the main level, and ensconced himself in a pair of rooms facing resolutely west.

41

"It's haunted, they say," Sorcha was leaning back, tilting a frail-looking chair to a dangerous angle. "Built by the ancients, when they first come to Penvarron. They say there's those in there that will never rest."

"Superstition," I said. Or tried to say. I had drunk rather a lot, and my speech was none too clear. Keeping up with Sorcha was a fool's errand, but I always gave it my best shot.

"All too right, dearie," she agreed. "I reckon it's just gloomy and damp, myself. Not that I been inside, barring to get my orders, those three weeks, and that was in daylight."

"Was Aidan sober enough to give orders?"

"Well, that's the odd bit. He was all right then. A little depressed, mind, and out of temper, but he didn't hit the bottle so hard then. At least not during the day. What he did at night I don't know, nor care. But one day, out he comes, tosses my things down the stairs, and says he'll have my rooms, thank you very much, and he's been drinking steady ever since. Not that I minded. Those stairs is killer, at my weight."

She refilled our cups, and we both fell silent. She was right about the tower. It was old, far older than anything else in Penvarron. It didn't explain the superstitious and obdurate behavior of the troops, though. Parts of Orliegh were as old as Penvarron, and nobody had ever suggested that they were haunted, except my brothers, who had enjoyed terrifying me when I was young, with tales of mad wizards roaming the hallways in search of human sacrifices.

"Superstition," I said again. "Ignorant, stupid soldiers' tales."

"I expect you're right dearie, but you can't change their minds, can you? They want to walk an extra ten miles a day making sure they don't go near it, well, you just chalk it up to extra training and live with it, don't you? Because when all is said and done, it does make the days go by."

The days did go by. One morning was much like another, and our afternoons were distinguished only by whether we had patrols to walk or some other duty, or were left, once or twice a week, to fill in our time as best we could, honing our weapons, mending our boots, or, in my case, taking Banshee out along the trails and trying not to think about anything. After a while, I found it was easier; the days merged with one another, the past began to blur.

I began to view it, when I gave it any thought at all, with an emotionless detachment, as if it had occurred to someone else, a long, long time ago. My rides out into the countryside confirmed my suspicions that Penvarron was a meaningless exercise in a military stupidity that said if you've got a fortress, you've got to staff it, and I could sympathise with the general disbelief in our own worth. If Camrhys had never attacked this place, never was going to attack it, and would be utterly insane even to consider it, it made it hard for those ostensibly defending it to take it seriously. Coupled with the reputation of the garrison, and the knowledge that we would likely spend the rest of our careers here, well, it did something to us all. The discontent in Penvarron was a tangible thing, sucked down with your evening ale, and sweated out of the very walls.

It wasn't all unrelieved gloom, of course.

There was one afternoon, out on patrol, the unit having backslid so far as to start nattering in the ranks, when I dismounted to give them a severe ticking off. I was just getting warmed up and enumerating their many flaws when I caught Ari rolling his eyes in a parody of long suffering, an expression so exactly like the one I had felt on my own face during my father's endless lectures on discipline that I stopped midsentence, lost my train of thought, and dissolved into helpless giggles.

This naturally set them off - we stood in an unlikely clump in the middle of bloody nowhere, howling with laughter. Every time I attempted to straighten up and start anew, saying "No, seriously," it doubled us over again, till we were weak and gasping, and I was leaning on a rock for support. We completed our route and got back to the fortress late but in a high good humor that lasted several days.

The countryside around Penvarron was not entirely without beauty, either. There is a powerful feeling to that kind of vast openness, and something wonderful when, on a clear day, you gazed out over the raw hills, knowing that there was absolutely nothing ahead of you for miles upon miles. It was only when, in my second month there, when the colder winds came whistling across those hills, that the walls of Penvarron's hopelessness seemed to close back in on me, and the sense of futility, the endless, pointless routines, began to chafe on us all.

But soldiers have held out in harder positions, down through eternity. To give in to this feeling was, by my father's teachings, simply wrong. I could be dead, I thought. We could all be dead.

One night, I tried to explain it to my patrol. The weather had turned chill and wet, we'd done four days of slogging through the mud of our designated routes, and they were at the stage where you wind up with quarrels that lead naturally to violence, just to break the monotony. I spent the last of my hoarded coins on another overpriced keg of ale, and rolled it into the barracks myself.

"Look," I said, when they'd settled down to serious drinking, and begun listing for me the reasons why they just couldn't stand life at Penvarron anymore. "Look, what we do is no different than any other soldier's life."

"Tell that to the latrines," said Ari. "It was never like this at Carthen."

"Maybe not. Out near the Camrhys border, well, that's bound to be different. But for most troops, that's not how it is. How do you think they fare out near say, Westfold? Some grand lord's troops? They aren't near the border. They probably haven't seen any action since Glaice was besieged and that's what? oh, twelve years now? If they're inland a bit, they don't even worry that a boatload of Istaran pirates will make it that far south. If it came to it, the lord would probably just pay the shield-fees for them and they'd stay right at home. Do you think they just loaf about, crying in their beer? They get up every morning, and do their drill, same as us, and march out some road that's as safe as being home in front of the fire, same as us, and," here I looked significantly at Ari, "They keep their blades sharpened, too. And they're no more likely to see danger than we are. But they keep on."

"The food's better," said Ari. We all laughed.

"I can't argue that. The pigs on my father's farms get better. But barring that, we're like any peacetime force. We just do what soldiers do, Westfold, or any place else."

"Maybe," said Wenna. "But they've got respect. And we don't."

"Respect? That's something you have to find yourself. You have to do the things worthy of respect. We have to do what we're paid to do. What the kingdom needs us to do. Maybe if we weren't here the Camrhyssi would try marching this way. Maybe being here keeps them off." And maybe those well-fed pigs would fly. But then I realized that I had actually convinced myself.

And them. It did make a weird, but elegant sort of sense. They sat silent, absorbing the idea. Then Wenna stood up and said "To Third East, then. And screw the Camrhyssi!"

We all laughed again and toasted ourselves and then Ari made a seriously crude suggestion concerning the sexual appetites of First North's captain, and we went back to being a bored and frustrated patrol unit with not much on its collective mind. We had been trained, and continued to train, for action, not sitting in a damp fortress growing mold, and since we knew it was not even a remote possibility, we could risk our dreams on battle and death.

Chapter 8

In addition to the daily patrols, once a month a party trudged the farther distance to Lesser Penne, a partly-collapsed fort about fifteen miles south. Sorcha kept it in minor repair, as best she could, and stocked with iron rations and a pile of wood. In case a patrol was benighted out along one of the southern trails, they were supposed to make for Lesser Penne for the night.

It had never actually happened; we were too canny and careful of our skins to allow ourselves to be trapped out in the open hills overnight without need, especially in winter. But if your squad drew Lesser Penne as a destination, you dragged them, complaining and bitter, over the downs, along with a pack-pony or two, spent a day or so doing whatever repairs necessary or possible, slept in its limited shelter, and then walked the same weary miles back. No-one liked this task, but its periodic appearance on the roster at least provided a change.

I had been at Penvarron for over two months when Third East's name came up for this duty. As the unlucky winners of Sorcha's roster-lottery, we duly checked our gear, shouldered our shields, and marched out before the sun had made its weak attempt to burn the morning mists off the hills.

Overall, though, I was pleased. For one thing, while the patrol had seen it as their Goddess-given right to grumble, they had done it while they were getting ready, not instead of.

And it was a chance to do some real soldiering.

We didn't get much variety at Penvarron. In the normal course of events, a squad is expected to do some guarding, some scouting, some mess-work, a whole array of jobs. Here, things had stratified: there were "soldiers" whose whole lives revolved around a single guard-tower, or a mess-hall, and one's work was jealously defended as the only really necessary function going on. It was stupid and it bred quarrelsome behavior, but it was so entrenched into the life of the place that you didn't even discuss a change, let alone infringe on someone else's patch.

We trekked the usual and by now, familiar trail south to a cairn of stones which marked the end of our normal patrol, and then struck out along the even narrower track that would take us to Lesser Penne. My map actually had had the fort marked, as one of its few major points, so I knew roughly where we were bound. As usual, it had got it wrong by a couple of miles or so, but Third East had done this job once before, and Tighe had warned me we would need an extra glass or so each way.

I was not much cheered by the first glimpse of Lesser Penne.

Once, it had been a real fortress, built around a hundred years before, with a good view of the rippling hills out towards Camrhys that would have been useful if we'd needed to have even earlier warning of an attacking force. Now, however, it lay desolate and empty, its walls crumbling with neglect and weather, and its ditch overgrown with grass. There were no effective guard towers left standing, the gates were missing entirely, and only one building was in good enough state to house our little group.

It was nearly dark; this late in the year, there was little enough daylight to patrol a short route, let alone cover double the distance in a day, so we made camp inside the ruined walls, and settled down for an uncomfortable night.

There were obvious leaks in the roof of our shelter; we were going to be very unhappy if the evening drizzle decided to upgrade itself to a full-blown storm, which seemed likely, given the signs. And, after I'd listened for twenty minutes to the patrol's ribald jokes and tired old grumbles, I realized I would be rendering the whole exercise even less appealing. They weren't going to like this one bit.

"All right," I said. "Let's set the pickets."

There was a moment of interesting silence.

"Pickets?' asked Colm. He was a nice boy, but lazier than anyone I'd ever met.

"Yes. You've heard of them, surely? What real soldiers do, when on the march?"

My honeyed tone wasn't lost on the others. They kept to a discreet and careful silence. Colm missed the warning signals, however.

"What the hell for? There ain't anyone here but us."

"Well," I said, "I'd bow to your superior knowledge, Colm, but you've never shown the Talents of a Seer before now. I believe I'll trust my own judgment on this, if that's all right with you."

Tighe, seated behind me, gave a snort that might have been laughter.

"That's right, lad. And you can take the first watch, just to show us how it's done. Seeing as how you have all this expert knowledge on when and why to set the pickets. Ari, you and Brighid go on out over the ditch there. You'll want someone on the back bit, Captain?"

"Colm can take that. And put a couple on the east approaches. Not too far out, mind you. Ari, wake me when you switch off. Three glasses apiece, and if one of you so much as blinks, you'll dig out the latrine-ditches alone come morning."

They were good about it, really. Wenna got caught up in a bargaining session about who would be on the middle shift, and managed, by trickily taking up a position of absolutely not wanting this least-favourable watch, to make sure that on the second night, she'd be able to sleep through the first two shifts, and be more or less rested for the long trek home. It was a nice piece of flim-flam, done right under Tighe's nose, and he appreciated it, even while complaining loudly that he'd been tricked out of his trews.

I didn't sleep much; despite taking the luxury afforded a captain of opting out of any assigned shift. Besides being awakened at every shift change, I needed to get up and walk the perimeter at random intervals to make sure they weren't curled up asleep at their posts. It had been far too long since Third East had had to act as though they actually had a job to do.

Nothing so much as a rabbit stirred in the night, a fact that Colm drew to my attention in the morning. I smiled and sent him to draw water from the one intact cistern.

We needed to fix the roof, but our resources were a bit limited: wood was not plentiful to begin with and we had no pitch to seal the makeshift repairs we did do. The rain had held off, but the wind had picked up in the night, threatening to destroy what little we could accomplish.

It was not a good day. Colm seemed to feel he was being put upon, not helped by Ari bestowing the nickname "Seer" on him. Then, Brighid fell from the narrow stone coping she had been standing on when handing pegs up to Tighe, and dislocated her shoulder. The only thing that saved us from murdering each other out of sheer pique was the promise of a really good dinner on our return to Penvarron. It was the usual reward for duty out to Lesser Penne, courtesy of Sorcha. She believed very firmly in the carrot-on-a-stick method of command.

The second night proved less dire than the first. The wind mercifully fell to a gentle enough breeze at sunset, and the idea of guard-duty no longer shocked them. The prospect of our return to Penvarron cheered me no end, which wasn't surprising. Despite its hardships, it offered a lot more comfort than Lesser Penne, and besides, it was beginning to feel like home.

When the second watch came off shift, I skipped my usual round, telling myself I wanted to keep them off balance. The truth was I was dog-tired, probably from two nights of truncated and irregular sleep. I'd had odd dreams, too, that kept waking me. I couldn't actually remember anything about them, other than being jolted into wakefulness with the distinct impression of impending doom.

Another of these nightmares dragged me into consciousness an hour later. I sat upright, my heart pounding, and my throat dry, then slowly the world came back to me. It was the unfamiliarity of my surroundings, I decided, that had me so out of kilter. I had never been prone to bad dreams before, barring a couple of rough nights just after Fairbridge.

After a few minutes, I got up, and made my way out to the ditch. Brighid and Ari were standing a few yards past a small knoll out front of where the gates would have been. I grinned as I went by, they were taking this piece of work with good-natured humour, even making up passwords of a rather crude and scurrilous nature, to challenge their comrades with.

The two out on the east side were also in position, although I suspected they'd been taking turns dozing in the grass, there was a bit of a depression, just about man-size, near the bit of stone wall beside them. Still, there weren't two spots, so they'd had the sense not to leave their post entirely. Whether they took this duty seriously or not was debatable, but at least they took me seriously. I let it go.

I started around to the back. Lucky Wenna, having drawn a full night's rest before her shift, had asked to be on the back, alone, as she had been on middle-watch the night before, but I couldn't see her.

Damn the girl, I thought. If she's gone to sleep in the grass, I'd have to make an example of her, and I couldn't think what an appropriate punishment would be. Normally she was a good soldier, taking what she was assigned with a good grace, not quarrelsome at all, and seemingly eager to learn new things. I moved out past the remains of a shed, which Tighe and I had decided constituted as good a perimeter marker as any, hoping she'd only thought to find a perch with a better view. Though how you could see much, in the misty beginnings of a false dawn, I couldn't imagine.

She wasn't there, as far as I could see. I felt a vague unease mixing with my captain's outrage. No lumpy silhouette in the shadows announced a sleeping backslider. There was nothing out here but grass and rock and the rubble of ruined walls. I turned to head back to the guard-point.

Just then, a figure emerged from a little fold in the hills to my right.

I breathed a sigh of relief.

"What the hell were you doing, leaving your post like that?" I said as she came up to me.

48

She looked tousled, and awake, but at my tone, she bristled.

"I was just taking a leak, Captain." Her own tone spoke volumes, mainly of resentment.

I relaxed. "Oh. Sorry. You shouldn't go so far, though. You had me worried."

"Well, but there's nothing here, is there? I mean, I understand about doing guard work, but Colm's right really. Not even the rabbits are hopping here."

"That's all to the good, Wenna. That's the point. We aren't sitting ducks for anything. That's what a picket is for."

"Yes. Well. Nearly dawn, now. Can't expect any excitement tonight, at any rate."

"You never know. All right, carry on."

She must be more tired than she let on, I thought, as I made my way back to my bedroll. She wasn't usually so snappish. Well, we were all tired. Good thing we'd be back in Penvarron tonight, with no work tomorrow. Perhaps I'd re-schedule morning drill for later in the day.

We were up early and packed and ready in record time, eager to put Lesser Penne behind us. Those who'd had an unbroken six glasses of sleep were cheerful and noisy. The rest of us just pushed our way through the business of breakfast (cold, since it seemed pointless to light a fire), a last check round to make sure that we weren't leaving some necessary bits of our belongings behind, and then setting out on the long road home.

It was, if that were possible, an even less eventful day than most others. In fact, the day before had been a welcome change. The excitement of Brighid's little accident, while unpleasant, and uncomfortable for her, had been the most unusual occurrence in our lives for days.

Being away from Penvarron even briefly made us feel better about the whole place and our lives, and the pickets, however useless, had had an effect on Third East. They were curiously happy. They felt like soldiers. They acted like soldiers. It was as good a lesson in command as any I'd ever gotten, and I felt even more respect for Sorcha, who had grasped this without any real training or the benefit of my father's long experience.

The sun made its first real appearance in days, burning away the last traces of fog, and even providing a little warmth. Wenna's spirits recovered, as did my own, our tiredness fell away, and we marched through the gates of Penvarron at sunset, looking more like a real patrol unit than we ever had before. Our dinner was nowhere as good as our imaginations had hoped for, but it was considerable better than our normal fare, and, helped by an extra wine-ration and our own comradely cheer, we had a riotous time.

Even a seven-day later, we still were in good spirits. Dawn drills were marked by a real effort to work in unison, even Ari made an attempt to keep his to his place in the line when we marched, and Colm stopped feeling aggrieved by his new monicker, but responded with careless good humour to queries on everything from tomorrow's weather to next week's menu.

The other units watched us with interest. Some of the watch-captains began to treat us as equals, which wasn't the norm in Penvarron. The watches, by and large, back-slid less than other units, they kept to some kind of ordered life, although their notion of what constituted an useful watch would not have impressed a seven-year-old manning the barricades on a snowfort anywhere else. But they turned up on time for drills and duties, and consequently looked down on the patrols, who had even slacker standards. Now Third East began to garner at least a grudging respect, even from the watch-captains, and I occasionally had someone congenial to drink with down in the tavern.

It seemed that Third East had beaten the company curse.

Chapter 9

I came awake suddenly in the night, with the sound of a whimper echoing in my ears. Lying in the darkness, though, I could hear nothing more than the sound of the wind sighing through the courtyards, and the irregular drips of rainwater from the eaves. My first thought was that one of the girls might have been raped.

It happens, even in well-run cantonments.

If someone, boy or girl, can't take care of themselves, or if the unit dislikes her, no-one will lift a finger to stop it, not even her friends, because otherwise, they might be next. I'd thought Wenna might be at risk, she seemed too passive and good-tempered to fend off unwanted advances, but the unit had gotten back its sense of itself, and lately I'd felt the danger had passed.

You never know, though. Some people just can't bear the idea of someone being beyond their reach. It isn't sex at all, just a form of bullying that has no remedy. She could have been waylaid on her way to the latrines by another patrol.

It wouldn't hurt to check. I got up and groped for my clothes in the darkness, dressed, belted on my sword, and eased open the door to the barracks.

There was no sound. As my eyes adjusted to the darkness I could see that they were all there, asleep and as unmoving as the dead.

I couldn't rest, though. The sound still trembled in my ears; it might have been a dream, or the wind, but I felt unsettled and uneasy, as though someone were watching me in the shadows.

I retreated back into my room and sat listening. It seemed unnaturally quiet, even for the hour. Penvarron was a place of almost continuous activity. There was no echo of guards calling out watch changes, or even of First East's ongoing dice game.

Just the wind, and the creaking of old, poorly made buildings, shifting in their foundations.

Finally I went out into the yard. The rain, an almost unfailing source of discomfort and inconvenience, had stopped late in the evening and it was a clear and moonless night, inky black, with only the wind to say that I wasn't dreaming.

I threaded my way down the twisting path of the sheds and barracks till I stood in the break between Fourth West and an abandoned shed, and listened for some sound, some sign to tell me that Penvarron lived.

The strange, soft whine came again, behind me. I turned, apprehensively, to the east and looked back to the gate. It was open.

We seldom used the east gate at all. The west gate was open all of the time, of course, so that officers and troops could come and go in the village at any hour, but there was nothing on the east side that was wanted. My first thought was that some poor idiot had decided to desert and, instead of walking out the unmanned west gates and losing themselves in the squalor and drunkenness there, had tried being clever. I squinted up to the walls, not very hopefully; no guard stood in view. Down watching Mag or the other whores from the fort walls, or else dozing in one of the towers. Stupid buggers, I thought and started for the gate.

My foot caught on some bit of rubbish, I skidded in the mud that covered the courtyard like slime, and went down hard and spinning onto my knees.

It was purest chance. I started to rise, lifting my head to look straight up the long rows of the Penvarron barracks, and a trick of angles and architecture had me staring, with a direct and unimpeded view, at Penvarron Tower.

I saw, in the cold starlight, its massive bulk rising up into the night. And there, about the second level, I saw the unmistakable flicker of light.

I wasn't frightened, not then. For some reason, my brain was moving slowly. I simply stared on, at the source of the light. There. There it was again, a little further to the left now. Unmistakably a light; a candle or a small, guttering torch, moving steadily upwards through the tower.

In, I thought, stupidly. In, not out. Someone had come in the gate.

I was on my feet and moving, not to the source of the light but back towards the barracks, stumbling over the uneven cobbles, and banging through my patrol's door, before I had another conscious thought.

"Tighe," I said, shaking him. "Tighe, get up. There's something going on." Then, as he grunted and blinked sleep groggily from his eyes, "Get them armed. And rouse the other units. Meet me at the tower. Move, curse you!"

Far away, I heard the sound of the watch alarm, and suddenly they were up and grabbing their kit. I didn't wait, but ran back out across the yard, and straight up the centre aisle of the bailey.

I was just rounding the foot of the tower, heading towards its one lone door, when I collided with a small mountain, which turned out to be Sorcha, fully armed, an amazing sight. Behind her was Aidan, with a motley collection of off-duty watch soldiers behind him still struggling with bits of clothing and kit.

"Right," she said, before I could open my mouth. "There's two dead, down by North Two's mess. Whatever the hell is going on?'

"Someone in the Tower," I said. "There's a light."

Aidan moved to the iron-bound door.

"Locked," he said. He looked remarkably sober and calm, as if this sort of thing happened daily.

"Window's not barred," said Ruan, Watch One's captain. "Garth, you're small enough. No, don't look at me like that," he added, as Garth's eyes widened. "You just nip in, and go straight for the door. Nothing to it."

"Wenna could," I said, as Third East came running up, but Ruan had already lifted Gareth up to the ledge and was shoving him decisively through the opening. I heard a grunt as the boy landed, the muffled steps, and then the soft creak of old ironwork moved, protesting, on its hinges.

I was behind Aidan as we entered. Above us, we heard steps and movement. Aidan went purposefully for the stairs.

The keep fell eerily silent. Then, as we began moving carefully up the stone stairway, I felt something. Faintly, from under my feet, the merest hint of a tremor, a vague shaking.

Then nothing.

Aidan motioned for some of the others to fan out into the rooms on the second level. The trembling, stronger this time, came again. And again. A little stronger. Like a heartbeat.

My own heart was beating strongly, too. I wasn't frightened, not yet. I was nervous, yes, apprehensive and on edge, the way you always are, confronting the unexpected, but I could hear more of our own troops coming in below us. Whoever was in Penvarron, they didn't have a chance.

We had reached the fourth level. The shaking under my feet was growing stronger still, becoming a sound now. Behind me, I heard Sorcha whispering to Ruan to send a few more people to check the rooms beyond.

Somewhere outside, I heard the sounds of fighting already started. I wondered briefly if Penvarron had at last gone mad.

The rhythmic pulsing grew ever louder as we moved up through story after story of Penvarron Tower. Aidan hesitated not at all, till we reached the last set of steps. It was ringing in my ears, echoing up through my bones, and at last I felt the first stirrings of fear.

Up till then, I suppose I had clung to the belief that it would all turn out to be another of Penvarron's garrison hoaxes. An officer's wager. A stupid prank gone wrong. But on the last landing, Sorcha's words about two dead, and the incessant drumbeat echoing up from the bowels of Penvarron Tower and rattling the stone walls, together with the open gate finally came together in my slow-moving mind, and the hair on my back of my neck literally stood on end.

Aidan seemed unshaken in his resolve. He stopped, peering up at the faint light reflecting down the stairs. Wordless, he looked back at us. He signaled a formation, and I heard the others shifting to comply. We listened, straining our ears, but only that incessant drumming, blocking out everything else, could be discerned. It was as if the rest of the Mother's creation had simply ceased.

Aidan looked at me. I nodded.

We started up the last flight of stairs.

Chapter 10

They knew we were coming, and had at least an inkling of what we were. We were walking into a complete unknown. I was glad, as we ducked and rolled through that archway, that it was only Camrhyssi soldiers. The tension of our climb through the tower gave way to habit. I kicked the knees out from under the man just inside the entrance, hacked viciously at the one behind him and grinned at Aidan. Behind us, Third East and the others were pouring through. Like most fights, it turned almost instantly to chaos.

"That way, I think," said Aidan, as the fight surged and eddied around us. He pointed to the door at the far end.

Certainly they seemed to be guarding it. We started across the room. The soldiers seemed inclined to stop us. It was bloody work, and damned annoying, I thought, as I slashed at one, stabbed at another. The door drew me. I wanted in and these lousy sons of whores, having disturbed my sleep, weren't going to stop me.

It was Sorcha who reached the door first. She tried the handle, then pulled back in alarm.

"Not locked," she said. She looked pale and uncertain. "Not locked but, something..."

I reached out, but my hand fell back, feeling as though it had touched something slimy and cruel. Then I felt a kind of anger, and stepped back a pace, and lunged, throwing all my weight and courage against that awful thing.

I fell, apparently into darkness.

The fall saved me. I felt the jar as my body slammed into the stone floor, and heard a crackling sound as if someone was frying bacon on a grill. Black sparks erupted around me, and there was a thick black mist covering everything, waist deep, and clinging greasily to the shapes in the room. I heard Aidan grunt heavily, as if hurt, but there was no time to look.

There were several people gathered there, got up in black robes, like some dreadful parody of the Goddess's rites for the beloved dead. They were grouped mainly around a big carved stone block, on a raised platform. Nothing seemed quite real, but vaguely, dreamily familiar. The edges of everything wavered, shifted, indistinct and ephemeral, but I could see that there were candles, and four of the intruders were chanting. Two more were at the head of the altar reading from an enormous book, and the rest were drawing swords and heading my way.

I didn't have time for them. I rolled and was on my feet, ducking past the first of my opponents, and hoping like hell that Aidan and the rest were going to handle them.

They were all, naturally, Camrhyssi. All but one, who was standing just beyond the altar, wreathed in that horrible black mist . That one was from Keraine, and his life and his death belonged to me.

It was Lord Uln.

One of the men at the far end of the room raised his hands and said a single, unknown word. Black fire shot out again, lighting up the walls and splashing outwards in those deadly black sparks. I ducked, just, and heard a scream of pain behind me. Uln drew his sword.

He didn't know me.

I could see in his face the grim amusement of a man who is killing a stranger. I moved steadily towards him, edging around, trying to get him off that dais and onto a space that I could fight in. Then suddenly he lunged forward, straight for the heart.

I only barely blocked it. We circled warily through the mist. The others were well into it now, I heard the sounds of battle all around me, muffled by the chanting, and the stones that still drummed that awful beat.

We clashed again, in a flurry of blows. He was good, actually. Fast and strong, and less weary than I was, after climbing those stairs and working my way through forty of Camrhys' best.

I parried, threw a couple of fast exploratory shots across, and began retreating desperately back towards the altar. Camrhys' best? The small voice inside me scoffed. Who'd bother sending their best to Penvarron? They'd been numerous and well prepared, that was all. In that instant I caught a block and turned my wrist, sending my blade slashing back up and slicing Uln's arm. Not deeply, but a cut all the same.

It was getting really crowded now. The chanting had stopped, as more of Penvarron's soldiers made it through the doorway and joined in the fray. Blood was everywhere and the floor was slippery and treacherous. He was still smiling confidently at me. I gritted my teeth and pressed in harder.

In a way, it's easier to fight in wars than in single combat. In a war, it's nothing personal; the man you face doesn't want to kill you, particularly. He just hacks at whoever is in front of him and if you move on, he just hacks at whoever replaces you. In a one-on-one, though, you know that there's only one end. One of you has got to die. I began to think it might well be me.

I couldn't seem to focus properly through the mist that swirled around me, and I kept thinking that he was far better a swordsman than his reputation and my own knowledge had led me to believe. We were circling again, as I tried to get closer to the dais. An inch or two of reach. That might do it. Why the hell wasn't he tired?

I twisted my body to ward off a really punishing blow, and skidded gracelessly in a pool of blood. Uln stepped in, and I punched up with my sword hand. I missed, just barely, as he pulled away in sudden alarm, and I fell forward. My sword skittered out, spinning away from me as I hit the stones hard.

It was all up, for me.

I had hit my head on the edge of the dais, and blood was coursing down into my eyes. Uln stepped over me with his sword in both hands. He had leisure now, we both knew I was finished. He gripped the hilt tighter, raised it high above his head, thoroughly enjoying his moment.

Everything slowed. I could see the dead and dying all around us. Over me, I saw through a haze of blood and black smoke, Uln's grinning face, as he savored his victory over an unknown and presumptuous foe.

Something in me rebelled. Why should I make it easy for him?

I was pinned half on my side, my arm just barely free. He was standing straddling my helpless, soon-to-be corpse. With the last shreds of strength, I pulled my shoulders over, lifted myself slightly, and punched directly upward, straight between his legs.

It's the kind of stupid move that no-one ever teaches you, because it almost never will work. If he'd been armoured, he might not even have noticed. But he was wearing a shorter version of those silly black robes, and damn all underneath.

Lord Uln made a curious sound somewhere between a wheeze and a scream, and toppled sideways. I was up and over him, dagger out and kneeling, pressing the blade into his heart, in a flash. His eyes were caught between pain and sudden terror. I put a little pressure on the blade, waiting for his eyes to clear.

When they did, and they widened in shocked knowledge and recognition, I pushed it in, my own gaze locked with his.

And when I saw with certainty that he knew me, was sure of just who had killed him, I pulled the blade free and let his life run out through my fingers.

It was over. All around me, there were the corpses of the invaders and of our own. I stood slowly, gasping for breath, soaked in blood. I listened to the throbbing sound falter and die away slowly into the night, watched as the black mist sank into nothing. The hazy edges of objects solidified back into reality.

"Nice goings-on, I don't think," said Sorcha. There was a nasty gash across her arm, but the two men who'd rushed her were worse off. They lay in a heap at her feet, their necks lying at odd and impossible angles. I wondered vaguely why she had bothered to draw her sword.

From the other room, I could hear Ari, giving a good imitation of a patrol second as he lectured someone not to be squeamish about heaving the Camrhyssi corpses down the stairs. I gave a shaky laugh.

"Did we get them all?" I had seen so little of the fight, I thought. I could barely remember what I had done myself.

"No," said Ruan. "One of them ran. Don't worry," he added as I opened my mouth in protest. "He won't have got past the others. We'll find the little weasel downstairs with his buddies, and a sword up his gut."

Tighe was staring at Uln's corpse.

"Here, this one's not from Camrhys," he said.

"Lord Uln," I said.

Sorcha gave me a strange look.

"Trust me," I said, sourly. "I know."

"What about this, then," said Ruan. He pointed towards the book, still lying on the stone slab.

"Don't touch it," I said, sharply. "No, really, don't. Think about it. What do you think they were doing here?"

We all fell silent, contemplating the last half-hour.

"We can't just leave it there," said Ruan, eventually.

"No. Here, grab one of those black robe things."

The closer we came to the book, the more apprehensive we got. Like the door to this room, it gave off a feeling of unspeakable evil. We swathed the thing in a purloined tunic, then in Tighe's shirt, donated after Sorcha agreed that the garrison would stand him a new one. Even wrapped, I could barely bring myself to touch it. The others refused.

Watch Two came in and we began clearing the bodies.

We found Aidan under a pile of the dead, with a gaping, blackened hole where his guts ought to have been. He lay still and unmoving.

"Poor man," said Sorcha, as she bent down to him.

He opened an eye, scaring us half to death.

"Get me out of here," he said, and fainted.

Chapter 11

We were having trouble making sense of it all.

Gathering the captains together, we met in Sorcha's room, with a barely alive Aidan propped on her bed, and the healer shaking his head over him like a prophet of doom. Not that it mattered, Aidan was under no illusions about his chances. He was dying; the only real surprise was that he'd made it this far.

There were precious few of us: our dead were piling up almost as high as the Camrhyssi. The tales that were coming in were as bizarre and wild as anything I had ever heard. If I hadn't seen the blackrobed chanters, or that horrible book, or touched that door, I would not have believed them. But I had, and standing in a corner of Sorcha's crowded quarters, I could hear the answer to this puzzle as clearly as if we'd been shouting the word.

Magic.

If I'd been frightened before, I was terrified now. Magic. Not the ordinary, homely tricks that your village hedgewitch sells, or the useful talents that people are occasionally born with. My father hired the local Finder regularly, when my mother lost her wedding ring in a pile of laundry or a bin of flour. But this, this was the kind of huge and malignant evil that the bards describe. We might never have seen it, never have actually believed it, but we knew it now.

None of us, of course, wanted to say the word out loud.

We hadn't found the other black-robed man. We knew how many there'd been when we entered that room, and the fighters who had been met outside the tower by small bands of Camrhyssi had been confronted by a couple more, but those were all accounted for in the heaps of bodies. We were one short, and we weren't at all happy about it.

It was however, one of many problems.

"Someone's got to go to Glaice," said Sorcha.

"Not Glaice," Ruan said. "They'd never believe it, and anyway, they'd still have to send to the Queen for orders. I, for one, am not sitting here for a month waiting to see what they'll throw at us next."

"Well, then. Who goes? And how many?"

"One person," I said. "It's faster. And we'll need every sword inside the walls."

There was a pause. I could feel the tension in the room. They were looking at me expectantly.

"No," I said. "No, I can't."

"Sure you can, dear." Sorcha said.

"No you don't understand. I'm the last person they'll see, let alone listen to. Ruan, you'd be better - "

"Not I. I'd be hanged before I got a mile past Eoghan's Moor. "

I appealed desperately to the rest of them. They'd been complaining for months, years, even, that they wanted out of here, but now that the moment had arrived, I found that none of them wanted it at the price of being associated with this disastrous piece of news. I was the newest. I was also the youngest. Somehow, over the next five minutes, after Sorcha resorted to the word duty, I found that I was being backed into a corner

"All right," I said. "All right, but we'll be lucky if I'm not thrown into a dungeon as soon as they hear my name."

"Don't give it," said Sorcha. "Just keep saying you've news from Penvarron that the Queen must hear, and don't back down."

"Even so, they'll likely think it's some fool's trick. Penvarron's no password to respect."

"Go to - Lord Cioren," gasped Aidan. We all jumped a little; I suppose we'd forgotten he was there.

"Cioren," he said again, and fell back against his pillows.

"That old man who came out last spring?' Sorcha's voice was puzzled. "What can he have to do with -?"

"Friend . Of the Queen. Lives near. Eoghan's." Aidan's voice was thin and wispy, and his breath came and went in short, raspy heaves. He looked dreadful, white and waxen, with a sheen of sweat on him. The healer looked grave.

"Get him. To believe. He'll tell them."

I looked at Sorcha. She shrugged.

"Old geezer," she said. "Come out last spring and poked around for a few days. Nice old man, but very odd. But if he's a friend of the Queen's, it'll serve. And," she rummaged around on her desk and produced a large silver medallion; "I'll give you this, too. We've only got the one, mind. Make sure you keep it safe. It'll get you past all the nosy-parkers on gates and such."

It was really just a version of my copper token from Prince Tirais. This one was stamped with the royal arms of Keraine. I'd seen one before, on a Queen's messenger, years ago, during the last real war with Camrhys. A Queen's pass, meant only for the direst of emergencies.

I sighed. They were all looking at me with such trusting expectation, their inadequate and unwilling savior.

"Where does this old geezer live?" I said resignedly.

It took a few moments for Aidan, half-fainting with the effort, to give me directions. I bent close to hear his whispered, halting voice. In the background I heard Sorcha ordering Tighe to get Banshee saddled, and send someone for my things. Aidan trailed off, fell into a fit of bloody coughing; and then lay still, his eyes closed. I looked at the healer.

"He won't live the night," he said. "It's just bloody will keeping him going now."

Aidan stirred.

"Not dead yet," he said. He looked up at me. "Got 'em in the end, didn't we?"

"That you did, sir." I couldn't help but be impressed; standing at death's threshold, he seemed calm and courageous, and nothing like the drunk and useless failure he had been. I hoped, if ever I was in his case, to meet my end so well.

"Always knew. That tower. Was poison." He fixed his gaze on me. "Go tell. The Queen. Save." But at this, his strength gave out once more. His eyes closed again, and his breathing, not strong to begin with, seemed almost to stop entirely. The healer pushed past me and knelt, touching Aidan's forehead.

"You'd best go. It won't be long for him now."

I nodded. The book that we'd found in the tower lay in a corner. As soon as we'd emerged, Sorcha had sent someone running for a flour sack and a leather dispatch bag. Wrapped, the thing had only just barely fit, but it was easier to handle now. I picked it up uneasily. It would have to come with, as proof, but I would have been happier with any other burden.

Out in the yard, Tighe was trying to hang on to Banshee's reins while avoiding her wish to take a chunk of him with her as a souvenir. She seemed more ill-tempered than usual.

Well, weren't we all?

Sorcha and I wrestled with Banshee's saddlebags, fastening my unwanted package onto her back. It took a bit; the mare was no more eager for this burden than I was.

"Sorcha," I said. "After I'm gone, you'll want to shut this place up as close as you can."

"Tighter than a girl before her Goddess-night," she agreed. "And I'll keep them on their watches, never fear. If so much as a rabbit jumps, we'll see it."

I leaned close to her, ostensibly to tighten a strap. "Sorcha, keep a watch inside as well." Her eyes flickered. I said urgently, "Someone opened that gate, Sorcha."

In the torchlight, I saw her pale eyes widen.

"Right," she said, grimly.

I gathered up the reins. Mounted.

"One last thing. Give me a seven-day. If you hear nothing, it means I haven't managed it somehow." There were little twitches, from Tighe and Sorcha both. Their thought was my own. Goddess only knew what was actually out there, besides a pissed-off mage from Camrhys. "Send someone else after that." I grinned. "Send 'em Uln's head. That'll at least get their attention."

I pulled Banshee's head round towards the gate. and as I rode down through the dilapidated collection of shacks of Penvarron village I heard, for the first time, the sound of the West Gate being swung to and barred.

It was slow going. I fairly itched for a gallop, and Banshee, unsettled as she was, would have obliged; luckily, sense asserted itself. I had a long road to travel and Banshee wouldn't last more than a couple of miles at the pace I was longing to put her to. I had no clear notion of where the Queen was at this precise moment; if she was at Kerris, the most logical of her many castles at this time of year, and if Lord Cioren proved to be absent or disinclined to believe my story, it could be a longer ride still. I let her canter for a mile or so, since she was so restive, then set her firmly to a pace that allowed for distance.

My back felt perilously exposed. Why had I insisted that a single rider had a better chance? I would have given anything, in that first glass or so, for a companion. Someone to even up my chances at survival.

After a while, this sense of vulnerability lessened. With every furlong, I was more confident of my chances, not perhaps, of seeing Queen Elowyn, or getting assistance for Penvarron's beleaguered forces, but of making it as far as Lord Cioren's place, and telling someone, at least, what had transpired.

I tried, on that lonely stretch of road, in the starlit darkness, to frame a way of telling this ridiculous and unbelievable tale that didn't sound like the ravings of a lunatic. It seemed barely possible that I could make Lord Cioren believe; both Aidan and Sorcha had left me with the impression that he had been quite interested in Penvarron Tower and had seemed to know more about it than those of us who lived in its shadow.

Quite a scholarly and courteous old gentleman had been Sorcha's description. She'd also said that he was mad as a coot, but then, Sorcha's opinions of her fellow man were cynical in the extreme. He certainly sounded eccentric, anyway, the sort of person who might believe my tale of death and magic. What this did for my chances of making anyone else believe it, or even stop long enough to listen to me, I refused to think about.

I had not gotten any further than "Sir, there's been trouble at Penvarron." and was considering not mentioning that bizarre weirdness in the upper reaches of the tower at all, but sticking to the idea of a Camrhys invasion, when the first small outbuildings of Eoghan's Moor took shape in the dim light of the false dawn.

On the edge of the town proper, where the sheep were penned and quiet, I saw the remains of two still smoldering bonfires. I remembered suddenly what day it was.

In Orliegh they would have had these fires too, and driven the livestock between the blazes, and walked the edges of the farms, chanting their thanks that they had had a good harvest, and drunk the ritual first pressings of the new year's wine, toasting the Fates.

It was the feast of the Merrydd. I was eighteen years old.

Chapter 12

Aidan's directions had been sketchy, but the track leading east from the main road was easy enough to find. It was narrow and winding and looked under-used, but after a half mile or so of thick bushes and rocky crags, it opened into a wide meadow. At the far end lay a small house.

Just a cottage, really. Some enterprising sheepfarmer, or a tenant of the Lord, it seemed, had tried their luck out here. There was smoke curling up from the chimney and the door, I saw as I approached, was open. As I slid off Banshee's back and started towards it, a man emerged.

"Excuse me," I said. "I'm looking for Lord Cioren's home, do you know it?

He looked me over. I flushed; there had been little time to worry over appearances and I was still covered in the blood and grime from battle, with a rag tied over my forehead to staunch the blood that had still dripped from my scalp.

"I am Cioren," he said.

I stared. The descriptions Aidan and the others had given me had led me to expect someone fat and balding, an absentminded, bookish man. The man before me was certainly gray-haired and past his youth, but he didn't appear in any senile. His eyes were sharp, under greying brows, and he looked as whippy as a ferret.

He was not dressed in the clothes of a nobleman, but in roughspun trews and a leather smock, the kind that blacksmiths or other labourers affect. I spent another moment trying to reconcile my imagination with reality, then caught myself. If the Queen's friends wanted to get themselves up like blacksmiths, or bog-trolls, for that matter, it was no concern of mine. I gathered my wandering wits.

"I-er- There's been trouble at Penvarron," I said. "Camrhys. There's a lot dead, sir, and I have to get a message to the Queen. Sir Aidan sent me, sir."

"You'd best come in," Cioren said.

We left Banshee to munch the grass, and Cioren sat me at his table, cut some bread and cheese, and drew two mugs of ale, while I tried to explain what had happened at Penvarron. Around mouthfuls, I answered his questions, as best I could. He seemed unperturbed. He certainly grasped the gist of it; moreover, he seemed to believe me. He also seemed, if not unsurprised, at least less shocked than I was myself.

"You're quite right. The Queen must know, and quickly, too. They'll all still be at Glaice, luckily. Not quite the ride it might have been if she'd gone back to Kerris."

I turned my mug in my hands.

"Do I need to go, sir? I mean, it'll come better from you, and I ought to get back. They'll need me, at Penvarron."

It was pure cowardice, of course. Something in his expression told me he knew it, too.

"Don't be ridiculous. I don't know the half of it. And there'll be questions. Ones only you can answer. I wasn't there. Well," he got up and began assembling more bread and uncut cheese, "We've a long ride ahead of us. Can you manage it?"

I swallowed the last of my ale.

"I'll have to, won't I?"

Around back of the cottage was a small shed, housing Cioren's horse. I helped him saddle up, and we walked back to where Banshee was placidly attacking some small shrubs. She was even less inclined to continue her journey than she had been to start it. Cioren watched as I cursed and fought her into a semblance of docility.

"Is she always so, ah, headstrong?"

I gritted my teeth.

"Worse, usually. She's a bit tired, thank the Goddess."

He laughed.

"Come on, then. You can tell me the rest as we go."

I don't remember much of the ride to Glaice.

I do remember hard, probing questions, and my own faltering, confused answers. I remember that I couldn't hide the strangeness of events from him, and that in the end I told him far more than I meant to. I had thought to keep my account strictly factual; a kind of take it or leave it report that left out my own speculations, but I was exhausted and vulnerable, I suppose.

Somewhere along the lines I found myself describing my fight with Uln, my slowness, my feeling that I was overmatched. I still didn't understand it; I'm no hero of the olden days, but swordcraft was what I had been trained for. It was practically the only thing I did well; I had never before spent so much of a fight estimating my slender chances.

The whole scene in the tower fascinated him. He coaxed a thorough description of it from me. When I explained about the book, he actually reined in and stared at me.

"And where is it now?" He sounded almost frantic, although that might have been my own apprehension speaking.

"Right here." I looked at the unwieldy burden tied to my saddle.

"Thank all the gods for that," he said.

"We thought we'd need it. For proof."

We rode on, after that, mainly in silence. My tiredness was beginning to tell; it was all I could do to stay in the saddle. We hadn't even stopped at midday, eating as we rode, but as the sun sank behind the trees, we came to a mean little village, and Cioren turned into the yard of a tiny inn.

I followed him into the common room, carrying his saddle bags. Cioren had taken charge of the sack containing the book; I was more than eager to shift that burden onto him. I sat at a table with him. Ate whatever was put in front of me. Rose and followed him up the stairs.

Somewhere before the top, he turned and looked at me. I don't think that I had said anything, or made a sound, but he said my name, sharply. It made no difference. The world fell away from me, I saw only blackness rolling in like a sea-fog, and I knew nothing more.

I was standing on a barren, desolate plain, the wind whistling through the featureless landscape like a knife, with the ground trembling below my feet as if to shake me loose and hurl me to the black and starless sky like a pebble. It was cold, brutally cold, I could feel the chill seeping into me, and I felt utterly alone.

The trembling died away and then, the earth shook again, harder, so violently it dropped me to my knees. I could see nothing but flat and empty rocky ground, glowing white from its own pallor, and yet I knew suddenly that I was not alone. Something was here with me; something evil and cruel. Something that wanted blood, and fear, and death.

The earth moved again, throwing me hard onto my side.

My eyes raked the darkness. The presence lay all around me, and I knew I was in great peril, but I saw nothing but the ground and sky. I pulled myself back onto my feet, bracing myself. There was, I knew, no past, no future, only this emptiness and this endless, terrible place. It hated me. It would cast me off high into that malevolent sky above, let me fall to the hard rock below, crush me in its arms, and leave me maimed and bleeding to die, unknown and unremembered, a shadow that had passed this way.

The earth beneath my feet gathered itself for another, yet more violent quake, there was a deep and soundless shuddering far within the bowels of the rock, a roaring filled my ears, and then something frozen and hard took hold of my heart, and *pulled…*

I woke, abruptly, to the sound of someone saying my name, and the feel of a hand on my shoulder, shaking me gently and inexorably awake.

"A dream," I said, bewildered. "A dream."

I sat up, my heart still pounding like a festival drum, trying desperately to remember where I was, who I was. It took a moment, then my mind cleared. I saw Cioren, his face grave.

"Sorry," I said, frowning. I couldn't remember getting to this room. By the light of a single candle, I saw that I was lying fully armed on a narrow cot. There was another bed, the blankets still neatly folded, and a tiny table bearing a tray with wine and some soft-looking biscuits.

"Are you all right? You rather scared me, dropping asleep on the steps like that." Cioren let go of my shoulder, rose and moved to the table.

"Oh. Yes, I think I'm all right. How long, sir, was I asleep?"

"Only a few hours. You likely need more, but we've a fair ways to go yet. I'm sorry."

"No, why? I'll be fine." My heart was quiet now. I could feel the memory of the dream slipping away. I could only remember that nothingness, and a queer and unsettled feeling.

I swung my legs over the edge of the cot, accepted the cup of wine he had poured me, and sipped experimentally. It was sweeter than I was used to, and smoother; after two more swallows I pushed my dreams out of my head and concentrated on the journey ahead.

In no time at all, it seemed, we were on our way again. Cioren retained custody of the package containing the book, which cheered me a little; even Banshee seemed relieved not to have that thing on her back, and had stood more or less quietly while I saddled and mounted up. Good food and a little sleep had done wonders for us both, and the chill of the predawn air, fresh and sweet, drove the last sleepiness from me. I began to think about what I was going to tell the Queen about Penvarron and Uln, and what I could safely leave out.

"Keridwen," said Cioren, when I raised this thorny issue with him, "You'll only have to tell the truth."

"If I knew what that was, I'd be happier."

"Well, the truth as you saw it, then. But," he half-turned in his saddle to look at me, "If you'd leave out the book entirely, I'd be grateful. It's the one thing that - well, it's not something I want to discuss with anyone. Not until I've had a chance to look it over properly. I'll tell the Queen about it. Privately. We won't be alone, not at this first meeting, I'm afraid."

"Oh." I thought it over. I wasn't used to prevarication, but I could see what he meant. Sort of. I couldn't explain what it was that worried me about the damned thing, not in words. You would have to touch it to know and I had been raised to think of Queen Elowyn as embodying what was right and decent about Keraine. Somehow, asking her to put her hand on that unspeakable nastiness seemed a betrayal. I applied myself to revising my description of the scene we'd met in Penvarron Tower to omit the book. It was surprisingly easy.

"Lord Cioren, do you understand what happened? I mean, I know in a way. But I've never seen anyone do something like that. And I had a dream…"

"Ah," he said. "I wondered. What you saw, Keridwen, hasn't been seen in Keraine for nearly five hundred years. Hasn't been seen anywhere, not even Camrhys, I'd wager, for that long, perhaps."

"But what was it? What does it mean?"

He was silent for so long that I thought I'd offended him in some way by my persistence, and wondered how I could apologize. Then he slowed his horse's pace to match Banshee's gait almost exactly and said, in a slow and thoughtful voice,

"How much do you know about the Kingdom of Averraine?"

Chapter 13

If there was anything left in the world that could send me spinning back into my childhood dreams, Averraine was the word.

In a single, flashing moment, I saw it all: the high graceful towers and spires of the ancient cities, the jeweled and graceful men and women, bright and shining in their flowing robes, the brilliant and decadent courts where Aenor watched as his brother the King went slowly mad and destroyed the world.

"I know what the bards say."

I knew more, in a way. I'd played, as children will, at being Aenor Machyll, and Bronwyn his daughter, heroes of my favourite tales. It was our heritage; in a sense, we were all Averraine. Keraine, Camrhys and far-off Fendrais had been, long ago, the three provinces, ruled from a magnificent city that now lay in ruin and decay somewhere to the south. I had seen it once, on an old map.

It was only when I'd grown up a little, that I'd let go of my sparkling visions of a noble past. There's a point you get to, I suppose, when you realize that the belief in being descended from wiser, more courageous ancestors serves mainly to bolster your belief that you are somehow braver and wiser yourself.

I said as much now, as we rode towards the border.

"Well, the bards aren't completely wrong," said Cioren. "They dress it up in colours we can understand, but the essence remains. The ancients were certainly more knowledgeable, about some things, and the great cities aren't a lie. You can see traces of them, in some places. They had great places of learning, and the riches of trade throughout the world to draw on."

"And magic."

"Yes, and magic, too."

"Like - like what happened at Penvarron?"

"Not at the beginning. In the beginning it was less ambitious; they understood what they could and could not do, and they used it well. It was only later, when greed got the better of them that they drew too much on the power of the land. They used it up, and still hungered for more."

"The bards never say that," I pointed out. "It's all just King Vaen going mad and making pacts with demons."

"There may be some truth in that. But I know that the power they raised in the end could not have been the work of one man. Nor of one demon, either. That kind of destruction takes a lot of work."

"But how - I mean, the stories say that it was the Goddess. She turned her back on the people, and Aenor swore never to allow magic again."

"Aenor's words only apply to Keraine," he said. "Camrhys went a different road. And anyway, you know there's magic. What the holy ones do, in rituals, is magic. They call on the Goddess' blessing, and they're very careful of what they do, but it is magic, all the same."

I considered this. One of my sisters was a priestess, so I did know, as he said, that there was magic, beyond simple charms and wardings. Siobhan used to light candles for us, when she was young. Later she wouldn't, having got grown up and serious, and full of the Goddess' mysteries, not to mention rather pompous about her abilities. But her small demonstrations seemed almost utterly unrelated to the terror I had seen in Penvarron Tower, and I said so.

"That," said Cioren, "was something else, you're right. I think that the book they used may well be an ancient one, one that tells of the ways our forebears harnessed the power and did those things that led to Averraine's destruction."

"All right," I said. "All right, I think I understand that part, sort of. But what I don't understand is what they were trying to do. What did they want to accomplish? And why," the words were coming before I properly knew what it was I was asking, "why did they come to Penvarron?"

"Well," he said, "What they wanted to do, I'm not sure. I'll need to study the book, to understand that better, I think. Why Penvarron is an easier question, I suppose, but not by much. You need to understand how magic works."

"It's a longish ride yet," I said.

I learned more than I perhaps had ever wanted to. I had lived my life in the belief that either the true magic was dead and forgotten, or that it had been much exaggerated to begin with. I discovered that day that I was wrong on both counts. It was on my lips a number of times to ask Cioren how he knew all this. I don't know what stopped me; partly, I think, I knew that the answer was the obvious one, and I wasn't ready to hear it.

"Power lives in all things," he said. "In the land, in the water, in the air, in ourselves. Those with talent can harness it, but it takes work. So much work that you can spend a lifetime just learning how to gather and use it without killing yourself in the process.

"But the power also flows and pools in certain places. And there, even those with little power of their own, and less learning, can create wonders."

For those with real talent and knowledge, the places where the ancient had found great pools and reservoirs of power made them almost limitless in their scope. Nothing, it must have seemed, would be beyond them, and only their own good sense and training could leash them.

It had not been enough.

In the beginning, they had understood that the power needed time to replenish itself, to allow the currents and flows of unused forces to collect back to the places where they worked their most impressive feats. Out in the open, a mage was limited not only by the power readily and finitely available, but to his own ability to withstand the magic he used. Only in the great citadels, and in the groves and wells of the ancients, could they work in safety.

They grew proud, said Cioren, which was understandable, and they grew reckless. They discovered ways to harness more and more power, and ways to draw the power into these places more strongly, and more quickly. And as they did more, they saw greater things ahead, and pressed even further.

They were caught by those most malicious of little sins: greed and vanity. Having more, they wanted more, and saw it as their right. They turned onto dangerous and unsafe roads, and later, into evil. In the end, they tore the power from the land, raised things from planes where in years previous they would never have gone even in thought.

It was inevitable, Cioren said, that they would lose control of what they had created. In one final act, someone, probably Vaen, had ordered some kind of spell or raising that required so much that it ripped through the channels of power, and recoiled, raw and untamed forces flashing back along the paths and burning out every source in its wake.

In the devastation that followed, it must have seemed to the survivors of Averraine that magic was dead. They had torn power even out of things and places that had held only tiny amounts to begin with and out of the people themselves, and they had felt as the blind must: that sight was a myth, even for those who still claimed to possess it.

The city of Averraine had been one of the principal places where they had found power. There were others: Kerris had been one, Evanion, in Camrhys, another. The Goddess' holy island at Braide had been well known. Quite a number of the holdings we still lived in, all over Keraine, had been lesser places that mages had gathered in, although the names had mostly been lost.

Only a handful of sites had escaped total destruction, mostly the smaller, more out of the way places, and even then, the power had been raped and bled out of them. All of the major places had suffered complete collapse, and most had never been rebuilt.

Those that had, had not seemed to regenerate, or else they did so very slowly; it was possible, said Cioren, that the paths and flows had been altered, and that power now collected in different ways, or new spots, as yet undiscovered. But the great centres closest to the source of the spells which destroyed them, those had been left behind, as the people fled from the destruction, and they had become evil, uninhabitable, places of ghosts and nightmares.

All, except, perhaps, Penvarron.

We were still some miles from Glaice, but the road was far more traveled now. Merchant-trains with loaded wagons moved slowly eastwards; despite frequent hostility and occasional wars, trade with Camrhys flourished. The weather had been cold here, and a hard frost had turned muddy roads to brown iron, but we were hampered by the traffic, and the need to thread our way through the carts and people who littered the Queen's Way. It was as good as a country fair, for me.

It made conversation difficult, though. I wasn't so sure I wanted to hear anymore, but there were questions still hovering in the air between us. Questions that, like my suspicions about how Cioren came to know all this, I was all too afraid that I already had the answers to.

Why the priests of Camrhys had come to Penvarron seemed frighteningly clear. The bards called what the ancients had done to the land "death-magic", when they gave it a name at all. Cioren said that this was as good a description as any; and that forms of it had turned into worship in Camrhys. Where Keraine had tried to repair the damage and gain the Mother's forgiveness, Camrhys had declared that if the Goddess turned her back on them in time of need, no matter what the cause, they would turn their back on her. They had clung to the belief that the power would return and that they would someday regain the forces and the knowledge that had been lost, and once more rule the world.

But with few places still able to retain the forces, and fewer still that gave the safety that those early places had, and with so much knowledge lost, there had been little danger of this ever coming to pass.

If the book was, in fact, an ancient *asarlaíoche* or grimoire, as Cioren seemed to think, then the need for a safe place of power was essential to them. And Penvarron had, for some reason, remained, not untouched - the power had been stripped from it as well at the time of the Great Breaking - but capable, and physically unharmed. The only other place equal to it that had escaped

73

serious damage that Cioren knew of was Braide, and that would have seemed anathema to the priests of Camrhys.

What Uln had to do with this, I couldn't quite fathom. I didn't see how he gained anything much by being a traitor, since he'd already had lands and a high position in Keraine. I knew, in a theoretical way, that people's motives for treason were not necessarily logical, that there were those who would trade everything in life for one moment of revenge over a tiny slight, but in my heart, I couldn't quite believe it. And I didn't know of anything in Uln's life that would constitute a slight anyway. Mind, I didn't know much of anything about him when you came right down to it.

It was all of a piece, anyway. All I had ever really wanted was a decent place in life. When that had been denied, I had settled for just some kind of place, and a slender hope that I could somehow build a respectable future.

What had I gotten? All the scariest bits of fireside tales, a collection of cuts and bruises, and a ride to see my sworn Queen with news that one of her nobles had not merely been a traitor, but apparently had dabbled in forbidden occult lores as well.

Why I couldn't seem to live my life in an ordinary way, but had careened from one disaster to another was beyond me. Perhaps I'd been cursed by a passing and easily offended mage, as Lady Aoife had been in the story of Bronwyn's Trials? It seemed more comforting than attributing it to my own poor judgment and inexperience, however more likely.

Chapter 14

The posting towers of Glaice's outer defense were now visible on the horizon, although I couldn't make out the devices on the pennons flying above them.

We'd fallen silent again as we navigated through the press of travelers; Cioren to think his own thoughts, and me left to contemplation of bearing the news that Keraine's fate might well be in the hands of every known thief, layabout, incompetent and misfit in Her Majesty's army. It wasn't hard to predict the initial reaction I would likely get. I watched Cioren's back, and hoped like hell that he had enough influence to get me a serious hearing after that.

At the outer towers, nothing diminished my growing unease. The guards didn't know him on sight, although his name and my Queen's pass got us through quickly enough. The closer we came to the main fortress, though, the slower the process became. Uln's treason had left its imprint; they were taking care not to allow our passage to go unremarked.

We came at last to the main gates themselves. Here, however, to my surprise, the pace quickened. Cioren's name alone worked a charm: the duty-officer came down, recognized him and we were let through to the stables while someone went running to the small palace that housed the royal family when they were here.

I squinted up at the banners as we passed. Glaice's own standard flew between two others: the arms of the House of Machyll, and the smaller, personal badge of the Prince.

My heart sank. He wouldn't have forgotten me, not in three short months, and the memory of my rash outburst of temper brought blood rushing to my face.

Maybe, I thought, he was out hunting, or inspecting the earthwork defenses on the border proper. I could hope so, although with my luck, it seemed unlikely. I was wishing myself back at Penvarron rather hard as we slid out of our saddles.

"Maireadh! How good to see you," said Cioren. A gentle-faced woman in leather trews and a faded blue shirt was coming out into the stableyard with her hands outstretched and a smile of welcome on her face.

"My lord. We didn't look to see you before Midwinter."

I busied myself with my saddlebags as they talked. My heart felt noisy and restive, and my stomach was queasy; I set down the bags and wiped my palms on Banshee's blanket. But now Cioren was turning and introducing me. I bobbed my head. Maireadh was apparently the Mistress of the Queen's Horse, a fairly important position, and despite her apparel, she was as noble as my own father, at least. Did all the Queen's friends go about dressed as peasants? I wondered. My own unwashed state seemed quite normal, in that case.

"Can we set all this somewhere? In your office, perhaps?" Cioren said this quite casually, between questions about Maireadh's son, and a jest about some girl named Lys.

"Certainly, my lord. Tell me," she added as we followed her through the door, "how are things down your way? We've had some excitement here, as no doubt you've heard."

"Ah, well," Cioren said, "Things are unsettled all over."

"Aren't they just? You wouldn't believe the time I've had, keeping them all mounted and ready, round the clock. And so many horses gone down, we've sent to Westfold for some youngsters, and naturally, they're never full-broken when you need them. I'll be glad when I get a moment to catch up on my accounts, which just shows how tired I am."

Maireadh's 'office' was an extra tack-room, with a table and chair in one corner. The remainder of the space was taken up by a haphazard collection of horse gear and saddles in various states of repair.

"Through here," she said, opening a small door at the end. "There's too much coming and going, I've not had time to clean up, but toss them on the bed there, and I'll send them up when you get settled. And you'd better have some decent wine for me when I do, Lord Cioren. You still owe me over a little matter of a wager, I believe. A bottle of Ilrai red, I think it was."

"I must have been drunk already, to bet against you in a horse race," Cioren said.

We went back out, the pair of them still bantering lightly over the quality and nature of the wine in question, and me tagging along at their heels like a half-trained pup.

Cioren did not wait, but with a wave to Maireadh, turned purposefully towards the central buildings. I followed still, gawking like any country yob at the unfamiliar livery on people's surcoats as they scurried about, intent on Her Majesty's business. It was as unlike Penvarron's slack and casual manner as anything I had ever seen: there was no-one idle here at all.

We stopped only for a moment at the main hall, while Cioren asked someone a quick question about the Queen's whereabouts, then we moved through halls and antechambers. The inner keep of Glaice was a maze of long hallways interspersed with beautifully appointed reception rooms; I lost my bearings almost immediately.

We were not, I gathered, allowing ourselves time to wash or change. At last we came to a door guarded by a man in the colours of the Royal House, who took one look at the pair of us and backed off. Cioren flung open the door and strode through, with me close on his heels, and I saw Queen Elowyn for the first time.

She was just rising, her hands stretched out in happy greeting, an expression that changed almost immediately to one of concern as she saw his face. I was behind, but I could guess that it was not reassuring; if it was anything like my own, it was probably grim and monumentally tired.

"Cioren," she said, and continued forward, with less certainty.

I had stopped just inside the doorway. There were others here. If I had written out the names of those whom I would rather not have met in these circumstances, I would have assembled this very guest-list. Beside the chair that Elowyn had just risen from sat Huwell, Baron Gallerain, looking sleek and comfortable, every inch the self-assured Queen's Counselor. Lord Gervase stood near the window, just turning to view our entrance. And to the side, lounging comfortably on another chair, his eyebrows raised in an expression of mocking inquiry, was Tirais, Prince of Keraine.

Perfect, I thought. Just what I need. This ought to be the most entertaining afternoon of my life. Just a little social call, my Prince, a little more career suicide before dinner, and then I'll just be on my way.

Cioren introduced me.

"Ah, Gareth's daughter." She said it warmly. Had someone neglected to fill her in on my summer's activities? Apparently so. Baron Gallerain frowned at me ferociously, and growled something unintelligible. Gervase looked me over with amusement.

Tirais' expression was unreadable and I had no time to figure it out; Cioren launched precipitately into a description of the doings at Penvarron, and whatever awkwardness I might have felt was lost in other anxieties as the Queen began to question me.

I kept my eyes on her. Queen Elowyn must have been, about this time, in her late forties, and she had never been accounted a beauty.. Tirais had her colouring, and her features, to a great extent, but there the resemblance ended. In him, the mix had resulted in the very ideal of masculine beauty.

For the Queen, well, the years had taken their toll. In fact, she looked quite ordinary: a middle-aged woman who had borne children, seen decades of war and manoeuvred through dozens of political crises, a woman who had weathered both joy and personal tragedies. It showed in her eyes. There was patience there, and strength, and tolerance.

I had to describe my behavior on the night in question, and each time I said the words "my patrol" or mentioned the orders I'd given, I could feel Tirais' amused derision like a slap. I glossed over the open gates as best I could; there's no excusing such idiocy, but I was loathe to blame the guards of Penvarron. No-one had believed in our importance here either; I could feel a slight disapproval, but we were on to more pressing matters. I described the scene in the tower carefully, and gave Aidan his due. When it had mattered, he'd done what was needed, and I didn't doubt that our limited success was his work.

But then there was Lord Uln. The very mention of his name jolted them from the slight complacency they still basked in: till then they'd at least known that Penvarron was victorious, if only temporarily. But Uln's appearance in the tale was something else again.

At first they didn't believe it. And that was my misfortune. The Queen asked me how I knew him.

"I worked for him all summer."

Up to this point, she had been gracious and kind, patient with my stumbling answers. Now her expression hardened. I was, it was true, too young and unimportant for anyone to have mentioned me or my treason to her before this, but now she wanted assurance that anything I told her could be trusted.

Cioren said, "Elowyn, she hasn't the guile to lie."

Oh, thanks, I thought. Now I'm a simpleton as well.

But Baron Gallerain's angry rejoinder that even a fool could betray brought aid, of a sort, from an unexpected quarter. Tirais said, in a bored and languid voice,

"If she says it, it's likely true. Whether she understands its import, Mother, is something else again."

Definitely I was being cast as a brainless fool. Still, my tension eased. If my wits were the price of getting the Queen to understand what danger lay in Penvarron, I was prepared to pay it. I resumed my description of the fighting. I knew roughly what had happened to the others, but it was my fight with Uln that they seemed most interested in anyway.

I kept it short. I skated carefully over the feeling I'd had, that he was a much better fighter than I was, that I'd felt slow and awkward. Then I said I'd gotten a lucky shot in - the memory of the cold-blooded way I'd ended Uln's life worried me and just thinking about it made me feel hot with anger even now. Cioren had said that I should tell the truth. I could feel his eyes on me, but he said nothing to contradict my terse account.

"We found some others," I finished. "Some of the watches stayed outside, and patrolled around, and they managed to kill them all. At least…but we must have. And there were more of the priests. We got everyone, I think, except for the one from the tower. I don't know how, or even if, he got out, but if he stayed in Penvarron, they'll have got him by now."

"I see," said Elowyn. She had lost the anger, and merely looked worried. Gallerain looked irritated. I didn't look at the others.

"And why," asked Tirais, still in that bored voice, "have you come?"

"We knew we had to send word." What did he take us for? On second thought, don't go there, Keri. You don't want to hear it.

"I meant, why you? Surely there were others?"

"Oh. I don't know. I'm newest, I suppose."

"You're the most likely to lie, you mean," This was Gallerain, still determined to cast me as some kind of villain.

At some point, they'd given me a low bench to sit on. I stood.

"I am not lying," I said. "Sir Aidan bade me go to Lord Cioren, who insisted I come with him. I've done that. If Your Majesty has no other questions, I can go back now."

"Sit down, Keridwen." Elowyn's voice was not unkind. I sat.

Cioren said, "Keridwen has it true, Huwell. She couldn't know those kinds of details if she hadn't seen them, unless you believe that she has spent the last forty years in Camrhys studying the old rituals. If she says Uln was there, he was there. If she says that she killed Uln, then she did. If she told me that he turned himself into a dragon and flew off, I'd be inclined to take it as holy words. We're wasting time."

Gallerain looked unconvinced. My anger faded. He was right, really. What was I, but a pardoned traitor, after all? If six months ago, someone had told me this tale, I would have felt the same.

"Sir, I know it's absurd. But it's true. I don't know why," here I mentally asked the Goddess' forgiveness for yet another lie of omission, "And I don't know how, exactly. But they came, and Uln was there. I got lucky and killed him. But we don't know if they'll be back. Penvarron can't hold out, not as things stand. They'll do their best, but we're under strength now, and, well, morale's not good."

Gallerain sneered.

"Morale? Pretty word for a garrison of cowards. I doubt there were more than a half dozen invaders, if there were any at all. In any case," he turned to the Queen, "We'll do best to keep this from Lady Angharad. We've no proof that her father's dead, nor that he was ever there. I won't have her caused undue distress. She feels her father's betrayal most keenly."

Angharad? Here? I sucked in my breath, and tried to remind myself that this was the Queen's business, not mine. Failed.

"My lady? Angharad's with you? Is that wise?"

Gallerain went slightly pink.

"You little - the lady is the Queen's ward, now that she's lost her father. How dare you imply - "

"She's the poxy bastard's daughter!"

"Your Majesty, must we listen to this rubbish?"

I was aghast. I knew Angharad. Well, all right, 'know' was a little strong. I had seen her, a number of times. Very lovely, the lady Angharad. And very proud and remote, with lowly troop captains.

I tried to choose my words carefully.

"My lady, it's just that she is Uln's daughter. And we don't yet know why he was-"

But here Gallerain stood up and loomed over me, his face now purple with rage.

"How dare you? You little guttersnipe, how dare you suggest that a sweet and innocent child had even the barest inkling of the treason her parent intended?"

"Why not?" I snapped. "You seem to think he confided in me."

There was one of those tense silences, where everything seems to stop. From the window, I could hear the echoing sound of casual conversation and laughter, and of birds singing. Gallerain sat slowly, heavily, back into his chair, his mouth agape at my audacity, his face a mask of fury.

Chapter 15

We were standing, Cioren's hand at my elbow. I heard the Queen saying in a gentle, courteous voice that naturally we must be very tired, and thanking me for my service. I felt the pressure at my arm as I was guided out the door.

We went, rather quickly and silently, through the halls of Glaice. I would have been hard put to retrace my steps, anyway, but busy with my own thoughts, I simply followed Cioren yet again along corridors and rooms without noticing where we were headed. When he stopped at last at a doorway and opened it, I followed him in, barely noticing where I was.

My anger consumed me. If Gallerain had been outraged at my very presence, I was equally enraged at the idiocy that seemed to have infected the rulers of Keraine.

To pardon Uln's daughter, absolving her of any involvement or knowledge of her father's betrayal, well, I could understand that. I had benefited from that same kindness myself. But to keep her beside you, close to the centre of power? To see her as yet another victim of Uln's treason, and assume that no harm could come of her presence, while castigating me for not noticing that something was amiss in my employer's plans? I saw my saddlebags lying on a bench inside the room we had entered, grabbed them, headed to a table where a pitcher of water and a wash bowl stood, and began stripping off my mail shirt and my tunic.

Neither Cioren nor I had spoken a word to each other. I scrabbled in my bags for my one spare tunic with a muttered obscenity. He could have defended me better, I thought. Left to face the wolves alone, I'd done as well as I could. If he found fault with my behavior, that was his problem. Curse them. Curse them all.

I kicked the bags under the table. Splashed water onto my face and arms. I could hear Cioren pouring out wine, settling into a chair. I scrubbed at days of accumulated grime and dust.

There was the sound of a door opening, then Cioren saying mildly,

"Don't you ever knock?"

"I'm a prince - I don't need to -"

I had turned, still naked to the waist, reaching for my clean shirt. Tirais cleared his throat, and without taking his eyes from me, said, "Sorry. You're quite right."

But he didn't move.

I picked up my tunic and shook it out. If he wanted to gawk, let him.

I'm not pretty. I've known it any time these eighteen years. But if I hadn't the pleasing features and soft curves of women who do more sedentary tasks in life, I'm not a monster, either. My face was reddened from the sun, my hair an unremarkable brown, and my eyes a dull, dark gray, but my body was muscled and firm from a short lifetime spent turning it into a useful killing tool. Men may prefer the rounded limbs of smaller girls with gentler voices and sweeter manners, and they certainly marry them more often, but they'll look at a woman like me all the same.

I pulled the tunic over my head. When I picked up my belt, Tirais had poured out two cups of wine and was holding one out to me. I took it with murmured thanks and we both sat down.

"Well," he said. "That was certainly the most entertaining half-hour I've spent in a long while. I thought Huwell would have a fit. Do you never rein in that tongue of yours? No, don't answer. There's no harm done. In five more minutes he'll have realized that insisting on your guilt will only beg the question of why he sent you to Uln in the first place, and think better of announcing your sins abroad."

"You believe me then?"

"Of course I don't believe you." His voice dripped sarcasm. "Traitors always ride hellbent for leather for two days to tell the Queen lies. And they always lose their tempers over royal policies that endanger the realm, and take the Queen to task over her errors in judgement. Happens once a seven-day at least."

"Oh," I said.

"I don't know why you can't keep out of trouble for a few months," he said, shaking his head. "I rack my brains for a way to put you somewhere reasonably safe and unobtrusive for a year or so, and what happens? Trouble follows you. To Penvarron, of all places."

"I've been meaning to ask you about that," said Cioren. "Why Penvarron? Surely there were other spots you could have offered her."

"Well, I was angry." he said defensively. "She won't shut up, you know. It was hard enough finding a reason not to hang every last one of them, and if ever there was a girl more eager to put her head in the noose…"

"I didn't - " I began, but then stopped. I had, in a way.

"You should have seen her," Tirais said to Cioren. "As proud and twitchy as Mother arguing with the Council. Five words of my speech, and she looked as if she'd come up and do the job herself if we didn't get on with it."

"I wasn't -" I tried again, but still couldn't find the words.

"Arrogant and annoyed, that's how she looked."

"It was probably boredom," said Cioren. "I've heard your speeches."

"Why didn't you? Hang us, I mean. I know that I said that we didn't know what Uln intended but still…?"

"Don't flatter yourself. I wanted to. But I didn't have time, really. The logistics would have been a nightmare. We'd've been hanging traitors till midnight."

I couldn't help it. Maybe it was the sudden and unexpected release of tension, but I could feel the mirth, building up inside, and I had no strength left to fight it. I put down my wine, bent over my knees with my face in my hands, and began to laugh.

I could hear the pair of them laughing too. After awhile, my hysteria subsided. I sat back up, and wiped my eyes.

Tirais was grinning across at me. "Not covered in your training, either?"

"Not even suggested." I felt much better, now. Peaceful, almost. But his next words put paid to that.

"Lucky for me I didn't go through with it. Your father might have killed me."

"You - You've heard from him?' I was suddenly, overwhelmingly terrified. My father's a patient man, but he has his limits. I had passed almost all of them months ago.

"Heard from him? Oh, if that were only all. He came boiling down the North Road like an avenging spirit not five days after Fairbridge, and don't ask me how he heard the news so soon. Mother says he has the most efficient spy network in the Kingdom, and that if there's anything you don't want Gareth of Orliegh to know about, it'll be the very thing he does know. And wants to discuss. Publicly. He raked me over the coals right out on the open road. That must be where you inherited your talent for insulting invective. I'd always heard that your mother is renowned for her gentle, courteous ways."

I was silent. If no-one outside of Orliegh had heard of my mother's addiction to hurling whatever small objects that came to hand when she was miffed, I wasn't going to be the one to tell them.

And if they didn't know about her ability to take an innocuous remark of a passing peddler and ally it with a bit of gossip from a servant to come up with an astute conclusion on Kingdom politics, it wasn't the time to enlighten them. My father despaired: my mother was often wildly wrong in her assumptions, but she was right just often enough that it was unwise to disregard her.

"Anyway, there he was, and in a hell of a temper, too. I don't know how many armed men he has to leave to keep his manor-rights, but he brought every sword he could have, I'm certain of that."

"Sixty-two."

They both stared.

"Sixty-two. It's what he has to leave, not counting the port fees."

They still looked bemused.

"It's the sort of thing he thought I should know," I said. "Uln's was one hundred twelve, but there were the free towns, and I don't know what they owe for service. But it's beside the point."

"Yes," said Tirais. "Quite."

"Was he, I mean, did he seem well?"

"Extremely hardy and his lungs in good repair," said Tirais. "Mind, it took Gervase twenty minutes to convince him that we'd done our best to keep you out of trouble. He wasn't too pleased about Penvarron, though. Which reminds me," he looked at Cioren with a speculative gleam, "Your name doesn't exactly inspire him with confidence, either. Did you really try to seduce his lady at their betrothal feast?'

"The merest flirtation," said Cioren, mildly.

I sat stupefied. One never thinks of one's parents as anything but one's parents. Somehow, the idea of my mother flirting with Lord Cioren, under any circumstances, was an impossibility.

"It was a long time ago," said Cioren, meeting my gaze with amusement. "We were all in love with her, or pretending to be. Huwell and I used to do it just to anger Gareth - he was rather possessive. But she was very beautiful; I suppose he had reason, in a way, although there was never any doubt who she wanted."

The things one doesn't know. I looked up, and caught Tirais grinning at me again

84

"So here we are," he said, leaning back in his chair. "At least you got your revenge, on me as well as Uln. How did you manage to kill him, by the way?"

"I told you, a lucky shot."

"You're a very poor liar," he said.

Cioren nodded. "He's right, Keri. You may as well have the truth printed up in a broadsheet and distributed in the streets. He'll just keep at you till he's got it from you anyway."

I sighed. "I punched him in the nuts, Your Grace. After that it was easy."

Tirais choked. "Very -er- creative. You don't seem happy about it, though."

I wasn't happy. But I couldn't find the words to describe my unreasoning anger whenever I thought of it. I felt confused and impatient, and curiously ashamed. I knew better than to make a man's death take longer than it needed. It's one thing to hate. It's another to use that hate to torture a foe's final moments. I shook my head.

"Well, let it be. I don't suppose it matters now. Someone'll have to go down there, I suppose. In winter, too. You really picked your moment, I must say." He rose, stretching his arms. "Get some sleep, Keri. You deserve better, but I'm afraid it's back to Penvarron for you, all the same."

I stood.

"It's all right. They'll need me. My patrol, I mean." Now why had I said that? I knew what he thought of my command ability.

"Oh yes. That patrol. You know," he said, as he headed for the door, "You do land on your feet, don't you? Well, they say luck is better than skill. Stay lucky, Keridwen. I think the kingdom can use it."

Chapter 16

The sunlight was streaming through the windows when I woke up. I felt rested, which was a wonder, considering the last two or three days: it took only a moment or two to remember where I was.

I was lying on my back contemplating not very happily the long ride back to Penvarron, when I heard the door open. It was only a servant.

I say that as if it were a most usual occurrence in my life. The truth is that I was unused to the presence of servants, barring those that had known me from birth and therefore treated me as an unimportant fixture in their own lives. My parents had never encouraged anyone to do for me what I could do for myself.

This servant was carrying a laden tray, from which I could smell the most delicious collection of aromas. Eggs, bacon, mulled ale. Some kind of fruit, too. I sat up.

"You're awake," said the boy, with relief. "Lord Cioren said to let you sleep yourself out. But Lord Gervase said you'd be hungry."

"I am. But I've overslept."

"It won't matter. They're making a big to-do. Something about sending a force south, I heard. They'll be at it all day, and half the night, I shouldn't wonder."

Dressed, I began eating, perched on the edge of the huge bed I had tumbled into, exhausted and a little tipsy, the night before. In addition to the food I had smelled, there were thick slices of bread, still warm from the ovens, and some small pastries filled with jam. The boy made an attempt to serve me, but after a couple of minutes I waved him off and out the door. It was easier to do this myself, and I was far too hungry to be patient.

I was starving. I couldn't remember when I'd last eaten, other than dried meat and hard bread in the saddle, and a vague recollection of an inn and something bland and boiled that seemed like a lifetime ago. Penvarron's food was reasonably plentiful, but it was sustenance only, designed to keep us going, not for the sheer pleasure of eating. I certainly couldn't remember eating anything like this recently: I stuffed myself, reveling in it.

I was still picking at the remains when Cioren came back from wherever he'd been. He eyed the empty plates with amusement, returned my mumbled good morning, and suggested a bath.

"Have I got time?" I said, around a mouthful of bread.

"Oh, yes. It takes nearly forever to make any decisions around here and even longer to actually do anything. If you're finished," here he watched me contemplating some apple slices, "let Alun show you where the bath-house is. You could use it."

I felt incredibly calm and peaceful, almost sleepy, and certainly disinclined to take offense at his implication that I was less than clean. I smelt, even to myself, distinctly of horse.

"How long have I got, really?" I retrieved my saddlebags from under the table, and began ransacking them for my comb. My arming tunic and trews were nowhere in sight.

"As much as you need. I can't see how they'll get anywhere before noon. And it's only a small force, for now. Tirais is in a temper over it, but he should know better. You can't shift an army in five minutes, not around here. Half the troops thought they were dug in till spring at least. They'll delay as long as they can, just on general principles. Here, don't worry over all that. Alun can find you anything you want."

I had dumped one of the bags out onto the bed.

"Have you, ah, spoken to the Queen?" It was impertinence, but it seemed important to me to know that Elowyn knew just what we were facing.

"Yes. She's inclined to think she may have wronged you, last night, but I wouldn't trade on it too much."

"No, of course not."

"I've looked at the cursed thing too, if that was your next question. It's what I thought it was. Not that that's much help. I'm not certain what they intended to do - if it's what I think, they were more than foolish. But it's in a safe place, for the moment."

There were things I still wanted to ask, but the look on Cioren's face, coupled with Alun's entrance, put me off. After a moment I abandoned the search for my comb, and followed Alun out and down into the courtyard.

Outside, there was, as Cioren had said, a huge amount of mainly useless activity going on. People looked busy, but it was the kind of business that would have earned me a clout on the ear at home. There were soldiers fussing over who was to do what, a couple of arguments were brewing, and a general air of "why are you making us do this?" was apparent all over the place.

I caught a glimpse of Tirais, dressing down a youngish-looking captain, and felt rather relieved that he had someone else to be annoyed with. I'd seen that expression of irritated contempt directed at me far too often. Practically every time I'd seen him, really. Even last night, when he'd been amused and expansive, I'd felt an undercurrent of frustration and anger.

Well, he had reason. I was the bearer of bad tidings, as well as being a reminder of Uln's treason. He'd every right to see me as a kind of carrion bird, meeting me only when things were at their worst.

The bathhouse was in a quiet corner, tucked between a small officer's mess and a stone archway leading to, Alun said, a practice-ground. The baths themselves were well appointed and mercifully deserted. Alun disappeared, and I managed to get completely scrubbed and sluiced down before anyone else came in.

Glaice is in the mountains, just overlooking the widest and most convenient of the passes into Camrhys, and it had been built over a hot spring - it had a pool full of steaming, sulfurous water for soaking that was piped in from parts unknown. It looked ancient and beautiful, with carved river-deities and flowing script I couldn't read. I had just settled onto one of the submerged stone benches, letting the warmth seep into my bones, my muscles rejoicing at the sudden loss of tension, when I heard Lord Gervase calling a cheerful insult to someone out the door.

I was too relaxed to move. Still, I didn't want to see him. I was trapped, not least because I was unsure of my clothing's whereabouts and the fact that there was only one door. Perhaps he wouldn't have time for more than a quick scrub-down? Maybe he'd just come in looking for someone else? I sent a quick request to the Goddess that he wouldn't notice me, huddled deeper into the water, and waited.

My hopes were in vain. I heard him grunt as he undressed, listened to the splash of water as he washed, saw his bulk as it dimmed the light at the archway into the alcove of the poolroom.

"Good morning," he said as he lowered himself into the pool. "Well, you've certainly put the cat into the chicken-run, and no mistake. They're all running about convinced the world's about to end, and there's no telling anyone different. They were just a whisker away from boredom, yesterday morning - you'd think they'd be glad of a diversion, wouldn't you?"

I couldn't think of an answer to all this. Fortunately, he didn't want one.

"Tirais," he continued, "is in full royal rage - he thinks his troops ought to be ready to move at a moment's notice. Why in twenty-two years he hasn't learned that an army thinks grumbling is the first order of business and foot-dragging the second, I can't imagine. I've spent his entire life telling him so -

but it's always the same. He's convinced it's personal. He's on the impatient side - you'll want to remember that."

"Will I?" I couldn't think why.

"Oh yes. He's going south with you. You'll have days and days of dealing with a man who thinks yesterday was invented for getting his most recent ideas accomplished." He was grinning.

I stood up, naked and dripping, thinking if that were the case, I'd better get myself dressed and ready.

"Oh, sit back down. Not that I don't enjoy the view, but truly, lass, you've got two glasses at least. If he shifts even one troop to the gates before noon, it'll be a wonder and a half. It's just occurred to him that the baggage wagons can't move faster than a crawl, no matter what their orders, and he's trying to find enough pack ponies to supply the main troops on the road."

I eased back slowly into the water.

"Don't look so worried. Tirais isn't an easy man to work with, I'll grant you, but he's fair enough, and kind when he remembers to be. Just try to keep your temper. His isn't the most long-suffering either, and you'll be at loggerheads with him forever if you can't curb your tongue."

"Oh. Yes, of course."

"There's no 'of course' about it. I've seen you in action, remember? Not that you weren't right, but that's no help. He's even worse when he feels in the wrong. Still, he's inclined to give you the benefit of the doubt, just now. Gallerain's been saying that Uln must have died at Fairbridge and Tirais is merely mistaken in believing he got away. Having you kill Uln in Penvarron months after is just what he wanted to hear. Huwell still treats him like a child, and that he can't abide."

The thought of Prince Tirais being treated like a boy and resenting it cheered me up no end. I was almost grateful to Baron Gallerain. In fact, I hoped he annoyed Tirais very thoroughly right up until we marched out of Glaice. Put him in a towering rage, I thought, dreamily, and he won't have the energy to even notice my presence. I'll just attach myself to the rearguard, and slip back into Penvarron, and he'll forget all about me...

"Don't fall asleep," remarked Gervase. He was standing at the edge of the pool, swathed in a couple of acres of toweling. "I've done it. Even if you don't drown, it's not the healthiest place for a nap."

Chapter 17

When I finally did get back to Cioren's rooms, I found that despite everyone's beliefs, I'd almost left it too late. A guard wearing the Queen's livery was waiting for me, with a message that said, stripped of its courteous phrases, to get my lazy butt down to the gate double-quick. My saddlebags were already gone, I followed the man back down the direction I had come.

I felt pretty good. After Gervase had left, I'd lazed in the hot water, digesting his words and trying to think of a way I could get through the trip south without attracting Tirais' attention, and reminding myself constantly to guard my unruly tongue. After about a half-glass at this, I noticed my skin was looking waterlogged and wrinkly, so I made the supreme effort and got myself out of the tub and dried off. In the outer room, I discovered my arming tunic and trews had magically reappeared, cleaner than they'd been anytime these last six months, along with a comb, and I got myself dressed. Alun then arrived, armed with a pair of tiny snips and the intelligence that Cioren thought I needed a haircut.

It was quite true, but it's not the sort of job you can do for yourself. I sat patiently, at first, while Alun got to work. He was competent, but slow; I had to work fairly hard, after the first ten minutes or so, to sit still under his careful, dogged work, without snapping at him.

Finally, washed and shorn, I put my chainmail shirt back on over my tunic, and belted on my sword. In addition to my own clothes, I was now the proud possessor of a good wool cloak, compliments of Her Majesty, who apparently did read Sorcha's reports. The lack of proper winter gear was a small legend at Penvarron.

Now, standing in the yard beside a beautifully groomed and rather feisty Banshee, I felt as though I was ready for anything. As usual, I was wrong.

Tirais, true to Gervase' report, was in a state of high dudgeon. He gave orders out with a kind of tolerant contempt, as though he had come to oversee a group of village toddlers playing at soldiers. It was obvious that this was, if not normal, sufficiently common as to occasion no resentment.

I thought it a little much. Anyone who's ever tried to put a group of people into full gear and on the road knows it takes time. How much time depends on how used to the idea your troops have gotten. Considering they'd had less than twelve hours warning, they were doing quite well.

I was watching, in amusement, a young man trying to get a column to move out of the way of a line of pack ponies that Tirais had decided might as well start down the road, since we'd overtake them in minutes no matter what kind of head start they had, when a hardbitten veteran with an interesting scar across her face and wearing Glaice's colours came up.

"Lady Keridwen?"

When had my status changed? I acknowledged I was Keridwen of Orliegh.

"Commander Olwen," she said briskly. "Prince Tirais says you were at Penvarron. He's given me the gist of it all, but I do have a few questions. Perhaps, when we're - wait, you," she began to yell at someone beyond my left shoulder, "Idiot! Don't put the damned things there. Get 'em off to the side. Sorry," she added, "Everyone's taken leave of their senses today. I just thought if you could give me some time as we ride, I could get a better idea of what's going on."

I began to say that of course I'd answer any questions she liked, but with a curt nod she was already off, yelling at the top of her lungs that if someone named Kathban didn't get his fleabitten arse in gear, she'd string him up by his guts, by Aheris she would, and I was left to soothe a restive and aggravated Banshee, who wasn't taking the commotion at all well.

No-one seemed particularly angry with me this morning; in fact they were treating me as if I was the girl I'd been six months ago: green and untried, but game, and with nothing questionable about me. It occurred to me that if I'd managed to refrain from chewing out the prince at our first meeting, he might have sent me to Glaice instead of Penvarron. I might still be heading south this morning - really unwanted errands always get shifted onto those troopers that have the least experience - but I'd have had three months of quite unobjectionable guard duty behind me.

Bit by bit, the small army Tirais had assembled began to resolve itself into a force that was ready to move. I was near the front of the column when finally, with no little shifting about and some cheerful cursing, the main gates opened and we started moving out. I could see Tirais at the head of the line, with Commander Olwen. They looked as though they were barely on speaking terms at this point, and my money was on Olwen overall. She looked as though she could give as good as she could get.

Cioren, on a fresh mount, cantered up the line and fell in beside me.

"You look all right," he said, by way of greeting.

"I feel all right too."

"Well, enjoy it. It'll be a longer ride, but I doubt less uncomfortable than the way here. And try to stay out of Tirais' way. He only knows what you've told him. I don't want him thinking about what we may have left out, and you're the least practiced dissembler I've ever known."

"I'll try," I said cautiously, "but really, Cioren, he is the Prince. If he asks, I'll have to say."

"I know. But until I know more about what's going on, it's useless for anyone else to speculate. If you're in a jam, can't you just say something outrageous? Pissing him off should direct his attention elsewhere." His tone was light and accompanied by a grin. I grinned back.

"I'll do my best, sir."

It was a mindnumbingly dull afternoon. Once we were onto the main road and truly on our way, the troopers settled down, and there's really nothing more boring than a long march. I didn't know anyone, hardly, nor they me, and I had no duties or responsibilities to occupy me. Cioren had gone, to ride up to with Tirais and Olwen, and I was left to keep Banshee from nipping at the heels of the rider in front of me.

The column wasn't making good time. I could feel Tirais' frustration from here, radiating from his stiffened back, and evidenced by the riders sent whipping up and down the line with curt demands for people to look sharp and pick up the pace.

In the first hour I at least had some things to look at.

I'd been too apprehensive, when we'd ridden in the day before, to take in the scenery. Now, at my leisure, I saw that Camrhys' invasion had left its mark. There were burnt fields here and there, and a couple of villages in ruins.

But considering the size of the force Camrhys had reportedly sent, the damage seemed almost accidental. I edged Banshee up to one of the guards riding ahead of me and asked about it, carefully trying not to sound like some gapemouthed country yobbo out to gawk.

"Aye," he said, and spat into the dust. "That lot went mainly north, like. Up by Caer Medhir, they took two forts. Burnt down a granary by Gosset, too, but it were empty, so no matter."

He spat again, and I let Banshee drop back into place.

I wondered what Camrhys had hoped to gain by it. We'd been fighting them off, in a desultory fashion, for most of my life, but the last time they had made any serious inroads had been when I was four years old. Even as a child, it had always seemed like a nuisance rather than a terror.

It was late when we finally bivouacked. Tirais had wanted to get as far as possible from Glaice, to get his troops into the mood for the morning. Otherwise they'd still be thinking about Glaice, and not the road ahead. It was good strategy, as far as it went, but it meant that we camped in a valley between two villages, rather than making for one of the smaller keeps along the way.

From the chatter I'd overheard, no-one seemed to know why we were headed to Penvarron. There was some speculation on subjects like mass desertion, although it was agreed that Tirais would have been far angrier if that were the case, and the idea of some grand master-plan to finally rout the Camrhyssi once and for all seemed to be more popular. No-one asked me my opinion, in fact no-one talked to me at all, until a soldier came up and said that His Grace wanted to see me.

He was camped on a little rise near the centre of things, and there were people assembling a fairly reasonable sort of meal on a table inside his tent. Cioren and Olwen were already there, lounging comfortably beside a brazier. It was warm enough that they had dropped their cloaks from their shoulders. I looked at the repast laid out and wondered, a little meanly, how His Grace would take to the food at Penvarron.

Tirais himself was not in evidence. At Cioren's invitation, I found a spot near the warmth, shed my own cloak, and was drawn immediately into a discussion of what had actually occurred at Penvarron, and what I thought the situation was.

"It's been three days," I said. "It'll be four more at least before we're there. Six if the weather's bad, or if the bridge at Eoghan's is washed out. And truly, Commander, I don't know what we'll find. I'm hoping not much - there was only one man unaccounted for, and with any luck, they found him the same night, or else he's running back across the border as best he can. Unless there were more out there."

"You didn't see anyone, and you weren't pursued," said Olwen. " I can't think that any invaders worth their salt would have let you get away with a message so easily. I wouldn't. It's madness."

"Ye-es. But it was Penvarron they wanted. Not even Penvarron itself, I think. Something that Penvarron has, or is." I looked at Cioren. "I'm sorry. I know you think that the least said the better, but you can't let troops march down there with no inkling of what they're walking into. And they'll know, after five minutes into the gates, more or less. Although the speculation will be out of hand by the time we get there; we live on rumors, in Penvarron."

"Any army does," said Olwen, before Cioren could reply. "But she's right, sir. We have to know."

"She's always right," said Tirais. I jumped, visibly, and cursed under my breath. He'd come up so quietly, I hadn't even noticed the tentflap moving. "It's her most annoying habit. What's she right about this time?"

"Merely that Olwen has a right to know what she's taking the troops to," said Cioren. "And I have to agree, insofar as we actually know anything." He sighed. "I know you think throwing more warriors at the problem is the answer, but truthfully, if manpower were the key, we wouldn't be here. Penvarron wasn't undermanned three days ago."

"It is now though. And begging Keri's pardon, and all, but those weren't the troops I'd have bet on in a bad spot." Tirais tossed his cloak over the back of his chair and sat. I was trying not to take offense at his words, and, as usual, failing miserably.

"Begging your pardon, sir, but we did pretty well. I'd say as well as your army does getting itself shifted on short notice. We were all asleep, nearly, and we got into that tower in less than two shakes of the tail after the alarm sounded."

He laughed. "You see? It's all right, Keri. I didn't say you didn't do well. Only that I wouldn't have expected it."

"Sorry. But the thing is," I hesitated, glancing at Cioren, whose face gave me no clues, "the thing is, I keep thinking that they wanted us there. They weren't trying to hide the fact that they were inside the walls. They left the East Gate open behind them. That's what woke me. And they used torches, once they were in. And no-one stopped us from going up the stairs. I would have put some people down on one of the lower levels, to slow us down at least."

"Unless they thought - no, that wouldn't work, either, considering what did happen. Oh, leave it be." Tirais sounded impatient. "Let's eat, and talk of something else. I'm beginning to hate the very word Penvarron."

Try as we might, though, we couldn't keep off the subject. It kept arising out of the most innocuous comments, while we worked our way around the subject of what had really happened and why, until Cioren got tired of our squeamishness. We couldn't bring ourselves to actually use the word 'magic', but he could, and did.

With devastating effect. Tirais stopped his knife midway from his plate to his mouth, put the slice of roast down, and gave him a look that said for two pence he'd hang him, Her Majesty's friend or no, while Olwen and I pretended we were someplace else.

Cioren ignored the look and said calmly that if any of us thought that not mentioning the most salient fact of the entire business was likely to make it go away, we were fair and far out.

"Take what happened to Keri," he said. "You can dance around it all you like, but you know quite well that some sort of spell was in action in that fight. Why else would Uln be so sure of himself? You and I both know his fighting skills were never great, Tirais. We may as well accept that the Camrhyssi, or some of the priests, anyway, have gotten far enough along in resurrecting the old knowledge to use battle-magic at least. If you're planning on beating whatever it is we're facing, you can at least be realistic."

It had been a long evening, from my point of view. I got out of there by the kindness of Commander Olwen, who said, after a few more go-rounds over some wine, that she'd pickets to inspect, and invited me to walk along with her.

Once out of earshot of the tent, though, she said genially that she couldn't have taken another five minutes of that crap, and guessed that I couldn't either, wished me good night and marched off.

I wandered back to the watchfire where I'd left my bedroll and huddled in my blankets, watching Aheris sink low into the night sky, and hoping that Tirais wasn't going to invite me to dine every night. Olwen was right. Another rehash of that one night in Penvarron, with all that useless conjecture, and I'd have lived down to Tirais' already subterranean opinion of me.

Chapter 18

Over the next couple of days I forgot my resolution to hang back with the rear guard, and consolidated a place near the front of the force, just behind Tirais' personal guard. Within hours, they had accepted my presence, making a place for me among them at their fire at night, getting me to sub for watches when Tirais' demands put a strain on their numbers and otherwise hardly noticing me at all.

We were moving more quickly now: once well and truly on the road, Tirais' troops gave me the lie. They were up before dawn, packed and ready before the word to march was given, and moving doggedly and with considerable speed throughout the day. Having settled into a routine, they gave it their best. We made excellent time down the main road, and the less-traveled road leading south hardly slowed us at all.

Still, it was the fourth morning before we saw the first buildings of Eoghan's Moor in the distance.

It was still only mid-morning, and we didn't stop, but rode through at a good clip, leaving behind us a cloud of dust, a half dozen or so amazed sheep, and our baggage train, to catch up as it could.

The day before, Olwen had organized a scouting party to ride ahead a few miles or so, reporting on the road conditions. They had crossed the bridge early, some miles ahead of us, but it wasn't long before we saw them riding back to the column.

They were moving fast. I felt the first stirrings of apprehension - it wasn't like seasoned troops to push their horses that way without need. Without thinking of the consequences, I urged Banshee towards the front of the column. It was a mark of my equivocal status, or perhaps more because I was nobody's particular responsibility, that no-one stopped me, no-one questioned my presence. In fact, they ignored me.

The scouts' faces were carefully blank, but I could see, even from several feet away, that they were pale beneath their tans. The youngest of them seemed almost incapable of speech but his eyes talked. He was seeing the world anew, through the lens of some unimaginable horror.

Much as Tirais and Olwen tried, they couldn't get much out of the scouts. Two of them managed to convey that they had happened on something, and that it wasn't good, but beyond that, refused to say more. The upshot of a quarter-glass of abortive questioning was that Olwen, the Prince and Cioren began heading out with the scouts, along with a few handpicked and bewildered guards.

And me. Cioren had noticed, but said nothing, when he'd seen me clinging to the edges of the little group questioning the riders. I fell in behind him. Whatever was out there, I reasoned, concerned Penvarron. I had a right to know.

I could have stayed behind. I wished, a short time later, that I had. But I would have had this moment in my memory, eventually.

The body lay, full out on the road. It was raining, and there was no blood about, although there surely should have been. From throat to crotch, something had rent that poor scrap of human flesh, raking it open like a sack of flour, and dragging the entrails out into the mud. The bits and ends were chewed and gnawed, as if some child had been nibbling at a cake.

There were only fluttering rags of clothing left, and a face set in a grinning rictus of horrified death, to say who this might have been in life.

Behind me, I heard one of the guards, losing his breakfast. We all must have been close to it. Olwen's face was green. I looked away, over the hills, and longed, not for the first time lately, to be anywhere but here. I looked back at the body, and noticed that there were tiny, delicate bites, along her neck and breasts. She hadn't been dead very long, by what I could see, and something had played with her, before she died.

I almost gave up my breakfast too.

"Mag," I said. "Poor Mag."

Tirais raised his head and looked at me as if I was a stranger.

"You know her?"

"One of the village whores," I said. What had she been doing here, so far from Penvarron? I thought how I had last seen her, in the Black Pig Tavern, dancing like a whirlwind on one of the rickety tables, a girl still, really, grown old early by a hard life and a harder profession.

"Cairn her." said Tirais. He sounded hard and angry.

"My lord?" Olwen said, blankly.

"Cairn her. Do you think I'm going to leave her here for more indignities? Or do you think that she had less right to protection, being a whore?" He was working himself into a rage.

I could see his point. It wasn't about Mag, not really. It was about fear and about helplessness. You could be scared, or you could be angry. You had to choose, and anger felt better to me too.

"You, and you. Ride on back and tell the others to make it here quick. And send a squad back to the baggage ponies and tell them to snap it up. We'll give them two glasses to catch up and I don't care if they kill every pony in the train to do it. They get here or else. Get moving."

I looked around. He hadn't actually lost his senses; there were plenty of stones for a cairn, and digging a grave, in that barren ground, was right out. I picked up a fair-sized rock and brought it over to lay beside the corpse. I heard Cioren sigh. I went to find another rock.

It doesn't take that long to cairn a body, especially when you have two hundred soldiers to do the job and an unlimited supply of stones close by. We hadn't got far when the rest of the column showed up, but it went quickly after that. We had been finished for over twenty minutes, and were standing around silent and useless and depressed when the shout went up that the supply train was in sight.

Tirais had worked as hard as anybody, dragging rocks to shield a mutilated and unknown whore's body from the elements. His hands were scraped and bleeding and raw but his hot rage had fallen away; he was in control now, but still coldly, calculatedly angry.

He waited for the ponies full of our belongings and supplies to catch up, then mounted, and without a word, spurred his horse down the track.

Alone, it would have only been a couple of hours to Penvarron. It took us over four to make the same trip, slowed down as we were by the laden ponies, and the discovery of a second corpse.

This one had tried to run, away off the track and heading south into the open country. We might have missed it, which would have been a relief, but the scouts had spread out in a straggly line to get a wider range of sight.

Much was the same about this corpse, except that it was noticeably and pointedly a man. About his naked legs flapped the tatty remains of a velvet robe. A black one.

"There's your errant priest of Camrhys," said Cioren, as I joined the unnerved little group gathered around this latest find. I swallowed. I could actually find compassion for the man, which seemed to make it worse. Despite the circumstances, I couldn't wish this on anyone. The dead man had a look of such awful shock, as though what had killed him had been a horrid joke, gone unaccountably wrong.

98

I found I was trembling. I tried to tell myself that it was anger, the same anger that had possessed Tirais a short time ago, but I lied, if only to myself. I was in a state of terror. If this was what lay ten miles from Penvarron, I could only imagine what was going on inside the fortress.

The wind was damp and chill. Within minutes of mounting up, the drizzle turned to a dirty, knifing sleet, and despite my new cloak, I was almost frozen when we neared the gates.

Even from a distance we could see that the village was deserted; nothing moved between the buildings, no lights shone out in the late afternoon gloom, and we heard no shouts from roistering soldiers.

Closer inspection revealed a town in ruins. There had been a fire here and three of the whores' shacks had burned, as well as the stouter house of One-Leg Denny's Pawn Shop. The Black Pig was boarded up and shuttered, but the rest of the makeshift buildings lay open and deserted, and there were bits and pieces of people's unwanted or forgotten belongings lying about in the muddy lanes. The wind moved a broken door, making a squeaking whine that sounded faintly human, like a baby left unattended. I shivered; my cloak seemed to do me no good at all.

We began moving up the hill, towards Penvarron's soundless gates, locked and barred, closed against whatever lay out here that had caused such havoc.

And closed against us.

There were people on the gates. We could see them; silent and unmoving, staring down at us like the dead.

Tirais tried a herald first. The man bawled out the Prince's titles, and demanded entry, in more or less the conventional forms.

There was little response. I could see a few of them moving slightly, and the wind carried down the sound of murmured discussion, but in the main, their silence held.

Gwyll tried again, this time throwing in some stuff about the might of Keraine as barely veiled threats, to no avail.

Tirais, by this time had recaptured his earlier rage. He rode forward, grabbed the standard from Gwyll's elegantly gloved hand and yelled out "Open the damned door, you lousy flea-bitten spawn of whores, or I'll kick it down and feed it to you!"

In a sense, it worked. A voice floated down to us with the intelligence that they had orders not to open the gates to anyone, not to the Mother of All, should she put in an appearance, but that they'd sent for their commander.

We waited. Short of mounting an assault on the gates, a fruitless task, as I've said, there wasn't any alternative. The sleet was coming down harder. I thought that Tirais would have a fit of some kind; his face was purple with unspent rage, but he sat on his horse in the gathering shadows and waited with us, mercifully nursing his anger against the chance that he could spend it on the hapless troops inside.

It wasn't completely fair. If he'd ordered troops to close the gates on all comers, he'd have been just as angry if his order had been disobeyed. It was the whole day that did it, six hours of increasing tension and disgusting discoveries, capped by this last quarter-glass of enforced waiting, that irked us all. We would have slaughtered the lot of them, given half a chance.

I considered, in the absence of any real information, who might be commanding Penvarron's forces. Sir Aidan was surely dead, and it had seemed as though the soldiers had been prepared to accept Sorcha's leadership when I'd left, but a lot can happen in a seven-day. Penvarron's useless and slavish adherence to a class and status base for its rules of command might have forced someone else into this thankless position. I hoped, in that event, that they'd chosen Ruan, who at least had some experience, and wasn't an utter ass.

I wasn't given long to contemplate this problem. There was a stir behind the parapet over the gate, and then a well-remembered voice calling down to us. We'd come at a bad time, it seemed.

There was a curse on Penvarron, said the voice. It wasn't that the troops wished to be disrespectful, or inhospitable, but, truly, they couldn't, in all conscience, open the gates and let us in to share their fate. If they were cursed, and hounded by the dogs of all nine hells, well, that was the way it was. They knew their duty, so they did, and here the voice trembled, with fear or exhaustion or both, and by the Goddess, they would see that we were spared.

Tirais looked like his rage would carry him off, then and there. He was still spluttering at Gwyll with some idea of telling them what he thought of this piece of idiocy, when Olwen stood up in her stirrups and yelled back to the watchers inside the walls.

"Is that you, Sorcha? Open these Goddess-forsaken gates, or I'll have you back scrubbing pots so fast your head will spin!"

"Lady Olwen?" Sorcha's voice ended in a happy screech. "Lady Olwen?"

There was a flurry of activity on the wall. I saw someone take a cuff to the side of the head, and moments later, we heard the sound of the bar being dropped away, and the scream of rusted hinges as the gates of Penvarron opened to us.

Chapter 19

There was confusion in the yard when we entered. Too many people were crowding into an already overcrowded space, and the five or six men in the gatehouse seemed unnaturally anxious to close the gates behind us. They began to swing them to twice before all the pack-ponies were in.

Part of the problem lay in the fact that Penvarron village seemed to have taken up residence in the courtyard. Tents and awnings lined the inner walls, and I saw Mag's little boy, Odhar, curled up on a mat in what looked to be the Black Pig's new digs. Cookfires turned the air smoky in the increasing downpour, and every soldier left in Penvarron seemed to be trying to fit into the remaining space.

The soldiers were milling around in knots comprised of their units and it seemed to me that there were faces missing in this press of humanity. My eyes raked the crowds for Third East, and found them, standing in a quiet huddle near the archway to the upper bailey. I couldn't see any absent faces, but they looked gaunt and harrowed, haunted by some unknown experience.

Gradually, a space was clearing in the centre of the yard. I saw that Tirais was there, with Olwen and Sorcha, who had knelt in the mud, her head bowed, waiting for the inevitable.

I pushed to the edge of the crowd, leaving someone else to deal with Banshee. It was Tirais' face that had me worried; I had seen that expression of unreasoning anger before and it seemed to me that someone ought to be ready to stop him from ordering her execution out of sheer pique. Sorcha had probably done the best she could. It wasn't her fault that nothing in her limited training had prepared her for a seven-day like the one that Penvarron had apparently had.

I don't know what I thought I would do, if the situation had warranted my interference, or why it never occurred to me that Olwen was more than fit, and ready to deflect Tirais' bad temper towards a more reasoned response. If anything passed through my mind at all, it was perhaps that he was already so used to being angry at me that I thought I might distract him from actually ordering Sorcha's death out of the need to do something, anything to revenge himself on a situation that had gotten way out of hand.

"I'm very sorry, sir," Sorcha was saying. "I didn't know what else to do. And you shouldn't have come, sir. It's true; there's a curse. I ought not have let you in the gates, Goddess forgive me."

"And what form is this curse taking?' Tirais inquired. His voice was deceptively calm and measured. He might have been asking after her health. It struck me as the kind of quiet that descends just before a storm.

"Death, sir. Every night, there's two, or more, found ripped to shreds, sir. We're being picked to pieces, it's a fact, and nothing to be done."

"You don't think," he paused, as if considering his words, which I would have bet my best dagger he wasn't, "You don't think, perhaps, that there is some other explanation? Some human agency at work, here?'

"Oh, no, sir. Not the way these bodies are. And there's more. The dead walk, your lordship. Hours after, you see them, on the walls, or in the windows. In the beginning we thought it was them sorcerers, out of Camrhys, but they don't walk, sir. Just us. We knew, sir, we knew then, we're doomed. And I was bound and determined, sir, that them as come after weren't to share our fate."

"Well, I believe that you believe in this - er - curse. But here we are. And I'm sure that whatever is happening here, my soldiers can manage it, as well as Penvarron's can."

"But that's what we're not doing, sir. Managing, I mean. We're being picked off one by one, and there's no hope for it. Penvarron, and all that's in it, is dying, and begging your lordship's pardon, but we know our duty. We ought not have let you in."

Tirais sighed. "Sorcha, if there's a curse, it's spread past Penvarron's walls. I'm sure you did what you thought best," his voice indicated he thought nothing of the sort, "But, nevertheless, here we are. We'll have stabling, and quarters. I'm damned if I'm standing out in this muck arguing the point any longer."

"Yes, sir," said Sorcha, rising. Her voice said it all. She'd tried, and failed, to convince him. In a way, it must have been a relief. It was someone else's problem, now. She bowed with surprising grace, backed off a pace, and then turned and began yelling at someone to get rooms ready in the main barracks.

I moved off towards where Third East still stood, a small knot of frightened faces in a sea of soldiers and baggage. How many dead altogether? And what was killing them? I thought of Mag's poor body, lying in the rain. Cioren had been too closemouthed, but I was beginning to guess at the source of our problems. It wasn't pleasant. It was nearly unthinkable.

"All right," I said as I reached them. "What the hell is going on?"

A half-hour later, seated in our crowded barracks, I felt as if I had even less to go on than I'd had before.

They had been reticent at first, letting Tighe, not a brilliant conversationalist at the best of times, explain in a disjointed way, what had been happening since I'd gone. But by the time we reached our ramshackle rooms, Ari had recovered enough to begin adding his bit, and once he became a leak in the dyke, so to speak, the floodgates opened.

The night I'd left, they thought nothing much had happened, beyond the obvious. They'd piled up the dead, shoving the Camrhyssi into a drainage ditch outside the south wall, and using some substandard pitch sent for roof repairs to set the bodies alight.

That pitch had been runny and useless for our purposes, and had always been considered a liability, being almost unbelievably flammable, so they hadn't been surprised when the pyre had gone up like tinder. Sorcha had been nervous about the stuff, and stored it outside the walls, so it was the obvious choice for the job, but when they'd begun burning our own dead, halfway through they'd run out of pitch. The third pyre had been lit with no real hope of catching on as the others, but surprisingly, it had gone up as easily as the first two.

Odd, but not unnerving.

Early on the second morning, they'd found a couple of North Two's soldiers dead in the culvert near our mess hall. At the time, it was supposed that they'd simply been missed in previous patrols of the fort, although it was a little strange. And they'd been horribly slashed, as Mag's body had been, but, sickening as that was, it could be explained away as a Camrhyssi savagery. They thought the cold weather had kept them from putrefying, but the corpses hadn't waited until a torch was lit before exploding into flames. A smoldering spark from previous fires, said Sorcha, firmly, to the startled troops.

It was on the third morning, when another pair of dead bodies turned up, one beside the West Gate, and one down by the latrines, that Penvarron began to panic. And by then, the village had been awash with rumors and terror, and were demanding protection, action, anything.

Tighe at least, had developed some kind of response for Third East, although he claimed he got the idea from Ruan. Stuck with a command he felt unequal to, he had had no qualms about getting outside advice. He split the patrol into two groups, put Ari in charge of one, and the patrol ate, slept and lived in two shifts, one always keeping watch. No-one in Third East went anywhere alone.

Four was deemed the minimum number, even for a trip to the privies. Ruan's Watch was doing the same, and so were a few others.

Others had reported seeing the dead walking the walls. Tighe wouldn't swear to it, but Brighid bet her life she'd seen Aidan on the walls, beckoning to her, the night after he was safely burned.

"The dead can't walk," I said, shaking my head. "Oh, I believe you saw what looked like Aidan, Brighid. But it's got to be a trick. What happened in the village?"

But here they balked. They hadn't seen it, and the witnesses had been full of garbled tales of a winged, toothy creature out of some lunatic's fevered nightmare, and a sudden storm of fire. Several villagers had been killed in the blaze.

In the aftermath, Sorcha had had no choice but to open the gates and let them in, once she'd warned them that things were no better inside. No-one had seen Mag since that night. I suspected no-one had thought about her overmuch; the news of her dead body miles away was greeted by silence, and shuffling feet.

So there they were, shoved into the courtyard like so many salted fish. People had continued to disappear, turning up as horribly mutilated corpses. They vanished in the night, and, as near as anyone could figure, only when they were alone, while the living continued, in desperate fear and dreary acceptance, waiting for their turn to be picked off, like herd animals patiently lining up for the slaughter.

It made no sense.

They hadn't seen anything. No clues to what or who or how the killings were accomplished. No cries of pain or terror reached their ears. Just the grim evidence, every morning.

I chewed it over. The only good thing I could see was that Tighe had kept Third East together and alive, and given Ari a chance at being a second, of sorts, a minor problem that had nagged at me for days.

"Right," I said, eventually. "You did well, all of you. Someone, drag my pallet in here, I'm not dossing down and waiting for whatever it is to turn up and make ribbons of me. As for the rest, well, that's what the Prince is here for. We'll just have to see that he knows what's going on, though I don't think Sorcha will hold back. Once she's told Commander Olwen the whole, they'll figure it out."

They seemed cheered, which was nice for them. I'd lied, of course. Oh, not about Sorcha, of course. But I couldn't think what Tirais could do about it. If in seven days no-one here had the slightest inkling of what was actually going on, I didn't think he'd make any more sense out of the grisly evidence.

On the other hand, Cioren might. I shied away from that thought. I liked Cioren, a lot; if he was what I thought he might be, my native prejudices were going to have to undergo some re-organization.

We'd just gotten my straw mattress dragged through the connecting door, and were contemplating the wisdom of nailing the damn thing shut, as a precaution, when Gwyll turned up, with a polite request from Tirais to attend him in his new quarters.

I hardly knew Gwyll. He was the Prince's Herald, and actually, we'd gotten as far, the other morning, of ascertaining that he was, in a roundabout way, a cousin of mine, by a marriage a couple of generations ago on my mother's side. But he was unbelievably aristocratic, eternally well-dressed, with the polished manners of a lifelong courtier. I couldn't see that he and I had very much in common, beyond a shared great-aunt, and his mere presence made me feel as though my bootlaces weren't properly tied, or that my face was dirty. Something like that, anyway. Inadequate.

"Wenna, Colm, you come up with me. There's no telling when I'll get back, Tighe, or what will come up meantime, so just carry on."

I'd thought it a bit of a come-down for Gwyll to be sent running an errand like fetching me when any passing soldier would have done as well, but as we trudged back into the main buildings, I began to think he might have volunteered, just to get himself out of the chaos.

The courtyard was still overcrowded with animals and people, and the halls of the barracks were just as bad. There were troops and baggage everywhere, and one of the village pigs had got loose, running through the archway leading into the main hall, and wreaking havoc in its wake. Arguments were breaking out all over, and the troops from Glaice were the main culprits. They had adopted an attitude of supercilious contempt, and seemed bent on putting Penvarron's soldiers in their place.

Inside the barracks was no better. Since only a few watch squads were housed here, there was plenty of room for the new arrivals, and Tirais had taken Aidan's old rooms on the second floor. Olwen was apparently down in the stables, trying to find space for all the additional animals, and Sorcha had been confirmed as Penvarron's quartermaster and was busy counting stores.

The rest of the troops were occupied in trying to outsmart each other over better barrack-rooms, or doing quick deals with One-Leg to get some extra cash for a sit-down in the tavern. There was gear strewn everywhere, and a hellish amount of noise.

We lost Gwyll to a vicious quarrel over precedence about halfway down the hall, and when we got to Tirais' rooms, there was another altercation breaking out between Watch Six and three of the newcomers over possession of a small but pleasant chamber next door to the Prince's.

The door was firmly shut. I left Wenna and Colm to enjoy the spectacle of Watch Six trying to match courteously-veiled insults with the soldiers from Glaice, knocked hard on the door, and when it opened, went in to see what Tirais wanted with me this time.

It was only the Prince and Cioren within. Tirais had apparently been going through Aidan's papers; there was a tidy heap on one side of the table and a smaller, less tidy one on the floor. He barely looked up as I came in, muttering an uncivil greeting, but Cioren gave me a smile.

"All settled in?" I didn't think it was politeness that prompted the question, but I nodded.

"So what does your unit say? More superstitious ravings? Have they convinced you that we're all doomed?"

"Well," I said, "If you want my opinion, this is the stupidest curse I ever heard of. Unless you count the fact that we'll be murdering each other by morning, there isn't anything that couldn't be attributed to a rather bloodthirsty band of assassins who are masters of disguise."

"Ah. And where are they hiding?"

"That is the trick," I agreed. "though if you look at the upper bailey, you could sort of see it. It's a rabbit warren, and half the buildings aren't really livable. You could hole up by day, I suppose, and do your killing by night. At least, I think you could. But that doesn't really fit the facts either."

"Are the killings only by night? No one's said, although," Tirais thought for a moment, "I suppose I didn't ask."

"According to Third East, it seems like it." I began to recount their version of the last few days. As I told them, the idea of a curse seemed even less likely to my ears. "Anyway, it's not like a curse in a ballad or anything. Those have some kind of point. This is all so random. And physical. I mean, apart from seeing people you know are dead wandering around, there's nothing to say that we haven't a madman running about. And the truth is, what with everyone in a state of terror, and all the funeral pyres, Sorcha's had no time to think of searching the place properly. Not that she could have got half of them to go looking anyway, considering all the corpses."

"Well, something's going on. I won't have my soldiers killed off like this without finding out what, either. Cioren needs to go into the tower, and I confess, I want to take a look at it too. Are you coming?"

I was silent. It made sense, I suppose. The tower was where it had started, in a way. But I didn't want to go.

Cioren said, "We can't force anyone to go in, Keri. But I need someone who was there."

I looked out the casement, down into the yard. The afternoon was drawing in. We would have to go soon, before full dark. I could just about stomach doing this now, in the remaining daylight. After dark, well, it didn't bear thinking of.

Tirais cleared his throat.

"We do need someone who can tell us what happened and where. Purely voluntary, of course. If you have other duties…?"

He meant, naturally, if I was afraid. And I was. Not of what might happen, exactly. I didn't think anything would. But when push came to shove, I didn't want to go back in there.

But I owed him. He was the Prince, after all.

And who else could they ask?

"Of course I'm coming," I said.

It was neatly done, I reflected, as I followed them down the stairway. Push me into a corner, imply, in the kindest way possible, that there was nothing unusual in my apparent cowardice, and what would I do? Put my head in the largest of available jaws without hesitation, of course. Tirais, if he ever gave up his claims to the throne, could have a nice career in extortion, I thought.

Chapter 20

We walked across the bailey, mercifully quiet now, as the troops settled into the evening routine. Tirais had his sword out already. If a madman lurked in Penvarron Tower, we were as prepared for him as we could be. What we'd do if there were several madmen was another story, but I thought I could die happy knowing that this disaster was the work of human hands. The alternative was too awful to contemplate.

Cioren looked calm. He'd no weapons, but it didn't seem to bother him, or Tirais. I loosened my own sword in its scabbard.

The door was still unlocked; I wasn't the only one who was reluctant to go near this place after that one terrible night. And Penvarron had had years of avoiding even thinking about the tower behind them. The gap showed merely a stone hallway, lit by the fading afternoon's light. It looked harmless.

"That's the window Gareth went through," I said, pointing. "There's no bars, you see. But they didn't pull the shutter closed. If they'd even wanted to slow us down a bit, they ought to have done that much."

"Yes, well, let's not speculate overmuch on their intent," said Cioren. "You're looking at this logically, and I expect logic will be useless, without more facts. Damn, but I wish they hadn't burnt those bodies. I might have learnt something."

I wondered what, not to mention how, but Tirais had already moved to the stairwell. It looked dim and bleak.

No-one had lived here for years. Even the fighting hadn't disturbed the cobwebs adorning the carving overhead.

"Well, let's get on with it," Tirais said. "I confess, I'm not keen on this place myself."

"It's no cheery summer palace," I agreed.

We started up the stairs.

I felt nothing. No hint of any danger assailed me, and no memory of the tremors that had shaken beneath my feet a week before upset my calm. It was just a place, a building. A well-made and poorly kept stone edifice, unused for a long time, but there's nothing evil in that.

There were some bloodstains. Places where Penvarron had chased some poor fool out of Camrhys down the steps into the arms of a trooper coming up the other way, or where an enemy had lain in wait for one of ours. But that's just the way of war. Soldiers die. In and of itself, it didn't bother me.

We came at last to the rooms at the top of the tower. I thought that if anything would upset me, it would be here, but the outer room, at least, struck me as ordinary. But for the debris of a few broken weapons, bits of kit, and some more obligatory bloodstains, it looked tidy, peaceful even.

Even the door into the inner room held no lingering taste of the evil we'd felt before. Over the lintel, the stone was carved with a tracery of knotwork ornament, and a script saying something in a language I couldn't read. It looked a bit familiar. A little like the carved stone of Glaice's bath house, perhaps.

Inside, everything seemed as it ought to be. A little dustier, I thought, than was probable in a seven-day, and there were some odd-looking marks, like scrapes, that I couldn't figure out, but beyond that, everything was, well, ordinary.

A chilly breeze blew in from the open door behind us. I crossed towards the stone altar. Stepped on the spot where I had finally killed a man I hated. And stopped, as if turned into a part of the stone walls around us.

Something cold and mean rose up into me, like a wave of icy water. I could feel anger washing through my veins like poison, and I leapt away from the grey stone under my feet as if I'd been burnt.

"What is it?" asked Cioren.

I shook my head. "I don't...I'm not sure. That was where I was, when I killed..."

"Ah," he said. "I thought as much. Try not to touch anything, and tell me just what you saw, when you came in that night."

I began going over the whole thing yet again, pointing out who was where, and when, while the pair of them listened, Cioren's face growing more shuttered and bleak as I spoke.

"So Uln was at the head of the altar," said Tirais, "When you came in. Like he was part of what was going on? Or more like an observer?"

"I don't know." I couldn't see how that mattered. "It went pretty quick. And nothing looked right. I couldn't see the edges of things properly. All that black misty stuff."

I gazed at the stone block, squinting and trying to pull a picture out of my mind of what I'd seen first off. The script on the mottled rock matched the script over the door outside, I realized. That must have been why it looked familiar. "They started after us right away, some of them. The other one, the one we found today, he was there," I gestured with my sword. "Chanting, with a couple of others. Uln was beside him, so he might have been part of whatever it was. Or he might have been just watching. I truly don't know."

"But he came right to you, when you went for him," said Cioren. "So it wasn't important for him to be there, I would suppose."

"Either that or his part in whatever they were doing was finished," said Tirais.

"The real questions are," said Cioren, just as if Tirais hadn't spoken, "What were they trying to do? And how far had they gotten?"

"Whatever it was, we stopped it," I said.

"They ended their part of it," he corrected. "There's a difference between ending and stopping."

"I guess." What did he care? I wondered. Uln was dead. The others were dead. If any had survived to wreak vengeance on us, they weren't hiding here. I was suddenly more than eager to go out into the bailey and start scouring the outbuildings for signs of the assassins. When I found them, I thought, I'd kill them. Slowly. Put them through what my comrades had been put through. Terror, and pain, and...

I started, looking up to find Cioren and Tirais staring at me.

"Are you all right?"

"Yes, of course, " I said impatiently. My hands were balled into tight fists. I swallowed, took a deep breath, and willed myself to relax my fingers.

"Well, I've seen enough," said Cioren. "Let's call it a day, shall we? Someone must have organized dinner by now, and I, for one, am starving."

It took a good part of my evening to get back to the main barracks, collect Wenna and Colm, organize Third East for a group march down to the mess, eat, and bring them back. The rest of my time was spent in listening to Colm's description and comments on Glaice's poor attitude towards the resident troops, and his opinions of soldiers who couldn't make do with barracks that lacked the extravagant comforts they were normally used to. It was actually very entertaining, considering that just ten days earlier he'd been the most vocal of the bunch in running down everything from the latrines to the mattresses as unworthy of even the lowliest peasant's lot.

Settling down to sleep was no simpler a task. The ten on Ari's night-shift had learned to be quiet enough, splitting into two five-man squads and taking up positions at either end of the room, but they kept shifting and stretching cramped limbs. Together with the unfamiliarity of these communal arrangements for me, and the groans of sleeping men and women in the privacy of who-knew-what hellborn dreams, and no amount of tiredness could help me drop off easily. Still, within an hour, I could feel myself drifting into a calmer, more restful state, as my mind gave up trying to find solutions to the problems besetting us.

My last thought was of Wenna, who seemed even more upset and tense than the others; she had dark circles under her eyes and a frightened rabbit look to her that seemed overdone, even in the present circumstances. I would have to try to get her to talk. Maybe she'd seen something more than the others; even Brighid, seeing ghosts, hadn't been as jumpy…my mattress wasn't doing any good at all, on the cold stone floor. I could feel the rock digging into my hips

There was smoke, and torches, and the sound of endless chanting, echoing up from the depths of a deep black pit. Under me lay the hard surface of the altar, and the glint of jewels and velvet in the flickering light.

I wasn't anywhere I knew. In fact, I wasn't myself, arrayed in silken robes that shone and moved with iridescent shimmers of light. I lay upon the stone, surrounded by people I didn't know, who smiled at me in triumph as the woman at my right raised a gleaming black knife above my heart. And I looked down in horror to see that the glittering cloth covering me was not decked with gold and silver threads, but with a thousand crawling, glistening, tiny maggots, moving and burrowing inwards to my flesh.

I sat up, with a soundless, endless scream, to find Tighe, leaning over me.

Chapter 21

In the morning, we talked. It was early, at least an hour to dawn, but Third East was trying to split the days up so that no-one lived permanently in the darkness, and it was tricky to arrange. Ari, settling himself for sleep said, inconsequentially, that it had snowed in the night, and wouldn't that just frost your mother's preserves?

My nightmare was nothing, to Third East. They'd all been having disgusting dreams, ever since the night of the invasion. Some of them were far worse than mine, involving close family members who turned into chittering demons or were being slowly tortured by the dreamers, who couldn't help themselves.

"It seemed so real," I said.

"Aye, they do. That's what gets to you." Tighe seemed resigned. Well, what can you do about dreams? You couldn't stop sleeping.

Outside, I heard the alarm being raised, but no-one here seemed to feel any urgency.

"Just more deaders," said Colm, when I raised the issue.

He was right. By the time the first group of five had marched up to the mess, they had heard it all. Tighe gave me the main points briefly as my lot waited in the inch or two of wet snow in the courtyard. Six of the new arrivals, gutted and flayed in the usual way, and one of Tirais' own guard still missing, presumed dead. Not a good night, from one point of view, although Tighe, grimly humorous, thought the score was not so bad for the curse.

I wasn't surprised when a couple of pale and shaken-looking guards found me as I hunched over a porridge-bowl, and said that Tirais wanted me up at the main barracks, as soon as I could manage it.

I finished my breakfast at a leisurely pace, resentful in a vague way that I couldn't seem to draw breath without Tirais wanting my attention, and hoping he didn't want to make another foray into the tower.

"Take them down to the practice ground," I said to Tighe. The busier they were, the better, I thought, as I left them and made my way past knots of unsettled soldiers, talking in hushed voices when they talked at all.

In Tirais' room, there was very little extra space. Cioren was there, as well as Sorcha, Commander Olwen and some of Tirais' guard. The rest, I guessed, were out looking for their missing comrade. Olwen nodded at me as I came in. No-one else seemed to notice my arrival.

"Well," the Prince was saying. "What do we do? Abandon the fortress to the Camrhyssi? Let whatever's here win, without a fight?"

He sounded as though they'd been talking about it for a while, to very little purpose.

I found a space just inside the door, and leaned against the wall. Let them come to their own conclusions. I couldn't think what they needed me for.

Olwen appeared to me to be doing much the same. She looked grim, but unshaken. It was her command; I didn't think she was prepared to let this go without a fight.

Nor was Tirais. After twenty minutes of fruitless conversation, thought, they were no closer to a solution that should have been obvious.

Part of this was because the dead bodies were not the least of it. One of the store-rooms had been found to be vandalized, grain and salted meat ruined and defiled. There had been huge and terrible claw marks at the doors, which lay splintered, like kindling. The loss of the stores was ominous; we had more mouths to feed than Penvarron was prepared for, although, as Sorcha pointed out without a trace of mirth, less than there had been the night before.

There was more heartening evidence, or worse, depending on how you looked at it. The doorway to Cioren's room bore more of those awful claw marks, as though something had tried to break it down. Whatever it was had been unsuccessful, though. This seemed to me to be a good sign; this thing wasn't completely omnipotent, able to work its will unchecked.

"I'm not running," said Olwen, when she'd had enough. "We know it must be something tangible, not some bodiless curse. A curse won't leave marks. And all the evidence says that the dead were alone when they died. Well and good; no-one's to be alone. Pull them all in to the main barracks. We can live here, in shifts, till we beat this thing."

Well, that was sensible. We'd be crowded, but the main buildings were just big enough to manage it, if we all doubled up.

"The watches can use the West Gates to go up on the wall. And they can watch into Penvarron as well as out. Sorcha, I'll need you to assign rooms. And put a crew onto sealing up all the entrances but for the main ones."

It seemed to be a dismissal. Sorcha and the others began drifting out, intent on new errands, and thankful to have something, anything to do. I pushed away from the wall, thinking it was nice that Tirais wanted me informed, but that I probably had better things to do. Cioren caught my eye, though, and I settled back. Apparently, there was more.

114

But his first words seemed to be purely social.

"How was your night?"

"Less eventful than yours, by all accounts." I said. I shouldn't have continued, it was none of my business, but I couldn't seem to help myself. "How did you manage it, sir? You're the first to escape this thing's destruction."

Cioren smiled. "I've no idea," he said pleasantly. "Perhaps it was just good luck."

"Be that as it may," said Tirais, "but this thing wants a piece of you, Cioren. You'd better take half my guard, for now. I don't want to risk you being unlucky in the future, if it's after you."

"Don't be idiotic. Your lot's understrength now, and we'll be living in shifts. I don't fancy telling your mother you died because I had borrowed the people who are supposed to be protecting you."

"It doesn't want me, it wants you."

"It'll take what, or who it can get. No, I'll bunk in with Third East if they'll have me. They seemed to have survived pretty well so far."

My eyes widened. But Tirais seemed in no way put out, he merely sighed and said, "As long as there's someone. Keri, is your patrol up to this? I know they must have had it rough."

"We'd be honoured, my lord."

I followed Cioren out the door, and off to find out where Sorcha was putting us. It hadn't escaped my notice how very pat and easy this had all been. I just couldn't figure out why.

The move into the main barracks was accomplished with far less fuss than I would have supposed, given Penvarron's history, and the new troops' general attitude.

Partly, it was shock: the soldiers from Glaice had lost that air of contemptuous superiority, and Penvarron was in a state of permanent shock anyway.

But part of it was also undoubtedly Sorcha. No-one felt quite up to arguing with her. Eight days of terror had given her a strength that went beyond mere size, and when someone attempted to use their birthrank on her, she gave them a look that must have frozen their blood in their veins.

Third East's disposition was delayed for some hours by Sorcha's determination to keep this to an orderly expropriation. She began by reorganizing those already living in the building, which was a delicate task. Watches that had spent whole lifetimes in the same barracks had to move to accommodate incoming groups, and hard-won deals from the previous day had to be declared null and void; in the three or four hours that this operation took, I went down to the waking members of my patrol out on the practice ground.

Just before I'd drifted off to sleep for the second time, it had occurred to me that we would need a different sort of training for this life. Whether we were spread out in barracks all over the upper bailey, as we'd been, or crammed into one building, it still held true. If we lived in shifts, we would have to fight in shifts.

In my unsettled, wakeful state, I'd reviewed every word I could dredge up of my father's lessons on group tactics. There were twenty-one of us. It would be easier to divide not into two, but three parties, and to train for fighting in ever-smaller groups. Who knew what lay ahead? Four men, on a trip to the latrines, might need to form up and cut their way out of a jam. If one were hurt, they'd be stuck with three, two even, if things went badly.

So as the rest of Penvarron shuffled their belongings around, fitting themselves into a building that had been meant to house perhaps half the number it would have to, Third East began to figure out how to create ever-smaller fighting units.

Around noon, Ruan's Watch came out to join us. Till then, the field had been deserted, but as they'd been settling into their new room, they'd seen us out the window, and Ruan himself came down to see what we were up to.

He looked as drawn and weary as the rest.

"Tell me," he said, after I explained my reasoning to him, "Do you think this will work?"

"I've no idea. But we have to do something. I can't just sit here and wait for my turn to be slaughtered."

"So much energy. Well, give it a couple of days. You'll be like the rest of us, after you've seen what it's like." But he grinned and called out to his men to form up in threes and show Third East how it was done.

He was good. He'd had training, and somewhere in the misty past, he'd had enough ambition to train his Watch up in the basics of close-quarter fighting.

About an hour later, Third East had had enough. They were tired, but the work had done them good, they looked less depressed and resigned, and more like soldiers again. I formed them up and we walked back to our old barracks, to wake up the night shift and give them the news about our imminent move.

The chamber that Sorcha had allotted us was at the end of a narrow, dim hallway, around the corner from Tirais' room. There was a stairwell just beside us, but on the theory that the less ways in and out the better, Olwen had ordered it blocked up. Two nervous-looking girls were hammering boards into place as we dragged our pallets along the hall from the central stairs.

None of us owned much. It took only two trips to remove almost every trace of Third East's occupancy from the old barracks, and the patrol seemed in reasonable spirits, cheerful even, as we hauled our gear into the room. It wasn't large. It was fortunate that we wouldn't all be in here at once.

"Leave a space at the centre," I said. "We'll need room for Lord Cioren. I don't think he has any more stuff than we've got, but he's a lord, you never know. Wenna, pull those three over by the window. I need more space to the front."

"Lord Cioren?' Ari sounded affronted. "What's this, then?'

"Oh, right, I forgot to tell you. We're to be his guard. He'll be sleeping here. I'm going to divide us into three squads, instead of two. One squad on general duty, one squad sleeping, and one squad with Cioren, round the clock."

"So tell me," said Ari, still a little put out, "Who is the old geezer, anyway? What good will he be, here in bloody Penvarron? He doesn't look like he'd be much use in a fight. Probably keel over in shock."

"I wouldn't bet on it. He seems to know quite a lot about it all. More than we do, I should think. And I think he has some ideas about how to fight it, and," I added, unwisely, "that doesn't seem to include going at it like a bull in the heifer's field."

Ari blinked. "But that sounds like a - a-,"

"A scholar," I said.

He stared, opening his mouth to say Goddess only knew what.

"A very good scholar," I said, meaningfully. His mouth closed. He rolled his eyes, dumped the armful of tunics and boots he'd been carrying, and sat down hard on one of the mattresses.

"Booklearning," said Tighe. "Just what we need. I wonder if he runs to bedtime stories."

"Don't get cute."

He grinned. "It might be good, though. Pleasant tales to send us to sleep without those dreams."

"Are you all having dreams?"

Cioren was standing in the doorway, of course. It was inevitable; we couldn't, with my luck, have gotten away with this conversation undisturbed. I wondered how long he'd been there.

I looked around. Third East returned my gaze expectantly. They certainly weren't going to talk to him, they said wordlessly. This was my puppy, apparently.

"I think we've all had them," I said. "Since that first night. Some worse than others."

He stepped over the straw pallet in his path, looking strong and assured. Like a king, almost. A lord, anyway, despite the homespun clothes. I wondered, not for the first time, who Cioren really was. Or what.

"Well, that may fade, in time," he said.

"Yes," I said, "but what does it mean?"

"Likely nothing. The strain of things, perhaps, or lack of proper sleep." He was being evasive, I knew it. His original query hadn't had the sound of idle chat. But his face gave nothing away, as usual. I turned back to the business at hand, which was how to cram twenty-two mattresses into a room designed to hold ten, at best.

My eyes fell on Wenna. She had dragged three pallets over to the spot I'd indicated, moments before, and now was crouched on one of them. She looked like death, and she was trembling.

Definitely I was going to have to have a talk with her. If a few days of terror put her into a state like this, what would she do if we were actually confronted by something truly frightening? We were all afraid. There was no ducking it; about half my last day had been spent in an excess of fear, but we were coping, more or less. It was only Wenna who seemed on the verge of breaking. I'd have to find a way to broach the subject without implying cowardice or censure, but I simply didn't know how.

Chapter 22

For two days, the new living arrangements worked and our luck held. We turned out no new corpses, and every soul in Penvarron made it to their breakfast hale and hearty, if not in the most glorious of spirits. Overnight we adapted to living in the most crowded of conditions; we learned to sleep through almost a continual barrage of muted noise, as the rooms became sleeping chambers only, and the waking conducted an almost normal round of gossip and gambling in the hallways.

Squads of Third East trailed around the fortress behind Cioren, who seemed bent on covering the entire keep on foot. Mercifully, he kept his wanderings to the daylight hours. I couldn't have answered for the results if he'd tried to make us patrol the grounds in the dark.

Nor did he go near the tower again, thankfully. We would have gone, and, indeed, we assumed that he would eventually drag us there, but he seemed to have lost interest in the place. Instead, we looked at the drainage ditch where the two bodies had been found on the first morning, searched a few outbuildings near the East Gate, watched him as he laid his hands on the stone curtain walls, and woke in the night to see him, still awake, staring out of the unshuttered window of our tiny room.

On the third morning, our short hiatus ended. The watch change found young Garth, dead at the foot of the stairs leading up from the guardroom beside the West Gate. His throat was slashed, his entrails dragged across the floor, and the scene was so bizarrely tidy and free of blood that it was hard to credit that he'd died at all.

I stood in the doorway, behind Cioren. It was my squad that had been up half the night with him, but we'd spent our time in the hall outside our room, drinking and dicing for wholly imaginary stakes in hushed voices. We'd heard nothing in the small hours to tell us that our doom was walking again.

Watch One's story was simple. The squad had just been going on duty, and had formed up in the guardroom, done a quick nose count for safety's sake, and started up the stairs. Garth had mumbled something about his boot-lace breaking, but the man he'd said it to hadn't paid much heed. It seemed likely, in the aftermath, that Garth had stopped to fix whatever was wrong, and that when the squad had turned up the stairwell, he'd been alone enough for whatever was hunting us to strike.

"You must have heard something," said Tirais, in exasperation. Watch One shuffled their collective feet, and said no, not really. Just their own boots, tromping up the stairs.

Ruan was still kneeling beside Garth's broken body, ignoring the overpowering stench that rose from the corpse. His eyes were blank, dazed, as dead as Garth's. He'd been asleep when the news had come, and I thought that the reality of it had only just begun to hit him. The once-removed import of it all was just beginning to hit me. I knew instinctively what he'd feel. Any decent captain would feel it.

Guilt. Guilt, and anger, and shame. You can't save them from everything, but this wasn't some clean soldier's death in battle. This was a dirty, wasteful end, and one that Ruan would pay the cost for, every day of his life.

A group of Garth's fellows were detailed to take the body out to the ditch beyond the walls. In the courtyard, people watched them as they took his wrapped and broken remains out into the open air. The villagers stood side by side with soldiers, numb and shocked.

After the gates had swung shut, Gioren turned and started back to the barracks. We fell in behind him, uncertain and confused. How could someone be killed this way, with no sound or sign? What could possibly have the power to do all this, yet leave no trace of their passing?

But we had no time to discuss it. At the top of the stairs we were met by Ari, his face grave, with a terse message that Wenna was in a state, and we'd better come up quick.

It had been in my mind that Garth's death would hit her hard; they were from the same village, and not far apart in age. She would know his parents, his childhood friends. They'd often spent their off-duty times together, splitting jugs of ale in the Black Pig and reminiscing about home.

Back in our room, Wenna sat huddled in a blanket, curled up on the pallet under the window, moaning and weeping. And the words she whimpered sent a chill down my spine.

I knelt beside her, but she shrank away.

"It's my fault," she mumbled. "All my fault."

"No, it's not, my girl," said Ari. "He joined up of his own free will. Who knew it would come to this?"

"It is my fault. All the death, all the dying."

"How so, Wenna?" I felt uneasy. Tears and ravings do that. I couldn't see why she felt responsible, but something about this nagged at me. I ought to have talked to her before, I thought.

"I did it. I let it in." She was near hysteria, or perhaps beyond it.

There was a collective stiffening as Third East took this in.

"You - what?" This from Ari, whose rough sympathy was slipping into frustrated anger.

I stood. I had a glimmer of where this might be going, though I couldn't quite credit it, and my first thought was that I didn't want to be the one to hear it.

"Colm," said Cioren, as if reading my mind, "Get one of those layabouts in the hall to go for the Prince. Tell them it's urgent, but don't you say one word about what. Brighid, have you still got that wine from last night?"

It seemed to take ages. Tighe brought another blanket; Wenna's shivering turned to shuddering, and her sobs grew more anguished, but we managed to force some wine into her and it seemed to help.

Tirais came, alone and quietly, thank the Goddess. He took one look at our faces, and then a harder one at Wenna, and his gaze sharpened.

I knelt back down in front of her.

"All right, Wenna. What's this all about?'

"I let them in."

"What do you mean? Did you use the East Gate and forget to drop the bar?" It seemed idiotic, and improbable, but nothing in Penvarron had ever made much sense to me.

"No. I meant to do it." And while we absorbed this, she went on, "He said it was all right. It was only supposed to be him. He never said anything like this would happen."

"Who, Wenna?"

"I don't know his name," she wailed.

"What the hell does that mean?" asked Tirais, not to anyone in particular.

I frowned.

"Well, where did you meet him? In the village?" Sometimes strangers did come through, trappers and such, dossing down at the Black Pig. But her next words muddied the waters further.

"It was at Lesser Penne."

"Ah," I said, as if this explained something. In a way, it did. "When you were on watch? You left your post."

It all came tumbling out then. Weeks of holding her secret in, and the fear and enormous guilt of the last several days, coupled with the death of a friend, unleashed a torrent of confession.

The very first night, she'd met a man. Why she had never questioned his purpose in wandering in a barren wilderness alone in the middle of the night remained a mystery. I let it go; I was cursing myself for having let the narrow back approach of the fort be manned by a single sentry.

"He - we just talked. He asked where I was from. He knew Penvarron a long time ago, he said. And he said he'd left some things in the tower. Nothing important. But he wanted to come get them. And he asked me to leave the gate unbarred. So he could just come in quietly, and be gone."

" And you agreed? Just like that?"

"Stupid cow," said Ari, venomously.

"Shut up. Wenna, didn't you think it was odd?'

She stared up at me, uncomprehending.

"You don't understand," she said. "He was nice to me."

Tirais knelt down beside me. He looked intent, not angry. I was surprised. I was having a devil of a time not slapping the silly bitch's face, myself.

"Wenna," he said. "What did the man look like? Was he a Camrhyssi, do you think?'

"No, of course not, " she said. "He wasn't a bit like them. He was tall, and handsome. Like you." The wine must be getting to her, I thought, irrelevantly.

"Anyway, on the second night, he said if I could leave the gate open on the night of the Merrydd, he'd just slip in. He said, no harm done. No-one would ever know, he said. He said nothing would happen to me."

Tirais looked at me. I thought of the numerous dead, and said, "Well, then. What's to be done?"

"Good question. I don't have an answer, though."

"Hang her," said Brighid.

Cioren said, in a gentle voice, "I don't suppose she had much choice in all this, Brighid. And I strongly doubt that any of you would have fared better against him."

"You think she was bespelled, then?" Amazing, how I could say this without a tremor in my voice. I must be going mad.

"Oh, yes. Something rather similar to the one Uln used on you, this summer past, I should think." And, when my eyes widened, he actually smiled, a wintry baring of his teeth, and said, "Come now. You don't think you accepted his ordering a massacre of innocent villagers because it made sense to you, do you?"

I stood. Something deep inside me, that had lain coiled and angry, so familiar that I'd ceased to even acknowledge its existence, dissolved. I felt unchained, loosed, freed.

"In any case," Cioren continued, "this man used her. Likely, he took pleasure in finding someone who was a good and hardworking soldier to corrupt. It's the sort of thing that people like that tend toward. And none of you would have done differently."

The silence that followed this lengthened. I could see us all, rearranging our thoughts, redirecting our anger. Ari sat down beside Wenna and refilled her wine cup.

Tirais stood.

"I needn't remind you all that this remains between ourselves," he said. "We'll just say that Wenna's worn out, and for the nonce, she's to be helping Sorcha with the stores inventory. She can read a tally, I suppose? Don't even think to yourself that it's anything else. Don't even whisper to each other in the privies that there's anything more to it. Can I be any clearer?'

They nodded. The wisdom of this seemed obvious. We couldn't be sure, even with Cioren's mage-bound explanation, that other units wouldn't decide to take revenge on the only culprit available. I wasn't so sure we'd restrain ourselves for long, even knowing what we knew.

I followed Tirais and Cioren out the door, with an injunction to the patrol to watch Wenna. It was still early, and most of Penvarron was awake and moving now; there was no serious need for larger groups.

If the two of them noticed me dogging their heels, they gave no sign. We turned into the main hallway, and went down the stairs and along the passage to Olwen's quarters, where she and Sorcha were engaged in a debate on how long Penvarron could manage without new supplies. They looked up; as the last person into the room, I slammed the door with considerable force, flung myself into a chair and said, without preamble,

"All right. I want all of it. And no more pissing about, either. I'm damned sick of being kept in the dark. What the hell is going on?"

Olwen and Sorcha went very still. Tirais raised those eyebrows, but Cioren merely said, "What do you think is going on?"

"I think that Camrhys sent those priests to raise a demon. And I think they succeeded, too. Why, I don't know. It oughtn't to have worked; we stopped them, and nothing seemed to be going on once we'd finished. But I think we've got a demon running loose in Penvarron."

There. It was out. Not that this felt any better.

"Well, that's succinct enough. No," he held up his hand at Tirais, who began to speak. "No, we may as well come clean. You're right about the demon. Does that help?'

I looked around. Olwen wouldn't meet my gaze, but Sorcha looked less terrified than I expected. I turned on her, frustrated.

"You knew? Of all the idiotic -"

"Stop it, Keri." Tirais' voice was like a whip. "You're only a patrol captain. You didn't need to be told."

"Oh, great. People are dying, and all you can think about is precedence? Rank? Let us take the brunt of all this, while you sit around watching?"

"Don't be an idiot. What does knowing it's a demon get you?" His eyebrows had moved even higher. Very aristocratic, I thought. He had a hell of a nerve, being snippy with me. "And if you hadn't noticed, this thing isn't particular about who it takes. We're all in this together."

"Could we possibly get back to the matter at hand?" Cioren sounded irritated.

"Fine," I said. "Tell me then, Your Grace, what you propose to do about it."

But at this I met silence. Tirais just glared across the room at me. Wonderful. They didn't have a clue. I made an effort to bring my anger under control.

"How bad is it, really?" First things first, I thought. Know your enemy. Suss out the terrain. My father's rules probably didn't have any bearing on the current dilemma, but I had very little else to go on.

"Not very," said Cioren. "He's quite a small, unimportant demon, as these things go."

I stared. "Well, I'd certainly hate to meet a strong one, then." My thoughts took a different turn suddenly. "Wait. Let me get all this in order. How did it happen? I swear to you, there was nothing that night that said we had anything other than a bunch of Camrhyssi running loose. What did we miss?"

"I'm not entirely certain," said Cioren, apologetically. "I'm guessing, but from your descriptions, I suspect that they'd completed enough of the raising to establish contact. Once that was done, they needed to feed it, strengthen the bond to this plane. With blood, I'm afraid."

"So that was to be us?"

"Actually, I doubt if who really mattered to them. Certainly not to the demon, which is why your killing Uln didn't matter. Although I suspect it surprised the hell out of him. I'd say that it's likely that they told their soldiers your deaths were what mattered, and that's certainly what they would have hoped for, but in the main, it didn't matter whose blood was shed. The Camrhyssi soldiers, and probably the lower ranking priests, were expendable. They just needed a substantial amount of violent death occurring at just the right time. And that may be where things began to go wrong. I think Penvarron reacted much quicker than they expected, and with much greater skill."

"I see. But aren't demons supposed to be under the raiser's control? Or is that just a bard's tale as well? I wouldn't have thought they'd have done this just to get themselves killed, whatever the damage to us."

"No, you're not wrong there. It's a separate spell, though, to bind the demon to your control. And the priest who escaped, he was the one who should have done it. I expect he hoped to be able to flee, once he knew he wouldn't have a chance to do it. But the demon stopped him. Luckily."

"Luck?" I couldn't believe my ears. "We have got a demon running around loose and you tell me we've been lucky?"

"Believe me, a controlled demon at the bidding of a Camrhyssi priest would be far worse. You'd never have survived the night."

"And Uln? What was his part in all this?"

"Other than treason? Well, it's part of the whole thing. They pick their priests carefully in Camrhys. Without the knowledge of Averraine, they need a lot of talent. And there aren't very many mages about with power to spare. The more smaller talents, pooled together, the better."

"Are you," I took a stronger grip on my fraying temper, "Are you saying that Uln was a mage? And that you knew it?"

"Oh, yes. Not a great amount of power, but it was there. He used to be quite interested in my research, years ago. Then he stopped. I'd thought he'd lost interest, once he realized that he wouldn't be able to harness any real power.

My mistake," he added, pensively. "I should have known anyone that ambitious would look for other ways to achieve his goals."

I thought of how Uln had tricked a few hundred innocents into treason, of how I'd spent three months in an agony of self-recrimination, of all the dead in Penvarron. I took several deep breaths, shaking my head, and forbore to point out that his mistake had cost nearly two hundred lives so far, if you counted the villagers massacred at Fairbridge. But he saw it in my eyes, and sighed.

"I know," he said. "I know."

"All right," I said. "All tolls gone to taxes, now. But it can't go on. We have an entire keep full of terrified soldiers. If they knew what they were up against, they might be able to combat it."

"No," said Olwen. "No, you're all out, there, Keri. They're half-ready to jump now, thinking it's a curse. Give them the truth, and there won't be six of them left in the barracks by dawn tomorrow."

"Are you suggesting they'd desert?" Tirais had managed not to leap out of his chair and throttle me, over the last five minutes, but he sounded perilously close to doing in Olwen over this implication.

"Yes, sir, I am." She sounded unafraid. "Look here, sir. As long as they think they might carry this with them, they'll see it through. But give them so much as a sliver of hope that they can run away, and it's fare-thee-well and good riddance to you. Never mind that they wouldn't get far, by all accounts. They won't see it, sir. They'll see their chance and take it."

"Maybe Penvarron's would," said Tirais, in a nasty tone, "But my troops are made of sterner stuff."

"I doubt that," said Cioren. "But even if you're right, it's Penvarron's troops that concern me. Most of them have a strong connection to the demon. As long as they're here, the demon's bound, by his own hungers, to hunt them first. The further afield they get, the wider the demon's scope."

"Hungers," I said. "Are we just meat, for this thing, then?"

"In a sense. It feeds on us. It needs blood and death, first off. But it needs terror, too. Fear and pain are like food to it. It grows in strength, as it feeds, but the stronger it gets, the more it needs."

"Will it weaken, if we - I mean, if it doesn't, well, you know - " It was hard to say the words.

126

"Ye-es. But that's all in relation to itself, not to us. Even half-dead with starvation, it's still incredibly hard to defeat."

"But it can be defeated?"

"I certainly hope so."

"It hasn't had it easy, these last two days," Tirais pointed out. "Only that poor boy, this morning. It must be getting a little lean, by now."

"It can live on fear and despair, as well," said Cioren. "And there's no shortage of that, just now. It prefers death and blood, but the rest will do to go on with."

The five of us mulled over these less than cheerful thoughts.

Sorcha had been silent and watchful through this whole discussion, although it was true that the rest of us had given her little room to add in her opinion. Now she stirred, shook her shoulders as if struggling under a great weight, and said, "Is it only people it hunts, then?"

This devastating little question stopped us cold. The image occurred to all of us, simultaneously, I was sure: all those horses and ponies, restive and bored, in the overcrowded stables. The implication was horrifying.

"It hasn't, so far," said Cioren. I could hear the uncertainty in his own voice; it scared me far more than anything else had so far, which was going some distance.

"Well, what does that tell us?" Tirais was business-like, firm.

"That he's a picky eater," I said, flippantly.

"Don't be stupid. It hasn't reached that stage for him yet, that's all."

I sighed. "All right, I get the point. But we're no closer to a solution. Cioren, you must know how to deal with this. Or at least have some ideas, at least."

"A few ideas, certainly. But it was never my main area of study, I'm afraid. I know a great deal less than you think. Certainly less than we need, at this point."

"Wonderful. Let me see if I have all this right. First off, we've got an uncontrolled demon running loose in this keep. As long as we're here, he'll keep picking us off and getting stronger in the process. Secondly, he feeds off our fear, too, so just not getting killed won't really harm him, over the long-term, it just slows him down. We can't tell anyone that he exists, because if they run, he'll chase them, and he'll kill anyone else that gets near him as well.

We don't have any idea what will stop him, and the only people who might are in either safe in Camrhys or dead. Have I missed anything?"

"No, I think that's about the size of it," said Cioren, "but I did say I had some ideas. Just very sketchy ones at present. There are some things, which might work, but they're risky. It isn't invulnerable, Keri. There are weaknesses."

"Well, that's a relief."

He ignored me. "For one thing, it's still bound primarily to this place. The raising wasn't completed properly, and it's having trouble maintaining itself on this plane. You notice it doesn't walk in the day. It hasn't learnt much, either. The lures it uses have been very crude, which may be why so many of you are still alive. It doesn't dare try its luck at more than one victim at the time, except for the night it attacked the village.

"And it hasn't gotten to the point where it can use forms it hasn't completely assimilated. Only the dead have been seen. I've questioned everyone I could, and no-one's seen any living soul where they couldn't actually be. Really strong demons can pluck a memory of a person out of your mind and mimic it so perfectly that your own mother wouldn't know the difference.

"If we have a chance, though, it will have to be soon. We can't count on it remaining this weak, and this ignorant for long. We need to find its lair, and defeat it, before much longer."

It was the longest speech I'd heard him make for days. And it wasn't just his words. You could feel the power crackling in the room. From under the misery that this last half-hour had swamped me, I felt a sudden stirring of hope. It wasn't strong, it wasn't all encompassing, but it was there. The barest feeling that I was not helpless. That there was a chance to fix all that had gone so horribly wrong at Penvarron.

The others felt it, too. I saw that Tirais no longer looked quite so furious, that Sorcha was nodding to herself, and that Olwen was rising up from her chair.

She said, "I'll double the guard on the stables, tonight. Just a precaution. And an extra half-ration of wine, I think. If the soldiers are happier, it may weaken this thing further, if only a little. Sorcha, you'll see to it?"

Sorcha nodded, and the pair of them went out.

Chapter 23

The small fire in the grate no longer seemed inadequate. The three of us lingered in its warmth, in relatively companionable silence for several minutes, until Tirais remarked that while he wasn't averse to laziness as such, there were some things to be considered.

We considered them. Well, one thing anyway. It wasn't pleasant, and I was not the only one, I noticed, who was less than ecstatic to be contemplating it, but it had to be done. In any case, it was action. It was doing something, instead of waiting around to be done unto.

Cioren had actually been giving it a lot of thought. And he'd come up with several possibilities. The worst one was, naturally, the most likely one. It would have to be tackled first.

And so, we made plans to go back into Penvarron Tower.

Cioren felt the fewer people exposed to the risks, the better, but Tirais was in command, so when we assembled just inside the upper bailey, all of the Prince's Household Guard not currently asleep were there.

My presence, as usual, was taken pretty much for granted. I might be only a patrol captain, but no-one, not even Gwyll, seemed surprised at my attendance. The more, the merrier, I thought sarcastically. Being unimportant was getting to be a Queen's Pass to danger, around here.

The idea Cioren had come up with was not one that held much appeal. He knew, from our earlier foray into the tower, that the demon wasn't living in that topmost room where its raising had occurred. Nor was there any evidence of it living in the lower rooms, nor yet in the abandoned collection of shacks that adorned the rest of the fortress. It certainly couldn't be living in the main buildings, stuffed with soldiers doing permanent guard shifts everywhere including the store-rooms.

Penvarron's demon had to be in the one place none of us had ever ventured. Most of us had never given a thought to its existence, but the place had to be there.

We were heading for what might lie underneath Penvarron Tower.

The snow had not melted; in fact, the continuing cold had left a hard crust on the surface, so that our boots made little crunching noises as we trooped out across the yard. It sounded unnaturally loud in the morning silence. We made our way down the empty rows of barracks and around to the door of the tower, tension filling the air as tangibly as the puffs of vapour our breath made in the chilly morning.

No-one truly wanted to be doing this. It seemed that Tirais' guards had been privy to the news that a demon roamed Penvarron, or else they were more astute than the rest of us, although I was beginning to think that quite a number of people must have figured it out by now. But our fear was overborne by our sense of outrage. Maybe demon-hunting wasn't what the Household Guards had signed up for, but the affront to their dignity as crack soldiers of Keraine gave them courage. We passed under the stone archway without the slightest of stumbles.

Tirais hadn't abandoned all caution, or hope that we might be wrong about the source of our danger. We traipsed through the entire building, from top to bottom, before beginning the search below. The idea that we might be trapped and set on from behind by purely human agency had to be eliminated first, he'd said, although Cioren had seemed to disagree.

But in the end, we were forced to conclude that no man or woman, as we understood it, had been into the tower since our last visit. We fetched up at the bottom of the stairs, walked down through the back corridor and stood before the narrow, doorless entry to the cellars.

Torches were already being lit. The faces around me were set and purposeful. This might be suicide; I didn't know, and I found that I was past caring. You can only be afraid for so long, really. Neither my body nor my mind could sustain the terror any more. I felt numb.

We began marching down the stairs.

Like the rest of the place, the way down was thickly covered with dust, and huge cobwebs festooned the rafters above us. The air seemed close and stale, and the walls here were rough-hewn, unlike the smooth blocks of the upper rooms. My shoulders brushed against them on the final landing, as we turned into what had once been the storage rooms of Penvarron Tower.

In the flickering torchlight we looked around at the empty room. There were the disintegrating remains of wine-racks and storage shelves, left too long unattended for even dirt and debris to have survived. It was dusty and cold and still. Behind me, someone sneezed.

Our tension dissipated; Tirais snorted with laughter, and we began to look around more purposefully, for the way to our enemy's lair.

It wasn't hard to find. In a recessed alcove, we found a door, not unlike the one in the chamber at the top of Penvarron. A carved stone lintel, fronted by an ironbound wooden block, and once again, looking as familiar as my own bedchamber at Orliegh. It had that same ancient script above it, and the same tortuous locked and flowing lines of ornament that the door upstairs bore. At Cioren's request, we moved back, and he laid his hands against the oak.

Nothing, apparently, lay in wait for us. At Tirais' command, the bar was dropped, and one of the guards pushed it gently open.

A wave of sweetish-sour air rose up from the blackness. It smelled like rotting flowers and fruit; torchlight showed us a flight of shallow stairs leading further down, but beyond this, there was only darkness.

We followed Cioren down the steps. The stench grew stronger, mixing with the smoky smell of the torches and overpowering it. At the bottom of the stairs we found ourselves in a long, empty space. The stone walls here were rougher still; the place had been hacked out of the bare rock, but the floor had been laid with carefully shaped and dressed stone, worn smooth in places as though thousands of feet had walked its surface for years uncounted, but at the very centre was a misshapen circle of stones, like a hearth, and inside that there lay a dark gap of darkness.

In the uneven light, I could see more of those huge scratch-marks that had marred the floor and walls of the upper chamber and that had been found outside Cioren's door that first morning.

It was almost a relief. My worst fears were being confirmed; it seemed that at last we knew what it was we faced.

Cioren produced a small leather bag and motioned us to stand away. We arranged ourselves in a circle around the walls and watched as he began dusting out a fine gray powder in a pattern at the centre of the room.

I felt a strange, expectant silence descend over us. Not even our breath stirred the cold air, and there was no sound beyond the faint whisper of Cioren's movements as he walked carefully around his work. Then, as he finished and took up a place at one end of the cavern, I felt the faintest, most tenuous of tremors beneath my boots.

Cioren stretched out his hands and began to whisper, in an unfamiliar yet almost recognizable language, a chanting singsong that I could barely hear. The silence stretched out, hardened, becoming almost a physical presence in its own right, while in the tiny well around Cioren, the sound of an ancient litany expanded and grew as if to balance this unnatural hush.

The torches, in that windless place, guttered suddenly, then flared. At the same moment, a huge rush of air roared silently past our ears. I felt my breath expel and die, as if I were a candle being snuffed. Cioren's voice grew stronger. It was all I could hear, that chanting, and the measured beats of my heart.

Something that was stronger and more overpowering than fear gripped my chest. My sword arm felt weak and shaky; my shield arm even worse. The rest of my body was strung as tense as a bowstring, trembling after sudden release.

Suddenly, Cioren's chanting stopped. For what seemed a lifetime, the whole world hung, waiting, in the balance.

And then I felt that tremor again. My feeling of weakness had passed and I felt more alive, more *here* than ever before in my life. This was something I knew, this shaking beneath my feet, and I knew what it heralded. At least, in my innocence, I thought I did.

The floor began to pulse, cracks between the timeless stones suddenly gaping, then closing. The polished slab I stood on rocked violently once or twice, and I nearly slipped, felt Gwyll's hand beneath my elbow, steadying me.

From far away, I heard Cioren call out a single syllable, terrible and cold. There was one last moment of that eerie, unbelievable silence.

And then all hell broke loose.

Out of the cracks, out of every tiny fissure and gap in the rocks around us, there came both sound and fury. A boiling, angry mist spewed out, red and black; the greasy, horrid filth of Goddess only knew what bloody abyss below us, crawling and screaming like carrion-birds. They were creatures, of a sort, hideous and malformed travesties of wild things that writhed and slashed at us, at once tangible and evanescent, in impotent rage. I hacked back uselessly as they formed and dissolved in front of me, while the stone at my back pulsed and groaned as if alive.

As if from somewhere else, I could hear Cioren, chanting again, new and terrible words that I could almost understand, but I had no time for it. All around me, the boiling detritus of all nine hells appeared to attack, in a confusion of snarling and biting ferocity, shrieking as they rose endlessly from the pits below.

The vaporous things began to crowd together as some unknown force pulled them into the centre of the pattern Cioren had drawn. We watched in fascination as they swarmed and pulsed into a mass of writhing, swirling shapes and began to merge. They were becoming less distinct by the second, dissolving and remaking themselves. The floor seemed to be dissolving too, as they pushed and fought within the circle, and the roar of an unholy wind rose up around us.

The creatures, twisted and contorted in that vortex, whirled into a blur of teeth and claws, and melded into a single fearsome entity. We stood, amazed and horrified, as that entity emerged, still writhing, from the nightmarish birthing.

It was huge, filling the cavern to the rafters, and it was, in the main, disgusting. Enormous leathery wings stretched out from massive, ridged shoulders; giant, razor-sharp claws slashed uselessly against unseen walls. Its tail coiled and recoiled, twitching and lashing out at whatever bonds still held it, and its long and pointed teeth gleamed in the torchlight.

But its face was the most distressing aspect.

As we watched in disbelief, the features squirmed and changed, from one all-too-human version to another. Garth appeared, and then Aidan, weeping and pleading, only to be replaced by Mag's horrified and gaping countenance. Face after face revealed itself, in the agonies of death, only to melt and disintegrate into another dreadful parody of someone else we knew.

I saw, without anger or pity, Uln's face form up, his teeth bared in some excess of pain. Then the face twisted again, becoming another, and another. And then, at last, it shifted once more, to a grinning contortion, almost human, but with a snouted nose, and curiously tiny ears, its fangs dripping red, and its glowing eyes fixed themselves on me.

I couldn't help it. In the sudden unlooked-for silence, I laughed.

It was not the right response. I wasn't amused for long; the thing seemed to swell and grow in the echo of my laughter, and began to growl menacingly. I gripped my sword tighter and raised my shield.

Not a moment too soon. Out of the corner of my eye, I saw that wicked tail twitch, and lash out. I thought the mage-bonds would hold it, but I was wrong, or else my good humor lent it some additional strength. There was a sound of an immense crash, the torches flared, and black sparks ignited in mid-air, as the tail lashed out.

I dropped, and felt the air move, hot and fetid, as the thing swept over me. On my right, Gwyll screamed in pain, and there was a crackling sound, all too familiar, as fire exploded into the cavern.

I heard Cioren's voice, as if from a great distance, saw the thing waver and shimmer, as if dissolving, and then it screamed in rage and became, for one eternal moment, so real and so present that my heart seemed to die inside me. Then, on the echo of the scream, it rose, hovering for long seconds over us, and was gone.

Chapter 24

I don't remember leaving that place. I could just barely feel my legs, running up the steps and through the wide hall in Penvarron Tower, but I saw nothing, heard nothing, save for Cioren's exhausted voice driving us up, away, out of there, and the rhythm of our feet on stone.

I came to myself as I tripped over the threshold of the tower doorway, stumbling to land on my knees in the snow, gasping for the sweet frozen air of the upper bailey.

"Goddess's tits," I said, inadequately, to the figure next to me. It was Tirais.

He gave me a pained look and hauled me up onto my feet. I saw that Gwyll was only just barely standing, his arm held awkwardly, blood dripping onto the white ground. All around me were the shocked faces of Tirais' guards, and beyond that, Cioren, looking grave.

No-one spoke again. As one, we moved slowly across the bailey and into the main hall, down the long corridor to Olwen's rooms, and sat about, silent, under her watchful eyes, while someone went for the healer.

The crowd in Olwen's commandeered chamber was gone. Gwyll's arm was only broken; badly, as it happened, but he was alive, which seemed pretty much a victory for us. The guards had been ordered to rest, but when I attempted to pull myself up off the floor to do the same, in the quiet of Third East's room, Tirais frowned me down. I relapsed, therefore, onto the rushes near the fireplace, and listened to Cioren give Olwen a rather well-edited version of what had happened.

"Well," she said, when he was through, "Nice place you've given me, Your Grace. A garrison of soldiers who are convinced they've been cursed, a demon running loose, killing at will, not enough stores to last us a month, and no way of getting more. Not that I don't like a challenge, you understand, but it's not the command you promised me. Is there a way to fight this thing?"

"Oh, yes," said Cioren. "I nearly had him, I think. And he'll be weak. We have the best chance I could get us, at any rate."

I stirred. "What did you do, then?"

"Cut him off from the source of power he's been drawing on. Penvarron," he added, turning to Tirais, "is tainted. That foul thing's been living right in the power, nearly. He's spewed his filth into the pool itself. It may recover, but it will need the holy ones, I'm afraid, to ward it properly. In the meantime, I've blocked his access to it. He'll need to feed, and feed well, before he can break that barrier. We'll have to stop him now, before he can get back his strength."

"You mean, it's still here?" I said.

"Indeed it is. In the day, it's still weak, and no matter how angry, its first instinct will keep him holed up somewhere till evening. Even then, it's our best hope, while it's hunger blinds it to any other danger. If it was less ignorant of it's own abilities on this plane, we wouldn't stand a chance, but right now, it's being driven by vengeance and mindless need. We won't get a better opportunity."

It didn't sound all that convincing. I might have laughed, back there in the depths of the tower, but truly, it was no joke. If that thing had been more solid, if Cioren's spells had not held it, even a little, we'd have been so much demon-fodder.

"So," said Tirais, "It's tonight, or not at all. Olwen, we'll want the place well-guarded. On the walls, in the yard, everywhere. Pull the villagers into the main hall, and put a guard onto them. The rest of the building's to be sealed off. I want everyone else on the walls, in big groups, ready by dusk."

"And then what?" she asked him. "Do we just wait around and hope we can take him?"

"No, of course not. I think," here Tirais gave me a wolfish grin, "We'll offer him something he can't turn down."

I didn't like that look. It reminded me forcibly of my eldest brother, tempting me into some childhood trap that always ended badly for me. But he was the Prince. It wasn't as though I had a choice.

I woke an hour before sunset, feeling not so much rested as less tired. Rest had become some luxurious memory. I couldn't think when I'd last had a decent night's sleep.

All of Third East had been ordered to stand down for the day; squads of other patrols had sat around our doors watching for us, and speculating on what the evening was going to be like. Tirais had chosen to tell the garrison a portion of the truth, and, despite Sorcha's dire prediction, none of them had decided to run. Yet. What they'd do tomorrow, if we were unsuccessful, was something else again. Of course, it might not matter, by then.

I dressed and went out onto the narrow outdoor walkway that ran along the second floor, above the courtyard, sucking in great draughts of winter air and watching the villagers below, milling about, waiting to be told what to do.

Cioren was up here too, doing much the same thing. He waved to me and I went over to the bench and sat down beside him, without a word.

After a while, he stirred.

"Well, this is it." He sounded calm. Nice for him, I thought, sourly. I wasn't hysterical, but I could feel the swell of it, just below the surface.

"Do you think we can do this?' I asked, after a bit.

"I certainly hope so."

This was less than inspiring. I cast about for something to take my mind off the immediate problem.

"Cioren, what should I do about Wenna? I mean, should she come with us, or - ?"

"She's as connected as the rest of you to this thing. Whether she would be safer with us or elsewhere, I don't know. I think you'll have to make that decision yourself."

"You're no help," I said, disgusted. "I don't know half of what's going on." Then, as he seemed about to lapse back into impenetrable silence, I added, "Come on. Tell me something useful."

"Tirais is right. You're like a leech out of water once you've got hold of something. Well, all right. What is it you think you need to know?"

"Well, that man she met. Was it Uln?" This struck me as probable. She'd said he was like Tirais, but I thought that she might have meant only that he was well born, or nicely dressed.

"I shouldn't think so. She would have recognized him, when they dragged the bodies out."

"Maybe not. What if he was disguised? Or he could have used a charm, or spell, or something." These words were tripping off my tongue with ease, I noticed. A few weeks ago, I would have said them with derision, if I'd said them at all.

"No, no. She would have known him, whatever he'd looked like. These things aren't so simple. If you bespell someone, they retain a sort of bond with you. They feel the pull of it, no matter what form the mage assumes later. You felt the pull of it yourself, that night."

"How do we know she didn't know him? Have we asked? I know I didn't."

"Well, you might have a point. But for what it's worth, I don't think it was Uln. She wasn't frightened by him, or intimidated, and that would have been

136

more his style. Uln was never a man to do his own dirty work, either, if he could help it. She liked him, and that may have been the magic, but somehow, I don't think so. I think the man she met was someone else."

"I'd give a lot to know who."

"As would I. It worries me. But we've other things to think of just now."

"Well, I thought I'd leave her below, with Sorcha. She's still shaky. But if she has a connection with all of this, as you say, perhaps she'd just draw the demon to her?"

"I don't know. I hope not. But if she's still in a state, she won't be much good in a confrontation, wherever it takes place. If she's with Sorcha and the villagers, she's probably as safe as she's going to be."

I sighed. I seemed to be no closer to a good decision than I'd been before. But after a bit, I cheered up. Whatever I did wouldn't really matter. We would either deal with what we confronted, or we'd die. If I died, I'd never even know if I'd made good choices. So it made no difference what I chose. I'd just have to do the best I could, and hope it wasn't the wrong thing. I decided to let Wenna go below with Sorcha, and put the whole mess out of my mind.

None too soon. A moment later, a soldier came up onto the parapet and said that the Prince wanted Third East to arm and stand ready, and I got up and followed him back inside.

Tirais' plan to offer the demon something it couldn't resist involved going back in the tower, which was what I'd suspected. I didn't care for it, naturally, but an order's an order. All of Third East, save for Wenna, would be there; strangely, this cheered me. Tirais' guards might be crack troops, trained within an inch of their lives, but I knew Third East. Not much on a parade ground, and they'd had precious little chance to prove themselves in battle, but they were mine. In the end, I found that I trusted them.

In the dying light of the winter afternoon, we marched across the yard and into the tower, climbing the stairs to the room where the fighters of Camrhys had met us that night, and settled in to wait for darkness. The Prince's guards were already there, along with Cioren, seemingly in a good mood, all things considered. We didn't really have a choice: we had to win this. We might as well be happy.

I could hear other patrols and watches, settling themselves on the steps below. They, too, sounded cheerful, as snatches of gibes and good-natured raillery floated up the stairwell. We'd left the villagers huddled in the main hall, armed as best we could manage, with Sorcha, Wenna, and the wounded Gwyll to keep them in line. Outside, I knew, Olwen had mounted double guard patrols along the walls, facing inwards to the courtyard. If the Camrhyssi wanted a good time to attack, this would be it, I thought. I rather hoped they would: I quite liked the idea of throwing them to the mercy of the demon they'd created.

The door into the inner chamber was open and I could watch the fading light as it moved across the stone floor, marking the time for me. We would have to go into that room, sometime soon. In Cioren's opinion, the demon would try to find a place where he could try to get a link to the well of power below Penvarron Tower, and the altar would be his first, best chance, especially if he thought he could feast on some unhappy soldiers along the way. He'd be mad with hunger and need, said Cioren, and there was a good chance he'd throw caution to the winds and go for the first available meat, just as soon as darkness fell.

What would happen if Cioren were wrong was something that we hadn't discussed. I, for one, refused to contemplate the idea. He had just damned well better be right, that was all.

The tiny patch of light drew closer to the edge, wavered, died. Sunset was almost on us. I drew my sword, took a tighter grip on my shield strap, and pushed my shoulders away from the wall.

"Well," said Tirais. "Now or never, I suppose."

Cioren moved to the door. The little leather bag appeared, out of some inner pocket, and we followed him across the threshold.

He began to lay out the pattern, around the altar, while we arranged ourselves around the walls. I felt nothing, saw nothing. The shadows lengthened, and the darkness deepened. Everything was quiet, you just could barely hear the sound of breathing, interspersed with the occasional creak or chink of armour, as someone moved.

We waited.

It could not have been more than a quarter-glass, although in the darkness it seemed far longer. The tension had slowly been growing, as we stood in the gloom, impatient and uncomfortable, trying to stay alert.

Then, from a great distance, we heard the sound of a watch alarm, out on the walls, and saw the reflection of some huge burst of firelight, exploding out in the courtyard.

"Damn!" Tirais yelled.

There was instant pandemonium. We rushed the door, and two or three soldiers jammed the exit.

I was against the farthest wall, with no way out. While the others screamed in anger at life, the demon, and each other, I turned and glanced out of the one lone window that looked out onto the courtyard and saw guards racing along the wall towards one of the towers.

This one tiny moment. It was such a little thing, but it was a fatal error. I looked back to the door to see the last soldier leaping through the opening and felt my jaw drop as he slammed it behind him. Heard in disbelief as the bar dropped. Turned to the only other human being still within the room with my mouth open and gaping, with no words to say at all.

There was a single moment of silence, no more than a heartbeat; then, as Cioren stretched out his arms, and said one soft, echoing syllable into that stillness, the very air itself trembled.

And in the next instant, my whole existence, encompassed by four stone walls, shattered around me.

Chapter 25

It was as though the room we stood in, the walls that bounded us, the stone we stood on, simply ceased to exist.

There was an immense crash, earsplitting in its intensity, and my entire world was transformed into a single, huge presence, an enormous, terrifying thing which rose up out of nothing, roaring out its anger. That evil tail whipped out, sweeping over our heads, as the thing clawed mercilessly at the air around us.

It was held within the circle Cioren had drawn, as it had been that morning, but I wasn't comforted by the thought. In fact, I had no thoughts, beyond that I had been horribly betrayed. My anger was almost total. I swung my shield up, and thought merely that I would like to kill something, anything, preferably Cioren.

The demon fixed his glittering eyes on me.

Well and good. It wasn't having me without a fight.

"Such a pretty little thing," it said. I twitched. Had anyone said it could speak? I couldn't remember.

"Such a brave soldier." The voice, if you could call it that, was hideous. Take a few cats in heat and then make the sound incredibly deep and very, very loud, that was about what it sounded like. The air around me reeked of death, of rotting corpses. I swallowed, nervously, and watched the tail as it flicked out. There was a shower of sparks as it hit the edge of the circle Cioren had drawn.

I couldn't see his lordship, but I guessed he was somewhere behind the beast. He'd better stay there, I thought. If he comes within sword reach of me, I'll spit him, I swear it. But the demon, having found his tongue, wanted to chat.

"Little warrior, you will be mine."

"Think so?" I had never, in any of my imaginings, thought of this encounter as being a conversation, but I saw that at the moment, I was safe. After a fashion. How long Cioren could, or would, hold this thing trapped, I didn't know.

"Oh, yessss." It had a snaky quality to its voice now, as if it was enjoying itself. "You'll be mine. You'll be tasty, when you scream."

"I shouldn't think so," I said, politely. "Very tough and stringy, would be my guess. Not that I know for sure."

It laughed. At least, I think that was what that sound was. I found I was chuckling, too. The whole thing had begun to feel unreal, or rather, even less real than it had been. From somewhere below me, a few wisps of white vapour drifted at my feet.

"Oh, I shall enjoy you!' it said. "When you howl for mercy. When your power becomes mine. I will have you, for an eternity!"

"But I don't have any power," I said. I watched as more mist curled up around my ankles.

The demon threw back its head, and bellowed with rage. I heard something that sounded like the word 'liar' in there but at the same moment I saw a tiny flicker in the space around the thing, almost like a fissure in the air, and instinctively dove for cover.

A rain of black sizzling sparks showered down, and something hit something else, somewhere, with a furious noise. I rolled, and hit an invisible but quite solid wall.

The mist was thickening, nearly waist-deep. I huddled into it, and watched as that deadly tail lashed out, seeking.

It screamed over my head, barely inches away. Cioren, I judged, wouldn't hold him for long.

I didn't know if Eater knew where I was, but it dawned on me that my best hope here lay in not being where logic might dictate. Reluctantly, I edged away from the comforting feeling of the wall, and away from where Eater had last seen me.

"Yes, hide and cower, little fighter." I almost jumped; the sound seemed to come from somewhere quite close to me.

Another flicker of movement caught my eye through the swirling mist. Cioren had also moved. I wondered briefly why the demon hadn't gone after him, but the thought was evanescent and fleeting. In my sword arm, I felt a strange, vague buzzing sensation and looked down: my sword was glowing, ever so faintly, pale blue.

Another of the crackling noises sounded, and above my head, near to where I had so recently crouched, I saw a shower of familiar black sparks.

Some instinct took over. I found myself scuttling back the way I'd come. It was a kind of dumb luck, or a suggestion from the gods, I suppose; moments later, yet another rain of sparks fell almost directly on the spot I'd vacated.

This was getting tiresome. The point, surely, was to kill Eater, so that I could finish off Cioren at leisure, and be ready to tackle Tirais and his guard. Pissing around in the mist wasn't going to further these ambitions. I nerved myself, and stood up.

The demon had grown. It wasn't really possible, of course, and part of me knew it. I might not be able to see the walls, but I knew the room I was in still existed; yet Eater seemed to tower over me, way past the ceiling, and filling a few extra chambers' worth of space.

The tail lashed out again, and even as I ducked under that massive flail, I saw another trembling in the air, and heard the beginnings of a huge and overpowering roar, like a thunderclap.

My instincts and the Mother of All had deserted me: I did the only thing I could think of.

I charged.

If Eater expected anything, it wasn't that. For one brief moment, I had the tiniest of advantages as he took in the knowledge, and I used it, smashing into his leathery leg with my still-glowing sword.

He howled. I didn't suppose I'd done him any real damage -it's fatal to assume your opponent is finished until you've slit his throat - but I yanked the blade away and dove into the mist for cover, while the sound of his anger and pain still echoed around me.

The whistle of Eater's tail followed me, and this time he knew at least roughly where I was. It tore across the mist overhead, and just as I congratulated myself on having escaped it, doubled back and smashed, with deadly accuracy, into my side.

I'd been moving in the same direction, which was all that saved me from death. As it was, the blow knocked me flying across the stones to land in an untidy, groaning heap, with no sense of where I was.

My sword, when I focused on it, was now a brilliant and incandescent blue. From somewhere a long way away, I heard Cioren's voice, chanting some strange and barbaric nonsense. I tried, without much success, to draw a breath, and saw, through a break in the white vapour that had hidden me, a massive claw, speeding down towards me. Saw Eater's loathsome, grinning face, saw my own end, ignoble, unremembered.

In a heartbeat, I squirmed, pushing myself into a small ball against the wall, and pulled my shield over myself, ignoring the screams of protest from my body. I set my sword against the impact of that merciless talon, and braced myself for the final assault.

I felt an enormous shock, and a sudden slashing burn across my leg, heard the burst of fire against my flesh, smelled the rot of hell on my own skin, and listened, in a detached way, to the mingled screams of Eater and myself. And in the same moment, my arm moved, without my bidding and my sword pressed upwards, into Eater's eye.

There was an instant of terrible, earsplitting silence. Then, as something unspeakably slimy began to drip away from my sword, Eater gave a roar, terrifying and desolate, and I heard a Word, and a high-pitched whining noise, and felt the earth shudder beneath me.

My heart lurched. I let go of my swordhilt, and tried desperately to move, but my body was beyond obedience, and I could only watch helplessly as Eater began to lean slowly, inexorably forward, to smash me flat.

I closed my eyes and waited for the inevitable.

Chapter 26

It never came. I lay, half-sitting, for one interminably long moment, as the sounds echoed away into nothing, and then cautiously opened one eye, to see Cioren standing over me, looking a trifle out of breath.

I glanced around for my sword. Not that I could do anything; my eyes seemed the only part of me able to move. The rest of me was screaming in agony. I felt as though every inch was covered with a flaming, burning suffering, and I still could not draw a real breath. Death struck me as preferable.

People will tell you that your body cannot stand pain beyond a certain amount. That when the hurt passes some undefined but known limit, your mind will take pity, and shut you down into unconscious oblivion.

It isn't true. I would have given anything to have passed out, but my brain, far from giving me that simple blessing, was sharp and clear, carefully cataloguing my hurts and registering each minute twinge, throb, and stab. I couldn't speak, beyond gasps of anguish, but my meaning was apparently clear.

"Don't try to speak," said Cioren. "You can kill me later, if you like."

I don't remember the next hour or so very clearly. This is fortunate; what I do remember is filled with agony, anguish and a complete loss of dignity. It's hard to maintain any semblance of soldierly fortitude when you are whimpering in pain or, in between times, puking up your last meal.

They got me, at last, out of the tower and into the main barracks. Not even the jolting as they carried me down Penvarron's winding staircase was enough to make me pass out; by the last landing, I had added a sore jaw from gritting my teeth to my list of aches and injuries.

I must have looked awful; Olwen took one look at me and sent someone scurrying for the healer and someone else to clear her stuff off the cot in her quarters, and Tighe and Ari, who'd been carting me carefully across the yard, laid me gently onto the bed.

Someone remarked, off in the distance, that my mail shirt would have to come off. I still couldn't breathe well enough to launch a coherent protest; it was taking all my energy just to keep from breaking down completely. I just clenched my jaws together and endured more or less, a nasty couple of minutes while I was propped up and my arms wrenched up over my head. I tried to look around, to see who was there, and mark them down on my list of people who would have to be eliminated later, but my eyes wouldn't focus, and one of them had begun to swell shut. I must have bumped it against my shield edge at some point. I'd cut my lip, too. I could taste the blood.

The world wavered. I was willing myself to go under, but my brain, idiotically, still wouldn't co-operate. Tirais' face swam into view, looking concerned. I made an ineffectual effort to slap it, but my arm refused to play. I was helpless, surrounded by people who had betrayed me, thrown me all unwitting at a demon for who-knew-what purpose, and now seemed bent on putting me through even more torture, cleverly disguised as a healer.

Someone began to examine my side, with gentle fingers. The pain was excruciating and I heard myself groaning.

The healer straightened up.

"It's her ribs," he said briskly. "The leg is the difficult bit. Here," he thrust a goblet into my face, "Drink this."

I gave a silent prayer that whatever it was would kill me. I didn't think I could take much more. It was wine, with a faintly bitter aftertaste of some herb. I sank back against the pillows and began to watch, with remote indifference, as he started in on my leg.

The wound was ugly. Blackened about the edges as if charred, with some greenish, suppurating pus oozing from it along with my blood. The healer remarked to his assistant that it would have to be cleaned, and I was so far gone that the words meant very little, until he produced a jug of the local poison we drank in barracks and upended it over my thigh.

I screamed.

Well, I tried to.

Cracked ribs aren't really that awful, but they hurt. Short of a truly serious break, where the bones press into your lungs, they aren't immediately life threatening, although people do die of it sometimes. But in the interim, a few cracked ribs can make you feel as if some giant blacksmith's vise has been wrapped around you and each breath feels as though the screws are being tightened. I couldn't get enough air into myself to make any sound worthy of the name, but I gave it a good try.

I'm not sure my agonized gurgle didn't scare them worse than a yell would have.

There was another one of those moments, where everyone stopped and gazed, a little shocked, down at my body, as if I had somehow done something completely unexpected. Then, they began all talking at once, in agitated and protesting tones, at the healer. I couldn't understand their words, and I didn't try. The commotion had one simple and delightful effect. Between the fire that erupted in my leg, the piercing stab in my side, the myriad smaller troubles afflicting the rest of my person, and the herbs Healer had laced my wine with, I finally and thankfully lost consciousness.

Chapter 27

In my dreams, Eater fell endlessly towards me as I watched. I couldn't stop him; I could do nothing as his enormous bulk crashed forever forward to my helpless body. I could feel the weight of that awful moment, pressing me into the stone, and my chest contracted under the pressure as all the breath in my body was expelled in one excruciating rush.

My mind fought its way back to consciousness, against my will.

The healer had gone. I was propped up on several pillows, with my torso wrapped in tight layers of bandaging to hold my ribs in place, and my leg, when I risked a look, appeared to still be there, although I couldn't really feel it. Somewhere beneath my muddled collection of throbs and aches was a memory of terrible pain, but the herb-laced wine had pushed it all to some far-off place I couldn't quite reach.

I sank gratefully back into sleep.

When I woke again, it was to the faint light of early dawn. My leg ached, and the rest of my body felt sore and tired, but otherwise, I seemed to be alive.

My one good eye fell on Tirais, seated on a hard bench near the door.

"You used me." I'd intended to hurl it as an accusation, but my voice came as a petulant croak.

He seemed unperturbed.

"Yes."

"Bastard."

"Keri, what would you like me to say? That I'm sorry? I am, but it was needful."

"Why?"

"Ask Cioren."

"I'm asking you." This wasn't going well, I thought. The least he could do was be ashamed of it. Instead, I detected amusement.

"Well, we needed you there. And angry. It seemed the easiest way."

"Who else - who knew?"

"Not Third East, if that's what you're thinking. I told them you'd volunteered to stay."

"And you couldn't trust me to do so?" That was better. My bitterness actually found expression.

"It wasn't that. Eater…all this - look," he said as I made a growling noise somewhere deep in my throat, "You shouldn't talk. The point is, it worked. You survived. Go back to sleep. I promised Donnach I wouldn't tire you."

"Bastard," I muttered. The room was wobbling and swaying around me.

"We are what we are," he agreed, as I slipped back into darkness.

My life seemed to consist, for a while, of similar interludes. Once, I woke screaming, because someone was changing my leg bandages and inadvertently poked at my wound; twice more I was propped forward to drink some nasty-smelling concoction.

At last, though, I found myself wide-awake, with no apparent agonies on the go. I felt tired, a bit, and bruised and pummeled, but nothing more.

Cioren sat near my side. He looked a little weary himself, as if he hadn't slept much.

I tried to speak and succeeded in a rusty mumble. I swallowed, and tried again.

"Tell me - "

"Yes, all right. Here, drink this first." He held a goblet to my lips, and I found myself obeying. I was unbelievably thirsty.

I settled back against the pillows and waited. He studied me for a moment or two, then said gently, "I know you're angry."

A masterpiece of understatement, that was. I wasn't angry. I was consumed by hatred, and a blind unreasoning fury, but underneath, I could feel a cold, sneaking suspicion that I was going to be cajoled out of my wrath.

"We had to get him, then and there, Keri. I needed him distracted. If he'd had a thought to spare for me, it would never have worked."

"But why not tell me? I'd have done it. Willingly."

"You'd have been too calm. Eater fed on anger. You know about that. If you'd stood there, all accepting of your fate, he might have noticed what else was going on. As it was, I doubt he even knew I was there, really, let alone what I was doing."

"So any old sacrifice would do, and there I was?" My voice sounded whiny and childish, even to me. I tried again. "I mean, wasn't there some other way? Wouldn't several angry people been a little better? Not to mention less risky?"

"No, it had to be you, I'm afraid."

"Me? I'm honoured. Is Tirais that angry with my lack of courtly manners, that I need murdering?"

"Don't be more of an idiot than you can help," he advised. "This was serious. And if it's any consolation, Tirais wasn't very keen on it, but he understood the necessity."

"Oh, good. Perhaps you'll explain it to me, then."

"Well, if you're prepared to actually listen, I will."

"I'm not precisely equipped to leave," I pointed out. "And I'm sure as hell not going to get much other entertainment."

He looked unconvinced. I sighed, and said, ungraciously, "I'm listening."

"All right." He settled back onto the bench. "Basically, it was because you killed Uln."

I considered this.

"Anyone might have," I said, finally. "I don't see the point."

"Try being a little more open-minded. Uln was a mage. He used some kind of spell or charm on you this summer, and it only barely worked, and not nearly as well as it should have. It must have bothered him.

"Then, two months later he throws battlemagic at you, and what happens? You kill him anyway. And Eater, just reaching this plane, takes his soul, and his knowledge, and his memories. Possibly, some of your emotions were in the air for him to taste as well. So there he is, wandering Penvarron, with a clear and distinct connection to you. Not to mention the uncomfortable suspicion that you may be a very powerful mage yourself."

"That," I said, "is the most idiotic and unconvincing piece of nonsense I've ever heard. Uln knew I wasn't a mage. The entire world knows I'm not a mage."

"Uln knew no such thing. He only knew that a young woman, with nothing much to recommend her beyond some tenuous family connections, didn't succumb to a very powerful spell. He must have been terrified, at the end."

I was silent, thinking about Uln's last moments on this earth. Cioren had a point, although he didn't quite know the truth of it.

"But when we came back," I said, "He would have known. I mean, I'm not a mage. Couldn't he sense that?"

"He sensed your presence, certainly."

"And then," I suddenly saw the light, "You stuck to me like a burr to trews. But if Uln was part of him, wouldn't he know the difference?"

"No. In time he would have figured it out. But after the first night here, you're right. I made sure I was with you whenever something happened. Eater wasn't very good at being here yet - he couldn't distinguish between us as long as we were together. I had to act fast, Keri."

"So you and Tirais set me up."

"I protected you as best I could. But I needed to filter my spells through you, and if you'd known that that was happening, Eater would have known it too. And if he'd gone after me, well, I couldn't have done anything. So I risked it."

"So how did you know I wouldn't be the first out the door? And how did you make sure that something happened just at the right moment, to get us all out anyway? More of your little tricks?"

"Tirais had something planned, as a diversion, but it wasn't needed. Eater managed that bit himself. But I - er - distracted you, momentarily. With a little trick, as you say."

I ran through my memories of those few moments. I hadn't looked out that window for more than a grain of the glass, I was sure of it. How had they all gotten out the door so fast?

"Well, why does your magic work so well on me and Uln's didn't?" I asked, more for something to say than anything else.

"It doesn't, actually. I had a damned difficult time getting you to look away at all. I have no idea why. You really haven't a particle of talent, yourself. By the rules, you should be an easy mark. But off the top of my head, I'd say it's at least partly you yourself... You're pretty hardheaded, and you focus on the essentials remarkably well. Perhaps magic can't breach the walls of pure practicality so easily. Most people's minds seem to wander far more and are just more open to suggestion than yours. Mind you, I've no facts for this, I'm simply guessing."

"So, I'm a wooden headed fool? Fair enough. Oh, all right, I see your point, and Tirais', too, if it comes to it. I don't have to be happy about it, do I?"

"Believe me, if I could have found another way, I would have taken it. But I don't have any more experience with banishing demons than you do, nor does Tirais. As a commander, wouldn't you have risked it?"

I would have. I knew it, and he knew it. Given the sacrifice of one against an entire garrison, I'd have hesitated not at all. As the sacrifice, though, I still felt vaguely miffed.

"Next time, give me a little warning, will you? I almost went after you instead of Eater, you know."

"Yes, I do know. But as I said, you keep your mind on the priorities. I figured you wouldn't kill me till Eater was taken care of. It seemed a decent trade-off."

I chuckled sleepily. My eyes were drooping and I had never felt so monumentally tired in all my life; I didn't notice when it was that Cioren left the room but turned my head into the pillows and slept.

I recuperated with surprising speed. After another day or so, I could sit up for reasonable lengths of time, and began to take an interest in my leg wound, which had begun itching like all the torments of hell. The healer remarked, rather unfeelingly, I thought, that this was a good sign, and recommended more rest.

While I was still cursing his ancestors for indiscriminate procreation, I got a visit from Sorcha. Having ascertained that there was nothing wrong with my insides, as far as anyone could tell, she smuggled me in a meat pie.

Healers are all united in the firm belief that anyone suffering from so much as a scraped knuckle requires a diet consisting of thin gruel and weak broth. Indeed, some of them have enlarged on the theme, and propose that what is good for the ailing must naturally be even better for the hale and strong. A healer passing through Orliegh had suggested such a diet might prolong lives; he was unimpressed by my father's sardonic observation that it might certainly *feel* as though you were living longer. Sorcha's bribe worked, in any case; I instantly forgave her any complicity in the plot to serve me up as Eater's dinner, and occupied myself with getting the meat pie inside of me, while she caught me up on what had actually occurred that night, and since.

Tirais had planned an explosion in the upper bailey, complete with fire and an extra dollop of smoke, but he might as well not have bothered. Eater himself had craftily unleashed those ethereal and frightening apparitions that had heralded his arrival in the cellars, this time all over the keep. They had been more corporeal than their first appearance, and considerably more lethal: in addition to a fire they'd started, we had lost several people in fighting them, and I was not the only invalid slowly recovering in the rooms of Penvarron. Sorcha was still bandaged at the shoulder from her own encounter.

As suddenly as it had come, the torrent of imps had vanished. As near as I could figure, it had been about the same time as when I'd sunk my sword into Eater's thigh. And when Cioren had done whatever he'd done to send Eater back to where he'd come from, the apparitions had reappeared, to flail uselessly around the courtyard, screaming like vultures, but to little effect, until, slowly, they'd winked out of existence, one by one.

The soldiers had spent the next day or so searching the keep for signs of demonic presence, and found nothing. Tirais had then sent north, for holy ones to come and purify and ward the tower, ordered up funeral pyres, and, incomprehensibly, kept a watch over my unpleasant bedside.

I felt a faint flicker of guilt over my accusations, but suppressed it. He had me at so great a disadvantage already; being angry with him seemed like the only way to hang on to even a shred of dignity.

Chapter 28

Tighe came to see me a day or so later.

By now I had become a most annoying and inconsiderate patient, and they'd given me crutch, for hobbling to and from the privies. Tighe viewed my distempered freaks with amusement, as I hurled an empty goblet at the healer's retreat.

"Well, then, is that how a captain behaves?"

"Oh, shut up. And where the hell have you been, anyway? Not even bad temper's contagious."

"No, sir." He sounded like he was enjoying himself far too much. I eyed him with disfavour.

"Ah, well, we've been away up to Lesser Penne. With Lord Cioren."

"Lesser Penne? What's there?"

"Nothing, and less. Thank the Goddess, or so Cioren thinks. Myself, I'd have liked a crack at a few Camrhyssi devils."

I looked at him. Really looked, I mean. When you see a man day in and day out, you stop noticing much beyond the general outlines.

He didn't look bad. Not exhausted, not agitated. But underneath that annoying cheer, there was something bothering him.

"All right," I said. "What's wrong? You look as if the prize-laying hen just went broody. Is there something I should know?"

"No, no. That is," he squirmed. "Healer said I weren't to disturb you, with gossip and such."

"You can't disturb me more than by hinting of dire things, Tighe. Come on, out with it, man."

It wasn't so bad. In fact it was damned good. Tighe was uncertain, but I saw at once how right it was.

They'd offered him a captain's place.

Third East, in fact.

It gave me a moment's pause, but Tighe hastened to reassure me that it was only on account of I would be going off to Glaice, with the Prince and the other wounded that could travel, and would probably be reassigned somewhere prestigious, that the question of the captaincy had come up at all.

"Take it." I said firmly. "Don't even think about turning it down, Tighe. You'll be great at it."

"But I'm nowise good at training and such. There'll be too much I don't know."

I grinned. "Guess what? None of the other captains know, either. We just do the best we can. And you know more than you think. You've actually done the damn job, anyway. You may as well get paid for it. Have you given any thought to a second?"

He had, which made me grin wider and Tighe actually blushed. Ari, of course, if he was willing. Which he most likely was, given that he'd had a taste of it, these last few days. We spent the next half-glass discussing the ins and outs of troop management, until Healer Donnach chased him away.

After another couple of days, Olwen got her room back, when Donnach agreed that I could manage Penvarron's hallways and stairs well enough. I was permitted brief intervals of sitting on a bench in the courtyard, chatting with the other wounded, and was even allowed to drag my weakened leg to the practice yard to watch other soldiers doing drills, but the food remained bland and uninspiring. Those of us still classed as invalids began a kind of clandestine market in decent comestibles, by bribing our friends and acquaintances for table scraps and sharing them amongst ourselves. Gwyll, his arm still splinted and in a sling, proved to be the most adept, although he steadfastly refused to reveal his sources for an unending stream of whole chickens off the spits and napkins' full of greasy cold sausage. I suspected Tirais was thieving them for him, in the interest of keeping us from wholesale rebellion.

Gossip cemented our little world together. Having shared food, as well as being the honourably injured, it was natural to share what little news we could glean. It was interesting, watching the class barriers breaking down before one's eyes: Gwyll chatting companionably with Dag from Watch Two over purloined bacon, speculating on whether Ruan would get a general pardon and be sent back to Kerris, where he'd once been a captain of Guards; or Lady Maeliss, who stood to inherit a barony and had been possibly the most snobbish of Glaice's incoming forces, sharing stray comments she'd picked up at the latrines that hinted Tirais intended for none of Penvarron's original garrison to remain here longer than it would take to rotate them to new posts.

Even Healer couldn't help but let occasional information drop, when he came to check our hurts. Tighe had been right; I would not be staying at Penvarron, nor could I keep Third East's command. Almost all of the wounded were due to be moved out as quickly as possible, some to Glaice, others to forts and stations along the way, to be reassigned or to wait for their units to follow.

I didn't see Tirais at all, at least, not to speak to, for several days.

According to Gwyll, those of us well enough to travel would be filling up the wagons that were due any day, coming down to resupply the fortress. The idea of being jolted over bad roads in winter wasn't an appealing one; I was hobbling about pretty well now, and after a couple days of thought, hopped along on my crutch to the stables.

Eater might never have attacked the horses, thank the Goddess, but his little helpers had been less discriminating. There were a couple of mounts that had had to be put down after being injured in the blaze that had started near the tack-rooms, and for two of the pack ponies, the evening's festivities had been too much - they'd turned mean and ornery, and would probably never be much use as beasts of burden again.

Banshee, quartered midway down the row, had survived well enough. Being mean to begin with, her general disgust with the world had not improved. She snapped at me, kicking her hooves against the walls, and a stable lad remarked that she had bitten a pony who had crowded her during morning exercise the day before. In short, she was fine.

I made a minor attempt to soothe her out of her sullens, with predictably limited success, and was just emerging from her stall, when I ran smack into the Prince of Keraine, just in from his morning ride.

His eyebrows rose, just a fraction.

"Good morrow," he said. I could hear the faint undercurrent of amusement. "You're looking rather better."

"Yes - er - thank you," I said.

He looked past me, into Banshee's stall.

"Yours?"

"Yes." My tongue, unaccountably, seemed leaden. Why did I feel so damned guilty, as though I'd been caught filching apples? I'd a perfect right to visit my horse.

"Rather an ugly little brute, isn't she?"

"Yes, but don't tell her original owner." I said promptly. "She was a gift."

He was quick; I'll give him that. The eyebrows twitched a little higher, but he said merely, "Indeed? I wonder what he was thinking?"

"Likely, he thought to do us both a service."

"Likely, he did," said Tirais, gravely. His eyes were dancing. "You weren't thinking of - er - riding, were you? Because I doubt the healers will give you a clean bill of health just yet."

"I wasn't proposing to ask, actually." The first rule of getting away with anything is to keep from actually saying you're going to do it.

"I wouldn't try it," he said.

I kept silent.

"I really wouldn't, Keri."

"Only a fool would," I said agreeably. We smiled insincerely at each other, without malice, then Tirais sighed and turned away.

But at our invalids' table in the mess-hall that evening, Gwyll slid into the spot beside me, examined the watery porridge on offer, and said casually, "How is your horse doing, Keri?"

"Well enough. She doesn't like anything at the best of times. I expect she thought Eater's little fiends just one more item on her list of reasons to be a bitch."

"Most of the mounts seem to have taken it in stride," he said. "Mind you, the gear didn't fare so well."

"So I've heard." I watched unenthusiastically as a stream of tasteless muck dripped off my spoon. No salt, no butter. Not that it would have helped.

"It's all lying in a heap in a shed out by Guard Tower Three," Gwyll continued, as if I hadn't spoken. "They'll have a hell of a time sorting out what belongs to who."

I glanced at him. He was looking at his porridge carefully, as if somewhere, somehow, there might be a reason to actually eat it.

"Tirais says they'll have to get a crew onto that in a day or two."

His voice was elaborately indifferent. Around us, the healthy were tucking into bowls of stew. The air was rife with the smell of spices and onions and rich beef gravy, but I was losing interest even in that. I pushed myself into a standing position, excused myself, and headed for the door.

Outside in the gathering dusk, I leaned against the stable walls, watching the two guards posted by the shed below the guard tower. The breeze had died down and the air was crisp and clear. I needed an excuse, but my mind refused to come up with one; instead, my conscience was busy pointing out that I'd been given a pretty clear order not to attempt this and I would be wise to heed it.

"Lovely evening," said Gwyll, companionably, as he came up beside me.

I nodded, my eyes still fixed on the pair of soldiers by the shed, wondering about the length of their shift, and what their precise orders were.

"Well," said Maeliss, behind me, "if we're going to do this, we may as well get on with it."

I followed them across the yard. They kept the pace slow, out of consideration for my leg, but it wasn't far. There was no time to form any idea of why they were helping me, except that they probably weren't keen on a week or more in those wagons, either. I wondered what Tirais would do to us.

"His Grace wants some of his Guards' stuff sorted out from the Penvarron gear, if it can be," said Gwyll, after a cheery greeting to the soldiers.

"Oh, aye," said one of them, producing the key. "There's a lamp, just inside the door."

We stood, in the midst of a jumble of saddles and so on, heaped chaotically about, while they lit it for us, and, after some commiserating remarks about making even the wounded earn their keep, went back to their post, letting the door bang shut behind them.

"That was good," I said. "About sorting out the guards' things. Very believable."

"Well, so we are. Sorting them, I mean," said Maeliss. "Look, there's Cam's saddle. We'll have to move those top three."

It took a long time, to find our own things. To keep ourselves honest, we piled any gear from Tirais' own guards in a new heap near the door, and started another pile of things that were too damaged to be reclaimed. It had not occurred to anyone that charred leather is of little use, or that wet harness will mildew. A lot of what had been saved was rubbish.

Banshee's saddle seemed all right, but I couldn't find a bit and bridle that could be reliably identified as hers. Gwyll solved this, however, by picking out some harness and tossing it down beside my feet.

"It's Bairre's, or was," he said, when I protested. "The dead don't care, at least."

At Maeliss' self-assured request, the two guarding the shed agreed to help us carry a few things out to the stables, to keep the doorway clear. That those things happened to be our own seemed to them to be an amusing joke, and quite understandable. I stopped worrying over what Tirais might do to us and started wondering what would happen to these two, when he discovered how easily we'd corrupted them.

But it was possible, barely, that they wouldn't be found out. There must be several shifts of guards on here, between now and when we left. My conscience fell silent; it couldn't approve of this attitude, but couldn't come up with a convincing reason to rat on Gwyll and Maeliss, either.

Chapter 29

The supply wagons arrived in due course, accompanied by four priestesses, a new Healer and a company of guards commandeered from the posting fort a little north of Eoghan's Moor. They were all agog to hear what had been going on at Penvarron, but Tirais' orders had been explicit. We held our tongues, said merely "Camrhys" as an explanation for the ruined buildings, and hoped that the bribes Olwen had promised One-Leg and the others would be enough to keep the worst details safely out of the gossip-mill. She'd offered them help in rebuilding the village, both in manpower and material, and the assurance of richer pickings to come, now that Penvarron had gained official respectability.

I had gotten to the bottom of the stairs without mishap, and was navigating my way around a mound of baggage in the hall, using my crutch to push a bedroll out of the doorway, when Sorcha came up, grinning happily and carrying a longish bundle wrapped in a scrap of leather.

"Well, its good-bye, isn't it, Keri?"

"So it is." I paused, searching for words. "Sorcha, I don't know how to-"

"Now don't start with me. Didn't I say you'd do? You take my advice, dearie, keep your head down, and watch yourself."

"You too," I said.

"Here, I brought you a sword, seeing as how your own just vanished, seemingly." She treated me to another of her wide grins. "I went through the storerooms for a good one."

Unwrapped, the blade gleamed wickedly. It had a plain guard, with new leather wrapped on the grip, the pommel decorated with a pattern of entwined gripping beasts.

"There were fancier ones, but I reckoned you'd prefer something you could use."

I was silent. It was a beautiful weapon. Much better than the one I'd stuck into Eater. Better than any I'd ever hoped to own.

"Don't fret," she assured me. "I'm not quartermaster for nothing, and Olwen knows, she signed off on the list without a murmur. Here, the scabbard's nothing much, but it fits."

I rested my crutch against the wall, and undid my belt. I was still awkward and unbalanced; Sorcha slipped off my old swordsheath and slid the new one on, and braced me while I rebuckled my belt.

"Take care of yourself, Sorcha."

"And you too," she said. "I look to see you a commander or better someday. Don't let me down, dearie, I've got money on it."

Tighe and the others came to see me off, carrying my saddlebags out to a waiting Banshee where Wenna had saddled her for me.

I'd endured several teary conversations with Wenna, who was indulging in an excess of remorse, until I'd lost my patience and pointed out that, yes; she was very much to blame, but that weeping and wailing wouldn't alter the past.

"If you want to make amends," I said in exasperation, "don't waste yourself being so sorry you're no good to anyone. The past is done with, Wenna. You have it in you to be a second someday, but only if you remember to be a good soldier, follow your orders, and be a credit to your unit."

She smiled, as much cheered by finally being yelled at as by my actual words, leaving my conscience to point out that I might do well to take my own advice.

Someone helped me into the saddle, and Ari dumped my crutch into a wagon meant for the wounded. I looked at Tighe, at the rest of them. I was going to miss them, I thought. All of them. Ruan was already gone: yesterday, I'd seen Watch One ride off to Lesser Penne, to start real repairs this time.

Tirais ignored me. For the moment I seemed invisible; I attached myself to the rearguard, and my leg didn't really bother me all that much, even when remounting after a hasty meal consumed along the roadside. I found a convenient rock, gritted my teeth against the protest from my ribs as I swung myself clumsily into the saddle and managed to hang on for the remaining hours of chilly riding until we ambled through the gates of Caer Druach.

My determination to stay out of the wagons posed a number of problems, none of which I had foreseen when I made up my mind to get to Glaice on my own terms. Gwyll and Maeliss were back with the Prince's guards, along with Cioren; I hadn't seen them, except from a distance at noon.

The wounded were unloaded and hustled into the main barracks. I followed the remaining troops into the stableyard, and watched as Banshee was taken off by a boy of about twelve, to share a stall with an unfortunate stable-mate. She went, however, without a single display of her usual bad temper, as if to drive home the impression that it was really only me who raised her hackles.

It was then that I realized what my pride would cost me.

All around me, soldiers were falling in with their units and being assigned mess-times and quarters. Leaning on my crutch, I watched as the courtyard slowly emptied. I had nowhere to go. There was no provision here for a lone arrival; Caer Druach had set itself for an influx of a known number of patrols and squads, and had arranged itself accordingly. There was no general mess or any convenient place for me to shake down for the night. No one paid me the slightest heed; I might as well have not been here at all.

I considered the stables, but even from the yard, it was clear that they were crowded to the point of bursting. In any case, the stable-lads would probably resent any encroachment; people are curiously jealous of what little terrain they can call their own.

It was the yard for me, and a cold, hungry and cheerless night; probably several of them, if Caer Druach was anything to go by.

It was utterly quiet now. I limped about uselessly until I found a spot beside the archway through to the main barracks. For a few moments, just being out of the wind was bliss. It felt briefly much warmer, but this was an illusion. The cold began to seep into my bones, and my stomach rumbled alarmingly.

The night deepened, and the chill increased. I couldn't sleep, of course, despite my exhaustion. I was shivering uncontrollably, my teeth chattering away like dice, I couldn't take my mind off my hunger, and I thought that if I had to endure more than one night like this, which seemed likely, I would very probably die.

I must have dozed in the end; after what seemed an eternity of dull disaster, I heard an angry exclamation, felt a shake at my shoulder, and opened my eyes to a fall of golden light from the barracks door.

"Of all the idiotic, ill-considered - have you no sense at all?"

It was Tirais, of course. Beyond him, as I blinked in the sudden light, I saw Cioren, looking grimly annoyed.

"You stupid little fool, what do you think you're doing? Do you want to freeze to death?"

"There wasn't anywhere else," I muttered.

"I ought." he said, "to let you die. You're far more trouble than you're worth. Come on, get up."

I struggled awkwardly to my feet, groping for my crutch, which had sprawled away into the lane.

"Can you walk?"

"Yes."

His arm slid under my shoulder, and I bit back a groan.

We moved to the door, following a silent Cioren through the wide hallway to a row of wooden doors. Tirais was still more or less carrying me; my legs were curiously weak, and it was all I could do to keep moving them.

"In here, I think," said Cioren, opening a door.

I saw nothing. Stumbling past Cioren as Tirais let go of me, I half-tottered, half-fell onto the narrow cot within. Warmth folded over me like a blanket, and my eyes refused to remain open. I could hear them still, a murmur of low, angry voices, and then, blessedly, nothing.

In the morning, I was rested enough to feel the embarrassment of it. To be found, not ten steps from the comfort of the main barracks, as if I were a mindless infant without the sense to come in from the cold, seemed to be the height of shortsighted imbecility. There wasn't any real reason to have done as I had; in the cold light of the morning, I saw that I could have at least curled up in the hallway, if I were too proud to search out the room set aside for the injured.

Cioren, out of kindness or disgust, said nothing to me at all. He arrived, with some food, dumped it onto a table, and disappeared out the door again, to return a few minutes later with Caer Druach's healer. The next half-glass is best forgotten: there is nothing more undignified than being pulled about by a girl one's own age who considers you a slow-witted collection of injuries.

I braced myself for a lecture when Cioren came back. It was what I deserved, after all; if I got off with a recital of my many faults and being forced into the wagons, it would be less than I expected. But Cioren looked merely tired. He sat down, folded his hands, and looked me over without a word.

"I'm sorry," I said, after a while. I had to say something. The silence was unnerving.

This, as expected, did not get a good response. He raised his eyebrows, quite in Tirais' style, but said nothing.

"Look, I know it isn't enough, but I just couldn't think what else to do. I was just more tired than I knew, I guess. I'm truly sorry if I caused any problems." It didn't seem that this would work. I suspected I had used up any good will still left in the world for me, and that if there was another garrison with a reputation like Penvarron's, I was for it.

Cioren fetched up another sigh, quite sarcastically long-suffering, as though everything I'd said was part of some already rehearsed scene.

162

"Keri, we can take it as holy words that you are six kinds of idiot. I don't see much point in going over it again, with or without your participation."

"Oh." He did not, in fact, sound particularly angry. I took heart. "Is Tirais seriously furious with me?"

"With himself, more likely, for not ordering you into the wagons at midday. You looked like death, even then. No, don't try to argue. As it happens, the healer says you don't seem to have done yourself any real harm, and old Donnach says he won't take responsibility for you, at any price, so you're stuck in the saddle for the duration. I've agreed to take charge of you, but only if you'll agree to abide by my rules."

"Oh." This seemed inadequate, but I couldn't come up with a response more fitting.

"You'll see Donnach every evening, as soon as we're settled in. If he says you're not fit to ride, you'll go into the wagons. No arguing, no protests. I want that understood from the start."

"Yes, of course."

"Right. And you'll do as I say, without question, or I wash my hands of you. I haven't got time to nursemaid a stubborn little fool."

"I promise." It was only till Glaice, I thought. What was in store for me after that was likely already decided, but I was too relieved to try worming that bit of information out of him.

The rest of our journey to Glaice passed without incident. It took rather longer than our race south, but my health continued to improve, and I tried to be as unobtrusive and well behaved as possible, so I wasn't relegated to the wagons. Donnach began treating me with a healer's disdain. I wasn't a dire enough case to warrant sympathy anymore, and my defection from the ranks of the really ill seemed to offend him; he changed my bandages without pity or even much interest.

I had some idea, I suppose, of being some sort of servant for Cioren, but I was fairly useless, really. For one thing, Cioren didn't need anyone to "do" for him, his needs were pretty basic; for another, I was still weak, after any day in the saddle, and needed far more than I could give. But we got along fairly easily even so; Cioren had an endless amount of quite fascinating knowledge, which he used to distract me from my aches and pains. By the time the towers along the border came into view, I had acquired a much better understanding of Keraine's history, some scandalous stories involving members of several noble families, and a number of unrelated facts about trade between Camrhys and Keraine.

The road into Glaice seemed much easier. The higher passes were now closed by snow, and much of the traffic that had slowed us before was gone. It wasn't surprising, when we entered the fortress proper, to be met with the intelligence that Her Majesty had already left the keep, having gone on to Kerris to celebrate Midwinter, and that she awaited us there.

I could feel my heart sinking at the news. It had been pure torture to get myself this far, and only pride had kept me in the saddle, these last two days. I had looked at Glaice as a haven, certain there would be a few days of rest and comfort before Tirais remembered me and sent me off to some other duty. The possibility that tomorrow morning I might be off again filled me with foreboding. Much as I wanted to see Kerris, I found myself praying that all Tirais meant by me was to leave me here as a Queen's trooper, in some minor and functionless squad of border guards.

It didn't seem, after the first hour or so, that any of us would be going anywhere anytime soon, though. Cloren and I were ensconced in the same rooms we'd shared a few weeks before. I gathered that these were his usual quarters, conveniently close to the Royal apartments, but on the end of a corridor, with easy access to the yard below, and out of the way enough to be quiet. Cioren took himself off almost immediately, with an injunction to Alun to see that I rested.

He didn't really need the order. I was tired enough, and the wide bed inviting enough that even my apprehensions took a holiday, and I slept the remainder of the afternoon out. It was blissfully quiet when I woke up to the mellow light of early evening. My nap had been deep and dreamless and I could look upon even our probable morning departure with equanimity.

I went to the window. The yard was empty of all but the usual traffic, a couple of dogs fighting over a scrap of meat and three off-duty soldiers crossing to the inner gate. Behind me, Alun fussed over my clothes.

"Oh, leave it," I said. My spare tunic was, if anything, filthier than the one I was wearing.

"The thing is, you're to dine with His Grace," said Alun. "You can't go in these."

"No-one will care. Tirais has seen me in worse." I didn't especially want to go to dinner with Tirais at all. I had the distinct suspicion my eventual fate was about to be revealed to me, and I felt too happy to spend an evening being told that my punishment would be for my own good. I would have liked to have suspended this moment of well-being, to push my hard realities into some distant future for as long as I could.

164

Alun grumbled that it would do him no credit to have me turn up looking like a beggar pulled in from the gates, and decided to take my clothes away to see if anything could be done. He was right, really. It was an invitation I couldn't refuse, and it would be all the harder if I turned up looking like something those dogs had been worrying. I might as well look presentable.

In due course, an hour or so later, I followed him down the hall to the Prince's rooms. My spare tunic had been tidied - it wasn't precisely clean, but the worst of the dirt was gone - and I was washed and brushed, and my boots had been scraped free of mud.

Tirais' apartments were rather larger than Cioren's, but they were no more finely furnished; indeed, since they contained perhaps even less, they presented a curiously barren appearance. They were empty of people, too. I spent a few minutes surveying my surroundings and realizing I was in for a quiet evening. The table was laid for four, which was a relief, I supposed. Having a full complement of Glaice's commanders to witness my humiliation would have been - well, humiliating. Still, the small number confirmed my belief that my future would be the main topic of discussion. I hoped Tirais wasn't as deeply offended by my conduct as he had seemed the night he'd tripped over me at Caer Druach.

I turned at the sound of the door opening. It was Tirais, alone for a wonder, and he looked me over for a moment as if he couldn't quite remember who I was.

"Pour me some wine, would you?" he said after a few seconds. "And sit down," he added after I'd complied and had moved off a pace. "It's annoying having to watch you prowling around like a cat."

"Sorry."

"No, why? This isn't a state occasion. It'll be a while, yet. They all seem astonished I'm here, I can't think why. Apparently they weren't expecting us, so they're a little behind in organizing dinner."

"Did you send ahead, to let them know?"

"Why should I? We spend half the year here - you'd think they'd be used to arranging meals for me by now."

I shook my head. The distance between Tirais' life and mine seemed enormous. My mother would have had some pithy things to say about courtesy and household organization, but it wasn't my job to explain to him why you couldn't just descend on a keepful of servants unexpectedly and assume you'd get the dinner you thought you deserved. At Orliegh, he'd be lucky to get bread and cheese.

"It's just as well," he said, after a bit. "Cioren's off somewhere, and Gwyll's down sorting out the wounded for me. Some of them are quite done in. You were probably right to insist on riding - the wagons seem to have made it worse for them."

I glanced at him. He certainly didn't seem angry. He was gazing off into the fire, with an abstracted expression on his face, as though he was trying to find a way to say something.

Here it comes, I thought. He's about to tell me that the Kingdom can do without my services. It was what I deserved, but I was nervous. I couldn't think what I would do for the rest of my life.

"You'll be glad to hear that we're not riding out tomorrow," he said, finally. "I'd meant to, but the horses need a rest, and that idiot Enan never makes a decision about anything if he can get out of it, so there's a host of little problems that need sorting out before we can go. Cioren says you need a break anyway. According to him, you'll fall off your horse if we push you any harder."

"No, no, I'm fine." What did he care? I wondered. I was just another of those little problems he didn't want to deal with. I couldn't think why my health mattered.

"Well, as it happens, Gwyll's not looking too fine, nor Maeliss either. I could use a good night's sleep myself, come to think of it. No, we'll take a day or two, then start for Kerris. You've never been there, have you? You'll like it. Much prettier than Penvarron, anyway, and at Midwinter, there'll be lots to amuse you."

I sat, slightly dumbfounded, as Tirais continued to describe Kerris at Midwinter for me. I scarcely took in a word. I was trying to figure out why, far from being punished for my sins, I was being rewarded. My mind could not quite get round it. I came back to the present only when Cioren arrived and Tirais appealed to him to help convince me that a few weeks at Kerris was just what I needed to regain my health.

"Well, I wouldn't go quite that far," said Cioren. "But it's true that a little time at court might do you good, Keri. And there are some things I'd like your help with. It might be useful to us all if you were there, and Tirais is quite right, Midwinter at Kerris is very entertaining."

"I'm at your service, of course," I said. The whole evening was taking on a bizarre shape. Gwyll came in, with a sheaf of papers, and the focus, mercifully, shifted from my immediate future, to Tirais complaining that

Enan, who commanded Glaice, couldn't choose a breakfast menu without someone's approval.

"Well, but you're here," said Gwyll. "He'd only let matters slide till spring. And most of it's on your orders, anyway."

Tirais glared at him, but said nothing. Cioren winked at me. I gathered that, far from letting trivialities mount up, Enan was doing his job as he'd been instructed, and I turned my attention to the servants, who were laying out a wide assortment of platters on the table.

The meal was an entertaining one. Once Tirais had finished signing off on various orders, he shook off his annoyance, and became an amusing host, full of diverting stories of his youth, much of which had been spent in Glaice's shadow. Gwyll, who'd been his companion for a greater share of it, chipped in with a few tales of his own, and I shared a couple of similar ones about Orliegh. Cioren had a few of his own as well, not at all to Tirais' credit, having been, for some of these years, a sort of royal tutor. It was illuminating, to say the least.

Sitting around over cups of wine, after the plates had been cleared, the talk turned, not surprisingly, to Penvarron. These last days had taught me something. I could see the point of my being used as bait, and my fury had faded. I thought, in retrospect, that it was at least far fairer than what many soldiers get. I had had some idea of what I'd been fighting, anyway, and Cioren was right about some of it. Knowing more wouldn't have changed anything for me, and my anger had served its purpose. Underneath, I had regained a bit of my pride: I'd done my duty, which is all a good soldier wants, in the end. That, a bit of praise and a decent jug of ale, and you could keep them working forever, or so I'd been taught.

But we had our questions and suppositions. The whole affair was odd, from Uln's treachery down to that mystery man of Wenna's, and scary too. What was Camrhys really up to? What did the return of such strong magic to what had only been a contest of arms till now mean, over the long haul?

"Well," said Tirais, "They won't try that kind of nonsense in a hurry again. They've lost a good number of trained soldiers, and not a few of those repulsive priests of theirs. And Penvarron won't be an easy target anymore, so I can't see that we're in any immediate danger from that direction."

"In fact," said Cioren, dryly, " 'All's well that ends well,' my Prince?"

"Or, perhaps, 'To the victor go the spoils', I think."

" 'The fast hound catches the hare'," said Gwyll.

"You might think 'No rose without a thorn', of course," Cioren sounded drier still.

" 'Method," said Tirais, reaching a bit, " 'Is heir to the Concept'."

" 'A stag within bowshot is worth a herd downwind', " I finished off.

We grinned foolishly at each other. There is nothing like four bottles of really good wine to turn even the most serious-minded into gibbering idiots.

Chapter 30

I was not precisely hungover in the morning, although my head felt none too clear and my ribs had taken a minor turn for the worse, from my imprudent decision to loosen some of my bandaging sometime in the small hours before bed. We'd spent a pretty riotous evening, after Cioren took himself off, trading "dumb luck in battle" stories, and my account of my fury and subsequent behavior when locked into Penvarron tower turned into a tale of hilarious stupidity in the face of danger. It was convivial, and enjoyable, and wonderfully cathartic to tell Tirais just what I'd been thinking in the aftermath of that horror.

In the morning light, I blushed. He'd taken it with spluttering laughter, after all that drink. I hoped he didn't really remember it. One of my father's dictates, about not getting drunk with your commander, floated back to me. I'd really have to start paying more attention to what I knew, or I'd be doomed forever to a life of backwater garrisons with poor food.

In the meantime, I had gotten a very good meal out of it, and the prospect of the Royal Court in full festival lay before me. I'd have to see Gallerain, of course, and he had no reason to like me, but the chances were high that our paths wouldn't cross much. Out of my league, Baron Gallerain was. I got out of bed.

My own clothes were nowhere to be found. In their place, there was a tunic and trews of very fine blue wool, beautifully trimmed in the red and gold of the House of Machyll, and a light cloak to match. On the table beside them, I saw a stamped lead token, the standard marker that you turn in to get your pay when you are employed by a really large army.

I dressed, carefully. My mail shirt was also missing, probably taken off for cleaning along with my clothes. Life was certainly a lot simpler, with Alun to worry over these simple details. Luxurious, not to have to fuss over it all, but to simply wait for things to reappear, cleaned and repaired, instead of wasting my time finding a sand-barrel and a brush, or a cistern for washing.

On the other hand, I didn't have anything else to occupy me. But that was a kind of luxury too, I thought. I sat down to another magnificent breakfast in my borrowed finery, agreed with Alun that it was a lovely day, and asked casually when my own things would be returned.

"Never," he said, grinning. "Those trews weren't good but for rubbish anyway. Old Mab's sorting out new things for you, from the stores. Prince's orders. And your mail's got big holes, they've taken it off to the armouries, to see what's to be done. I'll go and ask how long, if you like."

"No, that's all right," I said hastily. "You must have a ton of other work. But I need to turn in my pay marker. You don't happen to know where, do you?"

As it happened, he did. But Glaice being so large, it was quickly established that Alun's directions were nearly useless. Instead, I followed him down through the central courtyard, past the building that housed the infirmary, to the doors of Glaice's administration barracks.

Once inside, a man of uncertain years and poor vision scrutinized my token. I was then passed along through a succession of army clerks, who each gazed at the lead button as if it were some mysterious and arcane symbol. Eventually, I was ushered into a small counting-room, where yet another clerk examined my pay token, fumbled amongst a box of small leather bags, matched the insignia of my chit to those sealing the bags, and handed one of them over, along with a ledger to sign.

The bag felt rather heavy. I wasn't owed much, even without deducting my advance from Sorcha, and my decision to turn in the token had been partly for want of something to do, as well as a response to a much-quoted maxim of my father's on the subject of a soldier's pay. Of course, it might all be in coppers and beggar's bits, I thought, and stowed it away in my shirt.

Alun had disappeared, after my blithe assurance that I could certainly find my way back on my own. It turned out, of course, not to be completely true, as I got lost twice, but finally I recognized the gate to the courtyard I wanted and struggled up the stairs into my room.

The bag did not contain coppers.

Ensconced on the bed, with a cushion to support my aching leg, I stared at the pile of coins lying on the blanket. In addition to a quite unholy amount of silver, more than I'd ever actually seen in one place before, there were two gold pieces. They were the kind called 'ravens' because of the prophecy bird stamped on them, the obverse bearing a crown and the Queen's name. I counted it all very carefully, twice, and stared, thinking hard.

I knew what I'd been owed, after subtracting my advances. I counted that out, as close as I could. I knew roughly what a patrol captain earned in a quarter, even at a prestigious place like Glaice. I counted that amount out equally carefully. I was even capable of working out how much a full year might net me, and I moved another pile of coins to a place midway between my first collection and the large mound remaining. As near as I could figure, after carefully ascertaining what was left, my little pouch contained an amount in silver equal to two and a half years of duty in a good garrison.

I didn't even try to figure out what the gold ravens would translate into. I didn't want to know. Someone in the counting house had made a huge mistake, which would have to be rectified, but I wasn't quite sure how to go about doing that.

In any case, the coins made a very pretty picture heaped on the bed. I leaned back and gazed at them, while I tried to think who might be the best person to turn this matter over to. It was a pity Lord Gervase wasn't here. It seemed to me that he would know how to fix this without getting some poor clerk in hot water.

I was still trying to think what to do when Cioren came in.

"You don't look much the worse for wear," he remarked by way of greeting.

I grunted in response, my mind still preoccupied with my own dilemma.

"There's been a mistake in my pay."

He glanced over. "It looks like enough," he said, "But you'd know best what you're owed."

"That's just it. It's far too much. They've given me someone else's."

"Do you really think so?"

"Well, they must have. There's over two years' pay here, not to mention these." I pointed at the gold.

"You know," said Cioren, "there was a bonus for Penvarron soldiers. Tirais announced it, but I think you were still abed with your wounds. I expect that's the reason it seems to be so much."

"That might explain a little bit, but no-one gives common soldiers this much. They've mixed it up somehow."

Cioren wandered over to the side table and picked up the wine bottle.

"Keri, I shouldn't worry over it. You did hard service, and were wounded. I think the kingdom can afford a mistake in your favour, just this once. I would just accept it as good fortune, and let it be. Sometimes mistakes aren't worth the trouble it takes to fix them."

"That's all very well," I said, unconvinced, "But some poor counting-clerk could get into trouble for it. A mistake like this, he might lose his post."

"I tell you what. I'll drop a word in Enan's ear, and if it turns out to be an error, he'll let me know. And I promise you, no one will lose their place. Will that satisfy you?"

171

It would have to. I could tell he was rather bored by the whole affair. I wouldn't need any of it, not just now. I swore to myself not to spend even a beggar's bit of it, and began pouring the coins back into the bag.

Cioren handed me a filled cup and said, "By the way, Tirais said you may as well dine with him again. I'm off for an evening of dull gossip with an old friend, and he thought you might be at a loose end, otherwise."

I nodded. "Whatever you say."

"Whatever I say? Where does this sudden docility spring from? And what does it portend?"

"Well, I agreed to abide by your rules, didn't I?"

"That would comfort me, if I didn't know you so well. Don't quarrel with His Highness tonight. He's had a long morning, and the afternoon looks to be worse. Enan's caught a young recruit thieving from his mates, and that sort of thing makes Tirais rather angry."

More well-made clothes appeared in my room that afternoon, along with an elderly woman who announced that the things I was already wearing fit too badly to be imagined. I spent the rest of my day being fitted in new tunic and trews, these ones in a dark green with more gold and red embroidery at the wrists and neck, and having the blue ones altered to suit the seamstress' exacting standards. It was dull work but my part was over fairly early, and I filled in the remainder of my time sharpening every blade I owned.

The trouble with that sort of work is that it becomes rather obsessive. I lost track of time while getting the edge on my new sword to an unnecessarily razor-sharp keenness, and what with one thing and another, was late arriving at the door to Tirais' quarters in the evening.

He was alone, which surprised me. I'd expected Gwyll, at least, or some of his other guards, or friends who lived year-round at Glaice. But the table was laid for two, only.

Tirais cut off my apology with a wave.

"Goddess knows, after a day like today, I've no appetite left. At least not for food. I could eat a roasted recruiting sergeant, perhaps."

I said nervously that if he'd prefer to be alone, I could quite understand it.

"Oh, give it a rest. I'm not angry, just tired. But here, what would your famous father do, in a case like this? They take on a boy out of the back of beyond, and just because he looks good on the parade-ground, they put him into a unit full of rich merchants' sons and local landholders' daughters, and expect him to not covet all those lovely extras they came equipped with. And the poor lad just didn't get along of course, so it makes for even more temptation. And now they all cry "Foul" on him."

"Well, but you can't let anyone steal," I said. "I mean, he must have known better. But Da would never put someone into a spot that way. Not without being sure he could handle it."

"Anyone with any intelligence would know better," he agreed. "Except the idiot who didn't, in this case. And now they want to turn him out, entirely."

"So what will you do?"

He smiled. "You'll like this. I'm sending him to Penvarron."

I laughed.

"I'm hoping it turns out to be a little less exciting choice this time, of course. But between Sorcha and Olwen, I think he'll settle down quite nicely. He isn't a fool. That's a nice tunic, by the way. I like the embroidery."

I swallowed. "Yes. I ought to have thanked you before."

"Not at all. You can't go to Kerris looking as if you'd just come off the battlefield. People would be frightened."

"It's very kind of you, all the same."

"Is it? It seems very little, after all. Come on, you must be starved."

We passed a most pleasant evening, by most people's standards. I don't remember what we talked about, really. Border tactics, I think, and we wandered into a kind of philosophic byway about the difference between practicing and actually going to war, but by the end of the meal, when we were leaning back in our chairs and finishing off the wine, I was no longer aware enough to do much but pretend to listen.

I was conscious of Tirais' presence, in a way I'd never been before. I could feel my heart's rhythm; I noticed that my hands were cold as ice; I had to remind myself every so often to keep breathing; and I felt a chilling, exultant fear curling in the pit of my stomach. I kept up my own end of the conversation with difficulty, and, as soon as I decently could, excused myself for the night, pleading fatigue. I walked back to my room in a dazed and unhappy state, but once there, lying in comforting darkness, I could not sleep.

Somewhere in between my anger and my loyalty, I had fallen in love with Tirais of Keraine.

Chapter 31

It was nothing. It was less than nothing. The real miracle would have been if I had remained unaffected by so many days spent in his company. I was an inexperienced provincial, and he was a good-looking and powerful man, and he had held the power of life and death over me, and he had chosen life.

It was also disaster, and I knew it. There was nothing in me that would make him even look twice. If he had been nice to me, well, that was in many ways a situation brought on by enforced proximity, his own good manners and a sense of shared experience. I understood, without any difficulty at all, that there was nothing in this for me, not the least shred of hope. The best I could hope for was his continued friendship.

But even as I reminded myself of all of this, my conscience and my survival instincts taking a stern line as I lay in the soft bed turning it over in my mind, another part of me was looking cheerfully towards the next few weeks. I had Kerris and Midwinter before me, and days of at least seeing Tirais, before someone decided I was well enough to be sent elsewhere. I could be content with that, I thought, hugging my knees. I would have to be; it would be all I would have.

The next day was spent getting ready for the rest of our journey. I had, in addition to the new tunics and trews, been given a couple of linen shirts and a new arming tunic. It was of padded cloth with leather reinforcing at the elbows, and fit a tad too snugly over my rib wrappings. My mail came back, mended and polished to perfection, and with a message from the garrison armourer to be more careful; according to Alun, he had been very impressed with its fine construction. Like most armourers, he hated to see good workmanship marred by the realities of use.

Packing was a bit of a chore. I now owned far more than I ever had before, and getting my new clothes to fit into my saddlebags was a struggle. Finally, I rolled the lighter cloak I'd been given in with my blankets, and forced the rest of my things to fit.

Cioren came in as I was cursing at the buckle straps, which refused to close over easily; they were stiff with constant exposure to the elements. He was carrying a bag that I recognized with a sinking heart. The old friend with the taste for dull gossip had, I surmised, been keeping it for him.

I hadn't wanted to think of that package at all. I had actually forgotten it. Now, lying in the growing heap of baggage on the floor, it brought all the horror of Penvarron back to me in a rush.

Curiously, the sight and my own reaction did me good. My discovery of my own heart had occupied me, intruded on me, monopolized my thoughts even without my awareness. The thought of that book, wrapped in its leather bag, drove these feelings deeply underground. I gave it a sour look, swore again at the recalcitrant buckle, and said, "Oh. That again." and sat back on my heels and looked at Cioren as if it were his fault that it existed.

"Well, it has to be dealt with. I couldn't just leave it lying around. It's much too dangerous for that. But it needn't concern you. Pretend it isn't there."

"Oh, sure."

"You might be right, at that. Still, you know, Keri, it isn't your problem. If you had any talent for this sort of thing, it might be different, but as it stands, it's nothing to you."

"Thank you. Just having it in the room makes it my problem, though, doesn't it? I mean, if you need me for anything, if I'm of any use at all, it's to help you protect this…thing."

"You're far too quick," he said. "Yes, all right, since you've brought it up, I will admit, it had crossed my mind that your skills might give me an edge, if, in fact, there's any outside danger. But likely there isn't - only you and I and Elowyn even know of its existence."

"Yes, and a couple of hundred Camrhyssi priests."

"We don't know that."

"Maybe you don't," I said, flatly, "But I'm less willing to believe it. That book *came* from Camrhys, Cioren. What are the chances they kept it a secret from every other priest in Evanion? I wouldn't wager a beggar's bit on that one. And they had Uln as their creature. Who's to say there aren't more traitors just waiting for a chance at it?"

He looked me over. I rocked back on my heels and gave it back, stare for stare. If there was anything I knew about, it was that secrets are almost never kept. It takes most people barely a week to divulge the down-and-dirty, even if it's sworn to on the most sacred of oaths. The chance to hint that you know more than your friends is simply too tempting, and from hints to hard fact is such a tiny step as to be unnoticeable. The funny part is, half the time people don't even realize they've spilled the grain onto the threshing floor, and that's where the real mischief begins.

The silence between us grew. I didn't look down. I wanted him to understand how I felt. I wanted him to know that he could count on me, but only if I knew what was going on. It's impossible to protect something unless you're given the information you need, and I had the feeling that Cioren was much too used to keeping his own counsel to understand that easily.

"Yes," he said, after a bit. "Yes, all right, I see your point. But if you and I are watchful, I can't think that there's any harm to come. After all, there aren't ten people in Keraine who would recognize it for what it is. Or could use it, if it comes to that."

"I'm not worried about that so much. I'm worried about - well, never mind. I hope you have a good hiding place for it at Kerris, though. And if you want to avail yourself of my skills, may I give some advice?"

"Are you likely to hold it back?"

I grinned. "No. Look you, we can't discuss it openly. In fact, we ought not speak of it at all, but I quite see that you must, at least occasionally. But we need to be absolutely sure that there's no one about when we do. Out in the open is best. In rooms, like this, you can't tell who's listening."

He raised one eyebrow; it spoke sardonic volumes. I wondered suddenly if Tirais had caught that trick from him.

"You seem to have grasped the essentials of court politics rather suddenly," he remarked.

"It's only sense. I don't know who might be interested in this, and begging your pardon, my lord, but you don't know for certain, either."

But here I was given to understand I'd gone far enough. Cioren stood, pointed out the relative differences in our age, experience and sophistication, with a rider that I try teaching my long-dead grandmother to suck eggs. He clinched his argument, if that's what it was, with a recommendation that I go down and see the healers and make sure I was fit to ride on the morrow.

In the morning, I felt much better. The Glaice healer, a very different man than old Donnach, had given me a thorough going-over, said my ribs were doing fine and prescribed an evil-tasting herb tea to help my bones knit. He was even more encouraging about my leg: I had been afraid that there was permanent damage, but he felt the healing was going well, better than expected, in fact. Apart from its obvious weakness and wasted condition, his opinion was that in a seven-day or so I might consider giving up my crutch, and advised very mild exercise.

"No drill, just yet," he cautioned. "But when you feel that you've gotten some strength back into it, then just a little every day shouldn't harm you. I'll make up a salve for it; the skin feels a little tight. And I'll tell Lord Cioren to keep a watch on you as well, I know you young soldiers. One word from a healer that your wounds aren't fatal, and you'll be back on the field doing full-kit drills, I shouldn't wonder."

I blushed; he had me pegged and no mistake. I promised, therefore, to keep myself on a short leash, training-wise, and hobbled back up to our rooms.

It was the custom of the royal family to break every journey on the North Road at Ys Tearch. It's a very holy place, everyone who travels that way stops. It's something bred into our bones at a very deep level, being the site of Keraine's greatest triumph and tragedy. That one episode in our history marked us in some indefinable way, and gave rise to innumerable songs and stories.

Four hundred of Keraine's best and bravest died at Ys Tearch, for the sake of honour and the ideals that Aenor espoused. They held the fortress against overwhelming odds, without hope of succor, simply because it was their duty to do so. They were, at the end, overrun and killed, down to the last scullery-boy, and in doing so, enabled Aenor to fight off the Camrhyssi in the south, and march north in time to meet the second force coming through the pass that Ys Tearch guarded. He would likely have lost this battle, for the last remnants of the true mages were with the invading army, but here was where the story became something more than just a sad soldier's tale.

Just as Aenor's force reached the crest of the road leading to the fortress, the Camrhyssi had been putting to death the last members of the garrison. At this moment, according to those who witnessed this, the whole mountain above Ys Tearch gave way. Landslides do happen, but this was something much more majestic. It was said that the sky darkened at high summer noon, that the air became filled with thunder, and that the Goddess herself appeared, lifted up her hands and cried out in lamentation, and then, as she faded from view, an entire mountain collapsed, destroying all of the invaders not yet inside the walls, and burying a full quarter of the castle as well. The Mother of All had chosen a side, apparently, and it wasn't Camrhys'.

The landslide closed the pass. It was a huge thing, a frightening display, massive evidence of the power of the Goddess, and undoubtedly awe-inspiring.

It's also the subject of a long and very famous poem, recited in its entirety every Summer's Turning, the bane of every child forced to learn at least parts of it with which to impress their parents' friends around the hearth. One of my brothers was given the whole of it to learn after some youthful indiscretion, and due to his inability to commit it to memory without constant practice, I had, by the time I was six, learnt it as well. The lot of us spent a whole summer sepulchrally intoning "For an oath once sworn…" at every opportunity, until my father gave us a lecture on blasphemy and threatened us with dire consequences to boot.

Part of his ire was raised by the accepted belief that one of our forebears was among those who died defending Keraine, although by now nearly every family in the country could probably have said the same. There's no way of knowing, at this point, who was actually there, and as my mother once said in a moment of malice, everyone who found it politically useful seemed to have had an ancestor who died there.

Still, there are apparently some things that are just too sacred, and Ys Tearch was one of them.

It was less than a day's ride to the hostelry that had replaced the fortress. The castle itself lay higher up, tended by a priest sent from Braide, but a few miles below, in a sheltered valley, you could rest your horses, and find food and beds. It was free, having garnered many an endowment by wealthy patrons, as well as a sizable yearly gift from the Royal House, for the travelers who came in an unending procession just to see this place of destruction and sorrow that had given us a kingdom.

My window, like most of those commandeered by the Prince's party, looked east, up towards the silhouette of Ys Tearch against the granite skyline. It was early yet, midafternoon. One of the stable-girls had said it took mere minutes to ride up the track. In summer, they ran a wagon up on a regular basis, carrying pilgrims to see what remained of the keep.

Even from a distance, Ys Tearch looked hauntingly familiar, which was no surprise. The general plan was repeated, all over Keraine, in nearly every stronghold whose original construction dated from before the Breaking, Orliegh among them. A thick curtain wall, with towers placed at regular intervals radiating from a single main gate, enclosing a second wall, which was the castle proper. At Ys Tearch there were five towers inside, but only three were visible, and one was merely a toothy projection into the sky. There would have been two inner gates, and the towers would have been connected by long hallways built into the walls, with switchbacks, narrow stairwells and deadends placed at strategic intervals. Undamaged, it would have been an incredibly hard place to take; you could pick off your invaders one by one as they fought to take each square inch of the place.

" 'Ah, for those who linger here, Beneath these sorrow'd fields' "

" 'An oath once sworn shall always be, Impossible to yield.' " I said, without turning.

Tirais laughed. "Stirring stuff, if one didn't have to hear it so damned often. I came to ask if you'd a mind to go up. I always do, they expect it."

"I dare not miss it. My father would be appalled."

"Come on then. There's just time enough, and you'll want to see the whole of it, as it's your first visit."

Chapter 32

It was a small party that rode up the rough trail over the rubble to Ys Tearch, just Tirais, myself, Cioren and Gwyll, who said he felt obliged to pay his respects now that he knew something of what the defenders of Keraine had faced, five hundred years ago.

The track had been cleared through the bare devastation; nothing had ever grown over the enormous boulders that had destroyed the pass. They had constructed a simple gatehouse out of the local pines growing in the valley below, to house the priest who tended the shrine, and the members of the Queen's own guards who had been seconded there with him.

The four who had been sent to look after Ys Tearch might have been chosen especially for their ability to inspire a friendly impression. They were well set-up young warriors, openly cheerful and lighthearted.

The priest was a grim counterpoint to this jolly greeting party. He was extremely tall and austere, imposing a severe sense of the solemnity of our surroundings. We were led first to the memorial stones erected for the heroes and then given a dry and pious lecture on the nature of the Goddess' retribution, consisting mainly of propaganda regarding the iniquities of our mage-ridden ancestors, as well as a speedy overview of the castle's layout, before being allowed to wander freely among the ruins.

My instincts hadn't led me astray. I could have led us around blindfolded in Ys Tearch, it was so like Orliegh, although much larger. Parts had also been blocked off, due apparently to a distressing tendency for whole rooms to collapse without warning. Heavy ropes prevented us from entering the lower floors of one of the main towers, and the upper hallways leading into it were similarly blockaded.

The ancients had never built purely for utility. Everywhere I turned I saw evidence of their love of beauty; carved stone lintels, columns erected for sheer visual pleasure, and tiled floors one hardly liked to walk upon, so lovely were the designs. I soaked it up. When I went home some day, I would be able to show Da I hadn't wasted my time here, nor forgotten my family's honour entirely.

After a couple of glasses, though, the sights began to pall. There is only so much magnificence you can take, and the atmosphere of Ys Tearch, so oppressively holy and moral, overpowered you eventually. The crisp winter air began to feel a bit close and stingy. I couldn't envy those guards, stuck up here all the year long, with a priest with such an obvious taste for the darker, more implacable vision of the Goddess.

Tirais sensed my growing boredom; it must have been a relief. He'd been coming here for his entire life and for him it was merely another duty in an existence hedged at every turn by similar tasks. When I mentioned supper, he pounced with eagerness, and began leading us towards the shrine just inside the ruined walls.

We bought candles and lit them, and said the ritual promise of faith to the dead. The guards were gone; there was a warm glow from the casement window of the gatehouse and the smell of woodsmoke in the air, and the priest nodded without interest as we turned to go.

I forgot my troublesome ribs in my haste to mount, and they took their revenge. The sudden violent twinge caused my foot to slip in the stirrup, and Banshee retaliated for my clumsiness by shying abruptly and turning back towards the gatehouse.

The priest was still standing near the doorway, staring at Tirais' back, with a look of such blinding hatred that I nearly dropped the reins. A moment later, I would have sworn I'd been mistaken, his face was bland and impassive, and as I hauled myself into the saddle, he raised his hand in farewell.

We rode down to the hostel in silence. I couldn't understand the look, and I convinced myself, by the time I sat down to another rich and delicious meal, that I had imagined it.

Chapter 33

I had been in Kerris for nearly two days before I saw Queen Elowyn, or anybody else for that matter.

We arrived late, although by the time I reached my room in the palace and fell fully clothed into my bed, I felt as if I'd been arriving in Kerris for nearly my whole life.

The city crept up on you as you approached. It lay inland, at the point on the River Braide where it became passable for water traffic as the current flowed north to the sea. Consequently it wasn't walled and there was no clear place where you could say "Oh. This is where it begins." The farms and villages just grew closer and closer together until you found yourself in the thick of it, hemmed into narrow, crowded streets and surrounded by a wealth of exciting and exotic sights and smells. It was noisy, too; I thought I had never seen so many people crammed into one place in my life, and they all seemed to be shouting at each other. Fortunately for me, Banshee and I had been near the centre of the column and apart from keeping her tightly reined in and under control, I had nothing to stop me from soaking in the scene. Even after dark, the streets were brightly lit and full of life. I fell into a kind of stupor after a while, drunk on too many new sensations.

I slept nearly into the evening of the following day and woke with a start when Cioren came in to say that, for the sake of my health, I ought to eat something, at least. He stayed to watch me eat, then sent me back to my bed with a warning that I would be received by Her Majesty in the morning.

It was full royal court. I had worn the green tunic, it being the grandest I owned, and left all my blades off; it's considered a little rude to enter a throne room armed.

The Queen stood upon a black marble dais, in front of a gleaming throne. Tirais stood beside her, and down the length of that very long room was crowded every noble and peer of the realm available, and anyone else who could squeeze in. I saw only an endless sea of faces, none familiar, as I limped along at Cioren's side. I had left my crutch behind, it seemed the least my pride could manage was that walk without a rough-hewn stick to bolster me.

Elowyn came down the steps part way. I heard Cioren introduce me, as though our meeting at Glaice had never been. The Queen replied graciously, taking my hands in hers, and thanking me for my service to the realm. Then we moved off, the heralds already announcing some other business, and I saw, briefly, Baron Gallerain's face in the crowd about the throne. To my surprise, he smiled and nodded, quite affably, before returning his attention to more important matters.

All is forgiven, I though, confused but somewhat relieved, but before I could absorb the thought entirely, the court was surging towards the doors and I was being herded gently to the side. A servant lifted one of the huge tapestries to reveal another, smaller doorway, and I followed the others through, into the Queen's Council Chamber.

Gwyll and the other royal guards had collected to one side. I fell in with them, there really wasn't anywhere else that seemed right. The Queen's Council were arranging themselves behind chairs around the long table, including Cioren, and there were some subdued comments and questions drifting about. Then Elowyn and Tirais entered, there was a moment of stiff formality, the Council was opened, and they all sat down.

Tirais had a chair slightly off to his mother's side; as the heir, he was required to attend, but at the same time he had no actual function or power in this room, save what the Queen gave him. In this particular instance, he had a report to give, once Cioren had outlined the general state of affairs at Penvarron. Before he could do so, however, Baron Gallerain leaned over and whispered something to Elowyn, who turned and beckoned a servant over. Moments later, benches were being brought, and Gwyll and I were given permission to sit.

Sitting or standing, court manners obtained. Throughout my childhood, my mother had drilled me in them, ignoring my protests that I was a soldier and would never be required to use any of the courtly manners and graces or the complex skills she insisted I learn. It was quite lowering to think that she had been right, after all, in her firm belief that this training would come in handy. I was able to arrange myself fairly gracefully on the bench, relax my hands into a position that allowed for comfort, and assume a look of spurious interest in the long and dull rendering of what had transpired at Penvarron, and the inevitable questions and discussions that followed. I surmised that since I had been so intimately concerned, I was there as a witness, perhaps, should the need arise, and kept half an ear on the proceedings, while simultaneously letting my mind wander where it liked.

Cioren was outlining the events of the night Camrhys invaded Penvarron, although it sounded, from his perfunctory tone, that everyone present had heard at least a version of this before, and he kept it quite general. My name was mentioned, and a couple of faces turned to glance my way, then back to Cioren as he moved quickly on to the arrival of Glaice's forces and the discovery of the bodies along the road south.

The true courtly grace is to sit or stand through all this sort of thing without any fidgeting, which looks bad, should anyone catch you at it. Tirais, at least, had been doing it all his life, but I noticed out of the corner of my eye that he kept glancing at me, as if he expected me to scratch and shift like some country yob at a puppet show. Cioren was describing the state of the bodies found at Penvarron, not very accurately, I thought, and I began to consider what kinds of gifts I could buy for my family, seeing as how Kerris seemed to lack no end of things to buy.

I hadn't liked to press Cioren on the subject of my overpayment, but he had mentioned, on our last morning at Glaice, that Enan had found no discrepancies, and no-one was complaining they'd been shortchanged, so I had to accept that I had a lot of money, and nothing much to spend it on. It was late, but even late gifts at Midwinter would be appreciated.

Most of my family would be easy, I mused, as I heard Tirais begin giving a short speech on the state of Penvarron's garrison. My mother would be delighted by some of the rare and unfamiliar spices I had glimpsed on the stalls we'd passed in the night, and my brother Dion's second child had been just learning to toddle when I'd left; I could easily find a painted toy sword for her.

Cioren had taken up the trickier part of the tale now, dealing with the nature of what had haunted the halls of Penvarron. I let the words wash over me. It was done with, for me.

The hardest person to buy for, I decided, would be my sister Cait. She had made what Orliegh considered to be the match of the century, one of the north's most powerful lords, the Baron of Tor Gallis, having fallen for her after one encounter at a fair, last Summer's Turning but one. The general opinion of the world was that it was the greatest good fortune, and, simultaneously, no more than her due. Cait was beautiful, lively, and graceful, and also had the knack of making everyone around her feel more brilliant, better looking and altogether more joyous themselves. Argallen's family had been a little dubious, since Orliegh was rather beneath them, but by the end of the betrothal feast, they had become, to a man and woman, her devoted and adoring slaves.

It would have to be, I thought, as Cioren droned on about demonic presence, something impossible frivolous, something that would never make it as far as a fair in Dungarrow. Argallen could buy her anything she needed or wanted, in the normal course of events, but somewhere in the streets of Kerris at Midwinter, there must be something that she would love, something she would never have known she wanted until she laid eyes on it.

They were getting to the end now. My name got mentioned again. I didn't need to be listening to catch it, every head at the table swiveled to stare at me as Cioren began to describe that last desperate encounter with Eater. I managed a look of modest courage, figuring that I might as well appear in the best light I could. My eventual placement in a decent post might depend on these people's opinion. There was no point in wasting the moment.

Cioren made no mention of my angry unwillingness to be the sacrificial offering in that dreadful moment, or of my subsequent desire to murder both him and the heir to the throne. He gave a purely factual account, except that he had seen more of it than I had, and so was able to spice things up with a lot of horrifying details that made me look like a cross between an avenging spirit sent from on high and Bronwyn the Brave.

Hog-piss, I thought, but he was trying, I supposed, to do me a good turn. I allowed myself an expression of uncomfortable distaste, which was honestly how I felt anyway, and tried to look decently humble and unassuming. No one likes as braggart.

They all looked shocked and admiring. They hadn't had time to consider what an uncomfortable thing it would be to have a common soldier as their savior yet. All but one, a strong-faced priestess of the Mother, who grasped that aspect immediately, and looked briefly as if she would have liked to have strangled me. It would have been a coup if the Royal House had had to call upon the Goddess' servants to get them out of a fix.

They'd all end by hating me, I thought, and wished that Cioren and Tirais weren't laying it on quite so thick. I would have to simmer this down and save everybody's pride over it, else I'd make some enemies.

"It seems the realm owes you our thanks yet again, Lady Keridwen." Baron Gallerain's voice held not a trace of sarcasm. My father had once said that if you wanted to be a courtier, you had to cultivate an adaptable memory. I began to see what he meant.

"Not at all," I said. "I was glad to do my duty."

"But to have placed yourselves in so much danger," said the Queen. She looked at Gwyll and I, at our obviously battered condition. "We must be grateful to all of you."

"Your Majesty, all of us did only what we are sworn to do. And truly, it wasn't so much. Anyone who found themselves there would have done the same. It was Lord Cioren's abilities that did the real work, anyway. I was merely a diversion. A distraction, almost." There. That should shift the burden nicely.

It did, for the priestess at least. She bent her gimlet eyes on Cioren and said, "Ah, yes. How fortunate that you happen to live so close to the - er - scene of the crime, so to speak. We must all be grateful to Lord Cioren."

My flesh crawled. In a heartbeat, she had transferred everyone's attention from me, all right, to Cioren, and she made it sound as though he was, in some unspecified way, responsible for the demon arriving in our midst to begin with.

Cioren looked ever so slightly pained. "Indeed, but I knew nothing of what had transpired until Penvarron informed me of it. And after that, naturally, I did whatever was in my power to give aid."

No one questioned the form that his aid had taken, I noticed. The idea that there were powerful mages wandering about unguided by the Goddess was apparently common knowledge here, not worth mentioning. They might not like it; the priestess certainly didn't, but her ire seemed to be more about the lack of control than the existence of magic.

"Still, it seems to me that you might have saved many lives by seeking that aid from the holy ones in the area."

"Well, we might have, Dalriega, if we'd known what we faced, from the start. At the beginning, it seemed no more than an attempt by Camrhys to gain a foothold in the south. Once we knew for certain what we had on our hands, it was too late."

They began wrangling over who knew what when at that point and I lost interest. I was interested, though, to discover that quite to the contrary of my naïve beliefs, everyone connected to the affair seemed to wish to disavow any real responsibility or even close involvement in it all. Unlike the nobles in ballads, who were only too ready to take charge, the people around this table were busy trying to find some blame to attach to someone, somewhere. Lord Dunvarry, who was responsible for the defense of the lands lying just north of the River Varre, seemed especially eager to ally himself with Priestess Dalriega in finding a way to pin the whole affair on Cioren.

The argument had shifted. Balked of their prey, since Tirais and Elowyn were in no way disposed to allow the blame to be attached to Cioren, the Council started nitpicking over whose decision it had been to allow Penvarron to degenerate into a force that couldn't have fought off a cold, let alone an invasion. Baron Gallerain finally pointed out that since the slide into uselessness had been started by Elowyn's grandfather, it was hardly fruitful to quarrel over it now, and left it to the Queen to assert that in fact, Penvarron's much-maligned forces had done pretty well.

It all took an unconscionably long time. Those of us not on the Council were left to sit and stand, impersonating furniture, until Queen Elowyn cut the debate short by summing up the problem, designating several people to deal with the smaller questions that had arisen, a couple of others to devise defense plans, and dismissed them with an injunction to keep their mouths shut. She said it all more politely than that, of course, and left them all with the feeling they had actually been consulted, and that they were useful, which wasn't in fact the truth. Vital bits had been neatly left out, and none of the duties assigned served any real purpose that I could see, but they all left quite satisfied, even Dalriega.

I trailed across the yard in Cioren's wake, nursing my aching leg. The morning had been long, and my attempt to do without my crutch even briefly had taken its toll, but after two days of sleep, my body was restless with the need to move. When asked what I wished to do, I'd said that a visit to the stables to check on Banshee wouldn't come amiss. I felt a little guilty. She was mine; I ought to exhibit some interest in her. In any case, she might well have killed a stablehand by now, if her temper hadn't been soothed.

"Cioren, I'm sorry. About the meeting, I mean. I didn't intend for them to go after you like that."

"What, that? Don't give it another thought."

"Yes, but I truly only meant to, well, stop them from thinking about, well…"

"You wanted them to stop thinking about you. I understand perfectly. Don't worry, they would have gone after me of their own accord, sooner or later."

"But why? It can't be what you did, they all seemed to take that part quite well. And Priestess Dalriega really jumped on it, as if she was only waiting for her chance."

"Of course she did," he said, patiently. "The holy ones don't like me at all, which is understandable, although in Dalriega's case it may well have been personal."

"Yes, but - "

"Keridwen, leave it. You know why the priesthood doesn't like unbound talents roaming about. In the main, I agree with them. Look at what Uln managed to do."

"Well, yes. But still, you're on the Council. They must know you aren't like that."

"It makes everyone nervous. Confess it, it makes you nervous."

"Not so much, anymore. And they have no reason to be nervous right now, do they? Not," I had to slow down and phrase this carefully, "not knowing what they do."

We were halfway across the open cobbles. Cioren stopped.

"Your bootlace is coming untied," he said.

"No, I'm fine."

"I disagree. Your lace is definitely loose." His tone was amused. I must have looked mystified. "Retie it, Keri," he said, gently.

I caught on, finally, and knelt awkwardly on the stone, and began to untie and pretend to tighten my laces.

"You should know, I've found a place for our - er - little problem. Since I surmise that's what we're discussing."

"Ah," I said.

He told me where. I began to chuckle; it was arrogant to the point of insolence, that "hiding place", and it would probably serve quite well. I retied my bootlace, and stood.

"Yes, that'll do. Come on, then."

We turned down the wide alley to the stables.

"Anyway," I said, "it explains that priest at Ys Tearch."

"Explains what about him?"

"The way he looked. When we were leaving, he looked so angry. I thought it was Tirais he was staring at, but you were right beside. It must have been you he was glaring at."

Chapter 34

In the morning, I made my way through the yard and past the stable to the practice-ground Cioren had pointed out to me after our visit to Banshee. She had not been delighted to see me, of course; she had glared at me with evil intent, eating the sugar I'd brought her while making two attempts to bite me. The stablefolk were avoiding her, and no one would ride her. She wouldn't allow anyone near enough to saddle her anyway, so they just turned her out into the paddock at regular intervals, and kept their distance.

The rest of the day was dull. I heard from a servant that Lord Gervase had arrived, with his wife and daughter, but I kept to my room, alternately eating and sleeping.

In the chilly dawn, not very many people had gotten up for early practice, it seemed, although I knew that there were likely several other practice yards in a place this size. I did some stretches, trying to figure out just what my body was going to allow me to do, then went across to a covered shed and chose a blunted wooden sword and a very light shield.

Along one side of the yard, there were a number of heavy posts driven into the ground at spaced intervals, to use for training. I chose one at random, and started with the simplest of static drills I could remember. It had been a long time since I had used this sort of drill. My father didn't hold with too much practice that didn't demand that you face the risk of being hit back. He said it encouraged bad habits.

My ribs didn't allow for me to move my shield overmuch, though, and the thought of being hit there wasn't enticing. I concentrated on throwing shots; the shield was only because it's unwise to train too much without it. You risk forgetfulness becoming ingrained, and that can get you killed.

I couldn't move around much, either, because of my leg, which further limited me. Still, it felt good to be doing something so familiar. I hadn't gone so long without practicing since I was five, as near as I could remember, barring a couple of childhood ailments that had kept me housebound for any length of time.

There were more people on the field when I stopped to take a break, midway through. Gervase was there; he nodded and called out a greeting as he passed, and there was a young boy doing drills on the post farthest from me. I went back to running through basic throws until my leg told me that another minute of this and I'd be regretting I'd gotten out of bed at all.

Limping over to a stone bench near the open ground, I saw that Gervase was doing "hold the field" with a couple of younger men. He had been at it awhile, by the looks of things. All three of his opponents were red-faced with the effort of fighting him over and over again, while Gervase himself was battering them in turn without much exertion.

They were giving him his range; that was the problem. I watched as each of them stepped up to fight. Obviously nervous now and unwilling to press him, they allowed Gervase to set the distance. His arms being so much longer, and the fact that he favoured a sword that extended his killing zone out past where they could ever hope to land any effective blows meant that they flailed away uselessly until Gervase saw an opening he wanted and took it. The trick is to never allow your opponent that kind of an edge. You have to close. It's risky, but I could see that with another two steps they would have nullified his advantage and indeed, taken out his own weapon as a threat. If he couldn't swing through that wide arc, his sword would be almost useless.

"They say you're from the north."

I turned. The boy who'd been running drill on the farther post had come up to stand beside me by the bench.

"You must be Prince Connor," I said.

"Yes. How did you know?"

"You look very like your mother," I said, gently. It was true. I would have guessed his parentage anywhere.

"Did you know her?" His voice was wistful. "No-one speaks of her."

"I met her twice."

If I had wanted or needed a reminder of what damage an unrequited love run wild could do, what people could do to each other and a kingdom in the name of love, the proof stood here, in the person of a ten-year-old boy on a practice-ground at dawn. And his history was my own, in a small way, or at least, Orliegh's.

Orliegh and the rest of Dungarrow hadn't always been so tightly bound to Keraine. For most of our history, we'd been a kind of independent duchy, part of the kingdom in a nominal sense alone. And then, being so close to Braide and the centre of religious authority, Dungarrow had been a secular power in theory only. Gradually, the Dukes of Dungarrow had wrested control of their domain from the priesthood, but the experience had weakened their ties to Keraine, not strengthened them. There had been an uneasy alliance, a fealty that rested on the rulers of Keraine not asking for more than a formal adherence to that loyalty. The north, having thrown off the rule of priests, had been staunchly independent, and tried to walk a road of neutrality where Camrhys was concerned. Occasionally, forces out of the east had used our southern passes to launch raids into Keraine, and it had been to Dungarrow's advantage to turn a blind eye to it. So long as the raids caused few serious problems in Keraine and no damage to Dungarrow, it was expedient.

Elowyn's father had been the first to change the precarious balance. He had seen that Camrhys was growing stronger, and sought to bond Dungarrow ever closer to Keraine. My own father had gone south, to be raised, along with so many other lords' sons from the north, as a King's squire. It's a form of hostage taking, of course: who would counsel their overlord to allow Keraine's constant harassment when their own heirs risked being killed in the conflict? And it engendered stronger attachment southwards. Even Duke Einon had felt it; although he still would not patrol the passes, he stopped giving even tacit approval to Camrhys' use of them.

But when I was seven, rumors began circulating that Camrhys was massing for a real attack. Elowyn, newly widowed and none too secure on her throne, simply could not afford the risk of a second force slipping down from the north and surprising her rear-guard. She would have done anything, paid any price, to bring Dungarrow firmly under the kingdom's control, once and for all.

The duke's price was high, and Elowyn's daughter was the one who paid it.

He had seen her at some festival or fair. She was only fourteen, but beautiful even then, and although the queen had two children and had yet to name her heir, the smart money was on Merowyn. She was lovely, intelligent, and already known for her grace and wit. It only seemed logical that she should marry a lord with power and wealth, whose loyalty was so desperately needed.

The wedding-party stopped at Orliegh on their way north. It was a great honour, and especially exciting for me. As my father's squire, I was set to serve her, running small errands and such. She was lovely to look at, and full of laughter, and kind to a small girl, so I quite naturally fell under her spell. I spent two days being tongue-tied and shy, and utterly in awe of so much magnificence.

What my elders thought of a young and happy girl marrying a dour old man who had already raised two illegitimate boys to manhood, or what Merowyn herself thought of her fate, was never discussed. She had been raised knowing it might come to this and she knew her duty. I think she went to her destiny with a whole heart, ready to be pleased and prepared to be loyal at least.

What happened after was the stuff that bards love, although they prefer it well aged and decently distanced. No-one has yet made a story of that tragedy, though are some songs for Merowyn; sad and plaintive laments, with never a true name mentioned in them, and never sung in the halls of the great. It's still too raw, too hurtful, to call it legend and be done with it.

I saw the princess one more time, when she came south with her infant son, to meet his grandmother. She was older by only a year or so, but she seemed less lighthearted, even to me. She was still lovely, and her smile was still capable of breaking hearts, but she was different. Tired, perhaps, since her lying-in was only a few weeks in the past, but also less forthcoming, as if she'd learned a hard lesson about keeping her own counsel. She kept to her own rooms this time, and talked at length with my mother, soft, whispered confidences that later memory brought my mother to tears. I was kept away for the most part, but on the second evening, after I'd brought her some wine, she let me stay, while she sang her child to sleep.

She took a different route home to Dungarrow Castle, and I was set to learn a new kind of drill soon after. We heard little enough out of Dungarrow, or else it wasn't fit for a child's ears, and I forgot about her, as children will.

It was almost four years before things came to a head. Camrhys never did attack, at least not in force, but Merowyn's marriage served its purpose. The north was no longer an independent factor in Keraine's deliberations, and lesser holdings like ours were no longer torn between two loyalties. Merowyn would almost certainly be queen after her mother, and Duke Einon now had a strong reason to cleave to Keraine. His son would rule both Dungarrow and Keraine, in time. The borders were strengthened, and Camrhys lost easy routes to raiding rich lands in the south.

The end was as ugly as anything out of a bard's tale. I've never known much beyond the barest of bare bones, and I doubt anyone else living does either, but it appeared that Einon became increasing jealous of his wife. He accused her constantly of seeking to destroy him, of some secret plot with Keraine, of unspecified infidelities.

The really stupid thing, my mother always said afterward, was that Einon actually did love Merowyn. But he was a hard man, and his idea of love was bound up, for him, with notions of possession. Walled up in a cold, grim fortress lashed endlessly by the sea, cooped up for months on end with a young wife whose own position far outstripped his, and with his two older sons now dispossessed by the infant Connor, well, you could imagine the possibilities.

And one night, apparently enraged by drink and rumors that Merowyn had been carrying on a clandestine affair with his eldest son, Einon went on a bloody spree, beat his young wife, then murdered her, and in a fit of either madness or remorse, turned his blade on himself. All, apparently, in full view of his four-year-old child.

Einon's sons wasted no time. They understood that possession is nine parts of the law, and took Connor prisoner. They called it "protection" of course, but the simple fact was that until Connor's birth, Einon's sons had been entitled to equal rights upon their father's death. But with Connor's arrival, they had nothing save what Einon chose to give them. Seizing their moment, both men prepared to fight the local lords for control of Dungarrow.

I don't know how my father got the news so soon. He came in one night, shocked and angry, and was gone before dawn, riding out to every lord he knew. It was Orliegh's loyalty to Keraine that saved Connor, and Dungarrow: my father sent riders south to the queen and mobilized the entire north, in less than a seven-day.

Within another week, it was over. Einon's sons had not had the wit to understand that the lords would not meekly submit to Connor's dispossession or murder, or that Elowyn would not bargain over her grandson's body. Prince Tirais, now sixteen and in command of his own troops, had ridden into Dungarrow and rescued his nephew, while the lords of the north hunted down and killed Einon's sons.

It was this that sealed my father's reputation, in a way. He said afterwards that Einon had been a good lord to him, fair enough, if a little hard, but never asking that he divide his loyalties to his overlord and his queen. He would have accepted either of the duke's older sons as lord, if Einon had not married, but he said that he owed nothing to a pair of greedy bastards who used a child to gain what they had no right to.

And it's a tribute to my father's principles that no one, not even the servants, ever signaled, by word or look, that my father might have received any preferment in recompense for his loyalty to the queen. It occurred to none of us to suggest that he might have expected some new lands, or an abatement of taxes, or reward of any kind. If there were more cynical minds in Orliegh, they at least knew not to voice their thoughts.

I wept for Merowyn. I didn't understand it; I never had; how people could destroy something so beautiful, in the name of love. But I could understand it now. I could see, before my eyes, what the cost could be, too: a ten-year-old boy, too solemn and serious for his age, scarred by what he'd seen and trying still, after six years, to put a face to his sorrow.

I came back to the present with a heavy heart.

"She was beautiful," I said. "And she loved you. She sang you to sleep, in my mother's room at Orliegh."

"Orliegh," said Connor, slowly. "I know your father, then. He gave me a belt, last year, for my name-day. It's got a place for my sword, and a buckle made like a stag."

"Does it fit?"

"No, but he said I'd grow into it."

"He always does that," I said, grinning. "I've never gotten a gift I didn't have to wait two years to use."

He grinned back, squatting onto his heels in the dirt. "It's pretty, though, and it nearly fits. Next spring, at least that's what Grandmother thinks. I keep growing."

Gervase called him over, just then. I settled back onto the bench and watched him go two difficult bouts with a man who could have probably held off a small army single-handed. Connor, having little else to go on, made the same mistake as the three exhausted adults had, but for him the problem was compounded. At his size, he couldn't hit Gervase at all, and only his own quickness made the attempts last more than a few seconds.

Connor came back to the side, a little dejected, while Gervase took on all three of the older fighters at once. The prince was struggling with his shield strap, which was a little looser than is prudent. You don't want it slipping around; it's distracting even when it isn't lethal.

I knelt to help him; the buckle was hard to reach one-handed.

"Connor," I said. "You can't fight him like that. He's got far too much reach. Try, next time, to get your shield over you, and step in. Then stick your sword up under his shield and push, really hard. It's timing. You'll have to be quick."

He was listening hard, and his face was serious. He nodded.

"It may not work," I warned, as he lifted his shield back into position. "But it's worth a try."

He nodded again. Gervase had gotten two of his opponents and was merely playing with his third. We waited until they'd done and the man stepped away, breathing hard, and Connor moved back out onto the field.

He executed the move perfectly, having had the benefit of good training from his earliest days with a sword. He waited, fending his attacker off, till Gervase tried an overhand shot, then stepped neatly to his right, pushing his shield completely over his head. At the same moment, he hopped forward smartly

194

and stuck his wooden blade hard upwards, catching poor Gervase all unawares in the guts. I heard the gasp of surprise, and then Gervase called out, "Good shot, Your Grace!"

Connor danced back and let out a whoop of triumph. He had a right to be happy; three grown men hadn't landed anything so solid on the Lord Steward of Fairbridge in the last half-glass.

"Nicely done," Gervase said, much amused. "Now, don't gloat, Your Grace. It isn't polite."

"You're dead," Connor said, firmly.

"Aye, that I am."

"So, I don't need to listen to you, do I?"

Gervase laughed. "I'll have to watch you, from now on. It was well done, Connor." He looked across at me. "A trick of your father's, I suppose?"

I shook my head. I'd figured that one out myself, when I'd been about Connor's age. It hadn't been that long since I'd been the smallest, in a family where prowess with weapons was assumed. I could still remember how frustrating it had been, always being beaten. In those circumstances, you find a way to win, at least some of the time, or spend your life being trounced regularly by everyone in turn.

Chapter 35

Late in the day, I presented myself in the huge banqueting hall, as per Cioren's instructions. The Queen dined in state every evening during Midwinter, although she didn't stay late until the last few nights.

The length of the room was banked with tables, three deep, running parallel with the walls and looking out into the open space for the entertainers in the centre. At the top of the hall, a platform had been erected, with a long table for the highest in the land. Below it, facing the same way, was another table, for less exalted but still honoured guests and my seat lay there. It was far above my general station in life; my father would not have gotten so good a place.

They'd put me at an end, next to Lady Aileen, Gervase's wife. It seemed a little tactless, when four months ago I'd been part of a force that sought to kill her husband, but either she was ignorant of my perfidy or else had decided to overlook it; she introduced herself courteously, and we stood to await the royal arrival.

A pair of side doors opened. There was a blaring of hunting horns, noisy in that echoing space and we watched as the Queen, followed by most of the Council, entered. Standing below, I was aware of a swirl of brilliant colour and the gleam of jewels in the torchlight. I saw Cioren chatting easily with Dalriega, of all people, and I recognized Gervase, but just behind the Queen came Tirais, and, despite my best intentions and strongest resolve, I noticed little else of who was there.

The evening lived up to my expectations, which were mixed, to say the least. The moment those at the table above sat down, servants appeared with the first courses, and seconds later the musicians struck up a tune to accompany some dancers. I ate my soup and watched as they turned, swaying and clapping, around the hall. Behind me I heard the murmur of conversation from the royal party.

The dance ended and we were served with dishes of smoked fresh water fish. I looked down the hall and saw, to my surprise, a familiar face. Emlyn of Gorsedd met my eyes and lifted his goblet in silent toast, smiling.

It was unnerving. My family had conducted a bloody feud with Gorsedd for over a hundred years, begun over far less than Lady Aileen could hold against me, and although the two families no longer slew each other on sight, these feelings die hard in the north. Duke Einon had ended the killing, but Orliegh did not speak to Gorsedd; I had been warned repeatedly to avoid contact with Emlyn, who was only a year or so older than I was. His father had died of a

196

fever, ages ago, and Emlyn had once been scouted as a potential husband for me, to Orliegh's horror.

I knew nothing against him, really. By all accounts he was a pleasant young man who tended his lands and had wed a local girl in the end, busying himself with his children and his flocks. I would, I thought, have to get used to seeing people like Emlyn and learn to be courteous in public. I was a long way from home. I lifted my own goblet in response, and turned to answer a gentle query from Aileen about my wounds.

Gervase's lady was dressed in the fashions that the ladies of the court had recently adopted; her dress was tightly laced, and heavily embroidered at the neck, wrists and hem, and the sleeves were cut to show the fine linen chemise underneath. Her hair was caught up under a jeweled cap in a complicated style involving intricate braids and tiny curls. It must have taken her hours to prepare, even with help.

Despite her cultivated style and formal manners, she was an excellent dinner companion. She obligingly pointed out the powerful and well-known figures, some of whom had figured in Cioren's more amusing recollections of disreputable behavior, and her questions on the state of my health revealed that for all her constraining clothes, she knew a lot about bodily damage. She remarked that I seemed to be healing quickly, more quickly than she would have expected.

"So the healers at Glaice seemed to think." I said. "But it's slow going from my point of view."

"Don't rush it." She was distracted momentarily by an acquaintance across the hall, who was waving enthusiastically. "Odious man. Does he think I'm going to yell out a greeting in front of the entire court?"

I was saved from venturing an opinion by the entrance of a troupe of acrobats, who began tossing each other around the hall like so many blown-up pigs' bladders. Someone refilled my wine-cup.

There was a lull, after the acrobats, and a serving of roast goose in a sweet sauce. People had begun moving around, visiting each other from table to table to exchange gossip. Aileen and I settled down to discuss the harvest, which seemed a safe enough topic, as long as we didn't get too specific. What Uln's invasion had done to Fairbridge's crops, I didn't want to know. But we stuck firmly to generalities: the prices of barley, the state of the wool trade. To be polite, I asked about her daughter; mothers love to talk about their children.

197

The hall grew noisier, as more people got up and strolled about, greeting old friends and enemies with cries of surprise or joy. I could understand why Elowyn didn't spend long hours in this setting until she had to. Courtesy demanded that Aileen speak at least occasionally to her right-hand neighbour, so eventually, when we'd exhausted the amusing anecdotes about a three-year-old girl with an appetite for injudicious wandering and no sense of self-preservation, I was left to toy with the food still in front of me and nurse my wine.

I was longing for this ordeal to end. Between the wine, which was unwatered and far too sweet, the dizzying array of rich food set before us, and the heat and noise generated by too many people, I was becoming exhausted. I began to wonder how long it would be before I could slip away.

Yet another series of dishes was served, this time composed of sweets, fruits and cheeses. None of it appealed to me; I'd felt stuffed to the gills for the last hour or so. But it was cheering, all the same: we must be nearing the end of the meal, and if the Queen retired soon after, I would be free to seek my own room. I propped myself forward on my elbows and tried to stay awake.

Another blaring of horns roused me. The entire company stood, hastily and with much scraping of benches, and quiet descended. The herald announced that although Her Majesty was retiring for the evening, she desired us all to stay and make merry still.

Goddess be praised, I thought, as those at the high table began moving to the doors. The more robust or convivial members of her court were breaking off and moving down into the hall to join their families and friends, and I could see the signs of relief on many faces. The real carousing was about to begin.

My hope that I could escape any more courtly entertainment, be it wild or formal, was dashed: Gervase came to his wife's side as we stood watching Her Majesty depart.

"My love, the Queen's asking for you. And you as well," he added, smiling at me. "She invites you to join her, if you are not too tired."

Requests from royalty are, of course, nothing of the sort. I sighed inwardly and followed them up and out of the hall.

Kerris lay so far inland that the builders had had no need to think of defense, and had designed for living, not fighting. If any invader got this far, Keraine was lost; consequently it was laid out in far less confusion than Glaice, and had never been more than minimally added to over the years. A broad stairway led up into the gallery above the banqueting hall, and I recognized the archway leading to the Council-room and so into the hall where I'd been received the day before.

We went up one more level and along a torchlit hallway, and I was ushered into Queen Elowyn's apartments.

It was crowded. The Queen sat at one end of the room, surrounded by many of the people who had been with her at the feast. This was no stiff and formal audience: Gervase and Aileen split up almost immediately. Aileen headed for the Queen, and Gervase was left to shepherd me down to the other end of the room to where Prince Connor was describing his triumph on the practice-ground.

I had no objection. Tirais stood, listening with tolerant amusement to his nephew's account, although it was apparent this was at least the third time Connor had subjected him to it.

Our arrival gave Connor a chance to expound on his theme more thoroughly. He could now appeal to Gervase and I for confirmation of his success. This, of course, went less well than he had expected. Gervase cocked an eye at him and remarked that he wouldn't let him try that trick again.

"I'll be watching you, Your Grace. And that sword of yours, as well."

Connor looked crestfallen. This aspect of it hadn't occurred to him before.

"Don't worry," I said. "I know a couple of other things you can try. And some of them aren't so easily countered, Lord Gervase."

He rolled his eyes. "I'm done for, lads."

The men around us laughed. It was mainly men at this end of the room, standing and sitting, and discussing weapons and warfare. Not many people make fighting their life's business by preference, and in this, at least, women have more choices than men do. If he is physically fit to do it, a boy learns to make war in a warlike world, but no-one forces a girl to spend her days with a sword. Except, perhaps, my father, who had sent all of his offspring out into life with at least one killing art firmly mastered.

It was because it was mainly men here that I knew instantly when the ladies who attended Her Majesty entered the room. Every head around me turned, and by reflex, I turned as well, as a bevy of girls and women came through the door, laughing and chattering and swinging their skirts, with the lady Angharad among them.

She had the kind of fair, cool loveliness, coupled with such an air of vulnerable femininity, that she stood out like a beacon to any man's eyes. Her hair was of the palest gold, almost silver in the warm glow of many candles, her eyes deeply blue, her mouth so sweetly curved and her figure so slender and frail-looking, that despite her regal height, she gave an impression of wistful, fragile purity. It was the sort of icy, untouched beauty that turns men's minds just naturally to thoughts of violation.

Baron Gallerain claimed her hand, as if by right. She stood at his side, smiling tentatively, her whole posture one of grateful admiration. I could see on the faces around me looks of envy compounded by lust and longing. She was a prize, if you like. Who would not want possession of something so entrancing? She was murmuring something in response to Gallerain's soft queries after her health, forcing him to lean intimately toward her to hear, then, as he laughed at whatever she had said, she shook her head, letting her loose and unbound tresses swirl in lovely confusion about her shoulders. I felt the men around me move restively, as if they'd all sighed out at once.

It was an amazing performance, so subtly done that it seemed quite natural, as if she were unaware of the havoc she was wreaking. Unaware and uncaring; everything about her cried out for that innocence to be cherished, protected, shielded from the cruelties of her life.

But it was a performance. I had older sisters; I knew. I had listened to their long lectures on how to engage and hold a man's attentions. I knew how carefully one could time that little headshake, so as to obtain the maximum fascination; I had been told just how to pitch one's voice to draw a man close into your orbit, and how to look up through your eyelashes and make him feel as though he was the only man who existed in the world for you. My sisters had tried to teach me these tricks, especially when it was close to my Goddess-night, but the attempt, though laudable, had been unsuccessful. My interests always turned my conversation to weapons, or hunting, or the like, and when I practiced to be a seductress, I wound up in a fit of giggles. I wasn't the kind of girl who could pull it off, and I didn't have time for it, frankly.

Still, Angharad's methods were beyond anything I had ever seen. My sisters practiced these arts with restraint; they had to, in any case, since my mother would have beaten them witless for a performance like this, but they would have scorned to present themselves as victims, no matter how difficult their straits.

The entrance of the ladies mixed the company up a bit. As if it were a secret signal, the men moved forward into the room, and the conversation became more general as they paired up with their wives or engaged in flirtations with the single girls. This flow enabled me to look around. I saw that Tirais was watching Angharad, not with admiration, but with skepticism.

I became aware of Connor, standing at my elbow, watching Angharad as well.

"It's all right," he said. "I don't like her much either."

"Does it show?"

"No, but then, they aren't looking, are they?" Connor smiled, taking the sting out of the words. "She doesn't like me. But then, I don't see her much. Will you really teach me some more ways to fight?"

"Yes, of course, if I can. But don't you have a tutor?"

He made a face. "I used to. And when I'm at Dungarrow, Lord Agurne makes sure I train. But I'm only there in summer. They haven't got time to worry over me much here. Uncle Tirais tries, but he's been gone all winter."

"Well, I'll do what I can. But, you know, I'll likely be posted along, soon. Still, I'll be at dawn practice every day, if you are. And I can show you some things you can work on, after I'm gone, if you like. You won't be the smallest for long, you know."

We fell into a discussion on training, which was both natural and odd at the same time, for me. Natural, because my whole life had been spent in discussions of this kind, but strange, too, since I'd always been in Connor's place. The student, not the teacher, except briefly, when I'd trained my ill-starred troop for Lord Uln.

Connor was way beyond the sort of basic learning I'd given that odd lot of farmhands and sheepherders, though. In addition to swordcraft, he'd been taught to think strategically, which made our talk simpler. I didn't continually have to backtrack to explain why some things weren't useful, and he could follow my descriptions without constant demonstrations. Still, you wind up acting these things out, it's easier all round. We forgot our surroundings, as I showed him how to counter swings that came from your opponent's offside.

"Ah," said Tirais, as he and Gervase came back up to watch. "I know that one. Hard to beat, if you've got the speed, Connor. It takes practice, though."

"Everything does," I said.

"We'll all have to watch ourselves around you," he said to Connor. "If you're going to take lessons from Keridwen, we'll be eating your dust, I shouldn't wonder."

Connor grinned. "I hope so. Show me that one again, Keri. Will it work in close?"

Gervase groaned as I nodded and positioned myself to demonstrate the technique once more. We were gathering a little crowd, despite the ladies; for most of the men, and a few women, too, the social graces took a back bench to anything to do with war.

"I've seen that one," said Gallerain, who had strolled over to join us. "Your father used it in a tourney, once. I thought I was a corpse, for certain."

Angharad, standing beside him, shuddered visibly, and he turned with concern.

"Oh, my dear, are you chilled?"

"Oh no, no. It's just all this talk of war, and fighting, and - death. It's so silly of me..." She trailed off on a die-away note, looking, if anything, paler and frailer than before.

There was a general sort of embarrassed coughing and fidgeting, as if we'd been caught doing something vaguely immoral. They were all looking at this delicate creature with apology, and with everyone's attention on that and on Gallerain, who was fussing over her, saying "Quite right. Mustn't bore the ladies," and leading her away, she shot me a look of spiteful triumph.

Well, I'd known she was performing. But the malice puzzled me; I could hardly be considered a threat to her many conquests. Still, there are people who can't bear even the slightest scrap of attention not being on them, and it seemed Angharad was one of them.

The group broke up again, reluctantly, into small knots of conversations on less violent subjects. Connor trailed after Tirais, after making me promise again that I would meet him for early practice in the morning, and I turned to find the Queen beside me, smiling at his retreating back.

"It's very kind of you to agree to that," she said.

"Not at all. I've nothing else to do, just now."

"No?" She seemed amused. "Regaining your health might be your first concern."

"Oh, I'm nearly well, again. But I need to practice, more than anything."

"You mustn't rush yourself. Your wounds sounded quite dire, I'm surprised, really that you seem as strong as you do."

"So everyone keeps remarking," I said.

She laughed outright. "Well, if you're determined to be well, I won't contradict."

"I'm sorry. Was it rude? But you know, my parents never let me lie abed for long. Up and about, that's my father's cure for everything."

"So I've heard," Elowyn said dryly. "But then, I doubt he's ever been in quite as bad a state as you were, by all accounts. Still, if you don't find the prince irksome, and can give him a little of your time, I would be grateful. Connor's at rather a loose end here, these days. He's too young to be at court, really, but too old to be left out of Midwinter festivities."

"I'd be honoured," I said, automatically.

"You mustn't let him plague you, though," she said, a smile curving her lips. "I know how energetic and wearying a small boy can be, but Connor is alone too much as it is. It will serve us all, if you were to spend some part of your days with him. I want him to know Dungarrow and its people, since he'll rule there when he's grown, and I want him to see it in a better light. I'm afraid," she ended ruefully, "That the rest of us look less kindly on it than we ought."

"Understandable," I sighed. "It would be a pleasure, Your Majesty. I'm bound to Lord Cioren, at present, but I don't see that he's got much need for me. I expect I can put in a few hours in Connor's company."

"Thank you." She looked down along the room at the chattering groups. "You seem a little tired, Keridwen. If you want to slip out, I don't believe even my royal presence will notice."

I smiled my thanks, bowed, and watched her as she moved back into the centre of the room, to take up a seat beside Lady Aileen.

Finding my way to the door without attracting any attention was no difficult task; behind me, one of the Queen's ladies had been persuaded to entertain those assembled with a song, accompanied by a harpist, but as I slipped out, Gervase must have seen me go. He caught up with me in the hall, as I peered about, trying to think which way we had come and how best to get to my room.

"This way," he said cheerfully and opened another door.

It let onto a narrow stairway leading down. I followed the Lord Steward as he went.

"It goes to Tirais' rooms," Gervase said, by way of explanation, "And then on to the butteries, in case anyone wants aught in the night and such. Here," he opened another door, "We're in the Prince's apartments."

I crossed with him through an anteroom, through another door, this one massively carved and ornamented, and found myself in a long open corridor.

"Just straight along," he gestured towards the open gallery at one end. "Go on past the steps, and on to the corner. Cioren's rooms are to the right."

Chapter 36

Connor was waiting for me, still in high spirits, the following morning. The field was deserted; save for the prince and an elderly man in the Machyll colours, who was seated placidly watching as Connor warmed up. I was introduced; he rejoiced in the rather grand name of Parthalen, and he was a little deaf, which must have been a small mercy when he attended a ten-year-old boy.

I started Connor on moving drills, which he knew, stretched out my own cramped muscles, and ran through a couple of quick routines, mainly for form's sake, before settling down to watch and correct Connor's own form.

We moved on to specifics. He was an eager pupil and the time passed quickly; I looked up to find that there were several other people on the field, most of whom were strangers, and who watched our progress with interest. Well, Connor was Tirais' heir, until his uncle married and had children of his own. People were bound to be curious about him.

After he'd proven to my satisfaction that he could execute the basics easily, if not effectively, due to his lack of inches, I began to teach him a really useful little step-and-thrust trick that I still resorted to myself. It has to be adapted as you grow, but the logic presents itself pretty naturally, and, with a little practice, it's almost impossible to defend against. In its later versions, it has to be started with a fake, to get your opponent's sword out of position, but most fighters are willing suckers for misdirection. There's something about an easy opening in the midst of a really excited exchange of blows that makes it nearly impossible to resist. The best part of this particular shot was that even if it were unsuccessful, you weren't in any extraordinary danger; the technique itself put you into a protected position if you missed.

It takes practice, though. We were both dripping with sweat when I finally called a halt for the day. He had it partway, at least. In a week or two, he'd be pretty proficient. I'd have to teach him at least three other things, or he'd overwork it. A move only stays effective as long as your adversary knows there's something else you might be doing when you start to set it up.

Tirais arrived. I saw him out of the corner of my eye, just as I was letting Connor try the move "one last time", in this instance quite slowly, so I could see if there were any obvious mistakes that needed correcting. Keraine's heir stood near Parthalen, watching, until we were done.

Connor reached the end of the move, hitting his practice post with noisy force, returned to defensive position and held it, and called out, "Is he dead?"

without looking around. I'd taught him that first off. Even in practice against a wooden post, you never assume your victory.

"I think so. Well done, Connor. Don't put your weight so far across, and you'll have them every time."

Tirais strolled up.

"What a bloodthirsty child he is," he said by way of greeting.

Connor, coming over, grinned happily. "Did you see? Keri says you can't defend against it!"

"No, I said it's very hard to defend against, and that it gives you a couple of options even if you miss."

"Well, still…"

Tirais laughed. "I came to ask if you're free this afternoon, Connor. I'm taking out my new falcon, to see how she flies. If you're not too busy learning how to slaughter us all, you could join me."

"Oh!" Connor was momentarily deprived of speech, looking impossibly joyful and proud. "Oh, truly? I'd love to. Can Keri come, too? Uncle Tirais has the most beautiful falcon, Keri. He's been training her since spring."

"Certainly she should come. She looks rather pale. A ride will do you good, Keri, if you aren't too tired out, or sick of the very sight of Keraine's princes."

This sally drew a crow of laughter from Connor, who thought the idea of anyone being sick of him was a huge joke.

"Well, I need to see the healer, and I really ought to make sure that Cioren hasn't plans for me, but I would like to come."

"I'll go with you," said Connor, promptly. "If I go back to my rooms, Ninon will only fuss over my clothes and try to make me take a bath. Which is stupid, I'll only have to have another one before supper."

Tirais looked down at his nephew, as if to say that two baths might not be such an ill fate, then looked back over his head at me, smiling.

"I'll meet you at the stables, then, shall I?"

Down at the healers' rooms, I discovered that my ribs were healing nicely, and that my abandoning my crutch had done me little harm. Like most small boys, Connor found my collection of scars fascinating, and I was hard-put to explain to him that these were marks, not of heroic behavior, but of poor judgment, inattention, and occasional dumb luck. The healer helped out, as best he could, both of us ruefully shaking our heads at Connor's enthusiastic belief that scars showed some extraordinary skill. He wanted the stories behind the marks, and plainly disbelieved my tale of stupidity and overconfidence that had resulted in an arrow to the belly three years before.

Our return route to my room was circuitous, involving a brief stop at one of the guards' barracks, where Connor had made some friends, and a ramble through all of the Duke of Dungarrow's favourite hiding places and look-out spots. As a tour, it was conducted on no sort of plan or logical order, which was probably all the better. By the end of it, I thought I could have found my way around Kerris' central buildings in pitch dark.

Cioren was seated at a table in the main room of our quarters, reading a scroll that was overwritten and recrossed to the point of illegibility when we came in, still shadowed by the silent Parthalen. He looked up, amused at our noisy entrance, lent an ear to Connor's excited discourse on the morning's activities, and invited the prince to share a noonday meal with us.

"Oh, perfect," said Connor. "Now I needn't go back to Ninon at all. We're going hawking with Uncle Tirais."

"Fine. But I think you ought to let her know where you are, Connor. She may worry that you've drowned in a horse-trough, or been stolen by gypsies."

"Oh, she always worries. If I tell her she'll only try to stop me from going."

"Still, it isn't fair to her," said Cioren. "After all, it's her job to worry. I tell you what," he held up his hand to forestall Connor's objections, "We'll send Parthalen to let her know, after we've eaten. You'll be on your way, but Ninon will know you're safe. Will that content you?"

"Oh, all right."

Parthalen bared his teeth in what was apparently a smile. He seemed to share both Connor's desire to be free of Ninon's fussing, and Cioren's desire not to aggravate the poor woman. She sounded a bit of a tyrant; I had an image of an ancient crone, determined to keep Connor a baby, but when I hinted as much, Cioren shook his head.

"Ninon's no older than I am. But she's charged with Connor's well being. Don't encourage him to too much rebellion."

"No. I've no right to judge, any road. He's a handful."

Connor, meanwhile, was examining some of the objects in the room with interest. These were Cioren's permanent rooms at Kerris, and he left a lot of things behind when he wasn't in residence. I'd been fascinated by a number of them myself. There were books, of course, more than I'd ever seen collected in one place before, but there were also glass jars filled with odd-looking grains (hybrids, Cioren had told me, being experimented with in Westfold, to see if they yielded better crops) and some truly odd things; a stuffed owl, a wolf's skull, some glass beads filled with an oily-looking liquid, a host of things I'd never seen before.

There were more things, even stranger ones, in another room Cioren used as a workroom. I'd caught a glimpse of them, the other day. It was all both weird and worrisome. None of it said "work" to me, and it all seemed unrelated and not terribly useful. I could see the point of the grains, but the rest of Cioren's collection struck me as bizarre.

"Come look at this, Keri," Connor said. He was holding what appeared to be an ordinary gray rock, although it was abnormally round and smooth. I moved closer. It was only half of a rock, in fact. Turning the broken side towards me, Connor displayed its astonishing interior.

It was like a tiny cave, filled with shining purple crystals. The edges were like marble; polished and glowing, blue and purple striations shot with white. I heard my own gasp of pleased surprise.

"A dragon's egg," said Connor, smugly knowledgeable.

I looked back at Cioren, raising my eyebrows.

"So they're called," he agreed. "Although I have certainly never seen one hatched. Still, we don't know that it's not."

Connor left the egg to me, his attention already caught by something else. The remains of a crow, sealed into one of the glass jars claimed him, and after that, a pair of curved daggers. Cioren sat back down, and, after a moment, I joined him, still turning the rock in my hands and watching as the crystals caught the light.

"So, you're off hawking," he remarked. "I suppose that means you feel fit enough."

"Well, I've seen the healers," I said, defensively. "They've given me another one of their foul brews to take, but apparently I'm all right. And I've promised to spend time with Prince Connor. But if you've need of me, sir…"

"Oh, we're back to that, are we? Every time you get your back up, it's sir this and my lord that all over again. I'm not criticizing, mind you. I get little enough respect around here. Don't look so affronted. I'm sure a little exertion will do you good."

I grinned, unwillingly. Cioren didn't bring out the best in me, or at least in my manners. The trouble was, he and Tirais were both too casual.

Parthalen returned with a couple of servants and our meal. He refused to sit with us, but parked himself on a bench by the door to eat, while we fell to. After we'd demolished a couple of loaves, some cheese, a meat-pie and some fruit, Connor was eager to be off. He hopped around excitedly, while I washed and changed out of my armour. Nothing would induce him to do more than splash some cold water on his hands and face, but while he created a messy pool of droplets on the side table, I asked Cioren if he really had no need of me.

"No, no, go on. Tirais is right, you do look pale. You're used to far more exercise than you'll get around here. Try not to overdo it, though. We can probably skip this evening's festivities, unless you have a taste for big banquets."

"I haven't. Last night was enough."

"Well, you aren't done with them altogether. Elowyn expects everyone to attend at least some of them. But let it go, for now. We'll talk tonight."

We left Parthalen at the stable gates. In the yard, Tirais was already in the saddle and our own mounts were ready. Besides the falconer, there were a pair of grooms, on loan from Baron Gallerain's entourage, but this was an afternoon of freedom for Keraine's princes. Outside of these few folk, we were unaccompanied.

Banshee, having been neglected, was full of energy. She shied and twisted, and it took me a few moments to get her under control. I swore, wrenching forcibly on her reins, and sat hard into the saddle, and after ascertaining that she wasn't going to be able to scrape me off against a wall, she settled into being merely fractious.

Tirais and Connor watched all this with enjoyment. It always looks funny, when it's someone else's problem.

I had wondered how long it would take, just to get to some place beyond the city, where one could loose a hawk, but we left by a different road, and found ourselves quite quickly out in the wild. We headed northeast, towards the river and looking back beyond the palace walls, I saw that the city lay mainly west of us and amid that crowded view, I could just make out the silhouette of the famous stone bridge across the River Braide. On the other side of the river, the city resumed, but here, as we trotted along the track, we were in an open country of wide meadows and copses of birch trees.

The air was cool and fresh, filled with the tang of winter crispness, and the sky was a glorious, brilliant blue. I sucked the cleanness of it into my lungs, forgot the vague apprehensions that Cioren's last words had awakened, and gave myself over to watching Tirais fly his falcon.

A well-trained bird of prey, swooping down on a hare or other small game, is an exhilarating sight. We galloped in pursuit, cheering the falcon on and laughing uproariously at the grooms' half-hearted attempts to keep pace. I forgot that I was with the heirs of Keraine, forgot that I was a pardoned traitor, forgot the long and dreary months at Penvarron, forgot everything, in my sheer pleasure at being alive. Alive and in the company of a man I loved.

Stupid, of course. Even as we turned our weary horses back towards the palace walls, I felt the weight of it return, more crushing than before. He was a prince of the realm, and he cared nothing for me. Well, perhaps not quite nothing. I was a companion, and I had served his kingdom. I was owed something. But beyond that, I knew, he thought little enough about my presence, save that I was there, and could be made use of. I girded my heart in my pride, all the armour that I had against my inevitable disappointment.

Connor, unwilling to admit to the least suggestion of fatigue, was trying to convince his horse to do a kind of dancing step that young riders always try, emulating cavalry troops on parade. He paid no heed to our occasional warnings, but increased the pace, as his mount tried to pull the reins free in exasperation.

I wasn't watching all that closely. Tirais was explaining to me his theories on training a falcon, while the man who did the actual work for him tried not to contradict when appealed to for confirmation, and I was just turning back to look to Connor's shout for attention when I saw the young prince's horse stumble.

It went lightning fast: first, the slightest hesitant step, then a sudden jolt, and Connor went tumbling off, and his horse leapt skittishly away and was galloping out towards the river.

There was a sickening thud as Connor's head connected with frozen ground. I heard a shout of alarm from one of the grooms, but I hardly noticed: I was jumping from the saddle and rolling on the grass to come upright at Connor's side.

He lay very still. My own breath was arrested, from the hard jolt I'd given my tender ribs when I hit the ground. The frozen turf echoed with the receding thunder of hooves, and the wind, unnoticed till this moment, sighed out over the fields.

A second later, I felt Tirais' hand on my shoulder, as Connor rolled, moaning, over onto his back and tried to sit up.

"No, don't," said his uncle. "Lie still, you little idiot, till we know you're all right."

Tirais knelt beside Connor, and began looking him over. I moved back on my heels, shaky with relief, gazing around. The ground was barren and dead here, and the sparse grass flat and brown from the winter frosts. I brushed my hands along it, touching the coarse stubble, then I looked back at Connor, who was half-sitting, propped against Tirais' arm, and looking a little green.

"Rabbie, go after His Grace's horse, will you? Don't try to talk, Connor. It just makes it worse."

"Only a tumble," Connor whispered.

"That's right," agreed Tirais. "A tumble you could well have avoided, so next time don't tell me you know it all. You scared me half to death."

I stood. Connor's horse hadn't gone far, the groom had nearly caught up to him already. It didn't matter. Connor needed a few minutes more before we could even think about moving him.

But here he surprised me. He looked better already, the sick look having gone off, and some colour was coming back to his cheeks. He was sitting up on his own, though Tirais was still kneeling beside him, and they were arguing.

"I'm all right."

"Don't be stupid, Connor. That was no easy little fall."

"I feel fine." I heard an echo of myself in this, and smiled. Connor had courage. No sense, of course, but he did have courage.

"Look, we're not going back till I'm sure you can manage. And it's the Healer for you, first thing. Don't look daggers at me. It's only sense."

"It was only a fall," said Connor, doggedly.

"He could try standing," I suggested. "Just to be sure he hasn't sprained something. Only do it slowly. I've seen grown men faint getting up too fast."

This found favour with both of them, Tirais being convinced that Connor would feel like death on his feet, even if he weren't actually broken, and Connor equally sure that, upright, he would prove to be quite fit.

They were neither of them completely right: Connor paled at the effort of standing, and swayed, but this passed after a moment or two, and he did not seem to have damaged himself unduly. After ten more minutes, Tirais agreed that riding back under his own power would occasion the least amount of fuss all round, but was forced to appeal to me to convince Connor that seeing the Healer and being completely sure he was in fine shape was only sensible.

I couldn't argue. I wanted to know that Connor was not suffering from some undetected injury myself. Anyone who has spent time on the practice-ground knows how dangerous a blow to the head can be. Sometimes people seem all right, but they go to sleep and wake up dead. I pointed out that a good soldier always obeys his commanding officer, and that Tirais would seem to be his, and Connor, having gotten his way over his horse, finally agreed that he would suffer to be looked at.

It was getting late. The sky was gray in the east, with deep lavender smudged streakily over the west horizon, quite beautiful, really. I gazed at it all unseeing, as we rode back into Kerris. It was lucky, I thought, that I didn't have to sit through another banquet tonight. I couldn't have done it. I couldn't have spent five hours in that noisy, glaring light, wondering which of the gallant company assembled there would wish to murder a prince of Keraine.

Chapter 37

Cioren was nowhere to be found when I got back to my rooms. It was already dark, and it was possible that he had changed his mind and gone down to the feast hall after all, though that didn't seem likely. I washed and sat down in the room that separated mine from Cioren's own chamber, and tried to think sensibly.

It was no use. I had too little to go on. I needed Cioren's knowledge to be certain, and I realized, as the shadows lengthened, that I was hoping mightily that I was charging at phantoms, that what I thought to be truth would turn out to be smoke and moonbeams, brought on by too many strange things happening and addling my wits.

Connor had come through it with nothing more than a large bump on his head and the prospect of a scolding from the dreaded Ninon. Tirais, feeling responsible, had gone with him to his rooms, to explain, and try to stem the inevitable tide. I felt guilty, as well, since I was supposed to be looking after him, more or less, but neither prince seemed to feel that I had any share in the disaster.

They had closed ranks on me, Tirais pointing out with finality that Connor was bound to do himself a mischief, regardless of who might be minding him. It was true that even had I not been with him, Connor might have come to grief in the same way, but I wasn't convinced.

In the end, though, I had had to give up my guilt, since they were both adamant that I was blameless. I got a clap on the shoulder from Tirais, and a shamefaced promise to be utterly obedient from Connor, assuming I didn't refuse to have anything to do with him at all. This was spurious, though. He was blithely convinced of my continuing friendship, and he was right. I wasn't planning on abandoning him.

I heard a vague commotion in the corridor, and the door opened on Cioren at last. He was trailed by two servants carrying trays, and there was a confused few moments while they settled their burdens, arranged the table and made sure our needs were supplied.

Cioren was already seating himself, and reaching for the wine. I was suddenly aware of two things. One was that my suspicions were not really in any way justified and were going to sound idiotic. The other was that I was famished.

Thus we passed the meal in pleasantries. I couldn't hide the facts of Connor's accident without outright lies, but I thought that I managed to tell it as though I really thought it no more than a rambunctious boy's comeuppance, and we passed on to Tirais' falcon, the size of Kerris, and Banshee's habitual bad temper. Cioren broached a second bottle, and we relaxed beside the hearth, falling into companionable silence, until Cioren roused himself, sat up more sternly and said, "All right. What ails you tonight?"

I swallowed. I hadn't done such a good job of my tale after all.

"I - I don't know what you mean,"

"Don't try that trick with me. I'm far too old for it. What has happened to upset you now?"

"Nothing," I said. "Nothing except this." I reached into my shirt and drew out a tangled length of twine.

Cioren looked at it. He didn't, as I'd half-expected him to, burst out laughing. He gazed steadily at the string for a moment, then lifted his eyes to mine.

"Well?"

"I found it. Just at the spot where Connor's horse began to shy."

"It tells you something, this bit of string?"

"It looks," I said, carefully, "very much like the sort of charm Finders use, to draw out a hiding place. Even the twine's the same sort, and the Finder at Orliegh once said that it's got to be the right kind of twine, not just any bit of rope you find lying about. But it's different, somehow."

"And just what do you suppose that means?"

I swallowed again. It began to seem even sillier than it had when it was just my own thoughts. The idea of hearing the words outright was preposterous. Still, I had to say these words. I would never forgive myself if I did not, and something happened after.

"I think," I said, "that there might be a kind of spell that's similar. That would make a horse stumble. And I think perhaps it was left there to do just that."

Well, I'd known it was drivel. The fact that it sounded demented, when spoken aloud, came as no surprise. I sighed, and prepared to apologize for troubling him.

"Yes, you're quite right. There is a way to do such things."

My mouth dropped open.

"It's clever of you to notice the similarity between Finder's twines and this bit," he continued, ignoring my shock. "Few people would, even those with a little training. Still, I suppose a soldier's training is much the same as any other

213

learning, if it's put to use. The question is, though, whether it was put there on purpose, or merely happened to be there."

I shook my head, trying to clear it. I might have known Cioren, of all people, would go straight to the heart of it.

"I agree," he said, "I'm no believer in coincidence. But who was it meant for? And that's a wide stretch of land you were riding. It could have lain there for eons, really. If it didn't just fall there by chance."

"I don't like it," I said. "It just seems so unlikely, Cioren. Just after Penvarron, all of a sudden I'm surrounded by things that aren't supposed to exist."

"Just because you've spent your life being protected, away up in Dungarrow, where the holy ones keep a tight rein on this sort of thing, doesn't mean the rest of us live in ignorance. You had better face it: this stuff happens. With far more frequency than the priests would like it to."

"Still, calling it happenstance doesn't wash, Cioren. Connor might have been killed. What's more, it could easily have been Tirais. It was only that Connor was showing off, otherwise it likely would have been Tirais."

"But no telling that any of you would have passed just that way, today or any other day. And Connor wasn't killed, Keri. Falls from a horse aren't generally fatal. It seems a damned poor way to murder someone. If it was deliberately left, it was purely spite, on the off chance that someone might be discommoded, not a concerted attempt to end a life."

"Ye-es, I see what you mean. But it worries me, even if it's only spite. You could kill someone that way, and it would never be suspected."

"Not very sporting," he agreed. "Well, we're warned, now, aren't we? I hardly think that whoever left this, if it was done on purpose, will try anything similar. I expect they will try going to retrieve it, if they hear of Connor's mishap. And if they don't find it, they'll worry that it has been found, and that will likely end the mischief."

His unconcern relieved me somewhat. I had to agree that to continue leaving charms like this one about on the slight chance that the right target stumbled over it, and that the outcome was the fatality you wished for, was such a long shot as to be nearly useless. It wouldn't be Connor's neck that was at risk, anyway. I could make reasonably sure of that, merely by falling in with the Queen's wish that I give him my time, while I was here.

In the morning, I could see Cioren's point even more clearly. He'd said, to my surprise, that he would take it to Dalriega to handle, and that if it were just a novice playing tricks, it would be dealt with. My open astonishment brought a laugh from Cioren, who said that, Council differences notwithstanding, he and Dalriega were old friends. The tone in which he uttered this left me speechless. It seemed to me that the word friend didn't begin to cover it, and that besides being a mage, Cioren had unsuspected hobbies.

I know, of course, that neither romance nor lust is a province solely of the young. At Orliegh, in summer, we bathe outdoors, and there was that one summer my brother Dion had nearly given up washing altogether, when my aunt came to stay. Her undisguised admiration of his nudity had almost proved too much for his adolescent pride. And no one, growing up at Orliegh, could fail to be aware of my parents' adoration of each other, sometimes expressed rather too openly for their children's sensibilities.

But to be confronted by two unmarried and elderly people at opposite extremes of so many political issues, casually indulging in an ongoing affair, was a little perturbing. Cioren laughed at my unexpressed shock, called me a backward little provincial, and recommended I be a little less straitlaced. I apologized, trying to be dignified, but that only increased his amusement, and finally, I went to bed.

Meeting Connor on the practice-ground the next morning, I was inclined to be sympathetic on the subject of his injuries. He'd woken up stiff in every joint, which was understandable after a hard fall. I was a little sore myself, and we kept our drills on the short side. He was subdued, which was also understandable, having given himself a fright, but it wasn't healthy. I set out to cheer him up, a difficult proposition given my own tangled feelings over the affair.

Because of this, I agreed that joining the Palace Guard at breakfast might be entertaining, though I wasn't sure the guards would appreciate it. But they greeted him as an old friend, took my presence in stride, and made places for both of us and the ever-present Parthalen at their mess. They had already heard of Connor's accident, and teased him about it, in the way that soldiers will, and he began to see it as a joke as well. All the better. The barracks, I thought, was a safe place for Connor; it was always crowded and no one that sought to harm him by some random charm would attempt it there.

It was in the midst this convivial atmosphere of irreverent gossiping that I realized that, Tirais' stricture notwithstanding, everything of importance about both Penvarron and Uln's attack on Fairbridge was already common, if erroneous, knowledge.

The soldiers of Kerris knew all about what had happened at Fairbridge. They knew, in fact, of Uln's brief reappearance at Penvarron, and far too much about what had happened there. Tirais might as well not have bothered swearing the garrison to silence. It was all out there, at least the bits that we had been warned to keep shut about.

I wasn't really surprised. I hadn't thought it would work. There had been too many of us, and only a few had understood the true implication of it anyway, and asking such exciting things to remain secret was unrealistic. I wasn't even really upset by how fast the news had traveled, or by how far.

No, it was the conclusions that these men and women had come to on the evidence that dismayed me.

Far from seeing Uln as the self-serving traitor he was, the bastard was being pitied as a victim. Opinion varied as to how he had been seduced by sorcerous means into betraying his Queen and country, but the popular belief was that he had, in fact, been tricked into his treason by some person who had infiltrated his home and his confidence, and used Uln to commit these heinous acts.

I couldn't fight this. I could only listen, in shock and disbelief, as his reputation was salvaged, before my eyes. And there was no doubt in my mind where all this was coming from.

A gentle, rueful word, here and there. A sighing confidence, whispered into bemused and dazzled ears. And then, a man repeating it all to some friends. Perhaps there were servants about; servants hear everything anyway, sooner or later. It would be only days, before all of Keraine would know how one of Uln's people had been a Camrhyssi spy, bent on destroying a faithful servant of the Queen.

The guards in Kerris ate well, at least at Midwinter. Someone brought us gingercake, an apparent favourite of the Duke of Dungarrow's. He ate two helpings.

After this, Connor regretfully took his leave. He was due in his own quarters, for the next glass or two, apparently to answer official correspondence from Lord Agurne, who served as his Warden in Dungarrow. This was Duke-in-training stuff, and meant for his own good, but he didn't want to hear it. He was only consoled by my agreeing that if Cioren had no duties for me, I would spend the rest of the day in his company, so I walked as far as the main stairway with him, and watched as he mounted the steps to his own apartments, the picture of duty coerced.

My own thoughts occupied me as I walked down to my room to change. I couldn't blame Angharad for trying to reduce treason to mere stupidity. She was Uln's heir, and if she wanted to have anything to inherit, she would have to muddy the waters enough to be seen as both blameless and harmless. She was doing a good job, too. No, I didn't really mind, I thought. In her place, it was the only course available. Better to be the daughter of an idiot, too gullible and trusting to survive, than the offspring of a traitor. Hell, she might even be right, what did I know?

But the thought of unknown traitors brought me back to yesterday's near-disaster.

Despite Cioren's assurances, and my own common sense, I was still troubled by the thought that someone had planted that piece of mischief where they had. If the culprit had no murderous intent, it was still a disturbing occurrence, and no matter how common mage-craft was, you couldn't excuse that sort of careless disregard. I hoped whoever had done it was thoroughly terrified, especially if they had gone to retrieve the knotted string and found it missing.

Having servants was, as I'd suspected at Glaice, all too easy to get used to. Someone came into my room moments after I entered, to see if I wanted aught, and since I needed a bath, I whiled away nearly a full glass in pleasant luxury. Then, dressed and tidy, I sat down with a mug of ale and a book I'd borrowed from Cioren the night before.

It was a version of "Chronicles of the Kings", but written in a very different style than the massive tome used to teach me my history back home. It was irreverent and casual to the point of chattiness, and thoroughly engrossing. I jumped, when my door opened suddenly.

"Have you gone deaf?" asked Cioren. "I knocked twice."

"Sorry. I was reading."

"We'll make a scholar of you, yet. What have you got planned for this afternoon? I suspect not more hawking."

"No. I promised Connor we'd do something, though, if you've no need of me."

"I don't think so. Unless your handwriting is better than mine. I need to transcribe some notes."

"Oh. Well, I'm not considered much of a scribe. Sheep-tracks was the most common description, as I recall."

He laughed. "You'll be more useful tagging after His Grace and seeing he doesn't get up to too much mischief, then. He's probably free by now. I'll walk up with you; Elowyn wants to go over some of the - er - autumn reports."

I grinned as I stood up. "That sounds dreary enough. Better you than me."

We weren't halfway along the corridor leading to the main halls when what I'd been reading finally caught up with me. It seemed, from my vantage point, that Cioren was the most likely person to clarify my thoughts and put me right, in matters historical, and it was a long hike to Connor's apartments.

"Cioren, I've been thinking about what you said about Averraine."

"Have you, now?" His tone was not helpful.

"Well, it's that book you loaned me. I mean, all my life, I've been told that Averraine was so magnificent, and everything was perfect until the very end. But they keep mentioning border problems, and raiders out of Istara even before the Breaking. And come to think of it, even in the "Chronicles" back home, there's stuff about Iaione coming north to treat with the lords of Evanion."

"A king's life," said Cioren, neutrally. "Who else would treat with them?"

"But if we were one kingdom, why should he need to treat with them at all? Elowyn doesn't negotiate with each baron alone, as if they were every one of them kings. She goes into Council, and the lords have their say, but in the end, we try to do what's best for Keraine, don't we? I mean, I know each lord looks to his own lands' advantage first, but in the end, they obey their sworn Queen."

"Ah. Well, you're getting into the heart of it now, aren't you? You're right, Keri. It wasn't all as perfect as the bards and storytellers would have us believe. We didn't start out as one happy family, and we didn't end it that way."

"So Fendrais and Camrhys and Keraine weren't truly one people?"

"No. They began as separate tribes, and it's true, in some ways they never lost that separateness. Well, you've seen it yourself. Dungarrow still thinks of itself as independent from Keraine in many ways. If you read carefully, you'll notice that later on, when Averraine looked to extend their sway in the south, they left themselves open to more problems in the north. But why does this trouble you now?"

"It explains some things, at least."

"Does it?"

Encouraged by his interest, I said, "Well, it's been bothering me, why Ys Tearch is where it is. If we were one big happy empire, why would we build a fortress to guard a pass right smack in the middle of everywhere? No raider is going to hike a couple of weeks inland and wait around for a merchant-train to come through. It's too big to be just an outpost to keep off local robber bands, though. But if there were reasons for Keraine to worry over its neighbours, then it would make sense for the Ancients to build it. And staff it."

"But Glaice was never a fortress, not till after the empire's collapse. How would you explain that?"

"I'm not sure. Perhaps it wasn't as important. You don't try to protect what doesn't matter, so I'm assuming either they didn't care, or they figured Glaice wouldn't be the first choice for a battle, for some reason. Anyway, if there was unrest all over, it would explain why we have so many fortresses and strongholds that are so old."

"For what it's worth, I think you're right. Although I don't know why it worries you. Whatever reasons our ancestors had, it's all dead and buried now."

I quickened my pace, to keep up with him. "It isn't, though. If what you believe is true, then it's coming back to haunt us."

Cioren sighed. "Don't make more of this than you need. Bits and pieces of the past stay with us, Keri. But there's no reason to think that our entire history is conspiring against us."

I opened my mouth to say that there was every reason to think it, and that we ought to be prepared for the worst, rather than stumbling blindly from one crisis to the next, but we had reached the doorway to the royal apartments. A bored-looking guard struggled up from his bench, opened it, and I followed Cioren through.

Connor's rooms adjoined the Queen's, connected by an anteroom furnished with a series of marble benches along the sides and hung with several gaily-woven tapestries of hunting scenes, and strewn with fresh rushes on the stone floor. There were a couple of doors leading to both Elowyn's quarters and her young grandson's, the entrance to Connor's room being flung wide, and from it I heard the sound of light laughter and cheerful conversation.

It made a pretty picture. The Queen was seated on a chair, Connor on a low stool beside her. The ladies who attended Elowyn were scattered in charming groups about the room; several by the windows, two at the wide hearth, and one kneeling, her arms theatrically draped about His Grace, her eyes wide with pity and anguish, and her fair hair still unbound and maidenly, tumbling about her shoulders.

"But we must all take the greatest care of you, Your Grace," Angharad was saying. "I couldn't bear it if something were to happen to you, through someone's carelessness."

Connor did not look as if he appreciated the sentiment. He looked trapped, actually, his eyes panicky and wide, like a fawn surprised by a hunter. There was a smudge of ink on his cheek, and his face was red with embarrassment as he tried to wriggle politely away from his new friend and protectress.

"Ah, well, boys will take tumbles," said the Queen, comfortably. "Tirais was always covered with scrapes and bruises at his age. You will be more careful, though, won't you, Connor?"

The prince muttered something, lost in the rustling of skirts as Elowyn rose, greeting us cheerfully, and thanking me for my efforts on Connor's behalf. Angharad, now that her point had been made, abandoned Connor with alacrity, rising to arrange herself decorously beside the Queen.

Elowyn's words seemed to be a signal to the other ladies, who moved also to the Queen's side. They were, by Angharad's quick movement, made to seem superfluous and of lesser moment, though most of them would have been with Her Majesty far longer.

They were even less impressed with Angharad's stratagem than I was. I caught one of the older women looking rather put out, indeed.

But as the Queen turned back to Connor with an admonition not to give me reason to regret my spending time with him, I was less happy. Uln's daughter seized on the chance to add to her own eloquence, this time to me.

"You must watch and ward him most vigilantly," she said. "He is such a treasure to us all. I know that rough play seems only right to the soldierly class, but a prince is no raw recruit to be toughened up."

Elowyn turned back, an unreadable expression on her face. Angharad, having made her point, could not seem to stop, however.

"I expect," she continued in a honeyed tone, "that yesterday's mishap gave you quite a fright as well. I would implore Your Majesty to overlook Lady Keridwen's lapse, but I know you are so generous, there is no need."

"None at all," said Elowyn, gravely. "I think I know Keridwen's worth, Angharad."

"Forgive me," she said. "Keridwen will know I speak only as her friend. We are both conscious, I am persuaded, of Your Majesty's great forbearance."

It was neatly done, I'll admit. While Elowyn might not be taken in by this timely linking of my unwitting treason with Angharad's own precarious position as the traitor's heir, the other ladies were nodding as if my guilt was well-known. I could guess who had told them, too.

I made no rejoinder. It seemed to me that I could not. Anything I said now would seem only empty self-justification. I bowed to the Queen and her ladies, threw an irritated glare at both Angharad and Cioren as they followed Elowyn's court out the door, and swung back to look at Connor with sympathy.

He was flinging himself into the Queen's recently vacated chair.

"Oouf!" he said. Well, that was succinct.

"I know," I said. "But you kept your temper, at least. I'm not sure I could have. I'm not sure I did, actually; I hope your grandmother didn't notice."

He grinned. "It was awful. But she gave me an amulet against accidents. I had to say thank you, and that's when she went all weepy."

I looked at the braided ribbon around his neck. The charm itself was innocuous enough: every village wise-woman makes those little clay circles. But the complicated twists of black cord that wound around it seemed odd. Still, I'd seen a lot of new things lately, and Cioren had warned me I was ignorant and undereducated in these things.

"Well, you likely need it, riding the way you do," I said, wryly. "Anyway, it's done with. What would you like to do?"

Chapter 38

Connor had no plan in mind, other than to put a vast quantity of distance and fresh air between his person and the Queen's ladies. We went out for a protracted ramble through Kerris' grounds, starting with the kennels, where we debated the ancestry of some hunting dogs, and then along the walls to look at what ships were putting in to Kerris' bustling docks, before deciding to go out to the archery-range to do a little shooting.

The air did wonders for our respective tempers. After a glass or so of challenging each other to shoot from ever-increasing distances, and adding rather silly obstacles to our ability to aim, we had both forgotten our ill-humour, and began wandering the grounds in search of more amusement.

The Duke of Dungarrow was a surprisingly good companion, despite his young age. He didn't lack for intelligence, and years at court had given him a certain adult perspective and cynicism, which was highly amusing. What he did lack, I thought, as we traversed a winding maze of smaller buildings on our route back to the castle proper, was the companionship of children his own age. His scathing remarks about his elders might be funny, but it sat oddly on a ten-year-old's shoulders, and he had acquired a certain control over his feelings that was a little disconcerting in one so young. He needed to feel freer, looser, less constrained in his manner and less watchful of his tongue. It wasn't natural.

We rounded a corner into the small courtyard below the Mother's shrine, and stopped, both of us gasping in delight.

It was part of the oldest section of Kerris, and the shrine had been built above a tiled expanse. The pattern, exposed to the elements for so many centuries, had deteriorated, as these things do, and this winter, the priests had commissioned some craftsmen to repair it.

The damaged parts had already been dug up, and the ground prepared with sand, tamped down heavily to receive the new paving. It was gridded off with rows of thin strings set along it neatly, and the artist hired was kneeling on a board, with a pile of tiny, coloured stones beside him. Out on the cobbled way that ran alongside, there were more heaps of painted stones, sorted for size as well as colour.

We stood, entranced. The man's apprentice was carefully watering the sand, to keep it damp and ready to receive the bright blocks; when he'd completed his task, he was quite willing to explain it all to us. He led us through the entire process, showing us the cutting tools that his master used to shape the stones to fit exactly to their neighbours, and the roll of parchment depicting the proposed design. It had been carefully reworked, to come as close to what had been laid in, hundreds of years before, when Kerris was new.

Connor had hunkered down, as close as he could get to the man laying in the new work, and was chattering happily to the apprentice, full of questions and opinions, wildly enthusiastic, if a trifle uninformed. I looked at the brilliant, gleaming stacks of glazed tiles and it struck me, with piercing clarity, that this work bore a distinct resemblance to my life.

It seemed to me as if my whole existence, since leaving Orliegh, had shattered into so many fragments, unrelated and disparate. Events dragged me along, with no reason or sense, and I found myself constantly attempting to push them into a coherent whole. Nothing fit any pattern that I could see, and my existence, once so ordered and solid, had become as chaotic and muddled as the scrap heap of discarded stones beside me. The more I tried to force some order onto the mess, the more confused and murky it seemed to be.

At length, I stood. Unlike the artist, I had no neatly laid-out plan to guide me, more's the pity, I thought. A bell tolled out on the river, echoing faintly into the walls of Kerris. It was growing late, and I would need to change before I presented myself in the feast hall. I called Connor back to reality, reminding him of the time, and we turned back to find our way up into the palace.

The world, far from requiring me to bend my poor brain to its problems, conspired, it seemed, to distract me into unthinking pleasure. As the evening in the great hall wound down, and Elowyn departed, I was gathered up by Maeliss and Gwyll, and borne off for a night of carousing with Prince Tirais, who to be was the guest of honour in his Guards' barracks, on the outer walls of the palace.

There was a dice game already in progress when we arrived. Two men were struggling over a keg of ale with a stubborn tap hole, the wine was flowing freely, and the noise of off-key singing was deafening. It was rather crowded, mostly with strangers, and Tirais himself had not yet arrived. I scooped up a goblet of wine and a handful of raisins from the table as we passed, and settled in to watch Maeliss lose her uncle's money.

I saw some faces I did know, of course. Tirais' own guards were all familiar, and they called out greetings as they passed. I was one of them, in a peculiar way; I'd been through Penvarron and its horrors with them. I saw that Baron Gallerain had absented himself from the Queen's presence to do a little roistering himself. He stood in the midst of a small group of older men, telling what appeared to be an amusing tale, they were laughing heartily, at least. His servants, the same pair of bored-looking men who had attended us the day before, stood near the door, arms folded, with resigned smiles pasted on their faces. And I saw Emlyn of Gorsedd again. He was lending support, from a safe distance, to the pair wrestling with the ale-cask.

Tirais arrived, to loud cheers and some ribald remarks on his tardiness. He threaded his way through the crowd, calling out greetings and begging the abysmal singers to lay off, which had predictable results: they chose a new, rather lewder song and started up louder and more dissonant than before. He laughed and joined the cheering, still smiling, while an untalented soloist finished describing some impossible sexual feats and led the chorus.

Events of this kind are pretty common, of course. Every household troop gives them as often as they can, cloaking the desire to get thoroughly drunk and out of control under the pretext of honouring their commander. At Orliegh, the troops throw one every Summer's Turning, save for the year when we'd gone to the big fair up at Davgenny. They'd had another one later in the season, using my name-day instead. It was the first one that my father hadn't had a servant take me back to the keep early from, so I remembered it all the more.

The dice game was getting more expensive, and more serious. It became boring, for a spectator, so I refilled my goblet and headed towards the fireplace. The singers had worn themselves hoarse and had mercifully given it up, and someone had begun a story so openly boastful that his companions were threatening him with an alcoholic drowning. A few serving-girls, bringing trays of food in, were being chased away with promises of the usual delights in store if they lingered. As I said, it was a scene repeated all over the world, with few variations, in every barracks worthy of the name.

Gwyll, having done his duty in arranging these festivities, was seated on a bench surveying his handiwork with some pride. There were already two guards passed out in corners, and several people, including Emlyn, had developed noticeable lists to one side or another.

"Great party," I said, sliding into a spot beside him. "Do this every year, do you?"

"Yes. But this year's rather special, we thought."

I didn't have time to ask him why. Tirais materialized out of the smoky debauch and plunked himself down on my left, saying much the same thing as I had. We looked out for a moment on the drunken revelry in silence.

"To absent friends," Tirais said, soberly, and lifted his cup.

We hoisted our own goblets and echoed him.

"Having a good time, Keri? I hear Connor dragged you all over the castle today."

"It was fun, actually. And he needed a break."

"Yes. I left him preparing to write a new letter to Agurne. It seems he's come up with an idea for improvements to Dungarrow Castle."

"Not a pattern of tiles for his courtyards?" At Tirais' amused nod, I groaned. "I knew he was too taken with the work the priests are having done."

"Well, it's the first time Connor's ever taken any interest in Dungarrow. He's writing to ask if there are any craftsmen who can do this kind of thing locally, and if not, why not? He's quite excited, since Agurne's always asking him for his opinion on the improvements he wants to make. I don't think Connor understands the difference between what crops he ought to have planted and new paving for the Great Hall, but it's a start."

I laughed. "He won't find many people able to do that kind of work. Have you seen it? It's very beautiful."

"No, but perhaps I ought to go and take a look. It certainly got your attention."

"Anyone would be fascinated. Although I think it's partly how it's done that has Connor so enthusiastic."

"You could be right. He's been tossing words like 'tessera' and 'mineral glaze' at me."

I looked down into my winecup, reflectively.

"He needs more interests, I expect." I said. There was no response, so I plunged in deeper. "He needs friends his own age, really."

"Don't," said Tirais. His voice was low and intent. "Don't start this."

"Yes, but…" I trailed off. What did I know of raising princes?

"I know, and I'm not saying you're wrong. Just leave it, Keri."

"He needs a tutor, at least," I said, trying to salvage something for Connor out of this.

Tirais stood, disgusted.

"Does that sense of responsibility of yours never take an evening off?" he asked angrily. "Can you never just let a thing go?"

He walked off, leaving me miserable and deflated.

Gwyll slid along the bench towards me, watching as Tirais was swallowed up by the crowd.

"He's been fighting this war since last spring," he said quietly, after a moment. "The Council feels that princes of Keraine need to be held apart from the common herd, apparently. They failed with Tirais; no one could tell Bryan how to raise his children, but Elowyn has far more to contend with. They've blocked every attempt to give Connor suitable companions. And Tirais can do little, just now."

"But why? Surely Connor's life is his family's concern."

"Connor is still Tirais' heir, Keri. And even the post of tutor is hotly contested, since Searlat's death. Every lord in the kingdom wants to fill the place with someone who will do his position good, should it come to it."

"But Connor will only be heir till Tirais' marriage, surely?"

"Which he's shown no interest in as yet. Although," Gwyll looked out on the roistering throng, "that may change. It certainly looks as if it might, anyway."

I drank off the dregs in my cup. Of course he would marry. It had nothing to do with personal preference, and everything to do with policy. Likely, the Queen already had some ideas on this.

"Still," said Gwyll, "there's no need for him to be so tetchy with you. Nor for you to take it so hard. Perhaps you need a diversion."

"Kerris is one big diversion." I hadn't meant it to sound so bitter.

He laughed. "Ready for action? Well, I can recommend some young recruits who will likely be awed at your interest. Or some of the serving-boys."

"No, thanks."

"Fastidious, are we? You're like our Maeliss. Only knights' sons or better for her. She claims they've more stamina." He smiled easily. "If you prefer to sleep alone, so be it. Come on. I stashed a bottle of Aravel brandy under the stairs."

Two hours later, I was thoroughly drunk. I wasn't quite at the passing-out-in-a-corner stage, but rather close; I hadn't the head for brandy that Gwyll had, nor his long practice. At some point I threw off my gloom, and began taking Gwyll's suggestion regarding a quick tumble more seriously, but I was too far gone for that. Instead I had joined a group of Tirais' guards to trade some incoherent war stories, when one of Gallerain's grim-looking servants came up and said that Cioren had sent for me, and I made my stumbling way to the door.

The cold night air hit me like a slap. There was no one about; if Cioren had sent a servant to fetch me, they had not been told to wait. I took a moment to clear my head and then started off in the direction of the palace proper.

Kerris might be laid out in a more orderly fashion than Glaice, or other castles, but it was still huge. In my inebriated condition, I mistook a turning, fetched up at the stables and had to retrace my steps partway. It took longer than I would have thought; I got turned the wrong way twice more, and was actually, what with the night air and the exercise, almost sober when I finally saw a mess-hall I recognized, and regained my bearings.

I followed the colonnaded walkway along the palace wall to the gate, turned in, and crossed the main courtyard to another covered walk. The night was bright with the reflected light of a nearly full moon, and lights still shone out of the windows above me. I turned another corner, heading for the small garden below the west wing. Ahead of me, I saw another cloaked figure, just stepping into the open space of the lawn.

I was in no mood for companionship; my depression had returned like a black and oppressive cloud. I slowed my steps, to avoid catching up to whoever walked before me. Some of the shadowed corners moved, resolving themselves into three more figures that followed close on the figure's heels out into the grass.

The wine had made me stupid; it was the most obvious trick in the book. Still, I didn't quite grasp it, even as I hear the sound of steel drawing from scabbards and heard a muffled cry of alarm.

The attackers, now quite clear in the moonlight, advanced on their target, maneuvering him back across the garden to the farther wall. My hand found my sword hilt, and I began to run, in a not-quite straight or silent path, down the length of sheltered walk.

The intended victim was no easy meat. He was drawing his sword even as he turned to face them, and dropping into a crouch, flung his cloak away from his body to give his arms some freedom.

I careened off the corner of a pillar, stumbled, recovered my elusive balance, and ran in an erratic path towards the figures, still dim and shadowy in the moonlight, as they advanced on their quarry.

The trio leapt on him. I heard two swords crash in anger, and then, despite my weaving steps, I was on them, grabbing at the shoulder of one of the assassins and spinning him round to face me.

He looked, for just a moment, almost comically surprised. I raised my sword to meet his, only just in time, and the shock of it sent me stumbling back, nearly falling over my own feet.

He might have killed me, with his second blow, but we were, all of us, much too close. One of the fighters behind him stepped back in a parrying move and jogged his sword-arm, and he missed.

It wasn't skill, merely timing. For a brief second, my wavering sight steadied and I staggered back a half-pace, saw him teetering from the slight push forward, and hopped into the space that had opened between us, sliding my blade in a tight slant through to his throat.

I misjudged the distance, stepping in too close; instead of a high cut to the neck, my hand, wrapped around the sword hilt, smashed directly into his startled face, and he went down like a sack of grain. The attacker on his left whirled to face me, his sword already moving as he turned.

I felt my lips pull back in a ferocious smile, and I stepped forward into the fray.

And tripped over the man I'd just clocked.

My whole body lurched inelegantly forward and I heard my opponent's sword fly over my head, just as my head connected with a crack into his knees.

He fell, with a dull thud, his head smashing into a corner of the stone bench behind him.

It took a moment to pull myself from the tangle of inert limbs I was caught amongst. I heard from a distance, the sound of receding footsteps as someone ran lightly back across the garden and away down the paving beyond. I paid it no heed. My leg was screaming in reproach and my ribs ached as if kicked.

I struggled into a kneeling posture, my head reeling and my breath coming in short and painful gasps. The man who'd turned to take me lay still and unmoving; his head crooked at one of those curious angles that speaks of a neck irreparably damaged.

Beyond him lay the body of their prey, groaning. Blood was pooling around him and he clutched at his belly. No hope for it, I thought. There was no one else here to effect a rescue. I told my cramping and rebellious body to get up. I hadn't a lot of time.

After a moment, I managed to stand, to move over to his side, to lean down without throwing up or passing out, although my wine-soaked brain devoutly wished to do both.

"Come on, Emlyn," I said. "Come on. You have to get up."

Chapter 39

There were a lot of people in Cioren's room.

It had been dark and silent when I'd finally dragged Emlyn across the threshold, leaving a trail of blood all the way up the stairs, dropping him exhausted and still bleeding onto a bench and pounding on Cioren's chamber door to wake him. My head was no clearer than it had been, and my stomach roiled with too much wine and exertion, but I'd managed to gasp out the gist of the tale. Within moments, Cioren had roused the servants, sent for the healers and we'd dragged Emlyn, moaning in confused protest, to Cioren's bed.

Now I sat beside my family's enemy, as the healers worked on him. The wound looked bad, a deep gash across his belly, but Emlyn himself was, despite his pain, in surprisingly good spirits; when they cut away his tunic, he said with some humor, "A waste of good weaving, that."

The healer grunted, not much amused. He turned to his helper and asked for wine, not for Emlyn, of course, you don't just casually let a man with a belly wound drink, unless he's three parts dead already.

The room filled steadily with more people, buzzing with excitement at this strange and violent mishap. Tirais had arrived, with Gwyll silent and watchful behind him. I wondered who had alerted them to this little escapade. So much for discretion. That had appeared to have been Cioren's first concern once he'd picked the details from my incoherent account.

They were bandaging Emlyn up. The healer, stood, looking less doleful than he had at the start.

"He'll live, no thanks to his attacker," he said. He sounded annoyed. "It's deep, but it seems to have missed anything vital."

I smiled down at Emlyn.

"I might have known," I said. "Nothing vital about Gorsedd."

Emlyn's lips stretched across his teeth in a grimace of enjoyment.

"A little lower down, all my vitals."

"I knew it. Gorsedd's brains collect at the bottom."

Behind me, the healers and the interested onlookers departed. Their voices were muted, almost disappointed, as though Emlyn's survival was a letdown.

"Well," said Emlyn. "I suppose I must thank you."

"I suppose you must."

"Indeed. I won't be able to hold up my head, back home, once you've told the tale. Gorsedd obliged to Orliegh. It doesn't bear thinking of. My wife will be pleased though."

"That you're beholden to Orliegh? What kind of girl did you marry, Emlyn?"

"A kind one."

"Better than you deserve," I said, cheerfully. "Though I can't think her kindness extends to me. Likely she'd prefer you shrouded than owe your life to my handiness."

"You mistake her. I believe she views you with great pity."

"Pity? Why should Gorsedd's lady pity me?"

"Well, you lost me to her. She thinks you quite ill-used."

I laughed outright.

"Tell her it's your good fortune. You wouldn't have survived the wedding-night, else."

"So my mother thought. She'll have a fit, over this night's work."

"No less than my Da. He'd disinherit me, if there was anything left of Orliegh to leave me."

"I think," said Emlyn, suddenly, unaccountably serious, "you've inherited quite enough of Orliegh. Enough for me, at least."

I gripped his hand. "No debt, then. I just happened to be passing. Though if I'd known it was you, I confess I might have hesitated."

"Fair enough. I'll thank Gwyll then, for providing you with enough drink to cloud what little wits you possess."

Tirais cleared his throat in an expression of disgust.

"I hate to interrupt this little lovefest," he said, sarcastically. "But would you mind? What the hell happened?"

I shook my head. Waves of exhaustion were flooding over me. He knew as much as we did. Emlyn, between groans, could come up with no reason to explain the attack. I was, in fact, the only person in Kerris this winter who might have wished to kill him. He owed no money anywhere, had insulted no one he could think of, had ignored not even the tiniest courtesy to any man. Or woman either, he said, conscientiously. A paragon, Emlyn of Gorsedd was.

I'd seen no colours on the men. I had recognized none of them. The man I'd punched had disappeared before the guards' arrival and the corpse in the garden turned up no clues; according to Gwyll, he had been plainly dressed, and unknown to the guards who'd been summoned. He'd carried nothing to identify him. Not even his weapons were remarkable in any way; they were standard issue from some guards' armory, so determinedly ordinary as to be a cipher in themselves. They could have come from any fort or keep from Glaice to Westfold, and they showed no marks other than what might be expected from the single use they'd been put to.

The other two had vanished without trace; Kerris' gates had been warned, but since no-one had passed through them before the word to keep everyone in had gone down to the guards, it seemed likely that their escape lay in their obscurity.

"Put a guard on these rooms," Tirais ordered. "Gwyll, you'll see to it? Fine. I'll speak with you tomorrow, Keri, when you're a little more sober."

It was nearly dawn; I could hear the birds twittering in the gardens below. I wouldn't have thought I could sleep, what with the noise of servants waking, and the constant pounding in my head, but I was wrong. I was out before my head had hit the pillows, really, and I woke late in the morning. Someone had drawn the heavy curtains across the window to block the sunlight, and my second-best tunic and trews were laid out neatly on the chest at the foot of the bed.

I didn't have any real desire to get up. My headache hadn't gone off; instead, it had widened its scope to include my neck, and my recalcitrant body had added a bruising soreness in my side. I couldn't, for the first few moments, remember why it should be so, then the night had flooded back to me.

I sat, carefully, and swung my legs over the side of the mattress. A burning throb shot through my thigh. At this rate, I'd be a cripple by springtime. I found myself cursing Emlyn of Gorsedd as I struggled to pull on my shirt. Why couldn't the man have picked some other time and place to be ambushed?

My stomach hadn't settled itself. I threw up twice before I was completely dressed, and was still queasy as I stumbled into the main room. Cioren sat in pretty much the same place as he'd been when I'd left him, the night before, and covered platters and the remains of breakfast lay on the table before him. He looked tired and rumpled and was gravely nursing a tankard of ale when I entered.

"Emlyn? Is he - ?"

"He's well enough, and resting. Don't fret."

I sank into a chair. My head was making thinking difficult. I was glad, though, that Emlyn lived. I felt rather proprietary about him, actually. If he was going to be killed, I would prefer to do it myself, in a fair fight, than have him cut down by a gang of cowards.

Cioren handed me a steaming tankard; it was the unappetizing brew the healer had made up for me. I felt my stomach give me a warning lurch, and set it carefully on the table.

"I advise you to drink," Cioren said. "And have some breakfast. No, don't give me that look. I assure you, you'll feel much better with something inside you."

He was, to my surprise, quite right. I cut some bread, without any enthusiasm. I began eating the boiled egg he placed on my plate with even less enjoyment, and sipped at the hot mess of infused herbs, but halfway through, I felt my gut settling and the ache in my side recede to a minor throb.

After a bit, I even began to feel less cranky. Emlyn certainly couldn't have known he would be set upon as he'd strolled through Kerris' grounds, and it was only my bad luck that put me in the unlikely role of Gorsedd's rescuer.

My better mood was short-lived. Cioren, once I'd made some recovery that was visible to him, began to take me through the night's events once more, and my memory was unreliable, for the first part of my evening's carouse. I couldn't remember anything in any particular order, and I couldn't quite remember why it was that I'd left when I had.

We started at the beginning again, and my head began to throb in earnest. I recalled, suddenly, Gallerain's man, leaning over my shoulder saying that Cioren had sent for me.

"Why did you go to bed?" I asked. "I couldn't have been more than a half a glass, getting back."

"I tell you, I didn't send for you. I talked with Elowyn for mere minutes, then came down here, and went to sleep." He looked as though he didn't believe in my confused recollections. "Tell me though, did you see Emlyn go? He would have been only a moment or two before you."

"I wasn't watching him. Oh, but wait." I stopped, trying to piece together my intermittent mental pictures of the walk back. "I took a wrong turning," I said slowly. "I must have been an extra quarter-glass, at least. And they were waiting…" My voice trickled away into silence.

"So Emlyn left after, do you think?" It sounded so matter-of-fact; I scarcely took in the significance for a moment.

"If you didn't send for me," I said, "And Emlyn left just after...it would fit, but -"

"Yes." He seemed unshaken. Well, it wasn't his head on the block, here. "Yes, that makes a more sensible picture. Not by much, I grant you, but certainly more likely than Emlyn having someone with a grudge. I've never met anyone so inoffensive."

"Meaning I am?" I couldn't really take pleasure in the joke, though. Enemies are one thing. Assassins are something else. "Come on. Who would want to kill me? Gervase and Aileen, perhaps, but Lady Aileen certainly doesn't seem to hold a grudge. And you can't tell me that Gervase would stoop to hired killers. He could break my neck on the practice-ground, any day."

"You must admit, though, it puts everything in a different light. Where's that twine you found the other day?"

"On the window ledge, I think."

But it wasn't.

"I thought you had given it to Priestess Dalriega, anyway." I said.

"Who's had time? And she went off to the shrine outside the city that morning. I left it here, I thought. You must have moved it, or else I did," said Cioren. We began hunting through the eccentric trophies, to no avail. A thorough search of our rooms turned up no more, nor did a discreet questioning of the servants. No one had seen anything resembling our description, not for two days. After more than an hour's messing about, we were still empty-handed, and Cioren had assumed that grim and forbidding expression again.

"This is no good," I said. "It's gone, though I'm inclined to think that it went out with some other rubbish. You said yourself it doesn't prove a thing, anyway."

"Humor me. It might have proved useful, to my mind."

"But it gets us no closer to an answer, does it? Though I could make a guess."

"Don't," he cautioned me, "don't let your prejudices run away with you."

"Well, but who else would have it in for me? And here we both are, nice and snug together in Kerris. She's Uln's brat, when all's said and done."

234

"What could Angharad have to do with it, though? She's a pretty girl, rather sought after, with every hope that the Queen will make her a good marriage and give her lands back, which is all that's in her head, I've no doubt."

"Oh, I'll admit she's easy on the eyes, no question. That doesn't make her either stupid or innocent. In fact, I don't think you could find anyone less innocent."

"Easy isn't the word I'd have used," he said. I thought I heard a slight wistfulness in his tone, and felt a momentary disgust. "She's made very few friends, all the same. But an arrogance she's not entitled to doesn't make her a villain, or even rouse my suspicions that she's got anything to do with this. For one thing, how would she go about it?"

"How should I know? But she grew up with Uln for a parent. What do we know of what she was taught?"

"I'll concede the point, there. But she's only a girl, and she knows even less than you do about all that's happened. We can't accuse anyone, at this stage."

He was right, I supposed. Angharad was probably already in the Queen's custody by the time her father had crossed the border into Camrhys. I nodded, saying that I understood, and that I'd keep my mouth shut, if that was what was worrying him.

"But what's to do?" I finished off. "I can't just leave. I'm bound by Her Majesty's hospitality, at the very least."

"No-o. I don't know what to suggest, other than trying to stay in company, for now. Kerris is packed to the rafters, so that shouldn't be difficult, even after dark. We'll come up with an answer, soon enough."

I don't know why he seemed to think this advice would comfort me. I wasn't at all reassured, although I couldn't think that another midnight attack was imminent. Whoever was behind this seemed to use very different methods for each attempt. In fact, there was no guarantee that both items had any relationship; I might have two enemies, for all I knew. Or perhaps none at all. There was always a chance that these things had nothing to do with me.

Still, I was contented by the fact that both tries had been spectacularly unsuccessful, serving only to put me on my guard, if they were directed my way, and by the knowledge that no-one in Kerris, save for Elowyn, Cioren and I, knew of that evil grimoire that Uln had carried into Keraine. That, at least, could not be part of this mess.

Cioren had arranged for the healer to come and look in on poor Emlyn, still lying in Cioren's room befuddled by some herb-laced wine he'd been given.

Gorsedd's lord had watched our search of the chamber incuriously, washing in and out of consciousness while we crawled about to see if the twine had been swept under the bed or behind a chest.

After he'd given Emlyn more potions to drink, the healer insisted on seeing what damage I'd done myself over the last two days, and gave me a stern lecture on recuperation. Never mind that I hadn't gone looking for trouble, or that Emlyn would likely have died, had I thought to save my ribs the exercise; he expressed considerable anger over my disregard of my body's limitations.

Still, he found no evidence that I'd damaged myself further. I might feel as though I'd been pummeled into a pulp, but my ribs were still nearly healed, and my leg was bruised, but otherwise intact. I let his words roll over me, not paying them the slightest heed: if I'd gotten a raven for every time I'd wished myself otherwise and not involved in this sort of thing, I would be the richest soldier in Keraine by now, I reckoned, and nodded my head politely as he talked.

As if only waiting for the healer's departure, Connor arrived, with Parthalen in tow, and a basket of sugared plums. He knew Emlyn, of course; Gorsedd lies nearly next door to Dungarrow Castle, and Connor had been schooled well in the courtesies he owed his vassals. He had a boy's taste in gifts, though. I didn't think Emlyn would be up to an entire tree's worth of candied fruit, but held my peace.

I don't think he would have noticed anything amiss, he was too full of the tale of my daring rescue, gleaned from Tirais' guards and a few indiscreet servants. Why Emlyn should have been unsafe walking to his rooms in Kerris didn't come up as a question; Connor was merely thrilled to be on speaking terms with the principals of something so exciting, and eager to hear the whole.

I gave him as clear an account of the fight as I could. It wasn't enough, of course; mistakes that turn out lucky aren't very heroic. My half-hearted attempt to convince him that drunken brawling is neither wise nor efficient left him cold, as well it might. He eyed me with skepticism, convinced that I was being modest. I gave it up, agreed that it would be hard for Emlyn to hold to his family's anger at Orliegh after this, and after finding Emlyn still asleep, Connor departed, leaving Cioren and I to chuckle over a ten-year-old's appetite for violence and happy endings.

Chapter 40

Three days later, we were none the wiser.

The Feast of Aheris dawned, cold and brilliant with winter sunshine. The halls of Kerris were now so crammed with greenery that you could scarcely tell where outdoors left off and indoors began: the servants had spent the better part of the last days arranging boughs and branches of evergreen throughout the castle. Wintervine garlanded the stairwells and rafters, and the smell of applewood scented the air, as huge fires were lit in every hearth.

Kerris was crammed with people, too. Every noble lord and lady within a reasonable distance had ridden in to share the coming Midwinter revels with their queen, and many from much farther off had made the trip as well. Musicians from every part of the kingdom had converged on Kerris, along with travelling players, acrobats and the like. In the palace and the city, day or night, you were assailed with song and story. Assaulted with it, at times: the quality was uneven, to say the least.

I hardly had to try, to keep in with Cioren's wish that I not be much alone. It was all one could do to find privacy at the latrines, let alone anywhere else. Even some of the hallways had been turned into temporary sleeping chambers for the late arrivals.

It was no wonder then, that no trace of Emlyn's attackers had been found. In the crush of people descending on the Royal Family, anyone could have melted away into invisibility. After another day, the healer decided that Emlyn could be moved back to his own quarters and I had stopped worrying over shadows. In the press of flesh around me, I couldn't see how anyone could pull off another murder attempt, no matter who they were after, and I stopped searching the crowds for a man with a blackened eye.

Dalriega returned to the palace in time for the Feast, two days after the attack. Normally, I might not even have known, but she came to Cioren's rooms, full of angry concern, almost at once, not stopping to wash or change. A guard on the gates had been full of the tale, which had grown in the few hours of its life: a full squad of trained assassins was apparently roaming the corridors, and I was also mentioned as being about eight feet tall, and capable of breathing fire.

Dalriega was not amused. She discounted most of the gossip, of course, but the bare facts were enough to anger anyone. Consequently, she was spitting woodpegs even as she came through our door, furious at the very idea of assaults on guests of the queen. Most of her invective was aimed at the guards, who were, in her opinion, ill-trained, ill-mannered, and arrant fools, to boot, and could not have kept a cow-byre secure if their lives depended on it. It took her a few minutes to get on to me, but she wound up there eventually, asking acidly what kind of cuckoo Orliegh's nest had sent Keraine.

"Wherever you turn up," she said, eyeing me with disfavour, "There's been trouble. What is it about you, then?"

"Peace, Dalriega," Cioren came to my rescue. "Keri's guilty of nothing more than bad fortune. She can't help it if we keep inviting her to the feasting, so to speak. And all this might have been much worse, had she been elsewhere."

I wouldn't have thought this would stop her. She had been enjoying her temper. But it did slow her. She took a breath, looked me over and said begrudgingly that of course, it wasn't my fault.

This happier state of affairs didn't last. Cioren began explaining about the string-charm and Connor's fall, and we were right back at it.

"Goddess grant me patience! You knew where I was. Why didn't you send down to the shrine, if you were too lazy to come after me yourself? It isn't for you, Cioren, to decide what is important and what is not. Unfettered magery is a curse and a bane, and an affront to the Mother, and you have no right to keep anything like this to yourself!"

"And if I had sent for you, you'd have told me I was an anxious old fool. And that ten to one, it was just simple carelessness and bad luck."

"Well, ten to one, it is! But you say it's gone missing? Now, that I don't like. Though how you can keep track of anything in all this mess, I don't know. The servants will find it when they sweep these rooms out come spring, I shouldn't wonder. Tell me again what happened exactly."

But our second essay into Connor's fall, and another go-round of the late night attackers silenced her. Her face was stern and serious, and when we were done, she was quiet for several long minutes.

"It wasn't one of ours," she said, after some thought. "We train our novices better than that. And local charmers are too careful of their things to lose them rambling about the countryside. We don't let even the small Talents go throwing spells about without proper training. No, this was something meant to harm. But why?"

"Penvarron," I said. "It's the only thing I can think of."

She narrowed her eyes at me. "Penvarron wasn't so much."

I would have liked to have asked her what would constitute "much" in her opinion. In mine, Penvarron had been quite enough. More than enough.

"Keridwen thinks she knows who lies behind this," Cioren said.

Dalriega's gaze sharpened. Then, as she put together Penvarron and my own history in her mind, she blinked.

"No," she said, emphatically. "No and no. That girl is not behind it. I'd wager my life on it. Oh, she's a pain, I'll grant you that," she waved off my grunt of protest, "She's malicious enough, and a thorough-going little mischiefmaker, but the fact is, she isn't a Talent. She may have the nastiness to plan this sort of evil, but she hasn't the brains. No, Lady Angharad may wish you ill, and Goddess knows what else she yearns for: wealth and power, for certain, and none too particular about who she has to hurt to gain it, but she wouldn't know how to begin planning this kind of thing. She isn't capable of doing it herself, she hasn't the friends here to execute it, and frankly, she hasn't the wits to cover her tracks so well. Hers is the sort of background badness that hopes for your downfall, Keridwen, and would help it along, if she could, and certainly, she'll twist the knife, every chance she gets, but as for masterminding it all, or even taking an active part? No, I can't see it. Whoever's behind this has Power, to escape both Cioren's and my detection, and the money and brains to put it together. We're looking for someone far different from a silly little miss with a malicious streak."

I opened my mouth, then shut it. Half the people in this castle probably owned a charm like the one Angharad had given Connor. If there were something wrong with it, Cioren would have noticed.

Dalriega rose to go. "I'll put one of my people onto it. That one you killed, now. There might be something there. Tirais is sending us the sword he used, and some of his things. We'll find out who he was, for a start."

"I tried that," said Cioren, pensively. "Couldn't make out at all, which is odd."

"Ah, well," said the priestess. "I suppose there might be one or two spells I know that you don't, strange as that may seem to you."

Cioren laughed. "I'm sure there are. You're a stingy woman, Dalriega, doling out knowledge as if there might not be enough to go around."

She was already at the door, chuckling with restored good humor.

"Ah," she said, turning around. "I knew there was something I was forgetting. Here, this came while I was at the shrine. One of my priests dug it up, out by Ys Tearch, when they were repairing one of the posting towers. It ought to wait till Midwinter Night, but you can have it now." She drew a small, clothwrapped parcel from her sleeve. "Just don't tell anyone where you

239

had it. It's worth my reputation, to give away something like this to an Unbound."

Cioren took the package. Dalriega watched him open it with affectionate amusement, then, as he held the object, with undisguised pleasure, rising to give her an embrace of thanks, she laughed again, hugged him back, and said "That'll do. Merry Midwinter, my dear. I'll see you at the banquet, shall I?"

"Yes, of course," he said, absently, now intent on his gift.

"Mind he actually arrives down in good time," she said to me. "He'll be up all night, playing with it, if someone doesn't ride herd on him."

I said something, I can't remember what, but she was already gone, calling to her attendants in the hall, and the door banged shut behind her.

Chapter 41

Cioren's new toy was small, fitting neatly into the palm of his hand. It was metallic, darkish gray, and covered with angular, incised glyphs that were not quite letters, though they looked at first very similar to the script on those carved stones that dot the countryside, marking the Goddess' imprint on the land. He stood near to the window, holding it to the light and examining it closely, with every appearance of delight.

"What is it?"

"What? Oh, of course. You won't have seen one of these before. It's called a liarn."

"That's helpful."

He threw me a rueful smile. "Sorry. Are you really interested?"

"Sure. Why not? I can see how interesting it is to you, anyway."

He came back to the table, laying the object onto the cloth that had wrapped it, and sat.

"Liarns are partly focuses for power. But they also store power. You remember my telling you that power is dangerous, outside of the warded places? Well, our ancestors got round that by creating the liarn, to hold and focus raw power in a warded form that could be carried out from places like Penvarron, and used safely. Not a huge amount, of course, nothing like what you need to do truly important spells, but in the hands of a really Talented mage, it would be enough. You can filter your own Power through a liarn and augment what is there, without too much risk to yourself, even if you're interrupted."

"And we have such things, now?"

"A few. The priesthood keeps turning them up, in older shrines and so on. Most of them aren't useful, of course. Burnt out, mainly, or else created for such specific purposes that one can't do anything with them."

"But you've seen a lot of them, I take it?" I was a little confused. It was all like pulling on a thread on your tunic: the more you tug on it, the less tunic you seem to have. Knowledge apparently worked in a similar fashion: every time I thought I had it nearly worked out, I learned something that threw everything else into question, leaving me more ignorant and bewildered than before.

"Not like this one. I've got a few of the broken ones lying around. But the holy ones keep real liarns hidden away. This is the first one I've ever handled that appears to be in working order."

"But you could make one, surely?"

"Well, not so easily. Not like this. We don't know how they did it, really. I suspect they used the really powerful sanctuaries to actually make them. But we know the theory, more or less. I can make a temporary one, at least, but a permanent liarn, one that can have power restored to it after each use, that I cannot do. Nor can the holy ones. Or so Dalriega says. You can't always trust that, though. They keep far too much to themselves."

I gave it some thought, as he picked up the liarn and resumed his examination. Two things struck me. One was it was probably true that no one was able to recreate this kind of thing, else why would Dalriega have given one to Cioren? Affection wasn't enough, for someone like her. No, she had exhausted all the possibilities in the priesthood, and had decided that Cioren might be able to figure it out. And I could see why it might be important. Up against a Camrhys that could resurrect ancient skills and knowledge, a liarn might be a powerful edge in a conflict, sometime down the road.

The second thing that crossed my mind, almost at the same moment, was that Cioren, if he said he could make a temporary version of a liarn, meant, in fact, that he had done so. More than once, probably. And I could make an educated guess as to one of those times.

He was muttering to himself as he rose to take up pen and paper to make notes in his crabbed, tiny script.

My stomach felt cramped and sick. He'd actually said it to me, that he'd filtered his power through me. Made it sound casual, and benign, and said it when I was weak, injured and confused, so that I was unlikely to understand, or even much care, what it was he'd really done.

"That's what you did to me, isn't it?" My voice was harsh and angry. "At Penvarron. You channeled your Power through me, didn't you? Made me your liarn?"

"What? Oh, well, in a manner of -"

"Don't try to fob me off. You used me, Cioren. I was just a tool to you. Just another liarn."

"Keri, you know I wouldn't have -"

"You should have told me. You've used sorcery on me, every chance you had, without a single thought as to how I might feel about it. You're as bad as

Uln. Did you never think that I had some right as to how my body and soul are disposed of? Don't give me that crap about need. It didn't weigh with you for a second."

"I had no choice. You know that. If Eater had been able -"

"I said, don't give me that crap." I stood, trembling with outrage. "You had no right, and you know it. If you ever try that again, I'll kill you. I swear it."

I slammed the door behind me as I left. Even through the crash of the wood on the frame, I could hear Cioren say something about not being able to do it twice, but I didn't know if he meant to me, specifically, or something else, nor did I care.

I stomped up the corridor, kicking at a piece of foliage that had fallen from its perch in the beams overhead. I was in a thoroughly bad temper, although my inner voice said quite calmly that I ought to have known about this, that all the evidence had been there, and that in fact I had known it, if I'd stopped to think at all. It didn't help to know that the voice was right.

I turned onto the main hallway, still fuming to myself, and brushed past a knot of merrymakers coming up the stairs with an inward grumble. Merry Midwinter indeed, I thought, savagely. The highest in the land all think we're cattle and fools, to be used and dropped away like chaff from wheat, magic's running rampant, and here we all sit, making stupid jests and getting drunk in the feasthalls. We're doomed, if Camrhys has the slightest clue about it.

I had no destination, no plan. I was just going, trying to walk off my fury, and, in my anger, I went straight past the stairs and continued down the hall, not watching or even seeing where I was headed, until I nearly walked right over Maeliss, her arms wrapped about a handsome young man dressed in the finest of embroidered tunics and wearing an ornately made silver torc of rank.

I apologized. The blank look on their faces made it apparent their minds were elsewhere, but they disentangled themselves somewhat and we stood about awkwardly as Maeliss introduced me to her friend.

His name was Vere. Maeliss was only a couple of years older than I was, but this was sheer cradle robbing: Vere couldn't have been more than sixteen, and the torc, I discovered, was new. Vere's family was related to the Queen, and his father's recent death made him a close connection to the throne. We stood making idle social noises until a door opened behind us from Prince Tirais' rooms and Gwyll emerged, looking slightly harassed.

"Oh, hullo, Keri," he said. "Were you looking for Tirais? I wouldn't, if I were you. He's got a stack of reports to read by morning, and a foul temper to go with it."

"No," I said. "I was just wandering."

"Well, wander with us. We're off to the city. This place is crawling with petitioners and toadies, and if one more person tries to bribe me to get in to see Tirais, I'll do something violent, I'm afraid. A little hanging about with thieving merchants and innkeepers who water the wine, that's what I'm after. Give me an honest, out-and-out villain any day. These perfumed criminals and overdressed hucksters give me the pip!"

Around my neck hung a small pouch carrying about half the silver coins I'd been given at Glaice. I thought of the things I could probably buy, and smiled, my anger dropping away like autumn leaves.

"Sure," I said. "Why not?"

It was a glorious day. I don't mean the weather; overhead the skies were dark and gray and threatening snow, and the wind was howling out of the north, biting and chill. But until we passed through the outer gates of Kerris, and I felt my tense shoulders ease, I hadn't been aware of how the palace, and all that I'd been through, had oppressed me. The weight of guilt and worry dropped away as easily as my anger had, and I laughed with Gwyll over a silly jest thrown at Maeliss and Vere, giving myself up to enjoyment.

Orliegh wasn't poor, not in any true sense. I don't think I'd ever, until I left home, given a moment's thought to where my next meal was coming from, and I'd always been decently clothed. There was always a horse to ride, and amusements aplenty, that cost me nothing.

But we weren't rich. Coin was hard to come by, and gifts were generally things made by ourselves or local craftsmen, if they weren't simply the raw materials from our own lands. At fairs, or when tinkers and merchants came through, the estate's needs took priority: we bought only those things we could not make ourselves, and there was precious little left over for luxuries.

For the first time in my life, though, I had no reason to weigh need or price. I had more coin than my father saw in a year, and this was less than half of what I could draw on. The ravens and the remainder of the silver lay in some corner of Cioren's workroom. A safe place, he'd said, since not even the servants went in there. I had nothing to save for, really. I was free to indulge myself.

And my family. At a stall on a crowded corner, I debated over a variety of exotic spices brought from the east, appealing to Maeliss for advice when I couldn't decide, and not even feeling shocked when she said easily that I might as well buy some of each of them, since I had no idea which would please my mother most. I barely blinked over the cost of some delicately woven linen, worth more than a small field of barley: it wasn't much, compared with the money I had.

I couldn't shake my northern roots entirely, of course. I bargained hard at the cloth merchant's, and at the metalworker's when I found a pair of silver earrings that Siobhan would love. I was secretly shocked at the prices, despite my wealth.

The others were far more profligate. Maeliss in particular bought whatever caught her eye, at the first amount proposed, without any attempt to get at a true reflection of the item's worth. Gwyll, trying to choose between a throwing knife and an eating dagger as a gift for his brother, wound up with both, on the grounds that there was sure to be somebody he'd forgotten to buy a gift for.

Our arms were laden with packages and parcels when, hungry and worn out by spending, we reached a narrow alley, turned down it, and entered a small, clean-looking tavern called, amusingly, The Bull's Eye.

The innkeeper bustled over. She was a short, fat, middle-aged woman, with a happy smile creasing her face. She had a right to be happy: most of the tables were filled with prosperous-looking people surrounded by platters, tankards and plates. Innkeepers must turn a tidy profit, in Kerris at Midwinter.

"Lord Gwyll! And Lady Maeliss, too! Merry Midwinter to you both."

She hustled us to a table near the centre of the room, chatting pleasantly all the while of how busy she was, how all her rooms were filled, how she was pleased to see them both, and wasn't it all just awful, those evil Camrhyssi running amok and subverting the good nobles of Keraine with horrid spells? Lucky, we were, that Elowyn and Tirais were a match for anything, and able to stop it all in its tracks, did we intend to eat? She had a good lamb shoulder, just off the spits, and fresh bread and sweet butter.

Outside, in the fading afternoon, the streets were, if anything, more crowded than before. On every corner, I saw sights that surprised and delighted me: puppet-plays surrounded by eager, laughing children, dancers and singers, hedgewitches selling love-charms, players reenacting legends, complete with tawdry, garish costumes, and "mages" performing pointless, fascinating tricks.

I watched as a frail old man with a wispy beard pulled sprigs of wintervine from a toddler's ear, to the crowd's amazement, although there wasn't any mystery to it. Standing to the side and concentrating on the man's hands, rather than being distracted by his flamboyant gestures and rapid patter, I could see the tiny movement when his long fingers swept past the front of his tunic and twitched out a leafy scrap. It disappeared in a twinkling into his palm, only to reappear as he leant towards the child. From the front, though, it would look as if it appeared from nowhere.

Like everything else in life, it just depended on your perspective.

Chapter 42

Later that night, I presented myself in the feast hall, along with everyone else in Kerris. I had managed to skip quite a few of these tedious revels without comment; after the first couple of evenings, I had been moved to one of the long tables at the side to make room for more noble guests whose position demanded a central view of the proceedings.

But the Feast of Aheris, to celebrate the last full moon of the year, was not one I could avoid, not if I wanted to eat at all. Every servant in the palace was on duty in the kitchens or the hall, and every guest of the Queen's was stuffed into the place, packed together as close as herrings in a salt-barrel. Even Emlyn was there, looking pale but cheerful; I stopped on my way up to my seat, to ask him how he did, and exchange a couple of barbed and happy insults. I ate and drank, and listened to a rather dull story of some long-ago hunt from the man seated next to me. I drank some more and flirted mildly with Vere when he sauntered down from his place at the high table. I followed along in Maeliss' wake to another guard barracks and lost cheerfully at the dicing for an hour or more, then trailed along with a pair of Queen's guards who were off to a stint of duty in the main halls, crossing the wide courtyard in perfect safety.

I came up the central stairs in the silent night. There were still a few candles burning in sconces on the walls behind the open gallery, but there was nothing moving, and only the faintest echoes of sound from the hall below, as the few people still awake drank off the last of their ale and departed for their beds. But as I reached the halfway point, I could see, emerging from the hallway to the right, a slender figure moving onto the landing. The pale light caught and sparkled on her silvery hair and she wore a loose robe of some finely woven, almost sheer fabric that moved restlessly over her body as she walked.

My own progress up the steps startled her. She stopped, her mouth a round "o" of pretty surprise, and then, to my own astonishment, she waited, watching me, until I reached the top.

Some evil genius prompted me, or else I had drunk more than I knew.

"You're abroad late," I said.

"I had…an errand," said Angharad. She managed to infuse the words with mystery and innuendo, without changing the look of unmarred innocence that clung to her. I didn't know how she did it, and I owned, in my heart of hearts, that there was something impressive about it.

I shrugged. If she thought I would minister to her vanity by asking questions, she had miscalculated. Any question would be met with a lie or a half-truth, I reasoned, and anyway, what did I care? But even as these thoughts formed, I looked back along the corridor and realized that Tirais' rooms lay beyond.

Her eyes followed mine, and she smiled, that same spiteful smirk she had gifted me with in Elowyn's rooms.

"Indeed," I said, and shrugged again.

One of the candles guttered, then flared. I smelt the smoke, overlaid with something sweet and exotic. I really had drunk too much, I thought. My head felt thick and slow, and my stomach heaved, just a little.

She laughed. "He's a man of rather interesting…appetites, wouldn't you say?"

"I wouldn't know," I said. My voice was light and indifferent, to my amazement. If that was where his taste lay, well, I'd known there was no hope from the start. I could even understand it, in a way: she was beautiful, and it might only have been wishful thinking on my part, that he hadn't seemed to even like her. Still, I wished he had taken his pleasures with someone, anyone else.

"No? And here I thought you quite besotted. But then, you're not quite his style."

I felt one of my eyebrows quirk upwards and was amused, in my turn. It was catching, that trick of overweening superiority and hauteur, and it worked. Under that creamy complexion, she flushed, ever so slightly.

"It's an old game," I said. "And I've never noticed it works all that well. It's the queen you'll have to please, if you want your lands back. I doubt Tirais will champion your cause, however inventive you are in his bed."

"The queen," said Angharad, coldly, "was an easy mark. Poor old woman, she's starved for companionship of her own quality; it was nothing to cozen her. A sympathetic ear, and a few errands run, and she could not give me enough praise."

"But not your lands," I said, and smiled.

"They'll come. And more, besides. When the furor's died, I expect I will end up much to the good. Better off than you, at any rate. What will you have? A place in some garrison? A few coins, to buy your silence? The chance to die in their service? And meanwhile, I will be among the highest of the land, and sit in every council, and perhaps, even, decide your future."

"Keep talking, and you may yet convince yourself," I advised. "You aren't convincing me."

"Fool," she said. "It's already happening. They confide in me constantly. I know all that occurred at Penvarron."

"You, and every trooper and guard from here to Westfold," I said, still smiling. I could not believe my own voice, cool and dismissive. My face, I realized, reflected this. No hint of my inner turmoil showed, I was sure.

"Pah! Do you think I mouth the garbled gossip of those sots? I know more, far more, than even you do. They tell me it all. Even that book you brought, for all you think it so secret and safe. Ah, that's got you, hasn't it? But I am much in Elowyn's confidence, and in Cioren's, too."

My stomach lurched. She was right, this shock told, I couldn't help it. But I wasn't going to give her the satisfaction. I said, in as blighting a tone as I could muster, "I wouldn't, if I were you, read too much into pillow gossip. No, nor into what mistaken scraps you've picked up listening at keyholes. And I would wait until the charter for Uln Castle is in your hands before counting on your future."

For a moment, I thought I'd hit the mark. She blinked at my words, then recovered herself, and gave a bright, metallic laugh.

"It may be sooner than you think, at least," she said. Her hands made a curious little gesture, a kind of pushing motion, tiny and almost unnoticeable. I shook my head again; my mouth seemed suddenly dry and constricted.

"Or later than you would like." I said it with difficulty, though. I swallowed, but she was already moving off, as if suddenly bored with her sport.

"Good night, Keri," she said, and turned toward the stairs up to the Queen's apartments. "Sleep well."

She was wise, in this at least. I was in a dice-throw's distance of throttling her. I watched as she disappeared into the darkness and turned to seek my bed.

I couldn't sleep. My bandaging itched and my leg was aching, but these were mere trifles compared with the ache in my heart.

Cioren was still awake; I had seen the soft glow of light from beneath his door. But Angharad's words had reawakened my anger. He had promised me secrecy. He had sworn to me that the book would only be known to the queen, himself and to me, and that he would keep its disposition dark and silent. Goddess' tits, he'd gotten me to lie for him, if only by omission, and here was the daughter of our downfall's creator, being kept abreast of every detail. Likely, they'd a different definition of secret than I had. Likely, every spit-turner in the kitchen knew all about it.

I thumped my pillow in frustration. Not only did they seem to trust her, they seemed ready to embrace her. Indeed, the prince already had. The thought of him bedding that little garden-snake was sickening.

I got up, after a bit. There was wine, on the side table. I set my cup on the bench at the foot of the bed, pulled off my shirt, and began unwinding the wrappings that pinned my torso. It was the only one of my irritants that had a remedy, but after a minute or two of blissful scratching, my anger came back in full force. I swallowed some wine. There was something here that bothered me, beyond the obvious. I couldn't quite grasp hold of it, but somewhere, in my exchange with Uln's daughter, something had caught at my suspicious mind. Something not quite right about how she'd phrased it all, perhaps, or there was something else there that my conscious mind had missed.

I got back into bed, still sipping at my wine and replaying her words in my head. It was no good. Whatever had set alarm-bells ringing in my brain was too small, too subtle to catch. I finished off the cup, and pulled the coverlet over my head.

Chapter 43

In the pitiless daylight, I considered my anger. It wasn't necessarily Cioren's doing, I thought, that Angharad knew of the book. In fact, the more I considered it, the less likely it seemed. Cioren barely told me anything, even in response to direct questioning, and I couldn't see that even an outright seduction would open those particular lips for information. He was closer to Dalriega than he would likely recognize himself, when it came to doling out knowledge.

I hadn't seen him, to speak to, after our last, acrimonious encounter over the liarn. At the feasting, I'd kept my eyes resolutely away from the upper tables, still too bruised and resentful. But now, I felt ashamed. He'd done what he'd done, and he hadn't tried to hide it, really. If, as he'd occasionally said, I was a backward provincial who knew nothing of what pertained in the wider world, he couldn't be blamed for my misconceptions. And he'd been good to me, really. I blushed, thinking of how he'd taken me on, after Caer Druach. For all I knew, Tirais might have wanted to leave me there and be shut of me, once and for all.

I would have to apologize. The thought was not heartening. When you know you are really in the wrong, apologizing is the hardest part. And it might do no good. After my outburst, he might well consider that it was good riddance and fare-thee-well, and it was all that I deserved.

The door leading to the workroom was open, and I could hear him, pottering about. I swallowed, and walked over, peering in.

He was sorting through a small wooden casket that lay open on the overcrowded table, but he looked up at my tentative knock. I cleared my throat.

"Well?" he said. His voice gave me nothing, it was as flat and as expressionless as his face.

"I -er- I wanted to apologize," I said. My voice sounded strained and awkward. "For yesterday, I mean. I had no right, that is, well, I'm sorry, that's all."

He leaned back in his chair.

"Keri," he said, gently, "there's no need. Indeed, I should beg your pardon. You spoke no more than the truth. I did what I had no right to do, using you in that way. But truly, I was hardpressed to find anything that even resembled a solution, beyond what I did. There wasn't much time, and, well, perhaps I should have trusted you better. You certainly have much nicer instincts than I do. I was hoping to get away without actually having to say these words."

I laughed weakly, with relief. "I didn't want to, either. Can we just say it was my foul temper and have done with it, do you think?"

"Oh, aye, if you want the blame so much. I can afford that much generosity, at least. But come, have you breakfasted?"

"No, I've just gotten up."

"Then let's go down to the kitchens and see what we can scrounge. You won't get the service you're used to, these days. The servants are run off their feet."

Crossing the Great Hall, I caught a glimpse of Angharad, neatly gowned, with her hair hidden under a velvet cap. Baron Gallerain was with her, his head bent close to hers, deep in conversation. They didn't see us as we pushed through the crowds of hungover nobility swilling down their morning ale, which was a relief. I pushed my late night encounter with Tirais' mistress into the back of my mind and tried hard to forget that it had occurred.

We wasted a lot of time in the kitchens, where Cioren was an obvious favourite; the maids and cooks vying with each other to produce tempting dishes for him. We ate, therefore, far better than we would have if we'd tried our luck upstairs with the others. Instead of lukewarm ale and stale bread, we got buttered eggs, mulled wine, and sausage rolls, dripping with fat and piping hot from the ovens, along with a fair bit of entertaining gossip about the more important guests.

With Midwinter Eve only three days away, the staff and servants of Kerris were pushed to the limits and run fairly off their feet, but they were in great spirits, nonetheless. They joked and laughed their way through their work, despite the almost continual parade of visiting servants who trailed through with requests for special treatment for their own masters. There were some minor fits of temper, mainly from the cooks, who were at their wits' end as to how all these gentles could be fed at regular intervals while still managing to get an enormous feast for hundreds of people cooked and served in anything like style; and one of the spit-boys had slapped a ladies' maid who criticized his grease-laden smock in rather nasty terms. This was felt to be, however, a kind of triumph for the palace servants, as the woman retired, vanquished and in tears.

Finally, it became apparent that, loved as Cioren was, we were very much in the way and we left, retracing our steps back to the Great Hall. It was nearly deserted, compared to the multitudes that had milled around earlier, and Angharad was nowhere to be seen.

Just as we reached the main stairs, though, one of the Queen's servants caught up to us. I was wanted in the Queen's rooms, as soon as possible. Immediately, I surmised. The girl had been looking for me for some little time, too; she set an alarming pace up the steps, as soon as I'd been waved off by a distracted Cioren, who had been hailed from across the room by an old friend.

I came into one of the audience chambers, wishing I hadn't worn my arming tunic, and that I'd had time to comb my hair. I looked rather down-at-heel, but Her Majesty didn't seem to notice. She was holding a sheaf of parchments, listening to Baron Gallerain, who was droning on in low tones, but they broke off their speech as I came in.

I bowed.

"Just go on through to my workroom, please, Keridwen," Elowyn said.

I nodded, mystified. What Elowyn wanted with me was not clear. Doubtless she would explain, though; I crossed to the door she indicated.

As I began to push the door closed, Gallerain's voice floated to me.

"Really, Elowyn, do you think that wise?" His tone spoke volumes, to me.

I didn't hear the Queen's response. I shut the door firmly, without thought.

I knew what he meant. My shock was more that he knew it. Standing in Elowyn's untidy, crowded study, amid piles and heaps of account books and ledgers, I gazed at the mounds of paperwork that surrounded the Queen's days.

It's no easy job, running a kingdom. For every problem, there is a piece of paperwork to herald its arrival, and one, at least, to follow. For every item bought or sold, for every decision made, a record must be kept. And nothing is ever really finished with. Some of the books that littered this small room dated back to Elowyn's father's reign, or further.

It had been, to Cioren's mind, the perfect hiding place. If you truly want to hide something, plain sight is far and away the most secret. And what is one more book, among so many old and dusty tomes? In a stack of leather-bound ledgers, I saw the blackened, dried out spine of the book that Uln had died to bring into Penvarron, looking as innocent and unnoticeable as a harvest tally stick.

But Baron Gallerain knew what it was, and where. How secret was this thing anyway?

But then, I thought, how had I expected the Queen to keep it utterly dark? Gallerain was her brother-by-marriage, after all. He had led her armies, helped her raise her son and heir, bullied the less faithful nobles into submission, if not loyalty, and supported her through years of war and strife. Certainly, as the importance of the book's existence had become clearer, Elowyn would have confided in him. Perhaps I was merely insulted by his assumption that I was not safe with this knowledge. I could see his point. Who was I, after all, to be trusted with something like this?

Elowyn, opening the door behind me, recalled me to the present. She smiled, not happily, as her eyes followed to where mine had been drawn, and sighed a little as she seated herself, nodding to me to take the chair opposite.

"I don't know quite how to say this, Keri," she said, after searching among a pile of papers on her table, and not finding, apparently, the one she sought. "I'm very sorry for it, too. Ah, here," she extracted a thin envelope of oiled cloth, stamped with the Royal seal, and laid it on the top of the pile. "I'm not unmindful of the service you've done me. I hope I'm not ungrateful. Indeed, if things were other than they are, I would not even consider this. But, as I said, I'm sorry for it, but there it is. I can't always do what I wish."

I must have looked as I felt: completely bewildered. I hadn't a clue as to what she was talking about. It wasn't good, whatever it was. I could tell that much.

"Are you truly as insensible of this as you seem?" she asked. I didn't answer, merely waited. Whatever I'd inadvertently done, she'd tell me, eventually, I thought, confused.

"It has been in my mind for days," she said. "That Tirais was far too taken with you. Lately though, it's become rather more than that. You must see," she added, "That I cannot allow it to continue."

I stared.

"It isn't anything against you, Keri," Elowyn said, kindly. "You do see, though, how impossible this is?"

"Your Majesty," I said. Stopped. Swallowed. "Your Majesty, you must be mistaken. The Prince - I mean, he's never, - that is, I've never -"

"No? Perhaps you are oblivious. I, however, am not. He has not been closemouthed, to me, at least. His admiration, and his friendship, well, that could be overlooked. More than that is out of the question. Keraine's needs come first, Keridwen, as I'm sure you will agree."

I looked at my feet. She could not be right. Tirais had never treated me with anything but a kind of amused tolerance, interspersed with bouts of kindness and occasional comradeship. I said so, omitting his probable desire to punch me in the face every so often. Elowyn, very patiently, disagreed.

"I know my son," she said. "And I do regret this, but even assuming you were right, and that his heart is not engaged, an entanglement such as this must be avoided. Distance, and time, will let these feelings, whatever their degree, fade.

"Lord Raghnall is short a good troop second, out at Issing. It's a well-run garrison, if a little quieter than you've been used to, lately. It will do you good, to be away from all this, and somewhere where you can learn your trade at less than breakneck speed."

"I see," I said. I did see. I had been expecting something like this for weeks, although I'd firmly convinced myself that my eventual posting would be on the frontier, and in the ranks. It was far better, and far worse. It wasn't likely, out on the western coast, that I would see so much as an Istaran raider, let alone a Camrhyssi warband. Or a prince of Keraine, for that matter.

Less than a year ago, this would have exceeded all my secret hopes. Four months ago, it would have seemed like a fairy tale.

Today, it was as if I'd been kicked in the guts.

Elowyn's eyes were anxious as she watched me mull it over. She ought not have worried. Nothing in my training allowed for any kind of argument, or objection. I stood, took the packet she held out to me.

"I really am sorry," she said. "But it's for the best, Keri."

"Yes," I said. "I'll go and pack."

"You could stay till after Midwinter," she said, suddenly more distressed. "Certainly till then."

"Begging your pardon, Your Majesty, but it's really best, if I'm to go, that I go at once."

She stood. She looked as if she was going to apologize again, which was all wrong, and I couldn't have borne it if she had. She was right, according to her own lights, and I was so numb with the shock, that all I could think of was to spare her the trouble of her regrets.

She said nothing, however, but a gentle, slightly relieved farewell, and a request that I go in safety. I moved through the doorway and out into the audience chamber, filled with midmorning petitioners and various royal clerks and scribes, made my way through to the hall and down the stairs to my own room.

I packed quickly, without conscious thought. I went into Cioren's workroom and took my small pouch of coins and slipped the thong around my neck, then sat and wrote a quick scrawl, saying that I'd been posted, and where. I looked around vaguely, as if wondering if I'd left anything behind, but in reality, I was just wasting time, unable to grasp the truth of it.

Elowyn had sent word to the stables: Banshee was saddled and ready when I arrived. No one paid me the slightest attention, other than a groom who held out a package of bread and cheese and sausage, once I'd mounted. I shoved it into a saddlebag, and dug my heels into Banshee, hard, as she had adopted an attitude of complete immobility, and finally we cantered down the lane towards the gate.

Chapter 44

One can, in times of stress, do a great many things without any recollection of them. I have, still, no memory of leaving Kerris that afternoon. I have no idea of whether I spoke one word to the guards at the North Gate. I can't bring to mind a single image, as Banshee's hooves clattered over the stone cobbles of the bridge that crossed the River Braide. I don't recall turning her head firmly west as we met the main road. I only know that I felt cold and numb and invisible, as if I had died.

I came to myself on a deserted stretch of road, well after midday, and somewhere, just to my right, I could hear the sound of a brook, water tumbling over stones in a cheery melody that certainly didn't suit my mood.

Still, a girl's got to eat, and Banshee was unlikely to share my disinterest in life at the moment. I slid off her back and led her off the track in the direction of the sound, found the stream and a convenient rock to sit on and forced myself to swallow a bit of bread and some cheese.

I tried, during that lonely meal, to bring some order to my unhappy thoughts. The Queen must be wrong about Tirais' feelings for me, I thought. It would be too much to bear, if I were to believe that more than courtesy and kindness played a role in this. If Tirais cared, even a little, for me, well, that would hurt far worse. I couldn't afford any more regrets in my life; I had enough, what with these last months, without taking on a might-have-been.

I stood, carefully brushing away crumbs, and began to lead Banshee back to the road, thinking that it was ridiculous, really, for Elowyn to think that Tirais even noticed my existence, when he wasn't being furious with me. She must not know about his affair with Angharad, I thought, gathering the reins and preparing to mount up.

I was still mid-mount, one foot in a stirrup, and the other still swinging up, my body following, when it struck me.

I thumped gracelessly into the saddle, and nearly dropped the reins. Luckily, Banshee was in no mood to bolt, although it's debatable whether I would have noticed.

I sat, on Banshee's back, in the middle of the Queen's West Road, staring blindly into space, gobsmacked.

There is no other word for it. I just sat there with my jaw agape, while the evidence laid itself out before me.

Why would Angharad be walking the central hallway, heading for the gallery, when there was a perfectly good, and far more discreet staircase right beside

Tirais' bedchamber? Surely it was tailor-made for the Prince's mistress, if her room lay just above, in easy reach of the Queen's chamber, along with the other ladies of the court?

I saw, again, Angharad's hands, in a tiny gesture, pushing down and away, smelled again that sickly-sweet odour of smoke and something else.

The bitch had used magic. Say what they would, Cioren and Dalriega were wrong: Angharad had Power, a lot of it, she must have, to use it to hoodwink them into believing her no more than an annoying child with a nasty streak. And to confuse and anger me.

Across the hall from Tirais' apartments lay those of Baron Gallerain. I could see, in my mind's eye, the baron, his head bent to listen, as Angharad whispered sweetly to him. How many times had I seen them thus?

And Gallerain knew where the book was hidden.

Goddess' tits, we might as well hand the damned thing over to her now, like a Midwinter Gift!

A shout, from a farmer with a creaky wagon, recalled me to my surroundings. I blinked, urging Banshee to the grass at the road's edge, as he passed us. The sun was low on the horizon, and the breeze had picked up a little.

I turned Banshee back to the east. Whatever urgency I had was only to get to Cioren and tell him what I knew. I felt no anxiety, really. It was only that since I was posted to Issing, I needed to get back, explain my theory to him, and be gone again, hopefully before Elowyn knew anything about it. I could just about manage it, before the gates were shut for the night, and with luck, be off again before dawn.

I only just made it: the guards were changing as I clattered through the archway of the North Gate, and two of them were already heading towards the iron palings with a view to swinging them shut. The captain was one I recognized, and better still, he recognized me. He waved as I rode through, not stopping me to find out why I'd returned.

The halls were deserted. No surprise there: the feasting would have already begun. I hoped Cioren had forgotten to go. In fact, I was counting on it, and ran lightly up the steps and on down the hall towards his rooms.

The door to our common chamber was still open, but inside there was an eerie silence. A bench lay on its side where it had fallen, and a cup of wine stood, still untouched, on the table.

I turned, frowning. From somewhere, far off in the distance, angry, frightened sounds began to penetrate my ears.

I stepped back out into the hallway, listening intently. It came from above, from the Queen's apartments, and as I looked back along towards the gallery, I saw a liveried servant sprinting down the steps as fast as his feet would take him.

I began to move, running back the way I'd come as if every demon in the netherworld was at my heels.

Like the door to Cioren's rooms, the entry to the Queen's chambers was open and unattended. There were no guards to ask my business, and no clerks stood about, deciding who would get an audience with Her Majesty. The whole place was empty as a tomb.

But noisier: the voices were louder here, and I followed the sound of terrified confusion through a long hall lit with tall, white tapers into the anteroom that led to Prince Connor's bedchamber, and stopped, staring into that open door in horror.

The Queen's ladies stood about, weeping, some of them, and others shocked into white-faced silence. Gallerain was shouting at someone out of my line of sight, Priestess Dalriega was there, and Cioren, and Tirais, and against one wall I saw that Parthalen lay, as if felled by some unseen weapon, dropped in his tracks as he'd turned towards an overturned table and a spilled flagon of ale. There was a stain still spreading from the jar, but even from here I saw that he was drugged, not dead.

But it was the crumpled figure on the dark wooden floorboards beside the empty bed that drew and held every eye. The figure that Prince Tirais knelt beside, head bowed in anger and sorrow. The figure of Elowyn, Queen of Keraine.

It was a little like a puppet-play, I thought, dreamily. Any moment now, Elowyn would spring up, and we'd all clap our hands together and...

I gave myself a hard mental shake. What the hell was going on, anyway? I looked again, and saw the Queen's chest rise and fall, so slight a movement I almost missed it entirely, and I felt myself release a breath I'd hardly known I was holding.

I stepped into the tableau, and the play resumed.

There were a lot of screaming people here. Baron Gallerain barely registered my presence, and didn't skip a beat in his tirade, directed at a confused and sobbing Ninon. Several people tried to tell me what was going on. Since they had no idea themselves what that was, the accounts were essentially useless.

I gathered, however, that Elowyn had been found as she was now, that Ninon had been called away before the Queen's arrival here, by a summons to the Queen, which had turned out to be either a mistake or a trick (or a lie, as Gallerain was proposing) and that she had returned to find the Queen and Parthalen as they lay, dying, apparently, and Prince Connor missing.

There was someone else missing, but I didn't mention it.

I said, instead, into the first slight lessening of the din they were creating, "The Queen still lives."

I might have set fire to the bed-curtains, so startling was its impact.

Dalriega and Cioren sprang into action as if struck with a practice sword. One of the ladies swooned, and Tirais rose in one swift motion, turning in the same movement, with a look of such incredible and total disbelief and joy that my heart gave a hard, almost audible thump, and then pandemonium, as my words were confirmed, broke out once again.

In the midst of this chaos, my gaze fell on the small gray amulet, lying a few feet from Elowyn's hand. The rest of them were still arguing and calling for guards; I walked over and looked at it. I had just enough wit left not to touch it carelessly; I pulled a fold of my cloak around my hand and picked it up by the edge. I could see that it was a little different than the last time I'd seen it: at one of the carved, joint-like ridges, a small sharp metal tooth had appeared, covered with some sticky brown ointment.

I held it out to Dalriega. The rest had fallen suddenly, blessedly silent, and Dalriega made no move to take the liarn from my hand. She leaned close, sniffed at it, and said, with a mixture of horror and relief, "Vilrannis. Goddess' Mercy, vilrannis. I might have guessed.

"I want her to the shrine, at once. Quickly, you idiots. And send for the Healers to attend me there. Move, damn you! We haven't much time."

She took the liarn carefully, using a fold in her own robe to shield herself from the poison. One of the guards had already set off at a run to get the servants, another had knelt at Queen's side.

I looked at her. She was still conscious, you could tell by her eyes, which stared hard at me, telling me something. It was agony to her, you could see it. Immobilized by the poison, barely able to breathe, trying desperately to tell me what it was I must do.

The servants brought a board, to lay poor Elowyn on, but it took some time and Dalriega was no help; between her exhortations to be speedy and her demands for gentleness and care, it was slow work. I knew what vilrannis was, vaguely, but it seemed more complicated than I'd thought. The slightest mistake could kill the Queen, even yet, and Dalriega seemed uncertain as to whether she could pull her through it, even if she did get her to the shrine in time.

My heart felt as if it were failing as well; with every beat, it hurt more and more to look at Elowyn, yet I could not tear my eyes away from hers.

There was still far too much noise, and the vast number of candles lit in this room began to hurt my eyes. Too much was becoming apparent to me. I couldn't quite make sense of it all, and I was longing for darkness and quiet and time, to work it all out. Time that I didn't appear to have.

"Where's Angharad?" I asked. It was amazing, how simple words could shut these people up. I must have a knack for it, I thought, feeling laughter rising inside me, and knew that I was close to hysteria.

"What has that to do with anything?" Dalriega's tone was blustering, but underneath I caught a current of puzzled worry.

"Everything," I said.

"Nothing," said Gallerain at the same moment.

"Oh, really?" said Tirais. "Would someone like to tell me what's going on? Failing that, I'd like to know where you were, Keri. What the devil do you mean by disappearing like that?"

"I was on an - errand. For the Queen," I said, after a moment. Cioren opened his mouth, as if to contradict, then shut it as I said hastily, "It doesn't matter, now."

"Well, where is Angharad?" he said.

"Missing," I said. "Missing, along with Connor."

"I've had just about enough out of you, you little guttersnipe," Gallerain fairly shouted. "All your innuendoes and accusations, and not one shred of evidence!"

"No? I guess I'm wrong then, in thinking you told her all about the book and betraying the Queen's trust. I wonder how she knew, then? Because I rather think she'll have taken it with her, don't you?"

It meant nothing, to most everyone still listening. Certainly not to Tirais, who looked merely baffled. But to Cioren, standing beside Dalriega, it was as if lightening had struck. He turned, staring at Gallerain as if some new and shattering horror had emerged.

The Baron's temper deflated. He sagged visibly, as Cioren took one pace towards him, fists clenching, then stopped and said, sadly, "Oh, Huwell, you stupid fool."

I leaned against the wall, listening as another tide of angry shouting rose. Tirais began issuing orders, sending guards scurrying to the Kerris gates, and servants running to raise the alarm. What he hoped to accomplish, I didn't know. He still had no idea just what we were up against, he knew nothing of the book, or of any number of things that had been going on in Kerris these last weeks. I knew, though. I could have explained it all to him, but it wouldn't have mattered, and it would have taken far too long.

"And you," he finished, rounding on me. "I'll thank you to stay where you're put, this time. You don't move, you don't even breathe without my leave, do you hear me?"

They had succeeded in getting the Queen onto the board and had raised it. Four strong guards were carrying her away to the shrine of the Mother; as they passed, Elowyn's eyes fixed on me, pleading, desperate. I watched the men moving heavily across the room.

I turned back to Prince Tirais, still enumerating the things I would not do without his express permission.

"Yes, lord Prince," I said, not listening. "Yes, of course."

Chapter 45

I left them in the antechamber, still arguing over what it all meant. Tirais was giving orders to search the Queen's apartments, the grounds, the stables, everywhere, while Cioren tried, in as few words as possible, to explain a little more of this damnable coil to him. Gwyll had gone back in to look through Connor's rooms, to see if any clue as to his whereabouts could be found.

It was all quite useless, of course. Look how they might, they had so little to go on, they might as well do nothing. Unless Elowyn could tell them what had happened, they would be flailing in the dark.

I made my way to the stables. Banshee was still standing saddled in the yard, quite patiently, for her. I pulled the saddlebags off and dumped my clothes out onto the dirt. I wouldn't need them. People came and went, paying me no heed, and I barely noticed them either. I dropped my comb on top of the pile and shook the bags and a hard heavy object tumbled out at my feet.

It was round and silver, stamped with the Queen's seal. I ought to have given it back to Sorcha, when I'd returned to Penvarron, but what with one thing and another, I had only remembered its existence a quarter-glass ago. It must have gotten wedged into the fold of leather at the side; I hadn't noticed it still being there the last time I'd packed.

I had been wondering how I'd get out the gates, what with the long stream of orders Tirais had sent down. I looked at the Queen's Pass, and smiled. The Goddess still had a kindness for me.

I knew, of course, that there was no justification for what I was doing. Oh, I could tell my protesting conscience that I hadn't ever, in fact, sworn myself to Tirais or to the Queen, for that matter, but I knew that was mere quibbling. I was enough my father's daughter to know that the oath itself wasn't the important part.

I could say, with perfect truth, that there wasn't the time to waste trying to get someone to believe me, that Connor's safety lay in my ability to get to him in time, that a host of warriors would only slow me down, or that I owed Elowyn this service far more, but it was all nonsense.

I wasn't doing it for Connor, at least not completely. I did like him. I did want to save him. I thought with horror of what he must be going through, and prayed to the Goddess he would be safe.

I wasn't doing it for Keraine, though I could see how disastrous this night's work would be if Angharad succeeded. Nothing in my life conditioned me to accept a Camrhyssi victory while I still breathed, and I couldn't have let it go without a fight, but that was away in some misty future, and I wouldn't have claimed it as motivation had I been tortured and racked to do so.

I wasn't doing it for Elowyn either: she might already be dead, for all I knew, and revenge does nothing for a corpse.

I was doing this for completely selfish and petty reasons. I thought of Angharad's words, standing in the gallery the night before. She had cost me some bad moments with her lies and her witchery, had made me doubt any number of values that I held dear, and had very probably turned the Queen's mind against me so that I had been sent away.

And for that, I intended to kill her.

I slipped the heavy leather thong of my Queen's Pass over my head and let the medallion drop into place with a soft chink against my mail shirt.

"That should be a help," said a voice behind me.

I turned. Cioren stood only steps away, dressed not in his fine courtly gear, but in the leather smock and rough-spun trews I'd seen him in the day we met.

"Of course," he continued, "It all depends on whether you know where you're going."

"Yes. Well, I know that much, at least."

"I don't suppose that place is Issing. No, you're not that much a fool."

A stable boy brought his horse into the yard, saddled and ready. Cioren handed over the saddlebags he was carrying, not taking his eyes from mine.

I reached for Banshee's reins.

"Well," I said, and my voice was far more confident than any other part of me, "She's only a few hours ahead of us. With a little luck, we may catch her up."

They'd turned north, the Camrhyssi, when they fought their way past Glaice, last fall. Not south, to the rich farmlands that they had always coveted, but north, though precious little lay there for many miles still. Uln had fomented dissent and unrest, and finally a well-timed uprising, and the Camrhyssi had swarmed over the border, not for raiding, I realized, but to get to a place where the book could be used. Cioren had said that none of the great citadels of Averraine's greatness had survived. But Penvarron had. If Penvarron was still potent, then why not other places?

264

And other places, to me, meant old places. I could feel my months-long confusion, coupled with the recurring sense of familiarity I'd been assailed with at every turn, becoming almost tangible. The last of the pretty, painted tiles dropped neatly into place. It was all there, just at the edges of my understanding, and I could almost make sense out of it.

But it was more instinct, really, that drove me. I just knew. I couldn't have produced a single fact worthy of the name, but I knew where she'd taken him. Knew what place the Camrhyssi had striven for, knew why the place existed at all.

Cioren said nothing to me, as he followed me towards the gates. He simply watched as I flashed the Pass at the guards on duty, and they, poor credulous fools, pulled the way clear and waved us through. With all the urgent orders and confused rumors running rampant, a Queen's Counselor and an unknown soldier with a Queen's Pass must have seemed all of a piece, and orders to close the gates to all traffic had never included someone bearing that token anyway

Cioren's silence held, all the way through the city. It wasn't until I moved confidently onto the track that branched off to the east that he made any sound at all, and then it was only a long sigh of relief.

I felt my shoulders loosen, just a bit. It seemed my conclusion was the right one, after all.

"We'll be hardpressed for shelter, taking this route," Cioren said, after a time.

"I know. But I'm hoping to make up some of the time, this way. She can't have been gone long. Three hours, maybe? If she took the main road, she won't have made good time."

"I hope not. But she'll stay a little ahead of us all the same. Unless you have some secret plan."

"No," I said. "No, I'm just hoping to be close enough behind her that she'll have no time to - to do anything."

We rode for some time in silence after that. That there was nothing more I could do than to chase Angharad and hope to be in time to avert a worse disaster was depressingly realistic of me. I wished that I could come up with more: some grand and glorious piece of heroics that would save the day, but that was just childish, romantic dreaming. I wished Cioren could, but he looked to be as short of ideas as I was, and I thought it was rather childish, too, to keep expecting someone else to provide the solution.

We had gone a fair distance, out past where Tirais and Connor and I had galloped after Tirais' falcon, and the track was deteriorating into little more than a thin trail. I glanced at the sky. There was light enough, so far, to keep us on our path, but if the wind shifted and the sky clouded, we would have very little to guide us. Still, the way was open and plain enough. We needed to keep our course due east, until we met the North Road, which seemed a simple enough task. Even without a trail to follow, we could make it, cross-country.

With any luck, Connor would slow her progress down. There's a lot a ten-year-old boy can do, just naturally, that can hamper even a short journey. Assuming, and on this thought, my heart quailed, assuming, of course, he was alive and conscious.

Cioren broke into this unpleasant reverie, to my relief. The visions I was conjuring were not at all cheering.

"Just for the record," he said, "Where are you going?"

"Ys Tearch," I said, bluntly.

"Ah. Interesting choice, of course. You don't mind perhaps, explaining your reasoning to me? I'm not objecting or arguing, you understand. I'm merely - er - curious."

Knowing you're right is one thing. Telling someone what you propose to do, on the flimsiest of evidence, is something else again. If what I believed could have been said to have been based on evidence at all, which I strongly doubted.

"It isn't any one thing," I said, after a bit. "But I know that's where she's going. Ys Tearch was - is - a place of power, like Penvarron. It's the only reason it's so protected. And that priest. She must have witched him. You and Dalriega, I know you don't believe she's a Talent, but I know she is. She used magic on me. So she must have got to that bastard up at Ys Tearch, somehow. And to Gallerain, too."

He didn't say anything, not for some time. It was rough going here, the ground was stony and uneven, and we were both watching where we rode. But after a mile or so, the path grew better.

"You're right, of course."

The sound was startling, after so much silence.

"I did underestimate Angharad, of course, although not, perhaps, by as much as you think. Dalriega, well, I don't know what she may have guessed. But you are correct in this much: I didn't think Angharad was able to conceal the extent of her Power. Her father would have been her teacher, and he certainly lacked a certain, shall we say, finesse. And so I thought that if she did anything that might be dangerous, I would know.

"Ys Tearch, well, that's something else again. I've occasionally felt - but the priesthood doesn't permit much exploration up there. A mistake, perhaps."

Too many mistakes, I thought. But I understood it, all the same. I didn't handle the thought of real, palpable Power very well myself, even now. I could just imagine what most people would think, if they knew the truth.

"Could you tell me something?" I asked. He seemed inclined to talk, a real rarity, and I thought I might as well take advantage of it.

"If I can."

"How did the liarn get into Connor's room? Did you give it to the Queen, or what?"

"No, no. I've no idea, actually. But Connor came down, looking for you. He was quite upset, when he saw your note. I'd only just come back myself, you see, and I didn't think to conceal it from him. I rather suspect he may have seen the liarn there. I've had a few before, ones that don't work, of course, and I gave him one, once.

"I think," he said apologetically, "he may have just 'borrowed' it. Princes have a rather careless interpretation of ownership, I'm afraid."

"You mean, that was all a mistake? But that doesn't make sense, Cioren. There was vilrannis on that thing. It was a trap! How could anyone know where it would wind up?"

"That's the difficult part. And it answers some of your findings about Ys Tearch, actually."

"Oh." I said it almost casually. The liarn had come from a place near Ys Tearch. I saw that this was significant in some way. Obviously.

"I don't think Angharad 'witched' the priest," he said. "I don't think she needed to. The priesthood is quite a hotbed of factions, actually. One side, Dalriega's side, believes that the magic must be controlled, but only moderately, with some goodwill. They want the Mother's place assured, they want the power they believe is their due and their responsibility, and they want a say in the day-to-day affairs of the kingdom, to insure that place. It's not so cut and dried, of course; there's a lot of jockeying for power, and unspoken compromises going on.

"But there is a strong group who see the place of religion in much more decided terms. They believe that magic makes them strong, and that the strong should rule. They much admire the Camrhyssi way, where the priests control the nobility, even the royal family, and dictate almost everything from sunup to sundown.

"I think our priest at Ys Tearch is one of them. And to get him on her side, she would only have needed to lie to him. Not even that, perhaps, very much."

We were coming into hills, now, and our pace was slowing. It must be midnight, or later, I thought. We would have to think about stopping soon, if only for a time. We couldn't afford foundered horses.

"So," I said, "The liarn was meant for Dalriega, then. An assassination attempt, that's all. We've had bad luck."

"Yes. But unforeseen, even by its maker. After all, Tirais is not Elowyn. If the Queen dies, the priesthood will find themselves with a very different set of problems."

"But why did Angharad take Connor? That's the part I can't understand. I mean, she obviously planned it, but to what end?"

"I don't know. It may be that she wanted to hurt the House of Machyll badly, and this was the only way she could think of."

"Still, how did the Queen come to have the liarn? Do you think she just found it in Connor's room? How did it come to trap her? You didn't fall for it."

"I'm not entirely sure. I think Connor may have had it by him. And the Queen often goes in, to wish him good night. I think perhaps she found Angharad there, or maybe Angharad showed up later. In any case, Elowyn got hold of the liarn, and tried to use it. She would have known at once it was a usable one, not a burnt out useless trinket."

I sat suddenly, hard into the saddle, my hands dropping abruptly to my sides. The pull on the reins sent an irresistible signal to Banshee, who stopped dead in her tracks, as I stared at Cioren's back.

"You don't mean - oh, please, tell me I'm mistaken!"

He stopped, turned his mount, looking at me with amusement.

"What? You weren't aware that Elowyn is a Talent? Come, come, Keridwen. The House of Machyll is descended in an unbroken line from Aenor. Of course their Power is strong. It skips a generation or two, every so often, but everyone knows about it."

I choked.

"All right," he said. "Perhaps not everyone. But surely, your father knows. He was practically raised with her. Did he never say…?"

I shook my head, not trusting my voice.

"Well, now you know. To what purpose, I've no idea. We should," he added, prosaically, "look for a place to camp. Come on. There's a little vale just ahead that looks about right."

Chapter 46

We spoke very little from that point onwards. Only the necessities needed words, anyway: where to camp, whether a fire was required, who took what watch, things like that. We fed and watered the horses, snatched a little sleep, and continued on before the sun rose.

Near midday, we came across a hamlet that boasted a ramshackle tavern, and rested for an hour or so, ate, and looked after our horses. Conversation was still limited to essentials, but it no longer felt stiff or unnatural. It was merely that there wasn't much left to say.

It had taken us nearly three full days to travel a similar distance, with a full complement of guards and a small baggage train, but with only the pair of us, we had covered a lot more ground in less than two. But by dusk, it was apparent that neither the horses nor their riders could go on without a more protracted stop, and we made a proper camp. Over an uninspiring supper - we were neither of us good cooks - we considered how far we were from the North Road, and what our plans were once we reached it.

"I think we might have saved nearly half a day," Cioren said, swallowing a mouthful of rather burnt bacon. "And we should make good time once we reach the road. The question is, how did Angharad fare? We might want to consider what to do, if she's not there yet."

"You're optimistic. I'm not considering that until it's a reality."

"Well, there's always hope."

"I'm hoping I can kill the bloody bitch," I said calmly. It shut him up, rather completely, and I began wishing I hadn't said it.

But in the early morning sun, as we reached the steep hill leading down to the road, my spirits rose a little. We were closer now. On the other side of the muddy track, the mountains rose majestically away into Camrhys, and I began to think we might be in time after all.

I could even see, within the first hour, the blank, gray scar of Ys Tearch. We were still too far off to make out the fortress itself, but that huge expanse of stone and rubble was a clear landmark for many miles.

My eyes began raking the adjacent hillside for a way up to the ruins, a way that bypassed the hostel and the main road. I couldn't be sure Angharad hadn't worked some wickedness with the people who cared for the travelers there, and I was unwilling to risk the possibilities that raised. I wanted to surprise her, if I could; any advantage I could manage would help.

Cioren, when I voiced this to him, didn't really agree. He didn't say so, not in words, but it was clear that he thought me more than overcautious. But he had discounted my opinions before, and it had not turned out well. He merely gave me a look that said traipsing through the underbrush was not much to his taste, and let me have my way.

I found a game trail, eventually, that seemed to lead in roughly the right direction. I didn't know how far it went, or whether it would take us even part of the distance we needed to go, but we were getting too close, and I was beginning to get a little desperate. Time was running out. I could feel it.

Our luck held till we got to the top of the ridge. We could see clearly along to where the trees ended and the destructive evidence of the Mother's Power began, but there the trail fell away back to the north, and we were left to struggle the last few miles through coarse and brambly terrain, leading the horses, until we came to the edge of the forest and looked across at the vast bulk of Ys Tearch, rising up against the clouds.

It had taken much too long, I thought, sucking on a scratched hand, where a thorn had caught at me. I knew without a doubt that Angharad was already there. There and bent on some evil. It was too quiet, not even the wind was pushing the few scrubby bushes around, and there was no sound of pilgrims, coming to pay their respects to the honoured dead.

We walked on, skirting the huge boulders and picking our way through the barren rocks, until we came to the part of the wall that was still intact, and followed that around until we reached the gate at the end of the causeway. The sun was already sinking into late afternoon pallor.

I thought, a bit sardonically, that I had never expected to spend a Midwinter Eve like this, chasing what ought to have been phantoms and nightmares in the most sacred site in Keraine. Like my life these last six months, it was all a mean little joke, something a malicious bard had cooked up to amuse the hardhearted gods around some divine hearth.

We found the body of one of the Queen's Guards, sprawled just inside the archway, her throat cut, in a pool of sticky, congealing blood. She looked surprised.

I knelt, and touched the wet ground. In the cold, it was hard to say how long she'd lain here, but I thought not long. An hour, perhaps. I reached out and closed her eyelids gently, and stood again.

We tethered the horses in the broad, stone-flagged courtyard. Banshee was skittish; she was war-trained, and the smell of death and blood had roused her, and she was unwilling to stay put.

The second body was less shocking, we had, of course, been expecting this. His throat was cut too; cut down from behind, a coward's trick. The third corpse lay half inside a doorway and the job had been botched: instead of a quick and silent death, he'd obviously struggled. There were several slashes across his neck and his hands were cut up too.

I looked around in the golden light of late afternoon. Out beyond the tower we stood in, I saw the entryway of the main tower, its massive wooden door open wide, and started across the yard.

Cioren followed without a word. It was as if he was waiting for me to ask where we should go next, but if that were so, he would have a long wait. I knew exactly where I was headed.

Every way I had turned, these last few months, I'd seen things that had tugged at my memory, as if I had kept returning to the same spot, over and over again. And somewhere between my midnight conversation with Angharad and the discovery of Elowyn, collapsed on the floor of Connor's chamber, I had realized finally what it was I kept seeing.

Orliegh, as I've said, is old. It's one of the oldest keeps in Dungarrow, actually, built long before the Ancients fell from grace, and although it's small, it followed the same pattern that other structures of their making had.

I went cautiously through the door. The tall, arched windows, their shutters long since turned to dust, let in the light, in long, jagged shards splintering across the tiled floor. I crossed it in silence, with Cioren beside me, to the broad hallway beyond.

It was darker here; only thin arrow-slits opened themselves to the last rays of sunlight. I walked without hesitation along to the first turning, then onwards to the end, where the steps leading to the fortress storerooms lay.

The heavy ropes ought to have blocked this part of the keep, but they lay tangled in the dust. I ignored them, stepping over the fallen barrier without a thought. In the pale reflected light I noted that there was a gray scrape-mark, fresh and gleaming against the dark stone, that could only have been a sword, crashing uselessly on the wall and missing its intended target.

We stopped for a few moments, letting our eyes adjust to the darkness, although I hardly needed to. I didn't need light to know where I was going. I had, in fact, been here before.

Oh, not in Ys Tearch. But Orliegh had likely had the same builders, and if it were smaller, it differed so little from where I stood now as to be indistinguishable. I could remember going down into the cellars, twice a year, to help with counting the kitchen stores.

We came to the bottom step. I moved forward confidently, taking the left hand turning, and then, about halfway down, found the door I expected.

We moved through.

On the wall just beside us, a torch had been lit, throwing a fierce red glow onto the floor beyond, and falling on to the sprawled body of the fourth Queen's Guard, who lay there in a pool of blood. His blade was still clutched in his hand, and it looked as though this death had not been nearly as quick or as clean as the others. He had crawled, by the look of it, a few lengths, before death had taken him.

I looked about the room carefully. Around the upper edge of the wall there was a kind of frieze, a decorated series of stone panels, carved with delicate motifs and that same flowing script I couldn't read.

I thought of Orliegh again; of rows of smoked hams, of casks of wine and huge barrels of ale, and bins of barley, a kind of paradise for a small girl, playing silly games between the rows of foodstuffs waiting to be counted. And remembered the dark place, behind the stacked crocks of salted fish, where there was a carved stone door, all but invisible in the gloom.

I moved across the floor, skirting the spreading wetness from underneath the poor fighter who had died here. I even closed my eyes for a moment, although it wasn't really necessary; I knew where it must be, I could see where it would be, and I was right.

Halfway along the far wall, set ever so slightly back, and the carved decoration arranged so as to fool the sight into missing it, lay the faintest, barest outline of a door that matched the one in my child's inner eye. The exact mate, in fact, of the door beneath Penvarron's cellars.

I must have made a sound of some kind; Cioren, behind me, said something I didn't catch, but it didn't matter. I went close to the door, but waited for him. At Penvarron, he'd touched it, and known that it was at least moderately safe; if there was something lying in wait for me, I wanted some warning.

He understood, without words. He laid his hand upon the wood, closing his eyes, and, after a moment, drew it away and nodded.

All clear, then. I opened the door carefully. It made no sound; it was apparent that the aged hinges had been oiled, and recently, too.

There was a short flight of steps leading even further down, a black well of uncertainty that screamed of danger and trouble, and beyond that, just the faintest of reflected light, bouncing back out of the darkness yawning below.

I stripped off my shield. It would be narrow in that space, a shield would only hamper me and slow me down. I stepped carefully, quietly through the opening, and stopped, straining my ears into the silence.

Behind me, Cioren moved too, onto the tiny space of the top step.

I shook my head.

"Wait," I said, softly. He looked at me. "They may not know there are two of us. Let them wonder, then. If they kill me..."

He saw the point. They wanted us down there, they must be expecting someone, at least, and we had no choice. We had to go. In a sense, we were outnumbered, in that the initiative was all theirs. Keeping even the tiniest scrap of advantage or knowledge from them, even if only for a moment or two, might be the only way to beat them.

I went on, alone, down into the darkness.

My soft boots made no sound on the stones. I found that even my racing heart was quieter now, and my breathing dropped to shallow, noiseless intakes, timing themselves with a canny precision to my body's movements. My senses were keen and screaming in the shadows, every nerve straining beyond its normal bonds, and my focus narrowed sharply, to just this moment, just this place, with every emotion dropping away.

So, in the end, I knew when I neared the gap in the wall that my quarry stood just inside the door. I could hear his nervous breathing, and I could almost smell his anxiety. I stopped, soundlessly, just beyond his reach and listened, grimly amused, as he shifted his weight. The time would stretch, for him, seemingly endless, and I was content for it to be so.

He moved again, this time apparently relaxing, believing, I guessed, that there was less to fear with every passing moment. I let him have a few more happy seconds, and then stepped, neat and fast, all the way past his hiding place just inside the door, so that I faced him head on.

Not being a soldier, his expectations had been too predictable. He gaped with surprise, and then, as my sword whipped up and back, arcing towards his head, he dropped away, back into the room beyond.

If he tried anything, like the spells that had dogged me in my fight with Uln, I was too intent on my own goals to be deflected; or else he wasn't very good at them. My vision contracted to the things that mattered: the movement of his shoulder that predicted his next blow, the telltale placement of his feet that told me where he'd step to next.

But he turned out to be a decent enough fighter, when cornered. I'd expected it; the holy ones train everybody they get their hands on to the limits of their capabilities, regardless of what those are. We might even have been something of a match, on a practice-ground, or in a normal battle.

This wasn't normal. I felt as though my body was no longer mine to command, and real thought was gone, fled to some hidden recess in my mind. You've no doubt heard people say that they felt they were an extension of their sword, sometimes, but that isn't truly accurate: I was my sword. I had become, body and soul, a weapon. All of my training and experience and skill had fused into this single and incandescent sphere of time and place; it was a kind of epiphany of swordcraft, and it felt wonderful.

It was lucky that I'd had similar moments occasionally before; I might have been distracted by the sheer pleasure of it, if I hadn't known what it meant. Because all fighters have these moments at least sometimes, and it only means one thing: that you have cleared yourself, and come to terms with all that can happen, and accepted, without regrets or fear, that you will die.

I danced away from his blade, leading him on, as he twisted and turned, raining down blows like a spring storm. Wasteful, that; he wasn't in the kind of condition that allows for a long fight at this rate, but I let him have his time at it, flicking his blade away, without trying to retaliate, until he began to slow down.

And then I closed, making him fight a purely defensive battle, slamming my sword against his, harder and harder, so that each time his arm was a little slower, a little less sure, till he began to flail wildly at every twitch I made, and I heard myself chuckle.

That was unkind of me, I thought, absently, and stepped just a little sideways, dropped my body away under his last-ditch attempt at an overhand shot, and reached out with my free hand, grabbing his wrist and twisting it until the sword fell with a satisfying ring onto the stone floor, and my sword hand punched down hard on the back of his head.

I stood, with the body of at least one of our problems resting in a forlorn lump at my feet.

Cioren stood in the doorway, watching me with a question in his eyes. I shook my head, still caught in the pure joy of this strange state. I had just enough wit left to know that a death, here and now, could be dangerous. The priest still breathed, if a little wheezily; I undid his belt, turned him onto his side, and bound his arms above the elbows, with the leather strap. He'd be out a good little while, and then he'd have to waste precious minutes freeing himself, if he could, before he'd be of any use again.

Chapter 47

She was waiting for me, when I came through that last door. There were torches blazing on every wall, casting weird shadows into the corners and spaces of that long, pillared hall, and she stood before another raised stone altar, flanked by two smoking braziers.

The book lay open before her, with a gleaming blade, wickedly sharp, laid upon the page, and stretched out in the remaining level of carved stone, unbound and unmoving; there was a body.

Connor. For one impossibly long moment I thought I was too late, that he was already dead. Then I saw his eyes, fixed and frightened, and heard a tiny breath exhaling into the silence, and knew he lived.

Not that I could guarantee him even that, much longer. Angharad looked down the room to me, quite happily. She wore black, as those fool priests of Camrhys had; unlike their stiff velvet robes, the gown covering her was clingy and flowing, as though she'd dressed with care to seduce a lover. She even licked her parted lips, savouring this moment.

"I knew you'd come," she said. "I hoped for more of you, though. Have you run ahead, in your eagerness? Should we wait for the others?"

"What others?"

"Tirais? Full of righteous anger, to avenge the old harridan's death? Cioren? Dalriega? I promised that deluded zealot you killed their fates - a small disappointment for him, now."

This was vaguely interesting. Angharad seemed to have taken a number of deaths for granted here. But my mind and body still belonged to that state of self-induced battle-madness, and telling her the truth seemed pointless.

I said, instead, "I think this is between you and me. You can let Connor go."

"Oh, no," she said, and shook her head. Even now, she could not resist those delicately fascinating artifices. She might still be at Kerris, and flirting with Baron Gallerain. "I'm too close now. A pity about Tirais, of course, but I can manage him, after. But I do require Machyll blood, and Machyll blood I will have. Yours will just be - extra."

I walked forward, watching her carefully, calculating the distance. Could she pick up the knife and slit Connor's throat before I reached her? Perhaps, but she didn't seem inclined to do it. I guessed she had something more planned for him. Anger licked through my body, then died, abruptly. I didn't have time for it, and it wasn't needed. Something colder and more deadly had taken over.

"Stop!" she said, and I caught a note of impatience, and something else.

"Why? You won't let him go, you intend to kill him. Go ahead," I added casually, as the distance between us narrowed, "Pick up the knife."

If I could rattle her. If I could make her move away from that book. And from Connor. I kept going, even as she glanced down at the blade, and whatever spell she'd laid on Connor wavered, and he looked directly at me.

Something beyond me caught her eye, just as her hand began to move. She stopped and said, with some satisfaction, "Ah. There you are."

And she lifted one hand and said something else, in that unknown tongue, and smoke billowed out from nowhere.

A wind rose, cool and sweet, pushing back at the clouds. I reached the altar, grabbed hold of Connor's ankle, and dragged him towards me, risking a fast look backward, to see that Cioren was standing, just inside the doorway, his hands upraised, and a white and furious glow was on them.

It took him long enough, I thought. We had walked that last piece of hallway together, wordlessly, until halfway down, his footfalls had ceased, and when I'd looked, he was gone. I'd had to assume, in those last few minutes, that he had some kind of plan, but till this moment, I hadn't been sure.

I pulled Connor free. If there'd been a spell, she had dropped it to contend with Cioren. As he slid down, the braided ribbons caught on my hand and snapped. I heard the faint click as the charm clattered against stone and I shoved him, a bit roughly, into an alcove between two columns and turned to see what was going on.

It wasn't much. They seemed to have reached a kind of curious balance. There was smoke still pouring into the chamber, but it couldn't seem to move past a certain point, and the pair of them were locked into position, staring at each other, not moving at all.

"Keridwen," said Cioren, quite conversationally, as if we weren't standing on the very brink of disaster, "Go and get the book."

I rose. Angharad flicked a glance my way, and said, "I wouldn't. I can kill her as she stands, and you know it, even if she does not."

I hesitated. Only for a second, but they both caught it. Angharad laughed. "You're wise not to trust him. He would sacrifice everything for possession of that. And he will never tell you why, no, not until he has raised himself over us all, and you are each one of you his slaves. At least I admit my purpose."

"And what is that?" said Cioren. "To turn us over to the Camrhyssi? What will that avail you, Lady? They have no love of witches there. Do you suppose they will suffer you to live, once you have given them what they want?"

"Them!" she spat. She actually did, in a most unattractive fashion. "I am no such fool. I will have Keraine and Camrhys both, under my heel. And those who ride with me shall be as lords of this world, and laugh as you turn to dust beneath a sunless sky."

"With that book as your guide? I fear you have misled yourself. Nothing in that book will lead you anywhere but to destruction. Will the Goddess just let you take this world?"

"That beleaguered bitch? There are other powers, Cioren, and you know it. Other, angrier, terrible powers, who move, restive in their chains. Who will be freed."

His face blanched. The glow about his hands flickered, and in a moment of shifting light and shadow, I heard Angharad, laughing.

"They will love me, do you not think so? Am I not their fair deliverance? Oh yes, they will reward me well."

"I doubt it," said Cioren, and then all merry hell broke loose.

Fire shot out to meet the black smoke that curled about her. Brilliant sparks flew, and thunder crashed in my ears; I turned and crouched beside Connor, as terror swept through me. I could hear Angharad laughing still, the inhuman mirth echoing in the cavern.

Things began to creep around at the edges of the room, small, chittering, horrid things born of nightmares. The air trembled as Cioren and Angharad strove against each other, unmoving. You could feel the Power, as it writhed and pushed against itself, seeking weakness, searching for an opening.

Monstrous forms appeared in the battling mists. Things out of legend, that fought for becoming. The air itself seemed to shriek with the agony of birth and the forms rose and died, over and over again. The stuff of myths fought in the smoke; scaly lizards towered over enormous hounds with dripping fangs and glowing eyes, and claws sharp as daggers raked the fetid air.

It was a stalemate, all the same. Cioren was holding his own, sure: Angharad's little sphere of power was not growing, but her Power held, and I could see that Cioren could not last forever. Even now, a trickle of sweat dripped from his brow. I might not trust him utterly, as Angharad had said, but he was still my last, best hope.

Angharad moved her hands suddenly, in a gesture of impatience, and the smoke about her shivered, and then coalesced, hardening into a vast, dark maw that sucked at the flames. The air grew instantly chill, I heard a whistling sound, my blood seemed to freeze in my veins, and from a distance, I heard my own voice, crying out the name of the Goddess.

Cioren began to move suddenly, striding forward into the centre of this storm, and the blackness fell back. I saw Angharad's face change, as if baffled, and then, in an instant, she began to smile. She stepped just a little bit backwards, her hands pushed outward, and even as I screamed out a warning, that devouring mouth collapsed, and the Power rose up, drawing itself into a visible, indelible force that leapt from the seething currents around her, through her slender form, and out to Cioren's body,

The sheer, massive completeness of it dropped him. Smoke poured out in a rage from every crack and crevice in the room, and then sank away, into expectant stillness.

For a moment, Angharad just stood, unmoving. Her face was white and drained, and her breath came in shallow gasps, as we stared at Cioren's motionless body. Then even as I watched her, the pallor in her cheeks receded, and she turned to Connor and I, still crouched together in our misery.

"Come," she said. " The hour of Her weakness is at hand. I've work to do."

I put my arm around Connor's shoulder, felt his sobs as they wracked his body.

"Why should we?" I asked. I hefted my sword. "You come here and take us."

"You first," she said, as if she hadn't heard. "The boy will be sweeter, once his last hope has gone."

She moved back to her place at the head of the altar and looked down at the book, not even glancing our way.

I stood, suddenly. I wasn't sure what I intended. I can't even be sure that, in that moment, she hadn't conquered me with her Power, that I wasn't in the grip of some evil charm. I left Connor still shivering in fear, and walked calmly to the altar and stood at the base of it, watching her as she smiled at me.

I couldn't reach her, and she knew it. The long expanse protected her from any physical attack; even my sword would fall short of her heart, and her smile widened as I raised the weapon to her.

She drew a deep breath, lifting her hands above her head. I stretched my own arm out, the sword extending over the polished slab between us, and waited, as she dropped her eyes to the book lying open in front of her. I could feel the Power beginning to rise again, as she drew it into herself and formed it into words to shape my doom.

My sword tip had dropped, till it nearly touched the surface of the altar. Even as I wished for just a few more inches of reach, I felt my body lean, just a hair's breadth further.

The tip of my blade slid neatly under the leather binding, and my wrist turned delicately sideways, flipping the book closed.

I lifted my eyes to hers, and smiled back.

All the remaining colour drained from Angharad's face, leaving her waxen and ill looking, her eyes opened wide with shock. I could feel something, deep inside the earth, changing, gathering, transforming, and I stepped back without realizing I was doing it.

Her breath drew in sharply.

"You *idiot*," she said.

I could hear it now, a rumbling from the depths of Ys Tearch, the silent scream of stone on stone. Too late, I heard the echo of Cioren's voice, floating out of memory, saying sharply that there was a difference between ending and stopping. I thought, guiltily, that I might not have thought this completely through. Still, Angharad was certainly unhappy with what I'd done, and anything she disliked couldn't be all bad.

Could it?

"You meddling, imbecilic fool!" The shock hadn't sweetened her tongue, at least. She fixed a malevolent gaze on me, even as the patterned stone that she'd been standing on when she'd felled Cioren erupted into a black, boiling crack.

The altar rocked, with sudden violence, and we both looked in horrified impotence, as it split itself wide, like a pomegranate, and the floor opened in a jagged fissure, sending streams of foul vapour and filthy liquid shooting into the air.

And the book. It flew in a high arc out towards the abyss that had opened, trailing like an ungainly acrobat behind the silver sparkle of her knife. Angharad made one abortive movement after it, then stopped herself, and we watched as it landed in the muck and rubble of the growing breach between us.

It's a mark of the respect I had held Cioren in, that I actually looked, to see if I could reach it. It lay, fortunately, some several feet down, on a splinter of rock just above the emptiness that yawned below.

"You'll die here," said Angharad. She seemed quite composed for someone who, by the looks of things, was close to her own demise. "You'll die here, and the brat with you. I'm glad, too. I don't know what it is about Orliegh, anyway. Always poking their noses where they don't belong. But you, at least, will end here, unknown and unlamented."

The ground shook again. My knees felt weak, but I managed to stay upright.

"They will have Machyll blood, at least. He should have died years ago. We warned them the old man was too weak a vessel, but no. Those fools always think they know more. But they will see it, now. They will know that it was I who killed him. And you."

She chuckled, even as the rift widened, and the pillars protested in their foundations.

"They thought even that their little magics and tepid spells would serve them, those weak and puling priests of Camrhys. They lack the vision. Fiddling about in dark corners with trivialities, still frightened that the old hag will find them out. Well, but you use what tool comes to hand, don't you?"

She was much too calm. It was possible, of course, that she was merely mad; she certainly sounded as if she might be. Her tone was absent, distracted, almost, and her words made no sense to me at all. My desire to kill her had returned in force, but she was out of reach now.

As was Cioren's body. He still lay, beyond the barrier in the floor, not far from Angharad; he had not shifted at all, and not even the heaving granite blocks had altered his position. I had to accept that he was dead, as dead as the stone he lay on. Deader, actually: the rock seemed to be getting more animated all the time.

"I'd curse you," she said. "But it matters so little, now. The Dark Ones will have you soon enough."

That awful sound of grinding earth grew louder, she had fairly to shout these last words. I wasn't frightened, exactly, I had had death as a nodding acquaintance much too frequently these last months to find the prospect much of a threat, and I thought idly I had little enough to live for, in any case. But there was Connor to think of, and Cioren's death left me little choice. I was all the chance he had.

Before I could consider just how slim that chance would be, the roof caved in.

There was debris everywhere, huge piles of broken pillar and chunks of masonry from the ceiling, piled up in haphazard mounds. Something had struck me in the head, and I wasn't sure how long I'd been out for; I came to looking across at Connor, who still crouched in his tiny haven between two columns, his eyes wide and scared.

I forced myself to sit up. It hurt, and there was blood running hot and wet down the side of my head, but I could see after a fashion, so I couldn't be that badly off. It was a lot dimmer, but after a minute, I realised that was because most of the torches had died, and stopped worrying.

The part of the room that was most damaged lay on the other side of the rift in the floor. Where Cioren's body had been was a mess of tangled rock and old rafters, and Angharad was nowhere to be seen. The air was filling with the dust of ancient mortar, sifting out from between the cracks above, and obscuring my vision even more. The break in the flooring had widened further, and seemed deeper than ever, but I could just still see a tiny corner of the book, poking out from two massive pieces of misshapen stone. Well, it would be safe enough there for an eternity or three. I stood, and managed to totter over to Connor's side.

"We'd better get out of here," I said. He looked up at me gratefully. My voice had come out as cheerfully as if I'd been suggesting a stroll in the gardens at Kerris, and he got up without a murmur, and walked with me out the still-intact doorway.

Chapter 48

We passed the door to the room I'd left the priest in. It occurred to me that if he was still bound, he would die a rather difficult death, but I didn't see how it mattered. Despite my cheerful words to Connor, my hopes for leaving the bowels of Ys Tearch alive were small. Still, there was no point in sitting around waiting to be crushed to death. Whatever happened, I thought, would be easier if we were at least trying to live, and adding a murdering, traitorous priest of the Mother into this didn't hold any appeal at all.

We made it to the few steps that led back to the storerooms without as much trouble as I'd feared. There were some nasty moments, of course: large cracks were appearing without warning, under our very feet, sometimes, and once a piece of ceiling fell just as we stepped past the spot. But we crawled up into the ruins of the room that the last Sword had died in, and despite the real devastation there, made it as far as the hallway with no fresh disasters.

It was harder going here: much of the corridor was already falling in, and more of the castle's ruin blocked our path. We struggled over piles of broken wall, pushing bits of the fortress carefully away, and hoping there would be time to get just a little farther before the destruction behind us began to catch up.

The end of the hallway confirmed my worst fears. The narrow stairwell was choked with rubble; in fact, there was really no stairwell left at all, only an impenetrable wall of artistic rubbish. The tiled floor above had poured through the opening like water.

Till now, Connor had pushed along without complaint; now I heard him whimper, just the tiniest sound of despair. I was tempted myself, really. Having come this far, it seemed that the Goddess had been playing with our hope, and had now lost interest.

But there was no point in making certain defeat into a rout. I sighed, threw one last look up at the remains of our best chance of escape, and said, "Well, I expected this. No matter. We'll just have to go around to the kitchen side."

I was thinking, as we turned back down the hall, that if we were lucky, it would be a nice sudden cave-in, and we'd be dead before we knew it. There was a way out, if the wide tunnel that led, at Orliegh, from the storerooms to the outbuildings that served as kitchens existed here. But Ys Tearch had never been a cosy family dwelling, and the damn thing might not exist at all. Even if it did, there was every likelihood that it had already been destroyed. I thought lovingly again of a fast overhead collapse, and led Connor away, turning down the right-hand way that branched out towards the central ring of towers upstairs.

The hallway narrowed suddenly, and my heart sank. At home, this was a big, open concourse, with shelves that lined the walls, for everyday items like flour and onions and wine. Here it was barely large enough for Connor and I to walk abreast, and it was dark and dank. The noise of Ys Tearch's disintegration was growing louder all the time, and huge cracks were opening on every side. The ground shook and shivered in its death-throes, and my hopes dwindled to nothing at all.

We came to the end at last. The wall was a depressing blank, and on my right lay another, even narrower opening, piled again with the rock and rubbish of the fortress walls and ceilings. Gray light traveled over the tumbled stones, and it took me a long moment of blind, suicidal rage before I realized just what that meant.

The long slanted space was not completely blocked. Somewhere above us lay the inner bailey of Ys Tearch, and moonlight was pouring through that opening in sufficient quantity to show us the way.

"Right, then. Up you go, Connor." I tried to make myself sound confident and lighthearted. He was only ten. You shouldn't have to do this when you're only ten. You should especially not have to do this with an ignorant, backward and inexperienced nobody as your only guide. Connor, luckily, did not turn to me and tell me to get stuffed. He gave me a look that said he hoped I knew what I was doing, and asked politely if I could give him a boost up over the first lot of blocks that had slid into an almost solid wall and left very little in the way of hand-holds.

Once we were on top of the mess, though, it was much easier. The whole of Ys Tearch continued to shake and tremble, throwing new deposits of fortress wall onto us, and parts of what we crawled over were none too stable; one had to test each new spot carefully, and often what held Connor easily was unsafe for me, but we progressed, slowly, towards the vague glimmer of light and the promise of fresher, sweeter air, creeping along the broken surface like tiny ants at a hunting-party's picnic.

It seemed to take forever, that long crawl. Our hands were raw and bleeding, and my shoulders began to cramp with sustained tension. What remained of the ceiling was now within inches of my back, in some places, and for this bit, at least, Connor had an easier time of it. At last, though, I craned my head painfully around, and realized that nothing but open sky lay above me. I gave a groan of not-quite-unsullied joy, scrambled to the edge and we slid ourselves down the side of a massive fall of rock to the inner bailey and lay panting on the ground, half-faint with relief.

A lurch of that ground recalled us to our surroundings. We heard a low roar of unstable earth beneath us, scrambled to our feet and began to run across what had once been level greensward but was now pocked and cratered desolation, just as the opening we had emerged from crumpled into dusty slag.

Nothing remained, in the starlit darkness, of the places where we had been. The central tower was now a mountain of annihilation, a vast rubbish heap. Huge rips had appeared in the ground around us, as if torn up by giant hands, and black, oily liquid seeped out from ancient wells below, hissing steam and stench and vapor. Even as we ran towards the one narrow gate still standing, towards the outer yard and what I prayed might be safety, we could feel the world beneath us gather itself for another shuddering convulsion.

Terror lent us speed. We reached the vaulted archway, throwing ourselves through the opening in the wall like mad things, just as the wasteland behind us exploded. The mountains above us rained fire and rock, a hot wind whistled past my ears, and I heard myself, above the roar of the forces unleashed, screaming in despair.

The power of the impact threw us, by some strange piece of luck, the last few feet we needed. I stumbled, recovered, and stood on trembling legs. In that last moment of panic, I'd clutched at Connor's shoulder; I was still gripping him, and it took a moment to loosen my fingers from his flesh. He gave me a shaky smile.

"Well, that was a bit much," I said. My voice was hoarse, from shouting. I swallowed and tried again, but the world around me was so bleak and wretched that whatever I had been about to say dissolved into a sob.

The inner bailey had been worse, I suppose, but the picture out here differed only in degree. The south tower was still standing, more or less, but the walls around us lay in ruins. My eyes were drawn inexorably to where, not so long ago, Cioren and I had left our horses.

There was only a tumble of boulders where the mage's mount had been. I'd tethered Banshee some distance away, out near the centre of the yard, but it hadn't saved her. A stray bit of carved cornice had flown wide, and she lay broken and bleeding on the cobbles. She was already gone, her eye fixing on me with one last look of irritated, angry reproach.

I stared at her stiffening corpse. Somewhere, sometime, I knew, I would break my heart over this. But at that moment, I could only think that it solved at least one problem.

I could not have gotten her out. There was no gate left; what had been there had fallen into another small mountain of rocky destruction, when the already half-ruined tower had slid into extinction.

We walked over to the outer walls of Ys Tearch. Fear had come and gone, leaving me empty of everything except the knowledge that I had one last task: to get Connor out of this, if I could.

"Right," I said, kneeling down to him. "You've been very brave, Connor. Really. You have. I know grown men who would have perished, weeping, hours ago. You only have to be brave a little longer. I need you to do exactly what I say now, all right?"

"Yes," he said. It was little more than a whisper. Poor kid. I wasn't lying when I said he'd done better than most adults would have. It was only his presence that had stopped me from giving up back there in the cellars, myself.

"We have to get over the wall. It won't be that bad, I don't think, but, well, there's a lot that could go wrong. I want you to start climbing. I'll be right behind you, so that if - if anything happens, I'll be able to see where you - well, where you are. But you have to promise me, on your honour, that no matter what, you'll keep going. If I get hurt, you mustn't come back for me. You just get yourself over this wall, and down to the hostel, and don't look back, all right? Promise me."

His eyes locked on mine. I hoped he couldn't read the hopelessness in them. Even as I spoke, I had felt the stone flagging shimmying and swaying beneath us. But he said, quite calmly, "Yes, I promise. Honour of a Machyll, if you like."

"Good. Up you go, then."

The climb was a dicey one. Like the tunnel we'd clambered over to get out of the storerooms, the smashed walls lacked stability, whole slabs balancing precariously on pyramids of fallen rock. We inched carefully upwards, clinging to whatever bits we could each time the land erupted around us, and praying that the inevitable end would just hold off long enough.

At long last, we reached the top. It seemed to me we'd been doing this forever, that our whole existence had been one long, battered and futile exercise in trying to leave this hell. I couldn't quite remember how I'd come to this. Fortunately, there wasn't time to dwell on it.

There was a pattern to these awful quakes, I'd realized after a while. They had been so fast and furious, it didn't seem possible, but they tended to be in groups of five, each one stronger than the last, until the fifth one drew yet another piece of the mountain down onto us. Then there would be a short respite, where the ground and the very air seemed to vibrate, but this was less worrisome. There wasn't anything terribly destructive in it, other than that the shaking heralded another set of earthcrunching tremors.

I counted back, making sure I was right, and then told Connor to start moving.

"Remember, don't stop, except to hang on. Don't worry about me. I'll be right behind you. Now, go."

He wriggled out to the edge of the rocks, and let himself over the edge. I watched as he crept over the stones, feeling his way along as he searched for the best spot to drop down to next. It seemed reasonably safe. I let him get another few feet ahead, and then began to follow, hampered by my need to keep him in sight. It meant I couldn't turn completely away to let myself drop onto the next shelf of wreckage, and that wasn't the best way to do this. But it was imperative that I knew exactly where he was, in case the unthinkable happened. It was dark. If he were buried by a sudden fall of rock and earth, I needed to know just where to dig.

Halfway down, he gave me a fright, when he dropped over the lip of some projecting piece of granite and disappeared, just as the first in the latest series of jolts began. I was still screaming his name when the last one ended, with an annoying shower of pebbles onto my back.

"It's all right," he yelled. "I'm here."

I scrabbled and slid down the uneven surface, collecting a new set of scrapes on my knuckles, till I could see him.

"I'm fine," he said. He sounded aggrieved, as though I'd been babying him in some way.

"Sorry," I said. "I'm a little nervous, all right?"

He gave me the ghost of a grin.

"Keep on, then. We're almost there."

I was lying, of course, there was almost as much down left as we'd come already, and it didn't seem to be getting easier. But somehow, it began to look as if we might make it, despite my doubts. If we could just get to the bottom, we might have half a chance.

We were getting closer, though. The tremors had been gaining strength; each new set of quakes dislodging even more of the surrounding countryside down onto Ys Tearch, and not even the south tower's heights were visible anymore over the lip of the shattered wall. Just as I saw Connor jump excitedly down to within a few feet of what was left of the road, there was a terrible grinding sound, and then the fragile world of old stone blocks we inhabited burst apart in a roaring, fiery explosion.

I felt the rocks I clung to slipping away, as if melting under my fingers, and the earth threw me carelessly over, flinging me down the jagged stones as if I were a child's doll. I felt each jolt and crack, felt my bones slamming painfully into the unyielding shards, sliding and bouncing down the length of what remained below. I lost all sense of where I was; lost whatever breath was still in my body, lost everything except consciousness and the knowledge of the agony I was in.

I hit the uneven surface of the road below with a bonejarring shock. Every inch of my body was shrieking in protest, my head swimming in a sea of pain. I lay moaning on the pathway, wishing fervently that I could die.

Chapter 49

Get up, said my internal voice coldly. I opened my eyes. Connor was hunkered down beside me, an anxious frown creasing his own dirt-smeared face.

Get up, said the voice again, this time with some urgency. I saw that Connor was near tears, and tried valiantly to pull myself together.

"Well," I whispered, "We're out."

He did not look reassured. I felt the ground under me shiver a little, and managed, through sheer will alone, to roll over onto my side, despite the pain. I was bleeding, I noticed. From several dozen places. I pulled myself onto my hands and knees, and immediately threw up.

Get up. I have to get up I couldn't, at this point, have told anyone why, it seemed like the most annoying and trivial of concerns, but the voice wouldn't shut up about it, and more to silence that squawking than anything else, I ignored my body's reluctance and got shakily onto my feet.

If anything, this was worse. But my ability to stay upright, however badly, comforted Connor, at least. He smiled trustfully up at me, and took a few steps down the track.

Walk? He wanted me to walk? I could barely keep from dropping back to the stony bed of the road, and it began, in memory, to have seemed as soft as the best feather pillows, and this boy wanted me to walk?

Don't be an idiot, said my internal tormentor. Just do it. I stumbled a couple of paces forward, and my head began to reel. I felt my body begin to sway, my vision blurring, and thought, I can't faint. I'll fall down again and that would really hurt.

No. Fainting's not an option. Just keep going, I thought. One foot in front of the other. Never say die. The pompous fool who had come up with that one, I decided, had never actually been in any really bad case in his life. Death struck me as desirable. Like sleeping, only without the penalty of waking up again.

Step, step. I was moving, it seemed, without my own awareness. Left, right, just keep going. All this would have been much easier, of course, if the road had been content to stay where its original makers had seen fit to put it. Instead, it kept heaving itself up and slamming hard into my feet, trying, in its malice, to knock me down again.

Gradually, this distressing tendency on the road's part lessened. My aches and abrasions seemed to lose their sting as well, and my vision cleared, and I realized that we were now some distance from the devastation of Ys Tearch. We could rest now, I thought. We were safe.

The road moved again, a shower of rocks and dirt spraying up into our faces, and the thunder of the mountains behind us got suddenly louder. No, apparently we weren't safe. I kept going, staggering after Connor down along the path.

On a sunny afternoon, on horseback, the distance had seemed like a pleasant nothing. Bruised and battered, in the cold and the dark, with blood trickling from every pore in my body, it felt endless. I kept on, following Connor, and concentrating on not actually falling down. My breathing was difficult and sporadic, and my insides had not yet calmed themselves. Every misstep and stumble brought bile rising in my throat, but I was getting better: I no longer considered death as the preferable alternative.

We came, after this uncomfortable eternity, to the last bend in the track. I could see the gates of the hostel. There were torches blazing, and in the glare, as we came nearer, there were people, running about. Little shadowy figures, men and horses, scurrying around, very amusing.

It would be nice, I thought, as we approached the wooden walls, to lie down. Warmth, food, sleep. I could sleep for a week. I wondered suddenly about Elowyn. Was she still alive? If so, would her offer of a place at Issing still hold? I had been ungrateful, but now, the idea of a quiet, uneventful life in the prosperous West Ridings seemed like an unattainable dream. I pictured myself slipping into a dull old age, training soldiers and boring them with tales of long-forgotten heroics, growing fatter with each passing year. I hoped Lord Raghnall had a good cook. I had spent too much damn time going hungry, lately. Hungry and wet and cold and dirty.

He was standing at the gate. I recognized him from a long way off, and knew that for the rest of my life, whatever else came to me, there would only really be one 'he'. Uncomfortable, but true, nonetheless. I would go off, to Issing, or wherever else life sent me, and he would marry some nice well-bred girl with a turn for the kind of supportive, tactful diplomacy I so conspicuously lacked, but it would have to be that way, and I would have to live with it. I would have sighed, but the effort, and the probable pain that would attend it seemed to be too much, and not really worth it.

He didn't move to greet us. He just waited, as we dragged ourselves that last stretch, and slowed our steps to stand only a few feet away.

His face was set in angry lines, but he said nothing for one long moment. He looked away, finally, down at his bedraggled nephew, clinging to my hand, and said, "Connor? You're all right?"

"I'm fine," said Connor. The resiliency of small boys; he sounded quite cheerful. Whatever had gone on in his life, these last days, and I couldn't see Angharad treating him with any tenderness, he was bouncing back. It was amazing. I wished I could do it. I felt awful, and I guessed that I looked worse.

"Go inside. Gwyll's there, he'll look after you." Then, as Connor seemed disposed to argue, "Go on. Now, Connor."

The Duke of Dungarrow went, with a regretful glance my way. Tirais' tone didn't allow for disobedience, and Connor was, when it came to it, only a child, after all.

There was a long and uncomfortable silence. I should have gone in with Connor, I thought. Tirais wouldn't dress me down with all those troopers watching, would he? Risking a look at his face, in the torchlight, I wasn't so sure. He was furious, almost livid. I stayed put, and waited for the storm.

But he said, quite carefully calm, "Cioren?"

"Dead. I think so, yes." My mind coped, just barely, with the unexpected query. I had almost forgotten that part of the night's work; I struggled to bring my thoughts under control. "Angharad, too. At least - but I don't think she can have survived, do you?"

He looked up, away, over my head. The destruction was still going on, and from his vantage point, I reckoned he could still just see it.

"It was in the cellars," I said, by way of explanation. "They had an altar there. Like at Penvarron. Only not quite. Worse, I guess. That priest. I… I don't know what happened really."

My voice trickled away. I wished he would yell, scream, get it over with. I'd screwed up, all right, worse than he knew, even, and he had a right to be angry, if only he would just get on with it, so I could go in and lie down somewhere.

He transferred his gaze back to me. I wished he wouldn't. I probably looked as bad as I felt.

"You!" All his anger seemed to find expression in that one syllable. It came out like venom. "I would never have taken you for an oathbreaker."

I had thought I could take it, but the contempt in his voice was too much. My own temper took hold.

"I broke no oaths," I said.

"No? Your oath to Keraine? I told you to stay put, and you didn't have the grace to wait even a moment before haring off, without a word, and you say you broke no oath?"

"I didn't swear," I said wearily.

"You swore as a soldier. Every trooper swears to the commander of his garrison, and so to me. Or had that little item slipped your mind?"

"I didn't swear," I said again. "It's one of those things Penvarron was a little slack on."

I thought at this point, he might actually kill me. His face was white with rage, and he took a step towards me, then stopped, clenching his fists.

"Hairsplitting," he sneered.

I could have wept. It had been too long a night and I had nothing left. I was too tired to defend myself, to say that if I'd waited to explain, we might have been too late, that Connor might have died, that whatever Angharad had planned would have destroyed us all. I just stood there, and waited, too exhausted and too heartsick to respond.

I don't know when he closed the distance between us. I just felt him take hold of my arms, ungently, and he began to shake me.

It was too much, that pain, but before I could so much as whimper a protest, he let go of my arms and I felt myself leaning against him, my face buried in his shoulder, and his arms, not angry now, around me.

"How badly are you hurt?"

"Not too much," I said into the cloth of his tunic. "My ribs again, I think. And some other things, but I - I think I'm going to live."

I wasn't thinking very clearly. I could remember that there were reasons this should not be happening, but I hadn't the least inkling what they were. My mind took refuge in irrelevancies.

"Tirais, I'm filthy. I'm bleeding. I'm a mess."

"I'm getting used to that," he said.

I lifted my head away, trying to pull out of his embrace.

"Your mother - she'll be so - "

"She'll get used to it, too," he said firmly.

Whatever strength I'd had evaporated; I wasn't actually standing up on my own any more. Tirais' arms were the only thing between me and the hard ground we stood on, and finally I relaxed back against him, and felt his heart beating, in time with my own.

I don't know how long we stood like that. A long time, I think. Somewhere above us, the destruction I'd caused went on to its appointed end. The walls crumbled. The mountains continued to fall. You could still hear the thunder of that collapse for some time, echoing down into the valley as Ys Tearch, the most revered and holy place in all of Keraine, ground itself inexorably into dust and memory.

My parents, I thought, would never forgive me.

The End

About the Author

Morgan Smith has been a goatherd, a landscaper, a weaver, a bookstore owner and archaeologist, and she will drop everything to travel anywhere, on the flimsiest of pretexts. Writing is something she has been doing all her life, though, one way or another, and now she thinks she might actually have something to say.

But if you really want to know more, download "Flashbacks (an unreliable memoir of the '60s)".

Other titles by Morgan Smith

Casting in Stone – A Novel of the Averraine Cycle

Flashbacks (an unreliable memoir of the '60s)

Connect on line:

Friend me on Facebook:
www.facebook.com/morgansmithauthor?ref=bookmarks

Visit my blog:
https://wordpress.com/stats/morgansmithauthor.wordpress.com

CPSIA information can be obtained
at www.ICGtesting.com
Printed in the USA
LVOW13s0011310117
522614LV00011BA/1648/P